A HIDDEN ELEMENT

The Element Trilogy – Book Two

Donna Galanti

Wild Trail Press

For Mike. Who never stopped believing.

Acknowledgements

Special thanks to Teri Goggin-Roberts who helped me shape this book as I wrote it, and for cheering on "Team Caleb".

Thanks to my wonderful beta readers Randi Sherwood and Lisa Green, who know how to call me out!

CHAPTER 1: The Beginning

Silent dark hung under a star-filled sky.

The dark deepened as they headed into the forest. Ancient conifers towered over them, blocking out the moon. Rain fell cold and lifeless. The nearest town of Benevolence, Oregon, was five miles northwest.

Caleb Madroc's father stood across from him, waiting for his people to gather their belongings. Their pale faces glowed like orbs within gray hooded robes as they waited for his father's instruction.

"We head toward town," his father ordered. Caleb opened his mouth, but there were no words for his feelings of anger and loss at suddenly leaving the only home he'd ever known. It raged inside him, a tumult of emotion he must quell for now. At least his own black hair, like his face, was a constant reminder of his mother to his father. This made him glad.

Caleb shut his mouth and nodded, stepping in behind his father. Rain fell cold and lifeless. He fell behind as he helped the womenfolk with their bags. One young female sent him a furtive, desperate look as she touched his hand in passing.

I'm so scared. What will happen to us?

He smiled at her. *Keep your thoughts to yourself. It's safer this way. All will work out once we settle.* She bit her lip, her eyes full of tears, and nodded looking back down at her feet.

"Father, how much further? Some of the younger females are struggling," Caleb said.

His father's eyes stung him through the mist rising up from the forest floor. They were eyes so different from his, and from his mother's.

Caleb had often seen sadness and pity for his father in his mother's eyes. The day he had found her dead in the well her eyes held only nothingness.

"Can't we stop and rest, Adrian?" A few in the group grumbled. They looked wet and tired, a sea of gray flowing before him. His father glowered at their weakness. As Caleb scanned the sodden crowd a female smiled at his father, holding the promise of submission. Perfect for his father, who wanted to breed another son to take his place. A worthy son.

"We do not stop." His father's voice rose over the line of people before him, and he smiled back at the female and a strange sense of relief washed over Caleb. If his father did create a new prodigal son to groom it might remove his first born from his watchful eye.

With that thought, anguish over his mother's absence hit him fresh again. At eighteen and bigger than his father, he still needed his mother. She had been his kindred spirit, like Uncle Brahm. But now he was alone in this strange place. No longer did he have someone to be his true self with. He must step carefully.

His father continued to scan his flock. They stood still and silent, conveying their subservience. He nodded, apparently satisfied with their response. "You all took the oath to come here. Hard work lies before us in breeding our new community. Understood?"

They nodded in a collective wave.

Just like you bred with Aunt Manta while your wife lay dead? Caleb spewed out in his head without thinking.

His father moved closer, until his flaring nostrils touched his. Caleb stepped back, but his father gripped his arm. Dozens of eyes watched their battle.

Do not ever mention my brother's wife's name again, Son.

His father's fingers pinched him hard and his hot breath pulsed across his face, but Caleb couldn't stop. *Mother's dead because of you. And what about Aunt Manta? Did you kill her, too?*

I didn't kill anyone. And your mother should have been more careful.

You let her travel alone. She fell and died because she was alone.

It was your well, Caleb, she fell into. Your hideaway you carelessly covered up. Your fault.

His father's accusations stabbed him with painful truth. He sucked in his breath. *My fault. Yes. My fault.*

He looked around the watchful crowd as his head reeled with the agony of what he had done. His people stared back at him, their thoughts hid behind blank faces. Why did they come? Didn't they have dreams and wants and needs of their own, too? Or were they all obedient drones of his father?

His father thrust his arm away and turned around, plunging faster through the woods. Caleb hesitated then followed behind, trying to keep up. He envisioned himself standing still until everyone glided around him, leaving him to remain alone under a watchful moon.

Branches snagged his robe shooting him back to reality. His father's people followed in silence. If they didn't obey there would be consequences. As Caleb knew. He had no special privilege here as Adrian's son.

At last his father stepped out onto a paved road. It stretched far into the distance, where welcoming lights beckoned them across the final mile. They reached the main intersection of town. A car flashed by. A radio blared. Faces stared out at them. He stared back. They were so different from himself and yet…not.

He broke his gaze realizing how out of place this group looked late at night. The people here wore jeans and shirts, the shapes of their bodies outlined under tight clothes. The female's curves called to him, unlike his people who clothed themselves in shapeless robes to discourage free sexual thoughts. They were now to breed only with those chosen for them.

His father led them single file down the sidewalk. A handful of people sat behind windows drinking. They pointed at them as they walked by. "Gillian's Bar" flashed in neon green above the doorway in the late evening hours. A man and woman, heading into the bar, stepped back from the sidewalk to watch them pass. *Freaks*, he heard the man say. And his father erased the memory of the encounter from these strangers' minds in the seconds it took to pass them.

"Father," Caleb whispered in his ear. "Where are we going?"

A large building rose at the far end of a parking lot. "Ray's Lots" blinked over and over.

"Here is where we go."

A woman pushed a cart filled with bags to her car, the only car left in the lot. She stopped and stared at them. Her hair framed her face in tight curls. A blue and white striped dress strained to contain her breasts and belly.

"Good evening, brothers," she said with a hesitant smile.

His father motioned for them to stop. He smiled at her. She smiled back.

"Good evening, madam," his father drawled.

"God bless you." She grabbed his father's hand. Caleb swallowed a laugh at the way his father looked at her with such a serious, doting face.

"And God bless you, my child."

"What church are you with?" The woman fingered a cross at her neck. "Are you having an event in town?"

His father had said a church was the perfect cover. One of the many cultural ways learned before infiltration. All part of his father's master plan.

"It's the Church of Elyon," his father said.

The woman took her hand away and frowned. "Never heard of it. You're not one those crazy cults are you?"

Caleb stepped to his father's side. *Let me work her mind, Father.* "What's your name, Madam?"

"Sally."

"I'm Caleb Madroc." He shook her hand hoping his father didn't have some depraved mission in mind. Caleb wanted to get food for their hungry group and shelter and have as little interaction with these town people as possible. "We're simple folks. Our bus broke down outside of town. We seek food and a place to stay nearby. Can you help us?"

"What a nice young man you are. Of course I can help you." She abandoned her cart and pulled Caleb toward the store. "My cousin runs this store and can stock you up with food. And the Mercenary Motel is down the street."

He didn't understand her eagerness as she dragged him along then it was made clear by his father's mirthful laugh. His father had probed her mind and now controlled it—she would do whatever he commanded.

Caleb followed her into the store. Their people streamed in behind. Sally dragged him to a counter where a short red-faced man scowled at them. "Ray, these folks are here in town from a wonderful church. Their bus broke down and they need food."

Within seconds Ray's frown changed to a wide grin as Caleb's father continued his mind games. "Come in, come in. Time to close up anyhow." He flicked the sign on the front door and shut off the lights outside.

"Thank you," his father said. "I need food here for my flock before we find a place to stay."

"Help yourself to anything you want." Ray ran his hands over shelves. "Pretzels, baked beans, cereal, Ding Dongs. We even sell the word of the Lord." Sally and Ray beamed at them.

His father directed everyone to gather food and drinks. Sally and Ray stood by the counter, their minds blank except for what his father put into them. He dared not combat his father's powers. Not here. Not now. But someday.

"Ray, I need all your money now," his father said.

Ray clapped his hands together. "Of course." He pulled money from a nearby metal box.

When his father's bag burst full of items he handed it to a community member and cocked his head at Ray and Sally. "Time to go now, my new friends." He motioned his people out the door. Ray and Sally stood with stupid smiles on their faces as the group filed out into the parking lot. All, except his father.

"Come on, Father," Caleb pleaded, the dark knot in his stomach hardened. "Our job here is done."

"Not quite." His father moved toward the smiling cousins, a book in his hand. *The Holy Bible.* He thumbed through it to a passage and looked up smiling. "As for God, his way is perfect, is it not?"

"The word of God is true," Sally sang out, clutching Ray's hand. Her cousin nodded.

"Ray, isn't Sally lovely? Look at her." His father pointed at the heavy set woman.

Ray turned to Sally. His pants bulged and Sally's eyes widened. She tugged on her dress top.

"Have your way with her Ray, you know you want to."

"Father," Caleb whispered, clutching at him but his father stayed his hand.

Ray licked his lips and nodded.

"Sally, unzip your fine dress and show Ray what you've got."

Sally stepped out of her dress in a motion more fluid than one would have thought possible given her size. Her belly oozed over her thighs and her bra cut into her mountainous breasts. Ray panted, tapping his hands against his skinny legs.

Caleb moved toward the door.

"Stay, Son, I want you to watch this."

"I won't."

"You *will* or you know what will happen."

Caleb stopped and sighed, looking down at the floor. Eyes watched from the parking lot.

"Look."

Caleb focused on the dirt in the floor cracks. His muscles twitched with anger. His father thrived on his hate, wanted him to hate—wanted his son to be a Destroyer like him. They had hidden their true selves for so long and now were free here to unleash it. Not Caleb. He refused to give in to the dark inside. He tried to release the hate for his father, but it now filled his every pore. He made a vow right then and there, he'd never allow himself to be controlled. No matter the consequences.

He finally looked up. His father nodded, pleased, and turned back to his playthings. Ray massaged his crotch. Sally moaned, squeezing her mammoth breasts, and stepped out of her underwear.

"Take her, Ray. Bend her right over the counter. Dive into all her lushness."

"Lush, yes." Ray moved toward Sally, fumbling to unbuckle his pants. She squealed with glee and bent over the counter to receive him, her white bottom rising like a pitted sea of blubber. Ray mounted her, forged a path through her two white mountains, and slapped up against her in his glory.

"Lordy, Lordy," Sally sang out as she bounced up and down.

"Now that's wholesome entertainment." His father jabbed him. Caleb jerked away. "They're both enjoying it."

Caleb clenched his fists and shoved them in his pockets. "Can we go now?"

"Yes, Son, only one more thing to do."

His father pulled out something that looked like a handle. He flicked it open to reveal a small knife he must have picked up in the hardware section. He placed it next to Ray on the counter. Sweat flicked off the red-faced man's forehead as he plunged into buttery flesh.

"Ray, enjoying yourself?"

Ray grunted and grabbed on to Sally's hips, sinking into her expanse. She moaned again in delight as her buttocks shuddered.

"Good. When you're done fucking, kill the bitch."

His father strode out the door, pulling Caleb along with him.

"Father, no." Caleb struggled against him as his father shoved him hard through the door. Caleb spiraled his thoughts into Ray's brain. *Stop, Ray! She's your cousin, your family!*

Ray stopped his thrusting as if listening to Caleb, but his father's punch to his face ended his brain probe. Caleb staggered back, blood gushing from his nose. Ray straightened his head and rammed into Sally with a loud groan. Caleb drew his hand back but his father's fingers crushed his forearm. He fell to his knees. Blood spattered down his gray robe. The flock widened their circle, silent and watching. His father led as both law maker and enforcer.

"These lowly forms of life must be controlled," his father said. "We've studied their ways. Now, this first act is how we begin their demise and our rule. We will grow in number with our selected breeding and thrive as these useless beings die out. Watch this historic moment, Son, for anyone who turns away will be marked weak…and unworthy."

All eyes turned to the inside of the store as the desperate carnal scene played out to the end.

"I hate you," Caleb whispered, watching the forced lovers before him.

His father smiled at him in satisfaction.

Ray arched his back with a moan and finished his business. Sally squealed and pressed up against him. And when Ray raised his knife and plunged into Sally in new ways, she squealed again. And again. Her blood ran onto scuffed tiles and still she squealed. And then she stopped.

Tears filled Caleb's eyes and he closed them against the evil scene.

His father laughed. "Don't you see, Son?" He shook *The Holy Bible* at him. "I am their Way, their Truth, their Life—and Death."

Caleb did not answer. He remained inside his dark prison and swore someday he would end his father's rule.

CHAPTER 2: Seven years later

Laura Fieldstone eased herself up from the rocking chair. She bumped into the lamp. Lately, her belly poked out everywhere. She stretched, feeling the pain. Her back ached from sitting all day, but she had a deadline to get this book written before the baby came. It was the final one in a series of three. She would send it off to her editor and then take a long break.

She needed a break from the headaches that had returned. She couldn't tell Ben. He would worry, and she tried not to worry herself. Having a baby at forty was much harder than at twenty-six. Her body *felt* older as this baby strained within her. This baby, who took her unaware fourteen years after having Charlie. Long after Ben had a vasectomy.

Ben joked that one snuck through. Her doctor said it did happen, but her natural mother's adamant belief she had been a virgin filled Laura's mind as her belly grew. No one had believed her mother, and yet it had been true. Surreal. Had her baby also been created from someone other than the man she loved? When she allowed herself to wonder that awful reality she shoved the thoughts down deep inside. They were too horrific to define. *This child is mine and Ben's. We created him in love.* She said it to herself like a mantra as if to seal it in truth.

And so this baby grew inside her. A baby who kicked so much it seemed he wanted to break free early into the world. He stormed violently inside her. Would he be violent when he arrived? *No.* Their baby was perfect. Like Charlie had been. On the outside at least. She had seen the ultrasound. But what would he be like on the inside?

The thought of what her baby *could be* twisted in her like a sickness. During those times Ben held her and whispered calming things in her ear. There's only good inside you, he'd say. Our son will be fine, just like our Charlie. There is too much love in this house for anyone to grow up evil, he'd say.

Like her twin had. Like this child could be.

Sometimes Ben laid her down on the bed and showed her in sweet ways how everything was all right. They still drew fire from one another after fifteen years. She laughed. She was eight months pregnant and Ben still touched her with his flames. Even at fifty-one he couldn't get enough of making love to his very pregnant wife. But Charlie could be home any moment now from school, and that spiked her worry about him again.

She eased her anxiety by picking up the first children's book she had ever published, and rubbed her fingers over the cracked cover of a blue pony riding across the sky. *Big Brave Blue.* He was a flying pony who lived in the clouds. His colors blended into the sky and even as a runt he flew faster than any other pony, but he grew up lonely. His size and color separated him from his world's orange herd of giant ponies, but he had an advantage besides speed. He could blend into the sky making it hard for their enemy, the Dragon Beasts, to catch him when they plundered their land.

And when he faced the Dragon Beast leader and killed him in battle to save his herd, his own kind looked at him in a different light. When others like him were born, the herd realized they were evolving into an improved species, and they called upon tiny Blue to lead them into their new future.

She could hear Charlie's voice. *Again, Mommy. Read it again.* And she did. And then he would tug on her sleeve and quote his favorite line. *Being big doesn't mean you're brave—only big of heart does. Am I big of heart, Mommy, like Big Brave Blue?* She would look down at his little head and breathe his baby smell and say, *the biggest heart of all, Charlie.*

That was before he'd discovered his differences. Now her heart ached for him most days as he faced the bullies who saw them, too.

She peered out the bay window. The water raged rough across the Sound today. Waves ripped up and pounded toward land, a watery creature bent on blind destruction. The wind creaked through their ranch house. Wild and primordial and unfettered. Some days it called to her. It filled her with a deep yearning for something she didn't understand. On those days she felt unsettled, waiting for something, anything to happen. She wished to be the wild wind at times, unbound and free. The wind taunted and beckoned her at the same time. It's why she loved living on Puget Sound.

She had fallen in love with the grandness of Washington State. A place different from the Northeast where she came from, which held memories of her peaceful childhood. A place where she and Ben met. It had also been a place of horrific times. Of losing her parents, her friends, and nearly Ben. Their home now, in being so different, helped her forget her past.

She thought living across the country in Oregon was far enough to forget. It was home. She had persuaded Ben to stay on the west coast. His photography assignments allowed him to live anywhere, as did her author lifestyle. And they could leave behind their violent past that had flung them together. Close enough to be home. Far enough away to forget.

Today though, she urged the wind away. She had things to do before the baby came and didn't want to become lost in restlessness. Where *was* Charlie? She peered out the back door into the woods that their house backed up to. She hoped he hadn't taken a detour through the woods from school. She wished he took the bus. He spent too much time in the woods alone, as she had as a child.

The woods stretched deep for miles. A person could get lost in them. Or die in them.

Perhaps the wind blew a yearning in her son as well and the woods provided him comfort. She couldn't take this from him, not with the burdens he carried. Someday she would tell him the true meaning behind his abilities. But not yet. She wanted him to be old enough to handle it— and not let it destroy him.

There. Charlie's tall figure strode from the woods, hunched over. Taller than his father, he tried to hide his height. Being 6' 5" at fourteen was a physical trait that made him a target ripe for teasing. Not to mention his other features. She waved at him, but he didn't wave back. He put his head down and slowed his walk to the house. *Now what?*

Laura rubbed her belly and opened the door for him.

"Charlie, I was getting worried," Laura said. "You went to the woods after school, didn't you?" She looked down at his muddy knees, wondering what he had been doing out there this time.

He nodded but didn't look up, just shuffled in the door. She sensed his sadness, frustration, and anger. She wondered what he was thinking, but he seemed to have an innate ability to cloak his thoughts. Did she really want to know all the wild ideas that went through a fourteen year old boy's mind? Ben told her definitely not.

"What's wrong?" Laura hugged his waist from behind at an angle.

"That jerk, Brian, at school, that's what's wrong."

He turned around and set his backpack on the deacon's bench by the door. When he looked at Laura she gasped.

"Charlie, what happened?" His left eye had a cut above it and his lip swelled on one side next to a darkening bruise on his cheek. He shoved his hands in his pockets, but Laura pulled them out and sighed over his scraped knuckles. She pulled him to the sink and ran cool water over his hands, smoothing away the dried blood.

His nail-less fingers stretched long and thick in her small ones. Her pink painted orbs stood out in sharp contrast to his flesh-like pads. How she wished his nails had never fallen off as a newborn. He flexed his fingers and pulled away from her then plunked his large frame down on the bench. Legs and arms spewed everywhere like Bambi on ice. His silver white hair had streaks of mud in it. She got a clean dish rag and wet it, pressing it gently to the cut over his eye. He grabbed it from her. She saw flecks of blood on his shirt and hoped it was his.

"I'm okay, Mom," he said then blew out a big breath. "Didn't mean to grab."

Laura sat down next to him. "Tell me."

"I came out of study hall and ran right into Brian with his gang. He called me a Fieldstone freak and said I belonged in the *Guinness Book of World Records*. Giant albino pod-man. It's his newest nickname for me." Charlie stretched his long fingers out wide.

Laura took his hand. "You have beautiful fingers. They're—"

"No, Mom, they're not." Charlie snatched his hand away and held it up to her face. "I *am* albino pod-man. Look at me."

"I don't think so." She touched his hair. "Your dad doesn't think so."

"Yes he does. He thinks I'm a freak."

"He does *not* think you're a freak. He loves you."

"I heard him with you. He said I'm not normal and I'll never fit in."

Laura wished for the thousandth time Charlie had never heard their conversation. It had been late at night and they had no idea Charlie had been passing by their room then. Words to sting for a lifetime.

"He didn't mean it in the way you think, Charlie. He just doesn't want you to have a hard life."

"Whatever." He turned away and crossed his arms.

"We can do the surgery, Charlie."

"Like Dad wants me to have? Then everyone will know I have artificial nails on me, like I'm a girl or something."

"That we can change. Your hair color we can change. Your height we can't. Someday you'll be glad to be tall."

"Someday can't come soon enough." He sighed. She moved beside him and touched his hand again. This time he didn't pull away.

His teen years loomed long in front of him. How she wished she could make it better for him. Make all kids fair and nice. Sometimes she wanted to tell Charlie to pummel Brian, but she had to be the grown up and maintain self-control. It was the core of everything she taught her son.

"So then what happened?"

"He had an accident, sort of." Charlie smirked and bent his head.

"Accident? Really?" Laura crossed her arms and leaned back into the bench. Her belly ached, muscles pulling from all directions to hold up the weight she bore. One more month she had to get through.

"Okay, it wasn't an accident but I've had enough of him, Mom!" Charlie stood up and banged on the kitchen table with a sharp *crack*.

Laura frowned at him. "Remember what happened the last time you got so angry. You smashed the lawn mower to smithereens and it cost you all the money saved up to buy a new one."

"*Self-control.* I know, Mom." Charlie leaned up against the kitchen counter. "Sorry. Sometimes I get so mad. I hate having to control it. It's not fair."

"I understand, but you know what your strength can do. You didn't use it against Brian today, did you?"

"I tried not to." He shook his head. "I wouldn't do it to someone on purpose."

Laura believed him, but she wondered if the 'tried not to' would result in a phone call soon from Brian's mom. Charlie was a good kid at heart, sensitive to hurting others. He didn't want the strength that came with his powers. Laura never spoke of them as powers to Charlie though. She called them genetic anomalies. It softened them.

She told him they were part of an anger syndrome. His outbursts often triggered them, and Laura used this as a reason. Their pediatrician agreed and said Charlie had some anger tendencies and gave him techniques to combat them. His nail defects were explainable. Ectodermal dysplasia. A condition where a child is born with nail defects or no nails at all. But that's not what he had.

Some kids would have liked Charlie's abilities. Not Charlie. He hated being strong like a bully. He hated kids who teased. He never teased. He wanted to treat everyone the same way he wanted to be treated. He acted older in so many ways but immature as any teen. Laura never knew when he might exhibit maturity or immaturity. Right now she had the feeling the immature part was about to be revealed.

"So?" Laura raised her eyebrows at him.

"Well, his pants must have been too baggy as they kind of…fell off him in the hallway, in front of all these girls. He tried to pick them up but somehow his shoes got tied together and he fell over. Those tighty-whities mooned everyone. So sad."

"Charlie." Laura tried to sound angry as she overcame the urge to laugh.

Charlie shrugged. "Mom, come on. It was too funny. I'm sick and tired of him picking on me. He teased me last week for wearing tighty-whities in the locker room and now everyone knows he wears them, too. Besides, I didn't hit him or anything." He stopped smiling and looked down. "Well, not then anyways."

"What did you do, Charlie?" Laura was afraid to know. The memory flickered of their cat, Romeo, and an overenthusiastic five year old Charlie who liked to hug. Only he didn't know what his hugs could do. They buried Romeo in the backyard and told Charlie it wasn't his fault, but it didn't make Laura cry any less. She had loved that cat. There were no more pets from then on.

"He said I pantsed him and—"

"You did."

"Yes, but then he said he'd get me after school, so I thought I'd avoid him and take the woods home instead of the bus—"

"And because you wanted to let off some steam, right?"

"Yeah, okay. But not *at* anyone. I wanted to feel better. Not so…angry." He gripped the counter and bit his lip. "But Brian didn't take the bus either, he followed me. Him and his stupid friends. He hit me first, Mom."

"I believe you."

"I let him hit me. I told myself he's inconsequential, like you told me to think. I *did*. I tried to keep on walking and ignore him, but then the others started hitting me. It wasn't fair. Three of them against one." He clenched his fist, looked at it, and shoved it in his pocket. "I laughed at Brian and told him he's irrelevant."

Laura suppressed a smile.

"He didn't even know what it meant. What a dummy. So I told him to go find a dictionary. He hit me again and I hit him back. I tried to do it light, I swear, but—"

"But what? What did you do, Charlie?"

"I think I broke his nose." He blew out a giant breath. "Blood came out everywhere. I didn't know a nose had so much blood in it."

"Oh, Charlie." Laura stood up, pressing a hand to her back, and walked over to him.

"I hate myself." She took his strong hands. He stood tall over her with a child's heart trapped in man's body.

"Don't say that. I love you. Dad loves you."

"Why am I like this, Mom? I don't want to be *special*, okay?" He pulled his hands away. "I didn't want to hit him. I swear. You can have a doctor make me fingernails and toenails. Can a doctor make me normal, too? Take away these things I can't control?"

He jerked away from Laura and got a drink from the fridge. The phone rang. Laura sighed. It could only be one person.

Brian's mother.

CHAPTER 3

Charlie snuck back out to the woods after his mom got off the phone with Brian's mom. His mom acted so cool and calm about what he did. He wished he could be more like her and not like her at the same time. Did that make sense?

She left then to do errands and his dad was still out on some wildlife photo shoot in the mountains. She didn't say he couldn't go out to the woods so it didn't feel like disobeying. He just needed to get out his frustration. No Brian and his stupid friends. Charlie replayed the moment again where he had embarrassed Brian. Pants down. Butt in the air. Girls laughing. Awesome. But he did feel bad about hitting him so hard. He really, really hadn't meant to.

He needed advice and he hoped Ghost Man would be there. He had called him that since he first saw him at seven. The man said he was Charlie's special secret. As Charlie got older he felt odd not telling his parents, but how could he explain he'd been seeing this guy all these years?

It would make him even weirder. His dad would think so. He never understood him. He wanted him to be normal. He wanted him to have the nail surgery. *I'll never be normal! Why can't he accept me for who I am? Because I'm not good enough, that's why.* The main reason he didn't want the surgery was to defy his dad, even to spite himself, and so he remained the freak he was born to be.

His dad's words remained burned in his brain from that night a couple of years ago when he'd heard his parents talking.

"If only he weren't the way he is," his dad had said. "He'd have a normal life. He'd be normal."

"Don't ever say that," his mom had said. "I love him just the way he is."

"I love him, too, but…it's hard."

"Love always is, Ben, but you don't ever give up."

"Sometimes I want to."

Charlie had turned back to his room then after those last words from his dad. He hadn't wanted to hear anymore. That day the wall grew between them. He would never be the son his dad wanted.

But Ghost Man treated him like a son. Charlie wanted to keep him all to himself. Ghost Man understood him and helped him figure things out. He said he should embrace his anger and be himself. Charlie felt conflicted about it, but sometimes it felt so good to be angry and destroy things. And Ghost Man helped him practice his destroying powers. But never on people. Or animals. He still felt guilty about Romeo. If he did such a thing then, what power did he have now? It scared him to think about it.

He walked deep into the woods on the narrow path. It used to be a deer path that became his path as he trudged over it through the years. He liked knowing the animals made it before he came along, and now he kept it going. Gloom settled under the tall pine trees. Their great branches shaded all below. These woods soon blended into the national forest.

He stepped out from the trees into a sunny meadow. Often, when he was drained from practicing his powers he stretched out on the soft green waves. He wanted to lay there forever and be invisible. Invisible was good. Then he couldn't be called a freak. If his parents saw what he did here they would think he was a freak, too.

He touched his cheek. It throbbed still. He sat down on the ground and waited. He hoped Ghost Man came today. The meadow had become their spot. It's where he first met him when he got lost in the woods at seven. His mom and dad had been terrified and called the police, but Ghost Man directed him back home. It was the first time he kept a secret from his parents.

"Had a fight, I see, Charlie-boy."

Charlie jumped up. Ghost Man shimmered before him.

"Yeah, jerks. Called me a freak."

"I saw. Nice work breaking that kid's nose."

"I didn't want to but—"

"You needed to. I understand. I can show you ways to hurt him without touching him yourself. No one will ever know."

"My dad wouldn't understand."

"Yes, well, your dad doesn't have your special abilities. He's ordinary. You don't want to be ordinary like him, do you, Charlie-boy?"

"I don't want to be like him, but I don't want to be me, either." He tapped his foot, frustrated at being stuck in his life. He had nowhere to go, no one to talk to, and no one who understood him—except Ghost Man.

"Your dad is ignorant to the kind of abilities you have. And in his ignorance lies weakness. He knows you're a stronger man than he'll ever be. It's why he keeps you down about yourself, Charlie. He's your biggest oppressor."

Charlie had heard these words before, seeping into him for years building the wall brick-by-brick between him and his dad. But now Ghost Man's words hit him in the gut—they twisted there and formed the truth inside him which all made sense now.

"My dad is jealous of me."

"Yes. You're more a man than him. Wait and see. Your life won't always be like this. Your time to shine shall come."

"Like showing those bullies?"

Ghost Man nodded.

Charlie squinted. The sunlight streamed through Ghost Man in waves. "I don't want to hurt anybody, though. I just want them to leave me alone."

"It's your destiny to be powerful, Charlie. Don't you want to know how you're supposed to use your abilities? No one will ever call you a freak again. Not bullies and not your father—for that's what he thinks you are, isn't?"

Charlie nodded, feeling miserable.

"You can control others," Ghost Man said. "I can show you how."

"Control others? Sounds scary." *And awesome.*

Ghost Man moved closer. "Life is scary, Charlie, for most people. It doesn't need to be for people like you and me. I am a powerful being who others follow, and I can show you how to control that bully. I can show you how you can make him disappear. No one will ever know you did it."

Except my mom. She'll know.

"Your father can't show you such power, can he?'

Charlie shook his head and looked down, twisting his fingers in his pockets. He wasn't sure how to feel about controlling someone. His mom had taught him to control himself, not others, and to never hurt anyone. He had to be more responsible than other kids, she said. It wasn't fair. Ghost Man held out his hands to Charlie. His fingers flexed smooth and nail-less like Charlie's.

"I've been waiting for the right time to tell you. You're old enough now to understand. I come from Elyon."

"A made up place."

"No. A real place, where I belonged to a secret underground society. We planned to rule the world with our powerful genes. Others wanted to crush our dreams and almost did once. But we came back, more powerful than ever. We've come here to follow our dream."

"Is Elyon far away?"

"Further away than you can imagine."

"Tell me. Where?"

"In due time, Charlie-boy."

Charlie nodded, not pushing for more. He wanted Ghost Man to remain make-believe. The thought of him being a real person from a real place hung in his thoughts like an unwanted gift.

He held out his hand and touched the apparition before him. Tingling pulsed into his fingers from the fingers that mirrored his own. Rage filled him. He looked around. Alone. As usual. He picked up a rock and threw it hard with a shout. And another.

"You can do better, Charlie-boy." Ghost Man smiled at him.

Adrenalin coursed through him. He commanded his hands. Branches wrenched from the trees. They crashed together. He dragged rocks from the earth with his mind and pounded them into the ground. Sweat ran down his face. It stung the cut over his eye and that made him angrier. He screamed and flung his body about, inanimate objects battling each other. Drained, he sank down on the meadow floor. Ghost Man floated over him, smiling.

"Feel better?"

Charlie nodded.

"I can teach you how to make someone do anything you want."

"Anything?"

"Yes."

Charlie thought about this. "You mean I could make Brian do bad things to himself?"

"Yes."

"So it wouldn't be me hurting him but him hurting himself?"

"Yes. Do you trust me, Charlie?"

Charlie nodded. Ghost Man was his guardian angel. He watched over him and made him feel better. His dad made him feel worse. He didn't want to feel bad anymore about who he was.

Revenge filled Charlie with a sweet rush. "Yes."

CHAPTER 4

Adrian's community leaders had begun pressuring him to bring the boy and woman in. The man would be eliminated, but Adrian planned some fun with him first.

He looked up. Eleven silent elders in gray watched him. He didn't know what they thought. They all held a closed lid on their thoughts, including his son, Caleb, who stared at him expressionless.

"We do not bring in the woman and her family yet, but we will keep watch over them."

"Brother Adrian, the woman is pregnant and near birth time," Tollen said. "We must bring her in now before the child is born."

The others nodded at Adrian except Caleb; he continued to stare at Adrian with an eyebrow raised. Adrian pushed his chair back and strode around the table. He walked to the window and looked down at the vast courtyard filled with his people. In seven years they had grown to over one thousand. Twins helped boost the count with chemical protein formulated to split the embryos. Twins…like he and Laura had once both been, each with a counterpart to their own. No more.

His people bustled back and forth to their work in the many wings of the community. Children played tag, while the women chatted as they shucked the last corn of the season for their community dinner, stopping every once in a while to admonish the children. Each child was raised with the intent to trigger their Destroyer gene. Every Elyon carried it. Tapping into their hate and rage brought it out. And tap into it he did. Some resisted. The weak ones. They were beaten down until they gave in. The defective Elyons who didn't succumb to their Destroyer destiny were lobotomized—or killed.

It had all been controlled until a few fled, but the majority of his people were loyal folks who followed him as their great overseer. They were his flock, his creation, and their community was insulated in this rural setting. People in the outside world were made to think of them as a closed cult-like community and left them alone.

How *benevolent* of these people of Benevolence. How wonderful of them to hand their money over to them when requested on town trips. The cash helped build a new Elyon community. How easy to manipulate human minds. They had no idea they financed their own destruction. It was time to spread their seed outside the compound. Plans were in place. He saw his people's future here and it was prosperous.

"Father?" Caleb's voice brought him back to the tasks at hand. Perhaps it was also time to bring Laura in before she gave birth. But first he wanted the boy.

Adrian turned back to the community leaders. "Yes, all right. We bring her in, and I know how to do it."

He outlined his plan. All nodded. They would follow him. He had selected them with care before defecting from Elyon. They did not want their cause crushed in another Destroyer Uprising like on Elyon. Only Tollen questioned his authority—and they both understood why. They had both been in love with Manta, both had affairs with her. But she chose Adrian over him, just as the Destroyer leaders chose Adrian to lead over Tollen. And Adrian gorged on Tollen's jealousy. It fueled his power. It's why he had selected him for the mission.

Caleb remained silent as they finalized the details. His son's weakness remained a constant sore wound in his side. That and the fact he looked like his traitorous mother and claimed impotency. What young man could be impotent at twenty-five? Satisfaction surged through Adrian over the fact he had snatched his son away from the boy's beloved uncle—and his hated brother.

In one night he had dashed his brother's dreams and taken his son away from the last person he cared about. Caring about anyone led to weakness. Manta flashed through his mind like a burning arrow, but he put the fire of her memory out. He had to if he was to remain a strong leader.

The community leaders left but Adrian motioned for Caleb to remain.

"I am sending a female to you tonight."

Caleb's shoulders hunched inward and he hid his hands in his robe. "No Father, it won't work."

"A pretty one. Young. Nineteen. Brunette. You like brunettes, Caleb. I hear she is very accepting and fertile. Three children in three years she has produced."

"No." It came out a whisper.

Adrian smashed his hands down on the conference table that had been crafted by their carpenters from one large pine found deep in the forest. "Stop this nonsense. You haven't bred for years now. This must stop. You must arouse yourself to produce or at least use your transference powers to pass your seed on. It is expected of all Elyons and you especially as my son—and a Madroc. Weakness is not tolerated. *Will not be.*"

Caleb looked at Adrian with narrowed eyes. "Or what? I do your dirty work, isn't that enough?"

"No, it's not enough. It shows you are loyal but not strong. I am the one chosen to create our new Destroyer community here. Why can't you obey and do what we are all doing to increase our superior gene pool? You know what will happen to you. I cannot protect you from our laws."

"As our chosen leader you can change the laws, Father. And would you really lobotomize your own son?"

"If the leaders so decree it. Soon they will start to pressure me. I hear the whispers. And it makes me look weak."

"And I know *you're* not weak, Father." Caleb turned to walk away.

"I will have it done. Don't test me."

Caleb turned back to him. "I know you will."

Adrian's eyes widened. "Is this why you don't follow law? You *want* me to have you lobotomized? You want to lose your powers and work in a menial job forever?"

"It's better than living in this world. Don't you find it ironic that Destroyers were lobotomized after the Destroyer Uprising by our own Elyon community and now you're doing it to your own people here?" Caleb laughed.

"Do you prefer to live in the human world, Son?"

"Anywhere but here."

"You can't look to humans for help. Their greatest leaders fail."

"And happy is the man who has you as their god?" Caleb quoted back at him from the Bible. "Are you the god who keeps every promise and gives justice to the oppressed? I think not, Father."

Fury seethed through Adrian. His seed should be aligned with him, not throwing barbs at him. Adrian read the Bible every night since picking it up in that store on their first night in town. He had studied human religion before they arrived. Records were archived on the ship from Elyons' many trips to Earth via communication belts. They had watched and learned before choosing Earth as their people's final destination, and Adrian drank in human ways like an elixir.

He most aligned himself with Christianity, with God and his son. Someday, the entire world would see him as more powerful than their absent god full of empty promises. He had looked into the future and seen human kind replaced by Elyon Destroyers. He saw them overtaking the world in roles of power, crushing opposition with death and firepower. He saw himself as the American president at the White House—and he saw Laura at his side and all the sons they would bring forth. It filled him with power.

He locked eyes with Caleb. His younger children obeyed as willing learners. Never Caleb. Adrian wanted to see his son beg for pity, as he had once begged his own father.

Childhood memories overtook him—of cold, dark nights chained in the bottom of a well. His father had been an Underground Destroyer and deemed Adrian's weaknesses worthy of a night in the well.

Want to be lobotomized instead, Son? His father had scowled down at him from above with the ultimate threat, as Adrian shook his head.

Then his father's face disappeared. The silence had been the worst. No one came to unchain him. Only his father twenty hours later. By then his skin had shriveled, his body imprisoned in uncontrollable shivers from the rank, stagnant water that covered him to his chest.

He remembered trying not to think about what lay beneath the black water. He tried to sleep hanging onto the rungs which climbed up the well wall, but every time he nodded off his body jerked up right. His only savior was the sky above his stone cave. The stars had floated overhead in the night, calling to him with hope. He had endured those nights, but he had not given into his Destroyer gene. Not then.

A simple answer came to him. Caleb could be replaced with the boy. His anger drained. Yes. The boy would be his new challenge. He had courage and darkness in him. He was born to lead the Elyon people into a new world. But Adrian would give Caleb one more chance.

"I'll send the female tonight. I'll be watching."

Caleb smirked at him. "I know you will. You like to watch."

"Make a good choice, Caleb."

"I've already made my choice, Father." Caleb looked at him as if in pain. "And now I have your dirty work to do." He flung his robe back and left the room.

Adrian sank into his chair. He was so tired of leading at times. If Caleb didn't use the female tonight he would take her. He prided himself on the most offspring within their community.

Tonight he might add another.

CHAPTER 5

Caleb strode fast to his next job. He hated his father with the darkest depths of his soul. Hated how he had him brought here against his will. Hated how he ruled with cruelty. And he hated being part of the Madroc family. If he gave into this hate he would be giving in to what his father wanted him to be.

A Destroyer.

He would fight it even if it meant his own demise. He had seen the disobedient ones lobotomized. Labeled Unfit, they went about their jobs with blank smiles on their faces and were kept in a separate wing to be bred amongst themselves. They didn't seem unhappy. Would it be such a bad way to be? Innocent and content? But then he couldn't help his people in trouble—and he wouldn't know his sons. It was why he did his father's dirty work. It saved him from losing his mind—literally.

Caleb pretended for years to be impotent. It fed into his father's belief he was weak. It sickened him he had to "breed" and lay with females chosen for him. At times it was hard to resist as his teen hormones raged wild, but he assuaged it by relieving himself and using his mind powers to remove his desire.

He had lost his will just once at nineteen. She had been such a beautiful, sweet female. Rachel was her name. She was the third one his father had selected him to bond with as his "first" female in their community. The first two he refused and as a consequence was whipped severely, but the moment he saw Rachel he had to have her.

He succumbed to pleasure. And she had pleased him across a sea of soft nights, blending her flesh with his. He had fallen in love with her from that first night, possessing her body, soul, and mind. He tried not to think about how short their time would be together. The law stated each Elyon would bond with another for their first time before being placed in the breeding assignment pool. Never again would they be with the one they bonded with for their first time. It was his father's way of discouraging special relationships.

But Caleb memorized each moment with Rachel in his heart while begging time to slow down. And poems for her poured from him. He spoke them to her as he moved within her. One word at a time. "I. Just. Wanted. To. Set. You. Free."

And her moans grew as his words spilled over her, and when she cried out with release he spilled his life into her.

"Caleb, free me again," she murmured in his ear after their heartbeats slowed, chests pressed together slick from their loving. And he did. She took his hand then and silenced him with her tongue and lips. But never again would he recite a poem to her.

He fingered the worn paper he kept in his robe's pocket. The last poem he'd written for Rachel. He'd planned to give it to her one special night, but she never came to him again. Their bond was severed. She was sent to mate with another…and then another and another.

But she was already pregnant then with his children. Twins. Now five years old. Children who would never know him as their father. Children he couldn't love or raise with Rachel as his own. The babies were handed off to the other nursing women and passed around to feed. With so many twin babies he didn't know which pair was his sons. He watched the children in the courtyard for hours determining who his children were. As time passed he discovered two boys who looked like him. Jeremiah and Josiah. Caleb often whispered their names out loud as if sending up a prayer to be with them.

Oh, yes, he prayed to the human god. He knew the Bible as well as his father. He had since found his own copy during a town mission for money and supplies. He needed to understand this god humans worshipped. The god his father believed he was. Religion provided humans with purpose and peace and a sense of belonging to something bigger than themselves. All he desired. His father used the human Bible for his own power plays. Caleb read it to know what lay at the core of humanity and people's hearts. Their found strength in faith gave him strength and hope. He needed both.

But for now he had no time for prayer. He had to report to the whipping shack. He headed there through the wooded path near the perimeter of their compound. He reached the twelve-foot high fence which bound him to this place. Guards patrolled at intervals along the fence. The shadow of one walked now in the distance. Out there held freedom. The pine trees swayed free, their own master. Unlike him. Someday he would become his own master and take his sons with him. But if he tried and failed—they would die. If his father discovered his plan—they would die.

The screams brought him back to his world.

Caleb hesitated then pulled open the door to the rough-hewn shed. Thomas, a skinny young man, stood sobbing. He faced the back wall, naked with his hands tied over his head to a rope hanging from the ceiling. Savage red marks painted his pale back and buttocks. Blood streaked across him like a child's rough painting. His legs shook and urine trickled down them. Eli, an Enforcer, relaxed his leather whip—the end tinged crimson with blood—and frowned at Caleb as he entered. Whippings had increased by his father's decree.

"Not done yet. Your father ordered twenty lashes for the second offense of trying to desert. And ten more for self-healing yourself after your last whipping, weakling! I've got ten left to administer." Eli flexed his enormous muscles and massaged his wrist. "Got a wrist sprain from all this work lately." He grinned. Caleb did not grin back. Thomas continued to cry.

"Stop your blubbering, Thomas," Eli said. "This is well deserved, you know. Putting our community at risk. Where were you going?"

"Any…where…but here." Thomas cried harder. He swayed from the rope holding him up by his pitiful arms and his knees buckled.

"Yeah, well, after this it's the stocks for you all night outside. Caleb is here to take you over."

"No, no…please. The females will see me. They don't want me. No one does. It's why I had to leave."

"They sure will see you, Son." Eli winked at Caleb. "You know the rules. The females will have something to feast their eyes on in the morning as they go about their chores. And no self-healing, little Thomas, or they'll be a bigger whipping in store for you."

"I'll finish up here, Eli," Caleb said. He pulled his lips back in what he hoped fared as a smile.

"I don't know. Adrian was specific."

"Don't worry. I'll get ten good lashes in. Go back to your bunk and ice that wrist."

"I think I will. Thanks, Caleb." Eli handed him the whip. "Thomas, watch out no woodland animals visit the stocks tonight. They may nibble on your tiny member then there won't be anything left for the few females who'd have you." He slammed out of the shed with a roar of laughter.

Caleb stood quietly, the whip limp in his hands. Thomas bent his head down further into his chest. His sobs turned to ragged whimpers. Caleb took a deep breath and flung the whip out.

S-n-a-p.

It cracked the wall. Thomas screamed then twisted his head toward Caleb with a puzzled look.

"Nine more times, Thomas. I want you to scream with each lash, okay?"

Thomas nodded.

S-n-a-p.

Thomas played his part. Screaming was the easy part. Caleb finished then untied Thomas, who fell on his knees.

"Caleb…thank you."

Caleb lifted him up. "Let me heal those marks." He moved his hands down over Thomas's bloody welts. The marks and blood disappeared. Caleb handed Thomas his clothes. "Get dressed and then go back to your bunk."

"But they'll think I self-healed and I'll be whipped more!"

"I'll tell them I did it."

"Why? And what will happen to you if I don't go to the stocks?" Thomas's hands shook so badly he couldn't tie his robe.

Caleb helped him. "Don't worry about me. I'll deal with my father. But you have to do something for me."

"Anything." Thomas stood up straighter.

"I know you're behind on your breeding quota."

Thomas sighed. "I'm always last to get chosen for a female. It's not my fault."

"I'll send you one tonight. A good one. Make her feel special and she'll spread the word about you. The leaders will think you're a worthy breeder. Perhaps you'll be moved up the select list and have all the females you want."

Thomas nodded and clenched his hands together. "I—I don't know how to thank you."

"Do as I ask and happiness shall be yours. And Thomas?"

"Yes?"

"If you try and escape again it will be worse for you."

"I know."

"I may not be able to help you."

Thomas nodded and grasped his hands. "Thank you."

"Go."

Thomas ran out of the shed with a wave. Caleb stood in the dark torture chamber. He may be whipped himself for letting Thomas go, but he didn't care. How simple it would be if he could be like Thomas and the one thing that made him happy would be having females galore at his disposal. He wanted one of his own choosing, but he was destined to be alone.

He could live with that, if only he could be a father to his sons.

CHAPTER 6

Ben Fieldstone stomped the mud off his boots, removed them, and stepped into the foyer. He had spent all day taking wildlife photographs for a regional magazine. He stretched his arms, sore from remaining in the same position for hours. Unlike most people, animals were shy creatures of silence. Sacred yet soulless. To be in their presence required patience and hope. It's why he preferred them at times.

Even over his son.

He loved Charlie, but his son frustrated him. Ben didn't have the bond with him Laura had. The one thing that bonded them was their tempers. He might never break past his son's shell. He cringed, thinking again of how his words continued to hurt his son. *He'd be normal.* He wished he never said it.

"Laura?"

He walked into the kitchen. Cornbread steamed on the top of the stove. Ben breathed in the rich stew bubbling in the crock-pot. He flicked on the big overhead light. Early autumn darkness fell fast. There she sat, a vision in the rocker by the bay window with hands clasped over her pregnant belly as if protecting their child, her eyes closed.

Photo albums lay about open, one on her lap. Pictures he had taken of her and Charlie, when their son came into the world and then as a toddler. His son had loved him then. "Daddy! Daddy!" was all he heard when he walked in the door after a long day at a photo shoot. Ben would pick Charlie up and hold his wriggling warm body to his, as his son begged to be tickled. Now his son acted pained to be around him.

Something changed when Charlie was seven years old and from then on Charlie and Laura's circle remained unbreakable. Ben wasn't envious of Laura for it. He was glad Charlie found belonging with her, but he wished he could also find his own way to belong with his son.

And there strewn were photos of Laura. Her shining hair flowed in waves as she bent down to pick a flower on a meadow walk. She was his match. Together they were balanced. She had saved Ben from himself all those years ago. Saved him from a path of loneliness and loss and showed him how to live through love. She was stronger than him. She always had been.

They had both lost loved ones and suffered, but her heart had never closed. It had been open, ready to love again while he had closed his off in self-destruction. His heart was closed off now to a son he didn't understand. How could he open it again to him?

He stood for a while watching Laura, like the first time he saw her years ago singing away in a birch tree. She had been so beautiful then when he surprised her in the woods. She'd grown lovelier with age and maturity. He wanted to wake her, yet wanted to stare at her without her knowing. He bent down and embraced her from behind, her swollen breasts and belly caught in his arms. He squeezed softly and kissed her neck where chestnut curls hung.

She jerked and then relaxed.

"What took you so long? I've been reminiscing…now with the new baby coming." She pointed at the photos. "Wasn't Charlie adorable?"

"Just like you." He continued to kiss her neck, moving up to her ear. She moved into him and sighed.

"Remember our trip to the San Diego Zoo?" Laura said, flicking through album pages.

"Charlie wanted to release all the animals," Ben murmured into her hair.

"So they could be free to find their place in the world where they belonged." She sighed again. "Like Charlie wants to find where he belongs."

"Like Big Brave Blue?"

She nodded.

"He'll find it someday, Laura."

"He wants to feel he belongs with you, Ben. And he doesn't."

Ben stopped kissing her, but hugged her a bit tighter. He didn't know what to say about that. He needed to work on his relationship with Charlie, but it seemed as if some force kept them apart and he was helpless to break down the wall between them.

"Dinner's ready...although, I don't know where Charlie is," Laura said, finally ending their silence. She stood up, moving slow, and turned to him. "What took you so long?"

"I've been trying to get shots of the pair of bald eagles up there, among other things. They hid from me all day."

"They're huge and their nests are, too. How do they hide them?"

"I don't know. You, on the other hand, can't hide from me." He hugged her from behind.

"No kidding. Wonder when I'll ever be able to suck my stomach in again."

"Soon." Ben slid a hand into her shirt, stroking one plump breast.

"Ben Fieldstone!" She feigned indignation and an attempt to push his hand away.

"You said Charlie wasn't here." He stroked the other breast, her nipples hardening to his delight. "They're so in need."

She moaned. "I'm always in need with you around."

Ben pulled her toward the bedroom.

Laura resisted, looking out the window. "Charlie may be back home any minute. I hope he is. He got in a...well, he didn't have a good day and it's getting dark out there."

"A quick one. Charlie knows his way home. We'll lock the door and be quiet."

He led her into the bedroom and took her gently on her side, one leg flung over his. Her throbbing heat engulfed him, their child moving between them. A child he hoped would be like Charlie...and not like someone else. They didn't speak of it. Silence prevented many things. But in this act of love their child was safe for now, connected to both of them as their bodies fused together. All three of them were held close by threads too fine to see but taut with strength. He slid into her again and again, as if doing so harbored his son in a safe place.

Laura offered herself to him as she had on their first night so long ago, shy and innocent then in her love making. She had since grown into a sensuous woman, unashamed of her body and free in her sexuality. She moaned as he moved into her softness. Her warm breath pulsed on his chest. Her time of birth grew close and he held her tighter, wanting to keep her close forever. Wanting to keep her safe, their child safe.

"My perfect match," he whispered in her ear.

"Yes. Oh, yes," Laura whispered back, breathless as she neared release.

He sunk into her in a sweet rhythm, sucking on her breasts and caressing her tender spot. She clung to him in her moment, as she arched her back straining with her hips and her tight sex against him. He poured into her then and pulled her closer. Tears pressed onto his cheeks.

"What's wrong?" But he had the same fear.

"Our baby."

"I know." He held her. He had no other words. She carried his thoughts. He hid nothing from her. And over the years she had taught him how to read hers if she opened up her mind to him. At first he had been afraid to allow himself the experience but soon discovered it brought a deeper closeness to their relationship. And in making love it heightened intimacy. Their minds became joined as their bodies moved together in silence.

At those times he was not only inside her body but inside her soul. Lately she had been blocking her thoughts from him, and he felt a distance there that had not been between them before.

She moved away from him and sat up. He enjoyed her rounded curves and knelt behind her on the bed, his arms held her close. He spanned his hands on her immense abdomen. One more month. Would this child reveal himself at birth or over time?

Laura echoed his thoughts. "Our baby looks fine on the ultrasound but will he *be* fine?"

"Have hope. You were always better at it than me." Ben twirled her hair, but she pulled away and got dressed. He wished they didn't have to, but Charlie would be home. "We went through this with Charlie. We'll get through it again."

"I tried the belt again today. I had to see if they were still there."

Ben sighed and got dressed. He wished she wouldn't do that alone. "Did you get through?"

"Yes…"

"But?"

"I saw the shapes again hidden in the mist…and something else."

Ben waited. His heart knocked up a notch.

"A giant object not there before. A dark thing through the mist."

"A building?"

"Not sure. It's something they've built since the last time I got through. I thought they were all dead but maybe not. Maybe they live and will come here again." She sat back down on the bed.

Ben sat beside her. "And?"

"With our baby coming I want to believe they're still alive. Believe people from this other world are really coming. People from Elyon. From *my* place. Charlie's place. I've been waiting so long. Hoping for others and that—"

"You and Charlie wouldn't be the only ones?"

She nodded, tearing up. "I want to hope, but dashed hope can kill dreams."

Ben wiped her tear away. "Keep your hope close. You've only lost it once. Remember?"

She nodded.

"And you came back to me then, Laura. You had nothing to lose."

"Now I have everything to lose." She cried harder.

Ben took her hands, not understanding her fear. "Why, Laura?"

"Is this child ours?"

Ben dropped her hands, stunned. "What do you mean?"

Laura held her belly. "My mother had been a virgin…and she got pregnant. Then there's your vasectomy."

"The doctor said it can happen. No procedure is a hundred percent." It sounded reasonable and right to him. "Being pregnant can make you feel paranoid, Laura." He took her hands again and kissed them, willing her to believe his words.

She stared at him as she shook her head. "The headaches are back."

"Why didn't you tell me?"

"If I didn't tell you then I thought they would go away."

Ben nodded. He understood this. "But you said there hasn't been anyone on Elyon to contact."

"No one there…no." Her sobs trailed into gasps.

"You think someone's here?"

She nodded.

"A Destroyer?"

She didn't respond. He gripped her hands, not wanting to believe. He bowed his head to hers, his brain screaming with other possibilities.

The old fear hit him again in his gut.

CHAPTER 7

Charlie eased silently away from his parent's door, his mind reeling. How did his mom know about Elyon? He had thought it was a special place just him and Ghost Man talked about. And what was a Destroyer? And why was she so afraid? Her sobbing disturbed him. He planned to sneak back to the woods after his parents went to bed and hope Ghost Man appeared. He needed answers.

He set the table for dinner. Maybe it would make her happy. He disappointed her a lot, but he just couldn't control his urges all the time. He wanted to. He really did. She understood most of the time. His dad didn't.

He remembered a time when he and his dad weren't at odds. He had been a kid then. They'd go mountain biking along the wood trail. One time he had busted up his bike on a big rock going too fast. Speed set him free until he crashed. His dad had cleaned up the gash on his leg and put a big bandage on it. He never yelled at him or nothing. He took out his bike tools and showed him how to fix the problem. Charlie laughed when his dad wiped his face and left a big black smudge of chain grease on his nose.

Oh, yeah, Charlie-boy? You dare to laugh at me? His dad jumped him then, smudging his own face. He smudged him back and then all-out war followed. Charlie got full-on body tickled in the pine needles. He laughed so hard that his sides hurt. When they stopped they both looked like painted Indian warriors ready for battle. The same in look and spirit.

Not now. Not anymore. *Not normal.*

He was only normal with Ghost Man.

Charlie clinked the dishes and silverware together, partly in frustration and partly because he wanted his parents to know he was home. He didn't want to think about what else they might be doing in the bedroom with the door closed. His mom's pregnancy bothered him enough. He was excited to have a new brother even though he would be so much older than him. But sometimes his mom's big stomach grossed him out knowing how it got so big. He didn't want to think about his parents doing *that*.

His dad came out of the bedroom with his head bent down and Charlie saw a world of grief he didn't understand. Then his dad looked up and his face changed from a sad grimace to a half smile.

"Charlie-boy, where've you been? Your mom's getting worried."

Charlie fiddled to get the napkins lined up like his mom wanted them. It wasn't the time to remind his dad to stop calling him Charlie-boy. That was Ghost Man's name for him. "Hanging in the woods."

His dad came closer. "What happened to your face?"

Charlie looked up. "Kids at school. They followed me home."

His dad put his hand on his shoulder. "Why didn't you take the bus?"

Charlie twitched away and yanked open the cabinet to grab glasses. Fear, anger, and confusion mixed up inside him. Over his dad. The kids at school. The strange conversation he'd just overhead between his parents. He needed Ghost Man.

"Yeah, I'm okay Dad, thanks for asking. And I'm glad you worried too, not just mom. Thanks again." He slammed the glasses on the table. One wobbled and fell over. His dad reached over and picked the glass up.

"Okay, let's start over. Of course, I worry about you, too. And it's safer for you to take the bus, Charlie. Your mom and I don't like for you to be in the woods by yourself. The national forest extends beyond it for hundreds of miles. If you get lost in there we might never find you."

"Would you care?"

"Of course I'd care!"

"But Mom roamed her woods as a kid when she was younger than me." Charlie sat down, his anger faded. His dad looked old under the kitchen light. It carved harsh lines in his face. His hair had turned almost all gray the past year.

"It was—"

"A different time and place. Yes, *I know*, Dad."

"Let's get dinner on the table. Your mom will be right out. She's tired, so let's just have a nice dinner together. You can tell me what happened and we can figure out how to deal with this."

"There's no need for you to *deal*, Dad. And it's my problem. You can't help me."

"I can try."

"No, you can't. You don't get it."

"Help me to get it."

"You won't ever. You're normal."

"I never said you weren't normal, Charlie."

"You're lying!"

"I said to your mom once, in a private conversation, I wanted you to have a normal life."

"Same thing."

"No, it's not," his dad said quietly.

Guilt grabbed at Charlie. He turned away to get the water pitcher from the fridge and accidentally bit his lip. Tears formed. He didn't want his dad to see him cry. He had to get out of here. Go to his room. Something.

"I'm not hungry. I'll be in my room."

His dad looked at him, nodded, and turned away. And so did Charlie. Then he let the tears fall.

Charlie stood alone in the field. He peered up to the sky seeking out Ghost Man. He called Ghost Man's name over and over in a hoarse voice. The moon rose high amongst the stars. Charlie could wait all night if he had to, but he didn't have to wait long.

"Charlie-boy, what's wrong?"

"Ghost Man, I've been calling forever. Where've you been?" Charlie shivered.

"I've been busy managing my business. I have many people I oversee, Charlie."

"I need to talk. Bad. *Now*."

"Tell me."

"My mom, she knows about Elyon. I heard her talking to my dad. And about some belt and a Destroyer—whatever that is—and she was crying."

"Charlie—"

"She said 'maybe they're all dead'. Who's dead? And she said Elyon was her place and my place, too. It doesn't make sense."

"Shh…calm down, Charlie-boy. And let me speak."

Charlie puffed up his cheeks and then blew out hard. "Okay, okay." He ran his fingers through his hair and pressed his fingers to his brow.

"Your hair."

"My *hair*?"

"Yes, see how it's like mine? And your fingers. Hold them out."

Charlie stretched out his hand and Ghost Man reached for it with his. "You don't have nails either." Charlie stared at his own fingers then Ghost Man's. They shimmered along with his white hair. He glowed brilliant in unearthly light.

Charlie stared at him with wide eyes. "I don't get it."

"I've been visiting you for a reason. So you can know where you come from."

"I thought Elyon was a make believe place and you were some kind of special vision I created with my abilities."

"Elyon is real. A place far away. I'm from there. And your mother. And you."

"No. My Mom's from New York."

"Part of her is from Elyon."

"*Part* of her? What does that mean? And what about my dad?"

"He's just a human. Not like us."

"*Just* a human?" Charlie stumbled back on a rock. He shook his head so fast it hurt. "No, no. I don't know what you're saying, but it's all wrong. You're wrong!"

"It's true. I'm your mother's uncle. Your great-uncle. And I'm not from Earth."

"Stop it! I thought I wasn't a freak with you and now you're saying I'm even more of a freak. Just stop it!"

Charlie turned and ran to the edge of the field. *Come back to me, Charlie-boy.* Charlie heard him inside his head but didn't stop running.

The words shattered through him like hammer to glass. *Not from Earth.*

CHAPTER 8

Caleb watched the elders and listened as the council meeting went on longer than usual. They'd become unhappy with the recent number of attempts at desertion. And the new program did not seem to be working as planned. One of the leaders had been sent with a small group of trusted community members to set up their first church outside of their compound.

His father said the time had come to begin spreading their people throughout the world, but not all of the new community members thought so. Two members of the new church had disappeared and took their children with them, before new recruitment had begun. Caleb wished he was one of those parents.

But did those Elyons leave of their own accord or did his father find them unfit and make them disappear? After the Destroyer Uprising had been defeated on Elyon, his father joined the cause and rebuilt the loyal group in secrecy. Caleb had suspicions before about his father's membership prior to defection. Since being kidnapped his suspicions were confirmed, and he now feared what else his father could do—had done.

Adrian stood and banged his fists on the table. "Our plan changes. The next Elyon caught attempting to desert will die. Painfully. And those who refuse to breed will be lobotomized and bred through transference. Agreed?" He looked at Caleb.

The elders buzzed. Tollen looked down his long nose at Adrian. "And what about the new church out there?"

"Close it up. Bring the members back. We are not as ready as I had hoped." He sat down. "And seek out humans who may know about us. Erase their memory. We must cut off all enemies and destroy those who try to harm us. Even our own. Find them and dispose of them."

"You rushed this, Brother Adrian," Tollen said.

"It's been seven years of building a strong community. We must expand into the human world soon. In my lifetime. I must see this happen."

"It's for the good of all our people, not only one. We don't want our cause crushed again like on Elyon."

Adrian scowled at Tollen, who finally dropped his eyes, and sat down.

Caleb stepped in. "Father, with increased lobotomies we defeat the purpose of coming here to build our gene pool. Those lobotomized no longer have powers."

His father turned to look at him. "But they can still breed power, Son. Better than those who refuse to breed."

His father knew he had sent the girl meant for him off to Thomas after releasing the boy. Caleb hadn't been punished yet for his own disobedience. It would come. New scars would soon blend with the ones thick on his back already. He could bear the whippings—if he could spare the punished some pain.

Adrian called order and the elders voted on the new laws. Despair sunk into Caleb. They all had the power to heal but were denied this for themselves. This was the one law that enabled his father to wield the power of corporal punishment over his people. How ironic that back home Caleb was an outcast for not healing himself as expected when injured. He wanted to feel the pain, to feel human.

And here Caleb secretly saved the discarded ones, those his father punished and tossed aside like yesterday's trash. But how could he save every executed Elyon? At least a few were something. It was his one salvation. If he stopped a few souls' pain, it soothed the emotional pain he felt.

The pain of fighting against his Destroyer genes.

The pain of never knowing his sons.

The pain of never having love of his own choosing.

Would he soon be trash, too? And who would save *him* from being discarded?

Is this what his mother felt like in that well? He had only been seventeen the day he found her. He didn't know why she had traveled off the path and come across it. He had covered the old well with branches and leaves. It had been his hiding place back home to get away from the bullies—and his father.

He remembered the day he'd walked in on his father plundering Aunt Manta in their house, and hearing her moans of pleasure. He had stumbled out then into the cold rain, heading for his hideaway.

When he reached the well, a giant hole breached the brush he had last used to cover it. He shoved the branches aside and climbed down into his sanctuary, wary that some animal might be poised to greet him. Halfway down he paused, but sensed no movement. Heard no sound. The comforting dark reached up for him, and he longed to enter its embrace.

His foot reached the floor but didn't touch hard stone. He landed on something soft. He lost his balance and fell back, cracking his head on the side of the well.

He lay crumpled at the bottom, waiting for the pain to recede. As his eyes adjusted to the gloom, a face stared back at him. Not the bright eyes of an animal. Eyes he recognized, yet so different now drained of life. His mother's.

Caleb screamed and slammed back into the wall. Her head lolled to one side and her leg, stuck out at a crooked angle, lay on her travel bag. She leaned up against the wall as if someone had propped her there.

Why had she insisted on leaving alone? He should have walked with her. He knew these woods better than she did. She must have wandered off the path in the dark and fallen into the brush. He never should have covered the opening so carelessly. He should have told someone about the danger and had it sealed.

This was his fault. His own, dear mother's loss—all his fault.

Or was it?

Crying, he touched her shoulder. Like frozen wood. "Mother?" It echoed up the dank walls.

She didn't answer. He placed his hands on her stiff body and closed his eyes, willing her back to life with his healing power. *Please come back. You're all I have now. Please!*

But she was long gone.

No one heard her scream. No one came to save her. For days while he went to school and did his chores his mother lay broken and dying.

For days their search party combed the woods. He didn't want to see her down there. But later it became a place he went to. He sat there and talked to her spirit.

"Caleb?"

He brought himself back to the business at the table and realized his father watched him. He had to be more careful. He couldn't let his guard down and allow his father to read his mind. His father was a master mind prober, like a snake in dark halls that slithered unseen to uncover secrets.

"Do you second the motion to put these laws in place?"

The elders stared at him from around the immense table.

"I do," he finally said. "Motion seconded."

His father nodded at him. Let his father think he wanted to do his dirty work.

The elders left but his father motioned for him to stay. "I have a job for you."

Caleb waited, hands fisted under his robe. His fingers pressed into his palms.

"The first punishment delivered from our new law."

Perspiration rose hot above Caleb's lips. Blood pounded in his ears. He forced himself to reveal his hands and held them out as an offering. "Yes?"

"A deserter will die. It's your duty to make it so. She has been caught outside the compound with her children. Not far into the woods."

"How is she to die?"

"By stoning. The entire community will participate. It will be a warning to them."

Caleb pulled in his stomach. A sickness sprung deep from within him. He had to save her.

"And the children?"

"They will watch her die and then be placed back within the community."

Despair and relief coursed through Caleb at the same time.

"Who is the woman?"

"Her name is Rachel." His father smiled at him. "I believe you lay with her once. Long ago when your mind was strong and your body willing to do its duty."

His stomach churned. He shoved his hands back under his robe and pressed them to his gut.

"You must deliver her for the punishment. And when she is dead you'll bury her in the woods. Do you understand your duty?"

Caleb's eyes blurred. His father became a shadowy shape drifting before him.

"If you cannot, your sons will die, too. I know who they are."

Caleb's vision cleared.

"And you will throw the first stone."

Caleb nodded and pushed his way past his father. He ran to the nearest bathroom and threw up until there was nothing left.

He was empty inside. As he had always been.

CHAPTER 9

Laura heard Charlie come in. She turned over and looked at the clock. After midnight. What had he been doing? She tried to sit up but pain raged through her head. The migraines had returned. Her unborn child kicked angrily as if he too felt the pain. She fell back and sighed. Tomorrow she would question Charlie. Tonight she prayed for blessed relief from the pain. It had to be pregnancy related. She made a note to ask the doctor about it at her next checkup. The moonlight shed a soft glow through the sheer curtains. It hurt her eyes.

Ben moaned next to her. She wondered what his dreams held. Fear and terror like hers? She placed her hand on his arm. He moaned again. She pushed her belly into his side, needing to feel safe. She traced her fingers on the scars across his back, the physical evidence of his long ago night of suffering as a sailor in Hawaii. He had almost met his death then by a vengeful pimp who held him hostage and whipped him. And he had been saved by the man who'd watched over both of them in secret—Felix. It was a lifetime ago before he met Laura, when he had been another man.

She had to use Felix's communication belt again, had to know if others still existed there—were coming again like they had so long ago. With her child coming soon, uncertainty about his place in the world—about hers—filled her with growing anxiety. She needed to know her kind still existed in order to feel at peace. If they ever came to Earth and Charlie finally knew his heritage—could he accept it?

She slid from the bed and retrieved a box from her closet, hidden far behind clothes and under books. She sat in the wingback chair near the window and lifted out a wide, long belt of burnished steel. She peeked at Ben to make sure he remained asleep. His slow breaths comforted her as she ran her fingers over the belt's smooth texture. Its silver sheen glinted in the soft moonlight, rippling with iridescence. It changed color from dark gray to light then a deep purple and back to gray as it flexed between her hands with a life of its own.

She put it on and had to loop it on the last hole, her expansive stomach taking up most of the length. She took a deep breath and pressed a series of buttons on the buckle's panel that was the combination she had discovered years ago upon taking the belt from Felix. He'd helped her and Ben survive her twin's attack. Felix had been the only other person, beside her brother, who had been half-Elyon, half-human—like herself. He had died that awful night protecting her when her brother tried to kill her. But he left her one thing behind—his belt. Felix had told her it was a belt to their world. Elyon.

Take me to Elyon. She closed her eyes and in a whoosh was pulled through time and space. The tick of the wall clock and Ben's breathing left her. An almost unbearable silence filled her every crevice. She opened her eyes. Mist blew across gray rock. Stars twinkled above through racing clouds.

The vapor swirled away to reveal a black building, not square but angled and rounded. A figure stepped from an opening in it and moved toward her. Laura clutched her belly to protect her child, even though her body still sat in the chair back home. Her hands shimmered through her, like an apparition. If she pressed the large green button on the belt her spirit would return to her bedroom.

A tall, white haired man in a gray robe grew closer, his head down. He held a large bag and shuffled one hand about in it. The mist flowed around him as if it were part of him. He looked up and stopped, his hand frozen in the bag. He pulled it out and held it toward her. Laura inhaled sharply. She hadn't seen people here since Charlie was a young child and she had stopped using the belt. She had no need to then.

The man walked closer, his face puzzled.

You're Laura. His words came to her, clear in her mind.

Stunned, she didn't know how to respond and then the words came to her and she answered back with her own thoughts. *How do you know this?*

I saw you the day my brother spoke to you years ago. You were ready to bear a child then, like you are now.

You're my uncle, too?

Yes. My name is Brahm Madroc.

Your brother said your people were coming. I've waited and waited but heard nothing.

I believe he did come. The man's forehead wrinkled and he looked away.

What do you mean? The mist blew across the man, obscuring his sad expression.

He, along with Destroyer renegades, stole our people's ship. They could have only gone to one place, Earth, on their own mission. We crushed their Destroyer Uprising years ago, but we couldn't put their cause out completely. They rose again—and we believe are now on Earth. We can't know for sure. The thieves took our only communication belt.

Fear prickled through Laura. *When was this?*

Seven years ago. Right after my wife died in a lab accident. We were readying for our mission when it happened.

I'm so sorry.

The man nodded. *We had to start over with limited resources. Our new ship is almost ready.*

And you think your brother is here?

He always wanted to go to Earth, like our brother, Feo, his twin, who died in a crash there years ago. I assume he made it to Earth. And he knows all about your ways. We've watched Earth for many years through our communication belt. We've studied your culture. Your language. Your needs. Your desires. My brother has all this information now. He'll know how to infiltrate your society.

That sounds sinister.

Yes. His choice to stand with these renegades and do what he did can mean only one thing.

The fear that had prickled now grew to a stabbing frenzy inside her. *What?*

He is a Destroyer, too.

Terror shot through Laura at that one word. It's what her brother had been. A remorseless killer with a burning thirst for revenge. A monster with immense powers to destroy.

Brahm, what's your brother's name?

Adrian.

His face disappeared and moonlight through her bedroom window glowed down.

"Laura, what are you doing?" Ben knelt down, one hand on her belt pressing the button to send her spirit back here, the other on her shoulder. He shook her gently.

"They're coming." She gasped, stunned to be back in her room.

He rubbed her arms to stop her shaking. "When?"

"I don't know. I must go back and find out." She put her hand on her belt, but Ben pulled it away.

"No, Laura. Enough for now. We'll know when they come."

Fear over who would arrive made her quake inside. Were her headaches from this Adrian seeking her out? And for what purpose? When she spoke to him all those years ago through the belt he had been kind and encouraging. He had been nothing like her evil twin. He couldn't be a Destroyer. Brahm had to be wrong. And Adrian and her Elyon father, Feo, were twins, too.

Ben helped her take the belt off and put it away then led her back to bed and lay beside her. "What else did they say?"

She didn't tell him. If she did then she would have to think about it.

"Nothing else," Laura mumbled into his arm. He kissed the back of her neck and held her close, his hand stroking her hair. Pain wormed its way inside her head. Another migraine. Like the ones she had when her twin had once sought her out. Who sought her out now?

She gave into her exhaustion as her body's need for sleep trumped her fears.

CHAPTER 10

The man in her dream chased her through the dark mountain woods.

He looked familiar. Like her twin who once chased her. The man's white hair shone like a spotlight under the full moon. He raced around trees seeking her out. Once when she looked back his yellow eyes glowed with evil. He grinned at her, and in his grin she saw her death.

His pale, naked body rippled with muscles as he moved in fluid motion toward her. He seemed to fly over the mossy forest floor, his feet never landing on earth. She ran faster but her clumsy pregnant body defied her. She stumbled and grabbed onto a tree. She was naked, too, and in her nakedness she felt a deep vulnerability and shame.

Faster she ran.

The mountain trail zigzagged. The heavy growth grabbed at her, slowing her down. She plunged through a creek, slipping on rocks, and peered behind her when she reached the bank. He was gone. If—when— he caught her he would torture her slowly and rip her baby from her body. He would leave her here to die, with her child, in this wilderness. She would be forced to watch her newborn torn apart and eaten by wild beasts. And in this knowing, she would crush her baby's head with a rock before he suffered such a hideous death.

Pain sliced through her. Water gushed between her legs

The baby was coming. Here. Now.

In this ancient, godless wood with the devil chasing her.

She staggered up the bank seeking refuge. She doubled over and fell to her knees. *There*. A curved bush with a den inside. She crawled on pine needles to her sanctuary, scratching her knees and stomach.

She fell on her side and curled up in pain. Daggers ripped through her.

Breathe. Breathe.

Charlie had come so fast. This one would, too. The pain subsided and she rolled onto her back, praying the killer stayed afar. Moonlight stabbed through the branches, exposing her. She pulled herself further into her wooded cave. A lone owl hooted above, announcing her hideaway. Laura darted her eyes back and forth from tree to tree, but the woods remained empty.

Pain grabbed her harder, tightened across her belly like a giant fist pounding into her. She scrambled in the dirt for a twig, in between gasps and grunts. She bit down hard on a stick, swallowing sour grit. Pressure pushed all around. And such pain. She held her legs up, from underneath, widening the way for her child. She felt his head between her legs, pulsing to get out. Not here. Not now. *Oh God, help me.*

Then a laugh cut across her hell. The man strode up the creek bank toward her. His white skin glowed in the black around her. He stopped to watch the intimate scene. She was spread wide open to him, presenting him with her sex that had once spread wide open to Ben in love, presenting him with pleasure. Now her pleasure pushed out against her will. She had nowhere to run. Laura screamed from deep within as her child ripped her with each push.

"Finish your work, Laura. He will be mine."

"N—never," she sobbed.

Rip. Push.

She spat out the wood and screamed and screamed. Life pulsed violently between her legs. Her skin stretched over her child as he forced his way into the world. Her screams turned to moans. She bit her lip to stop herself from fainting.

Then the pressure disappeared. She cradled her child and pulled him to her chest, bloodied and alive. She wiped the mucus away, her tears spilling onto him. Ben's face. His lungs burst forth with a glorious cry. She placed him to her breast and his little pink mouth grabbed on. His suckling shot deep heat to her core.

"Benny, my little Benny."

Laura tried to stagger up but fell back, her child still connected to her.

"Please, let me save my child." She ran her fingers through the dirt around her, desperate for a rock. She finally clutched one in her hand, the other holding her child tight. His suckling noises spoke of beauty and life in this place of despair. She looked at the rock in her hand and looked at her son's tiny head. Would her killing him be a blessing?

The man sneered, his flattened features stretched across his face, and he moved toward her. She shrank back into her cave.

"He is mine, Laura. Ours."

He knelt before her, his monstrous naked form filling her space. She held her son tighter to her breast.

"Let him live. Please, let him live," she whispered.

The monster pulled her son from her in one swift movement. He chomped down on the umbilical cord with his savage jaws and ripped it in two.

"No!" Laura struggled to stand, but the man shoved her down. Her bloody and wailing baby branded the man's chest with stark streaks. The man's mouth was painted with her blood. Her son's blood.

"He is my son now."

The monster turned and ran through the woods. She crawled on the forest floor after him, praying the evil man would indeed let her child live. She tried to stand but fell. Her sobbing stole her breath. She gasped for air. Death was welcome.

She opened her eyes. Ben's hand closed around her throat. He knelt over her, his eyes burned fierce in hers. Hate filled his face.

"Ben," she sputtered out as he choked her. She flailed about trying to get free.

He pulled her up and slammed her down into the bed over and over. She clawed at his hands.

"Ben, please."

His eyes grew wide. Brute hands fell away. She rolled over and gasped for air, pushing herself up from the bed.

"Laura, Laura," Ben cried into his hands. He raised his face to hers, dazed. "What have I done?"

Laura stared at him in shock and confusion. "I—I don't know." She fell into the corner chair. Ben came to her but she sank deeper in the chair. His hands fell to his sides. His face twisted in torment.

"Ben, you tried to kill me. Our child."

"No. No." He sat heavy on the edge of the bed.

"You choked me." Laura rubbed her neck, her throat so sore. "Water."

Ben got her a drink and handed it to her. She took it with trembling hands, avoiding his touch. She watched him as she drank. He looked sad and terrified at the same time.

"Could a dream make me do something so awful?" He shook his head in disbelief.

"What was your dream?"

"I chased a monster that wanted you. He wanted our baby."

Fear poured over Laura in a cold sweat. "Then what?" It came out a whisper.

"I grabbed him from behind and choked him. But why did I choke you?" Ben reached for her hand. She stared at it then pulled away.

"Maybe it's me. My hormones from pregnancy conflicting with my powers and affecting you."

"But nothing like this happened the last time you were pregnant."

"I'm older now. Maybe my abilities are coming out in strange ways." She desperately wanted to believe that.

"Maybe." Ben didn't look so sure. "I read women can have pregnancy rage. For now, I should sleep in the guest room."

She wanted it to be hormonal rage affecting Ben and not something else. "One more month, Ben."

"Yes, one more month and everything will be normal again."

Laura knew he didn't believe it. He held her tight but she couldn't stop reliving the nightmare from long ago, where another evil man chased her through the woods. Only the man had become real. He had watched her from afar through his mind's eye in his cell. Her twin. And when he escaped and came for her she had two choices—redeem him or kill him. But he killed himself, a tormented man who believed he would never be anything other than a monster.

Now a frighteningly similar man chased her in her dreams again. Was he real, too? She grew faint from holding her breath wishing the idea away and moved into Ben. He kissed her once then left for the guest bedroom as promised. The door click behind him and took his warmth with him.

She stared out the window. The sunrise peeked over the trees, shedding warmth and light to their world in a comforting glow. Only their world now seemed dark. She closed her eyes and hugged her arms to her body. How would they find the light again?

CHAPTER 11

Charlie's stomach flopped with all the things Ghost Man had told him the night before. Now he was running late for school, but he had no intention of going there today. The woods called to him—and Ghost Man.

He got dressed and slunk down the hall to the kitchen. He hoped his dad had left for a photo shoot already and his mom had stayed in bed. No such luck. He turned the corner and there sat both his parents in the kitchen. His mom rocked by the bay window. His dad sat at the kitchen table and stared at her. No chatter. No breakfast being made. No radio on with his mom singing to some cheesy 80s song. His shoe squeaked on the floor and they turned to look at him.

"Charlie, where did you go last night?" His mom raised herself up from the chair.

He grabbed a muffin from a bowl on the counter and wolfed it down. "I had to think."

"You can think at home." She frowned.

"No I can't, okay?" He busied himself pouring orange juice. He didn't want to see his mom's angry face. He didn't know how he felt about her right now. Or himself.

"Well, for the next two weeks you will because you're grounded."

Charlie looked at his dad for help, but he sat there staring at his hands. "Dad?"

His dad looked up. "You heard your mom. Grounded." Then he looked past him through the window.

What was going on? This whole scene felt wrong. He'd rather his dad yell at him. Do something. But he just sat there and said no more.

His mom crossed her arms and looked over at his dad. "Your dad is with me on this one, Charlie. You're only fourteen. Nine is your curfew on a school night. You can't be out until midnight. I was worried. God knows what wild animals roam the woods at night."

"Wild animals are better than some people."

"They're unpredictable, which is why they're called wild."

"So are people, Mom." He shook his head and adjusted his back pack. "I gotta go to school."

His mom sighed. "Take the bus home today." She moved closer and stood on tiptoes to kiss his cheek.

"Yeah, yeah, yeah." He hugged her quick. She looked so sad. He opened the door and looked back. His dad still sat there, looking out the window. "Bye, Dad."

His dad looked up at him and nodded but didn't say another word. Charlie escaped the dreary scene and ran down the path, pretending to head to school by the road. When he looked back, his mom had resumed her vigil at the front window. She rocked and rocked. He waved once, but she must not have seen him. She didn't wave back.

He rounded the first bend and dashed into the woods. He hooked up with the trail and headed for the meadow. He needed answers.

A lone hawk soared overhead, piercing the sky with its cry. Chipmunks and squirrels bounced off tree branches as he passed. They nattered madly as if his presence disturbed their sanctuary. Then they ran off, leaving him with the mere sound of his feet crunching on leaves. His breath hung in the air, great frosty clouds leading the way. He reached the meadow. Ghost Man waited for him.

Charlie looked at Ghost Man across the field. *I could be a father to you,* he heard in his head.

Ghost Man walked toward him. "You know it to be true, in your heart, Son. Your darkest of hearts, Charlie-boy. A dark heart. Like mine. I can show you what you truly can be. Your real father never can. He is only a human. I can show you all the things you can have. Power. Acceptance. Belonging. Respect. And love."

"Love?" Charlie met him halfway across the meadow.

"Girls." Ghost Man smiled at him. "You *are* into girls, aren't you?"

"Yes." Charlie looked up at the cold, blue sky and shoved his hands back in his pockets.

"You can have all the girls you want."

Charlie stood before Ghost Man and looked down at his feet.

"And you won't be a freak anymore."

Charlie slammed a fist into his hand. "Good."

"And you can use your powers all the time. You won't have to hide them anymore."

"You can show me…in person? You're real then? You exist…somewhere?"

"Yes. I'm not far. And I'm coming for you, my Charlie-boy. I've been waiting all these years for you to be ready. Are you ready?"

Charlie moved closer. He reached out his hand to touch Ghost Man's apparition. His fingers moved through the ghost before him. "We are the same?"

"Yes. You belong with me."

"And my mom."

"Yes, she will be with us, too."

Charlie frowned and stared at him. "She never talked about you."

"She never knew I existed."

Charlie chewed on his lip. "What about my dad?"

"He will be welcome, of course." Ghost Man smiled at him.

"I don't want to be a freak anymore. My mom will want to know about you."

"Let's keep it our secret for now. We'll surprise her together."

"And my dad."

"Of course. I can help you see into your future."

"You mean I can see myself as a grown up?"

"Yes. See the man you will become. See a life of comfort and riches and all you desire."

All I desire. It made Charlie dizzy to think about having all he wanted. Money. Girls. Popularity.

"But my mom said everyone died though. Who's everyone?"

"Our planet is dying and our people there will too someday. I came here with others so our people could survive. You can be part of it. I lead the community, and you can help me lead. People will look up to you."

"To *me*?"

"Yes. Isn't it what you want? To belong?"

"I never belonged here. But I can't be an…alien."

"Yes."

"A freak."

"Not to me. Not to our people."

"Why didn't you tell me this years ago? Tell my mom…and my dad?"

"I had to be sure you were ready. I wanted your mom to be ready, too. In her own way. Are you ready then?"

Charlie looked around the silent woods and up into the sky, a place he had never thought beyond before. He looked at his fingers and back at Ghost Man. Was this all really happening?

"I need you, Charlie-boy."

He had come back for a reason. This had to be it. "I'm ready."

"Now, let me tell you everything."

"First, tell me your name."

"Adrian Madroc."

"Adrian." Charlie said his name slow, new on his lips. "Okay, now tell me everything."

And Adrian spoke to him as a father would to a son, with understanding and love.

As Charlie had always hoped his dad would.

Adrian watched Charlie head home under the bright, fall sky. The time had been right to reveal all to the boy. He could soon accept his destiny and become the true Destroyer he was meant to be. How amazing to guide his grandnephew through his breeding initiation. Together they would raise the standards of their people and build their empire. The day was coming when their community would be integrated within the human world.

He had described the rich history of his people to Charlie—of Elyons and of his secret society of Destroyers—and how his flock had flourished here on Earth without fear of persecution. He instilled a yearning and want in the boy to follow him. He answered the boy's questions with patience, dropping tantalizing seeds to grow inside. He had spent years building up trust in the boy. It would all pay off now.

By the time the boy trudged back to his home, the sun rose high over his head just like his new heir was rising—an heir to help him overrun Earth with their powerful genes. Someday in the far off future, Earth would be the new Elyon—a world of Destroyers.

And his plan to take back all that his brothers had taken from him would succeed. He was the strong one. His father had said so. He had survived to reap what his brothers had sown and lost—and more.

But first he would continue his fun with Laura.

And then it would be Ben's turn.

CHAPTER 12

Adrian knelt naked by his bed. He needed to endure pain to inflict pain on his flock. He could not be weak like them. He lifted the cat o' nine tails and flung it on his back in a familiar rhythm. With each whip he released a deep grunt.

Each strike was a gift he offered to fate as penance for the death of his mistress Manta. He did not seek penance for killing Tollen's unborn child that had grown within her. That was merely a casualty. Someday he would use it against Tollen. It would be his glorious, final playing card. For now he would let Tollen think it was Brahm's child who died. He did not need distractions. He needed to lead his people into this new world and breed the Earth with Destroyer power. Pain would make him strong then Fate would accept his pain and realign his path to greatness.

Forty lashes on his back. New scars over old scars painted his skin. Each strike of the nine tails pierced him with points of fire. He called to Manta with each grunt. She had understood him, loved him—and he had betrayed her. Blood ran like slow rain down his skin washing his guilt away.

And in the exquisite pain, his love for her skewered his flesh. He breathed it in with each lash. Frenzied love filled him up. It crazed his brain like an addicting drug. He had never felt it before except with Manta. It drove the harsh dark away, which ruled him. It filled him with soft light. But with the light came pain to endure Manta's death.

He could not let himself feel the pain of loss again. It was too much to bear.

He had caused her death.

Harder. Harder.

He groaned from the whip's sting and cherished the sweet physical pain that made him strong again.

He fell on his hands, breathing deep to push the pain away. Each morning he scourged away his sin. Day by day he became cleaner inside, stronger.

Time to finish. Adrian stood and faced the mirror. The lit candle sent shadows across his pale skin in the windowless room. He flexed his muscles admiring his physical attributes. Then he took a deep breath and resumed self-flogging. This time his thighs took the brunt. Streaks of red wound around his muscular legs. He called to his love again and again.

"Manta. Manta."

Caleb watched the courtyard fill up from under the side overhang. He soon would bring Rachel out. He watched her often with the other women doing laundry or working in the gardens gathering vegetables. She had been with many males since him and had borne more children since their time of passion six years ago. Did she think about it like he did? His last time of wild abandon. He had given in to lust and sweetness. She had been so open to him and full of beauty. It had felt so good to allow reckless release without care. Everything in his life now was done with care. He guarded his thoughts and actions to protect himself and others.

And now she would die. Could he save her?

The community members flooded into the square, silent except for the younger children. He scanned the gathering seeking two dark heads with hair of his own. He finally saw them. Relief washed through him that his children would live, but now he must lead their mother to her death.

Caleb walked down the open corridor to the prisoner's room. He hesitated at the door, unlocked it, and pushed it open with conviction. She sat on the concrete floor, naked and small, knees drawn to her chest. Her golden brown hair flowed around her, strands of pure bronze covering her in light. She looked up, eyes wide with fear. Tears dropped like clear pearls from her emerald eyes. Eyes he had looked into with desire and yearning long ago.

"Caleb," she whispered. "Help me."

"My father says you must pay for your desertion."

She put her head on her knees. "What will happen to all of my children? I wanted them to know I was their mother. I wanted to save all of them, but I could only take two. They were my first and I always knew they were mine."

Like I know they are mine, he wanted to say. Instead, he narrowed his eyes at her and walled himself off from her plea. "They aren't your children. They belong to the community."

"Mine."

"Not according to my father."

She looked up at him, sad and appealing in her bereft nakedness. "Will you watch over them?"

He pulled her up. She covered her breasts with her hair but not her sex. It had held him in a fierce blur of tangled bliss—and had given their sons life. He busied himself by binding wooden cuffs on her wrists.

"Come." Caleb pulled her to the door.

She screamed and fought him. Her hair flew like wild ropes about her, lashing him. He grabbed her shoulders and shook her. "It will be worse for you if you go like this."

She slumped against him. He felt her heart beat next to his and her warm breasts. So alive. Not for long. An ache struck him like his father's whip. He felt the pain deep inside now as his skin had felt many times from lashings. She moved closer into him, twisting his robe in desperation as if clutching onto him would keep her alive. Her thoughts shot clear into his mind. *I loved you once. I needed you then. Our sons need you now. My other children need you.*

"You needed a lot of other males after me."

She looked up at him. "Not like you, Caleb. You were my first. You knew I wasn't allowed to breed with only one."

Caleb nodded. He had loved her too, from afar. He opened his mind to her now. He dare not speak the words out loud. *I will protect the children. I promise. But I can't promise to save you.*

She cried harder then. He sensed her relief from his words. And hope. He pulled her then to the courtyard. She shivered against him from the early autumn air, bared to the elements. Free of coverings, as she had been when she entered this world. Adrian stood at the stoning gates. All heads turned to them as he led her to the stocks.

He locked her in, her head held tight in place with a wooden collar. He undid the cuffs on her wrists and locked her arms and legs to the posts in metal braces. Her eyes followed his every movement. She pleaded to him with her mind, but he closed off his thoughts to her. If he didn't he would go crazy, release her, grab their sons, and run. They wouldn't get far.

Red leaves shot down from the giant maple tree above. A gust of wind tugged the last of them from the old tree, blurring Rachel's face from Caleb for a moment. A burnt crimson ring encircled her. He stepped back and took his spot. The crowd surged forward, one entity. A gray-robed flock of death. The barrel of stones sat in the center of the courtyard. Each person selected two stones. When everyone had their weapons, Adrian and Caleb stepped forward and chose their stones. Rachel's sobs and the children's fretting cries hung over the silent crowd.

All eyes watched Adrian, waiting for his signal. He raised his hand and nodded at Caleb.

Caleb raised his hand also and closed his eyes. Then he let go.

The first stone flew.

CHAPTER 13

Laura wasn't being chased this time. It came as a delicious dream she had dreamt many times over the past year when she'd dozed on her bed, alone, under cotton striped blankets. She was naked and her breasts throbbed. She remembered how small they had once been before pregnancy. She had been ashamed of their size the night Ben first took her so long ago, thinking he wanted a full breasted woman as so many men did. But he had convinced her otherwise of their perfection. She lay back and stroked them now, enjoying the feel of her body as it held her child.

She closed her eyes luxuriating in content slumber, wondering about getting up, when hands covered hers. Ben. She smiled and kept her eyes closed. He gently pulled her hands away and caressed her. Slow warmth spread through her groin. Lips pulled on her nipples, fingers drawing them to intense arousal. She gasped, fighting the urge to open her eyes. Ben remained silent, fueling her fantasy.

Fingers trailed down her belly and pried her thighs open. She groaned and cried out when a hot tongue lapped at her in expertise as it had many times. It played with her as she liked best. Hands cupped her bottom, stroking, stroking. She twisted the sheets, legs trembling as she yearned for release. The heat flamed an unbearable ache, stabbing her with need and want.

The tongue fell away and she whimpered in loss, but then she was being pulled toward Ben. He opened her up wider to receive him. Her legs shook. She pushed into him. Hot flesh plunged into her core and she screamed, her need met. He thrust rhythmically, slow then fast, teasing her swollen sex bud that painfully throbbed.

"Ben, oh, Ben."

He covered her body with his, sinking into her, pressing his hard chest to her soft skin. His hand placed possessively across her swollen belly. She wrapped her arms and legs around him. Their sweat mingled together. Ben pulled on her breasts in sweet agony. Her body rose in the air. Breezes blew around her, embracing her, filling every crevice. She was so close. So close. Nothing bound her to Earth but this primeval fire. Space surrounded her, carried her. And still she refused to open her eyes. The dream was hers.

The explosion swelled in her and Ben held her tight. Her body bucked and he drove deeper inside her than he had ever been.

"Laura, open your eyes. I want to see you."

That voice.

The soft dream disappeared. Her eyes flew open. The pale demon stared down at her, covering her body with his. His yellow eyes burned in hers. Her body betrayed her, shaking with orgasm as she tried to claw out from under the monster. He held her fast, grinning down at her then plunged into her faster and faster. She screamed again and again. He arched his back and shot his dark seed into her with a mighty groan. It filled her womb and poured out of her, a gushing torrent of evil.

"It will be our son, Laura. *Ours*. He has been all along."

She woke up. Terror pulled at her. Her heart raced. She sat up and reached for the light, knocking it over. She pulled up the lamp. Finally, sweet light. The clock glowed 2am. She clasped her belly. It pulsed as if her child had been a witness to her dream. But her child was safe. Hers and Ben's.

A breeze tickled her face. The curtain blew up from the open window. She hadn't remembered opening it. She couldn't shake the dream. Her sex throbbed with heat. She put her fingers to herself. She was so wet and swollen there and her breasts ached. Could she be reliving the terror associated with her twin brother fifteen years ago in her dreams? Perhaps being pregnant drove her intense dreams and paranoia, as Ben had said.

She got out of bed and went to the guest bedroom where Ben now slept since the awful night where he tried to strangle her. She didn't resist his move. She had to protect her child.

She slid into bed beside him. He rolled over and pulled her to him.

"I miss you," she whispered.

"I miss you, too."

"You had another nightmare, didn't you?"

"Yes."

"Tell me."

Laura shook her head. "This one was different," she finally said. "It was you but then it wasn't you."

"Was it the man who chases you?"

She nodded, unable to speak.

"I've seen him chase you in my dreams. Like…your twin, X-10, did long ago. Only this man wants our unborn child."

"The man in my dreams wants our child, too," Laura whispered.

"X-10's gone, Laura. It's been over for fifteen years. There's no one chasing us here. Just in our dreams. It's natural to worry when you're pregnant. Your hormones are raging along with your fears our son won't be…normal. And *that* is all normal. It's been a long time since you had Charlie."

"I know, but we've had a good life for so long now. I don't want it taken away. Like everything was taken from me back then."

"It's just fear. Nothing else. Don't let it overshadow the good we have now. The bad doesn't have to come back."

She wanted to believe it. "Charlie! I have to check on Charlie." Laura threw back the covers and swung her legs to get up, but Ben stayed her with his hand.

"I just did. He's asleep in his bed."

"You're sure?"

"I checked on him right before I came in here."

Laura eased back on the pillow and closed her eyes. She pulled the blanket tighter to her, chilled even though the furnace had kicked on warming them against the early fall chill. "Something is happening. I can feel it. My migraines are back. My nightmares are back. Someone is here. Someone who wants to harm me…and our child."

"Laura, how can you be sure?"

"I can't."

"There's no physical proof. No murders of those you love. No cryptic notes telling you this time to use your powers."

His words soothed her. She knew she sounded like an irrational, hormonal pregnant woman, but his actions the other night had truly frightened her. She opened her eyes to Ben's kind face, trying not to see the face of another. A face filled with hate and revenge. A face like her dead brother's. He had been the hunter and she had been his prey. She didn't want to be hunted again.

"Stay with me, Ben." She reached for him and he pulled her to his chest. "I need you."

He lay her down then and placed a hand on her belly, claiming her child as his like the monster in her dream had. "I won't fall asleep, I promise."

She looked up at him, eyes shining. "I don't want to sleep."

He smiled at her, rubbing a breast that swelled from her nightgown. "Are you sure?"

She nodded. "I want you in me."

She needed to chase the monster from her mind. She needed Ben inside her, stroking the terror away as he filled her with his purity and strength. She undid her buttons, offering herself to him. He undressed quickly and she pulled him closer, eager for him to be inside her.

"Now, Ben." She pushed into him, needing him to fill her with his goodness. He sunk deep, his face buried in her breasts, and took her in all the gentle ways she needed.

She made sure to keep her eyes open.

CHAPTER 14

The crowd moved away. The community members went back to their daily chores. Washing, child care, compound repairs, cooking. They all had their jobs to do. Now Caleb had his job to do. Taking out the trash. Only Rachel wasn't trash. She had been loving and alive. Someone's mother. Someone's lover. She had his heart once.

He stared at her figure in death.

He had no time to waste if she were to live again.

He unlocked the stoning gates and gently removed her from the iron braces and wooden neck collar. Her pale, bruised body fell into his arms. Her heart no longer beat against his chest. Her breasts no longer pressed warm to him. He picked her up, cradling her head to his. Her hair fell in the waning sunlight, the one sheath adorning her. Time hung precious. He strode across the yard, when his father stepped from the shadows. His robe's hood covered most of his face.

"Take her far past the perimeter fence. Bury her."

Caleb nodded as twisted emotion burned through him. He had to close off his thoughts so his father didn't see his true plans for Rachel. He continued through the courtyard.

"Caleb."

Caleb turned and faced his father again.

"Watch yourself." His father pulled back his hood and smiled at him. "And when you're done report back to me."

"Where?" It came out a deep whisper.

"The whipping shack. Penance for Thomas."

Caleb nodded again. He turned and strode off. He turned back once. His father still watched him. Caleb turned a corner. His legs pumped faster.

Time was running out to bring Rachel back to life.

Charlie slowly pushed open the back door, looking for signs of his parents. Both cars sat in the driveway. He stayed in the woods most of the day again talking with Adrian. Ghost Man seemed so real since he now had a name. He was out there, somewhere in a real place, waiting to meet him. It all tumbled inside Charlie. He didn't know how he felt about it, but anticipation for something filled him up. For what, he didn't know, but it rose inside him waiting to spill out. He couldn't tell his parents about this. Not yet.

He shut the door quietly behind him. He wasn't supposed to be home for another twenty minutes, but he had been freezing in the woods all day and was starving. He had practiced his powers for a while. Then the temperature dropped. It felt almost cold enough for snow. He placed his hands on the radiator, warming them in the toasty kitchen.

He hoped the school hadn't called about his absence and he checked the new phone messages. Lucky him. The secretary had left a message. He deleted it. The second time this week. Running water hummed. His mom or dad in the shower. Probably his mom. When her back was killing her she said a hot shower made her feel better. His heart slowed a bit. He might get away with skipping school today.

And then screams hurdled through the house. He dropped his backpack and ran toward them. His parent's room.

Another piercing scream ripped through his gut.

His mom.

Charlie burst through the bedroom door. Steam curled out from under the bathroom door. He reached it in two steps, expecting to push the door open. Locked. He slammed up against it.

"Mom, I'm coming!"

The floor shook.

"Charlie…no." His mom's words came out a gurgled whisper. Glass shattered. Wild grunts called to him.

He kicked. The door cracked. The jamb shredded. He used his hands to pull the wood apart with his mental commands. Splintered shrieks filled the air.

"Mom, hang on!"

Wood exploded. Charlie pushed through the shattered door and fell into the bathroom—and a dark figure. He beat on him, grabbing his shirt. Steam billowed all around the mad man.

It was his dad.

And he was strangling his mom.

Caleb darted between trees toward the mountain bog. He passed the new well his father had recently ordered be dug. Its stone walls rose harsh and cold, an unwanted stranger in the woods. Why had his father built it? He'd said they needed it as a backup water source. It had to be a lie. Their other well was full. It had to be for a form of punishment. His father enjoyed finding new ways to punish and oppress. This had to be part of his plan. No time to think of what that plan involved now.

He moved away and headed east toward the road, a few miles away. It was the one road into the town of Benevolence—and away from it. His arms burned with the weight of Rachel. She grew cold. He had to stop soon and save her. A little further. He needed to be far enough away from the compound. He blocked his thoughts to hide his whereabouts. An icy wind cut ruthlessly across him with the promise of a harsh winter.

He forgot the bog began at the edge of the woods and plunged into wet muck. He stumbled and nearly dropped Rachel. He steadied himself and backed up to go around the marsh, when something stuck out of the mire before him. In the brown and green moss of the bog it jarred his brain. He stared at it. A pale, elegant hand. Female.

He sucked in his breath, gripped Rachel tighter—and ran back to the safety of the woods. Trees flashed by. Far enough.

He fell to his knees, hugging Rachel to his chest. Dead pine needles cushioned his fall. Deep breaths. In and out. He had to be strong for her. He unbuttoned his robe and laid it out on the forest floor, placing Rachel on it. Her blue bruises lay ugly against her pale skin. He tucked the robe around her to warm her cold flesh. He kissed her chilled cheek and pressed her hand to his face. Then he began his healing.

He moved his practiced hands over her curves. Using the incredible powers of his mind, he willed warmth and life back into her. He caressed and kneaded her sweet limbs. *Please let her live.* Was there really a human god out there watching over Earth who could answer his plea? Did this god watch over Elyons as well? And would he doom Caleb to a human hell?

He wanted to redeem himself either way through sparing others pain. Sweat broke out on his brow. Was she too far gone? His stomach tightened. He moved his hands faster over her. *Come back, Rachel. Please.* Her head lolled to one side. He stroked her hair as he worked and spoke to her.

"I do love you, Rachel. I never stopped. I wanted more, but it wasn't meant to be. I had to think of our children first." She remained cold beneath his hands.

This gift he had. Perhaps it was not enough for her. Many Elyons had healing powers but not like him. He lived as an anomaly. The others could only heal the living. Caleb discovered at an early age how to bring the dead back to life. He did not share this information. It would be used against him, especially by his father. In secret Caleb had practiced on dead animals he found, learning the time limits of death for his power to still work.

The first time he attempted it on an Elyon the fear of being caught and punished ensnared him. It would be more than whipping he received. He might not survive, and he had to survive to use his gift to help those in need.

His first save had been a man caught stealing. Adrian used him as an example to warn the community by whipping him to death. Caleb brought the man back to life in the woods. He was so amazed he had brought an actual person back to life he thought he would have a heart attack and die in the man's place. The man had shook his head and stood up on shaky legs, like a stunned animal.

Caleb shoved clothes at him that he had stashed in the woods and told him to head for the road and away from Benevolence. Find another town. Suspicion would grow if deserters kept showing up in one place. Mind control would get them only so far.

The man, awaking from his shock, had fallen to his knees and kissed Caleb's feet. Caleb pulled him up and directed him away. No thanks necessary, just his silence.

Seven more times he had done this. He imagined those Elyons out there in the world having a second chance at life. Living and loving and being embraced by humans who cared. Caleb had never failed to heal one of them until now. He bent over Rachel and pulled her to him, straining to bring her back. He rocked with her, willing his life into hers. Giving his heart to her as he once had.

She trembled beneath him. Color rushed back into her. Her bruises faded. She arched her back and gasped.

He held her to him. Her breath infused his neck with warmth.

"I just wanted to set you free," he whispered.

"Caleb," she whispered. "How did you save me?"

He pulled her up and put his robe on her. He would pay for losing it later. He had stowed his extra one nearby. "It doesn't matter. You must go. Head to the road and away from town. You must reach another town and ask for help. Before night comes. Tell no one about this. Pretend you have no memory. Find a church. Someone will help you."

She looked at him with watery eyes. "My children."

He grasped her arms. "I will watch over them. You need to go. *Now*."

She just stared at him. He shook her. "We'll both die if you don't."

She nodded and hung her head. Caleb lifted her hair away from her face. It shone dark gold in the sun flickering through the trees.

She pushed her hands in his robe pockets and then drew out a piece of paper. He watched her unfold it and read it. He knew it by heart, this last poem he could give her like he'd once given her his love.

She read the last two lines aloud. "Wrapped up in my heart with no place to go. Come, unwrap my heart and set me free in you." She looked up, a solitary tear rolled down her cheek. "You unwrapped my heart too, Caleb Madroc."

He pulled her close. Pine cones plunked around them. The wind blew a sweet, mournful song through bare branches. Yellow swirled down. The last dying leaves of autumn. In that moment he believed they were together, out for a walk in the woods before heading home to mate by the fire. A normal life. Somewhere else. Not here. He bent down and kissed her. At first, she didn't move and then she pressed herself into him. He stroked her hair and took her mouth as a token then he let go and pushed her off him.

"Go. Now. Be free!"

She stared at him with wild eyes and stumbled away, his poem clutched in her hand. Then she turned and ran. His cloak flowed behind her, protecting her. He watched her go. He unraveled his full heart and sent it with her. It did him no good in this place.

He wanted to leave with her, but he had to think of their sons. If he left, his father would kill them. The sun faded behind clouds. He still had work to do. He headed for the tree line to dig a fake grave. He pushed the image of the hand in the bog away. He didn't want to know why it was there—or who put it there. There was just one person who would, but he couldn't face that now.

It was time for his punishment for saving Thomas from humiliation.

His father would add to Caleb's scars.

Those scars Caleb could suffer with.

The scars of Rachel and his sons seared his heart forever.

CHAPTER 15

Charlie beat on his dad's back. His mom's wild eyes stared at him as she gasped for air.

"No!" Charlie summoned his strength and pulled his dad off, shoving him into the wall. It cracked with the force. His mom fell back into the tub. His dad turned around, anger blazing in his red face. He looked like a monster. Then he rushed at Charlie.

Charlie grabbed him by the throat and lifted him off the ground. He choked him, enraged. He wanted his dad to die. They stared at each other in battle. His dad's arms swung at him.

"Charlie, stop!" His mom pulled herself up from the tub. He squeezed his dad's neck.

Tighter. Tighter.

His dad slumped against him. Charlie threw him down on the floor. He turned to his mom and handed her the flowered robe on the hook, averting his eyes from her nakedness.

"Charlie, what have you done?" Her voice was raspy, as she tied her belt.

"Me? Dad tried to kill you. What's wrong with him?"

His mom bent down to his dad, pushing broken glass from the mirror away.

"Mom, let's get out of here. Come on. We've got to call the police." Charlie tried to pull her up but she clung to his dad.

"No police. Help me, Charlie. Help me heal him. Not his fault."

"What do you mean, heal him?" Charlie shook his head. He could move things, break things…but heal? Could she?

She placed her hands on his dad's chest. He looked so pathetic sprawled on the floor. He didn't look capable of what he'd done. He had acted strange for days and now this. It was like he was hiding something. Or ashamed of something. He never knew his dad to be ashamed of anything.

Charlie bent down. His mom took his hands and moved them with hers.

"See? Touch him. Now wish with all your heart for him to be healed and wake up. Send your strength and life force to him."

Charlie pulled his hands away. What had his mom not told him about their shared abilities? Some genetic freakish thing? Jesus healed. God healed. People didn't heal. Did they?

I can't do this.

His mom pulled his hands back and looked at him with a determined expression. "Yes, you can. We can."

Oh, my God. My mom can read my thoughts, too!

She nodded. "And now we need to save your dad."

Stunned, he moved his hands with hers over his dad whose chest rose and fell with shallow breaths. His dad lived and yet he'd almost killed his mom.

Rage infused Charlie again. "Mom, if he wakes up and tries to hurt you again, I'll kill him. I will."

"He didn't mean it, Charlie."

"Like some kind of tumor pressing on his brain making him do crazy things?" Charlie had read about such things. "And he almost killed you…and the baby."

"No, he wasn't. And it's not a tumor."

Charlie said no more. Water still poured from the shower head. Steam spewed around them in a tropical hell, his hair and clothes plastered to him. He let his anger fade away and willed his dad to be strong again. He had no idea what he was doing, but he did it for his mom's sake.

"Laura? Charlie?" His dad opened his eyes. He looked up at them and then his hands. "What have I done?"

"It's okay, Ben." His mom kissed his dad's hands over and over.

"No, it's *not* okay," Charlie said. His chest hurt. *Breathe. Breathe.* "You tried to kill Mom!"

Charlie helped his mom up and pulled her back to the door. His dad slowly stood. They all dripped from their shower struggle. His mom turned off the shower. Could this be some kind of mental disease his dad had? A disease he would have someday? Fear, distrust, and anger mixed together. At his dad. At his mom.

"It's not me," his dad covered his face. "It's not me. Someone is making me do it. I'm so sorry."

His mom moved further away, clutching her robe and her stomach, her face pinched. His dad reached for her, but she stepped back.

"Laura, help me. I'll leave until the baby comes."

"Yes, you need to leave, Ben."

Charlie looked back and forth between his parents. "What is it, Mom? What's going on?"

"I've heard that before."

"What?"

"It's not me." His mom stared at him, but her eyes were somewhere else.

"It's *not* me," his dad repeated.

"I don't know for sure it's not you." His mom moved back another step.

"Who else could it be, Mom?" What were they talking about?

"Someone who may want me dead," his mom said. "Again."

His dad stared at her, his hands reaching for her, pleading, but she shook her head. "You need to go, Ben. I have Charlie to think of now and our baby. Just go!"

Rage flared in Charlie. His mom's words cut through him like fire. He grabbed his dad. "You heard her. Get out, Dad!" He shoved him into the bedroom and out the hall door then locked it.

"Laura? Charlie?" His dad banged on the door.

His mom moved toward his voice. Charlie pulled her back, but she shook her head at him and he let go. She placed her hands on the door and leaned into it. "Go to the motel in town. For now." A sob broke from her. "We need to be safe from you."

Silence hung heavy. Then a fist slammed into the door from the other side.

"You're wrong. I know you are. And I'll stop this, Laura. I will. Charlie, you have to believe me!"

A final bang reinforced his words. Footsteps moved away. Silence. Then a door shut. His mom leaned against the wall and cried.

Charlie hugged her. What had just happened? Would it happen again? And his mom was like him. Why hadn't she ever told him? And his brother would be dead now too if he hadn't stopped his dad. He felt life and death decisions hanging over him. He wasn't ready to deal with this and be a man yet. He was just a kid suddenly terrified of his own dad—and his own destiny.

CHAPTER 16

Adrian faced the community leaders. Some looked unhappy. Some looked worried. But Tollen's face held scorn. Caleb walked slowly into the room and stood by the fireplace. The flames shot up the chimney as if announcing his arrival. Adrian knew why he didn't sit. The pain from his whipping prevented it. He had never cried out, which had enraged Adrian even more. His son must learn not to interfere with his leadership, like letting that stuttering idiot, Thomas, off. Showing mercy only made the weak weaker, and he would be seen as weak if he could not control his son.

"Brother Adrian, we must address the deserters." Tollen frowned at him. "Their number is growing. And they are all female."

"Perhaps we need to actually catch the deserters—if you can Brother Tollen—and either lobotomize or stone them."

"It doesn't fix the problem, Brother Adrian. You can't kill or lobotomize the entire flock. You'll be erasing our purpose for breeding here. Erasing our powers, our strength, and our ability to build our world on Earth. I have looked into our future and it is changing. And not for the good."

The other community leaders nodded and began talking at once.

"You knew the rules set forth before signing on to this mission. Would you rather be back on Elyon in hiding on a dying world, persecuted for your beliefs?"

"No," Tollen said calmly. "But we can't lobotomize our entire flock and risk losing our community we've strived so long to build."

"If you follow the rules you'll have no fear of lobotomy here," Adrian said with a smile. "Besides, it's a small number who desert. You are overreacting to the situation, Brother. Even if the females reach the outside world, they are too terrified to speak about our community. And we self-destructed our ship when we arrived. There is no trace we ever came here. The humans wait for our return. They will never find us. All will be well."

He wanted to draw the subject away from the female deserters. If they knew the truth his leadership could be over. Even he had to follow rules. And Tollen could not become leader. He held him under his authority. But for how long? At times his visions of the future became hazy, lost to him. He could not lose all that was to be. He had to forge ahead to rule the world.

Caleb moved closer to the table. "And what if more than a few want to leave, Father?"

All eyes turned to Caleb.

A chill rolled through Adrian. The fire didn't kill the cold that had blown in with fall. Adrian stood up and looked down at his leaders. "Then we will deal with them. For now, we must expand the perimeter security. All who leave from now on and are caught will die by stoning. One example is not enough. This should reduce these traitorous deeds. Agreed?"

He asked for their permission, as if he needed it. He did not, but he let them think they were part of the decision-making process. Soon he would have another by his side to help him lead. One he had spent years grooming. One with powers as strong as his own. Charlie. A true Destroyer at heart, unlike Caleb. And when Adrian's new heir was born another son would ensure leadership for generations.

The leaders looked at one another and nodded.

"But Father, how can you encourage the flock to stay without death hanging over them? Your laws are too heavy for them. You don't let males and females choose one another. They don't want to be assigned anymore. They want to live like humans, free. And the women want to raise their own children."

Tollen nodded. "Yes, *Madroc,* they want it so badly some have been caught mind bending elders to get them to do what they wanted."

"And they were whipped severely for it," Adrian said. He rose taller, angered that he was not addressed with respect. They faced one another, eyes locked. "Serves them right for disobeying the rules. Perhaps you would choose to break the rules, too. Perhaps you would let the flock do what they want without being mind bended. If so, we can arrange for the same punishment for you, *Brother.* Perhaps we should do it now, as a deterrent so you won't be tempted to break the rules. Caleb can escort you to the whipping shack and we can all have a good show. Yes?"

Tollen's jaw twitched and his nostrils flared. Then he let out a big breath and looked down. "No, Brother. I would never disobey the rules."

"Neither would I."

Adrian looked at Caleb as he said it. He had whipped him extra hard for losing his new robe. He wondered for a moment, if indeed his son had lost his robe or given it to one of the flock members. *Weak.* He was tired of battling a weak son, and at near sixty he felt himself getting old, but he needed his mind and body to stay young in order to succeed.

Adrian looked out the window. The trees stood half bare now. Winter lurked. And in winter, problems within the community grew as the flock became restless indoors. Crime against each other rose. Fights, thievery, and the occasional rape. This would serve them well against humans but not themselves.

The leaders watched and waited in silence.

"We've created a church-like community to blend into this world. And our community is based on laws. We have these laws for a reason, to establish ourselves on this planet. Our leaders before us created them so we could survive." Adrian turned back to the table. "We cannot deviate from them. If we do, we will not survive. Chaos will reign. More will leave. We will be strewn to the world. We will be diminished. And our leaving Elyon will have been for nothing. Would you rather be back on a dying planet hiding from our society? Many of our fellow Destroyers died or were lobotomized in the Destroyer Uprising for our cause. Do you want to suffer through it again?"

"But our first church in the human world has failed. It's been seven years. How are we to expand into the world as a community if we can't control our people?"

"We must try again. Brother Tollen, I want you to create a committee to start another church amongst humans. Those who apply must have a flawless record here of work ethic and law abidance. They must also have leadership ability."

Tollen smiled at Adrian. "Very well." Something in his smile made Adrian uneasy.

"We must offer the flock something of their own, Father."

"What do you suggest, Caleb?"

"A festival of dance and music and food."

"I agree with Caleb," Tollen said. "Create a community outlet of release before winter comes. Allow them some fun. Let them forget any worries. It will solidify us as a family. We'll have it in the courtyard."

Adrian sighed and nodded. All the community leaders agreed. Let the flock have their distractions to take their mind off desertion and death.

The leaders left but Caleb remained.

"A festival is not enough, Father. You must let the flock make some of their own life choices…if you want them to stay. They don't want to be oppressed."

The fire crackled and wind howled down the chimney blowing up giant flames that licked at the brick.

"I am creating this world here, Son. This is not a human democracy. Once you understand this you will have an easier time here."

"Tell me, Father, why is it only females desert? They must be awfully crafty to slip past the perimeter guards."

Adrian stared at Caleb. His son's face betrayed nothing. Did he suspect him of something? Had he misjudged Caleb all along?

"Like I said, they are weak."

Caleb said nothing but finally nodded. "Yes, I'm sure that's it, Father."

Caleb walked stiffly to the door. Adrian hoped his pain burned deep. He could not heal himself or he would receive a double whipping as part of the punishment. Those whipped were checked on a daily basis. One man who had defied this recently, almost died from his second whipping.

"I'm sending another female to you tonight. Although in your condition, I doubt you'll be pleasing her much."

Caleb turned back. Hatred shot out of his son's eyes. He wanted it to be so. In pushing his son to hate, he could succumb to his Destroyer genes. But he refused.

"I will never have an easy time here. I'm branded your son but not by choice. Other choices I make will be all mine. Not yours."

"Watch it, Son. The choices you are making will lead to your end."

Caleb stared at him for a long moment. "So be it."

His son slammed out of the room, leaving Adrian alone. Perhaps Caleb would change his attitude after a long, cold night in the new well. Something told him Caleb would never come to be the son he had hoped for. They battled wills. They always had. His son was too much of his mother.

Adrian warmed his hands by the fire, his thoughts full of all he had to oversee. The final crops to be harvested before winter. The firewood to be cut and stacked to heat the compound's many quarters and rooms. The breeding to be assigned. One in particular. He had a girl in mind for Charlie. One practiced in the art of love. He had enjoyed her many times.

He couldn't wait to share her with the boy.

Very soon.

CHAPTER 17

Charlie sat at the kitchen table. His mom busied herself getting some tea, after she had bolted all the doors in the house. They had both changed into dry clothes. She kept glancing at the door as if expecting his dad to return any moment. That moment with their hands pressed to his dad's chest wouldn't leave him. They had healed him…somehow. He couldn't make sense of it. A deep foreboding hung over him like an ominous cloud. He wished he could see into the future now like Adrian could. What would it bring?

He looked out the bay window. Dark was here already. Branches screeched on the glass as if warning them winter was nearly upon them. He gripped the mug of hot chocolate his mom made him. Its rim burst up with melted marshmallows, the way he used to like it as a kid.

She sat down and blew on her mug. He blew on his. Marshmallow froth flew off. His mom laughed nervously and wiped it up with a napkin.

"Mom, what's going on?" He still wanted to call the police but she had refused.

She looked into her tea as if seeking answers herself. "I have things to tell you, Charlie. Things you may not believe. May not *want* to believe. I had hoped to tell you when you became older, but it seems the time is now."

Charlie jumped up. Electric jolts seemed to zap at him. He couldn't sit still. He walked to the bay window. It looked over the black nothing. Somewhere out there the water raged across the Sound and Ghost Man—Adrian—waited for him. As he always had. He had listened, given him advice like a real dad. Not like his dad who had tried to kill his mom. What if he came back and tried again? The thought barreled through Charlie like boulders tumbling down on him.

"Things about me?"

"Yes. And me and your dad. And things that happened long ago."

"What does it all have to do with now?"

"Everything. Or nothing."

Charlie took a deep breath, trying to squelch the fire running through him. He turned back to his mom and sat down at the table, squeezing his hands into fists. She unfolded them and held them in her dainty, normal hands. His looked so monstrous next to hers. Charlie wanted to tell her what he did when he went into the woods, and about Adrian, but something held him back. He didn't know how to put it into words. It was still jumbled up inside him and now the incident with his dad smashed about uneasily alongside it.

His mom's thoughts flew into his head. *You and your dad are my whole world, Charlie. I won't let anything happen to you. I promise.* He felt overwhelming love cover him, easing his anxiety.

"You have mind powers like me."

She nodded.

"What about Dad?"

Your dad doesn't share what we do, but your dad saved me.

"What do you mean?"

"I guess I should start from the beginning."

Adrian got up from the bed in disgust.

"We can try something else?" The young female sat up and twirled her pale hair that flowed down perky breasts. He looked hungrily at her sweet, hard nipples poking through curls of spun gold. So young, so lovely. And best of all, eager to please the leader of their community. But her body and tongue had done nothing to arouse him. The thought of being impotent like Caleb enraged him. It was for the soft of body and mind. And he was strong. He turned back to the female.

She got on her knees, her white bottom presented to him. "This way?"

He pulled her up. Let pain infuse his libido and drive out the weakness.

"Not yet. Use these on me." He pulled out his cat o' nine tails and held them out.

Her eyes widened. "I—I don't think I can."

He scowled at her and she shrank back. "You must. I demand it. Now hit my thighs and chest." He stood tall, legs shoulder width apart and put his hands on his hips.

"Now!"

She nodded and moved forward, striking him.

He closed his eyes and grunted. "Harder!" She obeyed.

Each point burned fire in him. Each lash struck him, driving the softness out of his mind and body. And soon his staff grew as hard as his spirit. As it should be. He opened his eyes. She dropped the whip. He pushed her down on the bed. She opened her legs, offering her warm cave up for him to sink into.

His blood dripped on her from the whipping. He licked it off her breasts, her belly. She moaned and raised her legs. He spread her wider, eager to plunge into wet delight and leave his seed behind to grow. His cock touched her used maidenhead and instantly shrunk. He howled at his flaccid failure and shoved her off the bed. She screamed and cowered on the floor.

"What kind of female are you?" Adrian smashed his fists on his thighs to punch away his failure.

"It's not me," she whimpered. "It happens sometimes to the older men."

Adrian moved toward her. She shrunk further on the floor, covering herself.

"You think I am like the older men, do you?"

She looked confused. "No—no, of course not but it can happen."

"Get out. You'll be punished for this. Sent to the fat and ugly males."

The female clung to his leg. "Please, it's not my fault."

"Then you're saying it's mine?"

She stared up at him with pathetic eyes and shook her head.

"Get out, useless female."

She pulled herself up and stumbled for the door. He threw her robe at her and she ran out the door. He watched her flee down the dark corridor. His anger deflated. He bent down and picked up the cat o' nine tails. He had to drive the weakness out. If that female told others he was weak he would not be able to control them. It was time to bring Charlie in. Together they could stand strong. And soon his new heir would be born. Two sons to shape and mold to take Caleb's place. One a man, one a babe in arms. Two sons to ensure his continued leadership—and his plans to rule Earth.

But sudden fear now of losing his power struck deep.

He positioned himself and raised his hand.

The flagellation began.

CHAPTER 18

"I'm adopted, as you know," his mom began. "My mother was a runaway and died the night I was born."

Charlie nodded. She had told him before and also about her adoptive parents who'd raised her. As a kid he used to ask his mom to tell him her childhood stories over and over. How she lived in the country and had chickens and climbed trees to sing from. How her mother made the best apple pies and giant pickles in huge crocks. How his mom roamed the woods and walk along rock walls. But he especially loved hearing about her lake. The one she rode her bike to early in the morning where she wrote about sunrises. And where she'd met her friend, Mr. B, who lived at the lake. He sounded like a cool, crotchety old dude. Charlie waited for her to tell him more.

"But I wasn't the only one born that night," his mom said.

"What do you mean?"

She blew on her tea again, although it must be getting cold by now.

"I had a twin. Born before me. He was given away. A man who took him to be raised somewhere else."

"Where did he grow up? Did you ever meet him?"

His mom was a twin! And he had an uncle out there he never knew. He had the feeling his mom had a lot more to tell him and he had to be careful with his thoughts. He wasn't ready to share Adrian with her. He had kept him secret so long.

And then unease filled him. Adrian had taught him to hide his thoughts over the years. He said no one could know about him. He said there were others in the world who could read minds. And if they read

Charlie's mind and found out their secret then Adrian would have to go away. Charlie didn't know anyone who could mind read, but it became a habit to cloak his thoughts. He didn't want to chance losing Adrian, even if it was all a game.

As a kid he'd pretend he was a spy and the enemy was trying to infiltrate his mind to get information. He had no idea the spy was his mom. Had there been times he hadn't used this skill? Had she read some of his thoughts over the years? He'd heard his father's thoughts over time but never his mother's.

His mom stared at him for a long moment. "Yes, I met him," she said.

"Why didn't your parents adopt him, too?"

His mom stood up, holding her back. She had a twin, had mind reading and healing powers…what other things hadn't she told him?

"They didn't know about him, Charlie. No one did, except the government. They took him away and raised him in a secret facility."

"But why?" It sounded like something from a spy game.

"Because he was—" she stopped.

"A freak, right? A freak like me?" Charlie jumped up and pushed his chair hard against the table. The mugs clanked together. His mom came to him and took his hands, but he shoved her away. She stumbled. Guilt surged through him and he caught her before she fell. "Sorry, Mom. I just get so mad."

She looked like she would cry but then images of him as a little boy flooded his mind from hers. The day he lost his first tooth and rode his bike without training wheels. The day he'd cut his hand falling from a tree. There had been so much blood. It seemed he should have gone to the hospital but he didn't. Why? He remembered his mom hovering over him, touching his hand and the pain had gone away. She had healed him, hadn't she? He let go of her arms.

"Yes, I healed you then," she said. "And many other times. You were all boy. Falling, running, jumping. Wanting to get somewhere faster. Your mind racing to the next thing. Your body unable to get there as fast. But never a freak. Not to me."

She sat down again and sighed, but he paced the kitchen.

"I go to the woods to do things, Mom. Not bad things." He looked over at her. She waited for him to go on. "I can, well, I can move things with my mind."

She nodded. "I know, Charlie. So can I."

And the surprises kept on coming. Her words empowered him to want to know more. She made him feel less alone in his differences but also angry. "Why didn't you tell me that you could do all these things before? I wouldn't have felt like such a freak my whole life knowing you were like me."

"I'm sorry," she said, pleading with her eyes. "I was waiting for the right time for you to be able to handle all this. There's no handbook for moms on this subject."

His anger faded. He had the truth now. Or some of it.

"You and I come from another place, Charlie."

"What do you mean?"

"Another world."

Charlie sat down. He looked at his strange fingers. "Why aren't you like me?"

"I'm a mix. Half human, half Elyon. Like you."

"Alien?"

"No, El-ee-on. A place far away. Too far for us to travel to but not for them. They had discovered a travel technology that broke time barriers. We don't have their technology. We can dream. Perhaps they'll show us someday how to travel deep across space."

Charlie wondered about it too, but it all sounded insane. Yet Adrian had talked about Elyon too and his mom didn't even know him. How many others were out there like himself, like his mom, like Adrian?

"You don't seem upset by the news."

"It makes sense, Mom. Now there's a reason why I am the way I am."

His mom looked at him as if trying to figure him out, or his thoughts. Hearing about Elyon from his mom hit like a real punch. Her saying it drove the truth home.

He came from another planet.

"I know it sounds like a science fiction movie." His mom took his hands again. "But it's true. A long time ago a spacecraft from the planet Elyon crash landed here on Earth. The planet was dying and they sent a team in search of a new planet to start over. My father, who piloted the craft, was fatally wounded. He came in contact with a runaway girl—"

"Your mother."

"Yes. He passed himself on to her before he died."

"What does that mean?"

"He transferred his...seed to her. Impregnated her but without having sex. He—"

"Okay, Mom, I get it." He pulled his hands away. The wind howled around the house. It sounded as empty as he did. And sad.

"The government knew about this planet already because another spacecraft had crashed years before. They came in then and cleaned up the site but kept watch over the area. They told the town a meteorite crashed. And they found out my mother had become pregnant through a 'virgin' birth. They believed she got pregnant from the alien they had found on board and wanted her child for testing."

"How'd they know that?"

"Because the government had experimented with Elyon and human babies before."

This was becoming more and more like a science fiction movie.

"So why didn't they take you?"

"They didn't know my mother carried twins. The doctor who delivered us sold my twin to the government but kept my birth secret and gave me up for adoption. And that's how my parents came to raise me."

Charlie shook his head. All this bizarre information swirled inside him. If the kids at school heard about this they would really call him a freak. Pod Man from Outer Space.

"But what does Dad have to do with all this?"

His mom looked into her tea as if wondering how to answer him. She pushed her hair away from her face. For a moment she looked like a young girl. Like she might have looked when she met his dad.

"His parents were crushed to death under the so called 'meteorite'."

Pity for his dad tugged at Charlie. He'd known his dad's parents died on vacation but he never the details. What must his dad have felt like? Losing his parents and in such an awful way.

"It's why he never talks about them," Charlie said.

"Yes. He had a hard time in foster homes growing up."

He couldn't imagine how that must have been, but it didn't change things between them.

"Dad thinks I'm a freak."

"He never thought of you as a freak, Charlie-boy."

A lump formed in the back of Charlie's throat. "That's what Dad calls me."

"I know."

"Dad wants me to be normal but I can't be, can I?"

"Your dad wants you to enjoy all the normal things a kid should enjoy."

"You mean the things he didn't get to do growing up?"

His mom nodded.

Charlie drained his hot chocolate which had grown cold. It left a slimy feeling in his throat. "So why'd he try to kill you tonight, Mom? I don't understand."

"I'm getting to it. My brother had powers like us and—"

"Had?"

"Yes, he died before you were born. He grew up as a science experiment. Alone, unloved. And angry. So very angry."

"And he could heal like us."

"Yes. But he didn't use it for good."

His mom held his arm. She scared him. Images of death and pain crashed into his head. Of a man who looked like Adrian. His mom took her hand off and they faded.

"What else could your twin do?"

"He was a certain type of breed of Elyon, a Destroyer."

"Sounds scary."

"I know. There are three kinds of Elyons. Seekers, who can seek out people and the future. Healers, who can heal and move objects with their minds, which is what I am—and I think you are too, Charlie. And Destroyers. These kind have all these powers and something else."

"What's that?"

She twisted her fingers together. Her wedding band glinted in the kitchen light and it reminded him of his dad. He couldn't make sense about how he felt about him right now. He was mad at him, felt sorry for him, and didn't want to see him, yet wanted him home all at the same time.

"They have high testosterone levels."

"So?"

"So it meant they have a predisposition toward violent rage."

Like me, Charlie thought, cloaking his thoughts again.

"Only a small percent of Elyons were Destroyers," his mom continued. "But I have often wondered if all Elyons had the ability to be Destroyers. If it was bred in them and certain events or environment could trigger their Destroyer ability. Just like we humans can choose, or not choose, to do wicked acts. Can they?"

He didn't think she expected an answer from him. And he had none to give. "What happened to him? Your brother?"

"He sought me out with his powers. He hated that I had a normal life while he grew up in a cell. He wanted to kill me. To hurt me. And he did. He killed my parents, my friends." Her voice faded off.

Charlie's head pounded and he tapped his fingers on the table. His mind couldn't settle on all his mom had told him. Her brother killed his grandparents and others? And how did Adrian fit in with all this? And his dad? And him? He wanted to escape into the woods and scream for Adrian to take him away and make him feel safe and normal.

Unable to contain his agitation any longer he jumped up and paced the kitchen again. He understood now why he and his mom had always been so connected. They shared powers—and another world.

"You told me your parents died in a house fire."

"They did. My twin burned it down with them in it."

He looked at his mom with her eyes full of tears. It must have been so hard having a brother who killed your parents.

"How did he die?"

"He escaped his government prison to find me and a man came to help save me from him. Someone who'd been watching over me, and your dad, for years. We called him the Man in Black, but his real name was Felix." She paused then rubbing at some spot on the table.

"And?"

She jerked her head up as if she'd been lost in thought. "Felix was…half human, half Elyon—a Seeker. He was the one who told me all about Elyons. He was the product of a human-Elyon breeding experiment from the first Elyon spacecraft which had crashed years before my father's. Felix had been raised as a government experiment as well and worked for the government doing the undesirable jobs. He was there the night I was born, and he took my brother away."

"What kind of person does that?"

"A tormented person. One held prisoner by the government. Felix was a good man. He saved your dad and me. And Mr. B. Dear, Mr. B."

"Mr. B knew about this?"

"Yes. He was my only friend left who helped me. But he died, too, the night Felix saved us all from my brother."

Charlie was so confused. All these new names and people coming together for one purpose. He crossed his arms to stop himself from shivering. He looked down at his mom. She looked so fragile and small.

"I know it's confusing, Charlie, but you need to know this now. You see, as a Seeker Felix saw into the future about me and your dad. He said we'd carry on the Elyon line and he had to make sure we came together and had a child. And we did. You."

She smiled up at him. But he didn't smile back. And he didn't want to think of his parents being brought together to do that. *And so I was created like Felix from an experiment?*

No." His mom cut off his thoughts. "You grew in me before I knew about all this."

He wanted to believe her.

"So Felix watched both of you for years?"

"Yes, and he knew my brother would kill me if he found me. He stopped my brother from killing me and your dad, but in the end my brother took his own life. He couldn't see himself as anything else but a monster. I tried to convince him otherwise."

"Why would you do that after he killed your parents? Your friends?" Charlie would have killed him, not saved him.

"It wasn't his fault. I believed he could have overcome his murdering tendencies if he'd been raised with love, with a family who cared for him. But he had no one. And I was his only family."

"Where did this all happen?"

"At the lake where I grew up in New York. At the site where my father's spacecraft crashed long ago. And Felix told me something long ago I never forgot, Charlie." She paused.

He looked at her as he bounced from foot to foot.

"Fate seeks to realign itself to its correct path, no matter how bad the outcome," she said.

"What does that mean?"

"Our destiny is already set. Fate will find a way to achieve its set course. We have to follow it, but sometimes it's not the outcome we desire."

"Can't we make a difference? Change the outcome?"

"Sometimes."

"Then sometimes not, right?"

"Right."

"Good is supposed to win out over evil, isn't it?"

His mom didn't respond. He sat down and this time he covered her hands with his. She gripped them. And he felt what she felt. She would do anything to protect him. She would kill for him. It shocked him. He had thought he was the violent one. His mom had seemed soft and sweet. Maybe they weren't so different. Or maybe he was more like her brother.

"What was your brother's name, Mom?"

She gripped his hands harder. "The government didn't name him. He only had a number. X-10."

"X-10." It sounded like a robot. Or a monster.

"But I called him Charlie." She looked away with a sad smile. "He wanted to be called Charlie."

CHAPTER 19

Caleb hung back in the shadows of the courtyard and watched in frustration as the community members dragged the stoned Elyons off to be buried in the woods. There were too many deaths now to deal with. A work detail had been formed and Caleb was not part of it. Fear struck him that they would discover he never buried any bodies up on the tree line— and fear of then being lobotomized.

If that happened he could never save anyone again, including his sons. He would be an empty shell used for manual labor and breeding. He wasn't blind to the irony as it summed up his life now. If he didn't comply with the order to breed soon, he would be lobotomized.

Caleb scanned the original community members that gathered after the stoning. Doctors, engineers, farmers, cooks, carpenters, seamstresses and more. They understood their duty and accepted it. Brought here under false pretenses, he did not. These were the elite, chosen by his father from the Underground Destroyer rebellion. They had named his father their great savior and leader. They would follow him and do what he ordered. Not Caleb.

By the time Caleb had been drugged and strapped down on this secret mission, escape was futile. His mother was dead, he had no friends to miss—but still he had not chosen to come. Not this way. He had dreamed of coming here, yes, but to travel with Uncle Brahm on a mission of good—not on his father's mission of evil conquest.

How he missed his Uncle Brahm. He had been a kindred spirit who fed his soul with acceptance, love, and wisdom—all the things his own father never gave him. In his final days on Elyon, Caleb had helped his uncle get ready for his mission to Earth. And then his life became a dark void—his mother died, he found his father in bed with Uncle Brahm's wife, and he was kidnapped by his father.

He would have given up his dream to go to Earth and stay with Uncle Brahm if he had known of his father's plan to steal the ship and go to Earth. His father deceived him because he knew Caleb's choice would have been to stay with his uncle—and he'd come to understand his father never wanted his hated brother to have anything of his. Especially his own son.

He remembered knocking on his uncle's door that first day to assist him with preparations for the Earth mission, hoping for his own ticket to go.

His uncle greeted him then with a wide smile on his round face and pulled him into a big hug. His uncle's hair was white like his father's but all over the place—like his scientific inventions.

"My boy, Manta and I are off with the others. Starting a new path for our world to follow."

"I'm happy for you. Everything will work out on this mission, right?" Caleb felt bad the moment he asked.

His uncle's smile faded. "My brother Feo's crash was over forty years ago. He was a young Madroc, just out of youthhood." He paused and shook his head as if reliving his youth. "But we have better technology now."

"I know."

"I often wonder, if your father's twin, Feo, had survived the crash, would your father be different."

"Not likely. He was born the way he is."

His uncle shook his head and looked down. "No, your father was much softer in his youth. We had been brothers and friends then."

"I didn't mean to make you sad."

His uncle looked up and smiled again. "You never make me sad, Son."

Caleb was desperate to move on from talk of his father. "So, taking any volunteers?"

"Aha, I don't think your mother would take to it well."

But in the end it didn't matter. She died that week, having fallen into the well and breaking her neck. Aunt Manta died, as well, in a laboratory explosion. The mission to Earth was delayed, and a few months later his father's Underground Destroyer uprising had stolen the ship to Earth—with him in it.

His father had lured him to the ship late at night under the pretense Uncle Brahm planned to take them on a special secret tour before the launch, but it was all a lie. Upon entering he encountered the Destroyer defectors and, under protest, was strapped down in a holding cell and drugged. When he awoke the dark woods of Earth greeted him—and his hate for his father consumed him.

He saw Uncle Brahm once walking through the mist back home on Elyon. Desperate to contact home, he had stolen his father's communication belt. He tried to get his uncle's attention, but he never looked up to see him watching him from afar, a sad look on his bowed face. Then he faded into the fog, but seeing him was worth the whipping he received from his father when he discovered him using the belt.

Could Uncle Brahm have helped build another ship with his people? Would they be able to seek a new life as planned for their people before they died out? He held on to the tiniest hope he would see his beloved uncle again—and when that happened his father would no longer be ruler.

But he was here now, alone, on this new world where their people were fleeing once again to a new life, away from the forced life they had here. He had heard the whisperings around the compound. Many Elyons wanted to become part of the human world. They didn't want to take over Earth and destroy its native inhabitants. They wanted to blend in and belong. To live a life of their own choosing. Like him.

He watched his sons' heads now as the community women took the children back to the main childcare room. *Jeremiah and Josiah.* He whispered their names to himself. They were so small, so innocent. He had to get them out of here. No child should have to participate in killing. Many children smiled, as they threw their stones, as if it were a game. Emotion tugged at him when his sons didn't smile. They both closed their eyes and threw their stones, only after a 'mother' had forced their hands up to do so.

Caleb had closed his eyes, too, wishing his aim would go far off course. In closing his eyes together with his sons the distance closed between them, but it was still an impossible chasm to bridge. Someday he hoped to be able to go to them, smile down at them, and tell them he was their father.

He tucked himself away now under the corridor overhang, pulled his hood over his face, and listened to the community members whispering nearby.

"They didn't need to die."

"A fit punishment, if you ask me. They are endangering our way of life."

"What life? This is no life. Our first community failed in the human world. We won't make it like this."

"Maybe we could bond with the humans. Befriend them. Be part of their world."

"Yes, in doing so we can create our own world, too."

"Or maybe they'll just experiment on us.

"Shh. We'll be heard. Stop this talk and thinking. Do you want me throwing rocks at you, too?"

The community members wandered off. Caleb stayed and watched the last of the dead being dragged away. He wondered if he could dig them up in the night and revive them, but nighttime was hours away. They'd be too far gone by then. He only had a short window of time to bring someone back to life before they finished passing on to death. And he didn't know if he had enough energy to save them all. Giving life drained him of life.

"Caleb." His father dismissed the elders and called Caleb over. Tollen, the lead elder, tilted his head at him in passing. Caleb pulled his hood back and moved toward his father, shielding his thoughts in preparation. His father smiled at him. A pit sunk into Caleb's stomach wondering what dirty deed would be required of him.

"Yes, Father."

His father continued to smile at him. Caleb hid his hands in his robe and squeezed them together.

"Tonight it is time. You must breed. I am sending a special girl over."

Caleb shook his head. "I do all you want. I dig wells. I bury the dead. I won't do this. I won't."

His father's smile disappeared and he grabbed Caleb's robe then let go. "You *will* do this. My flock is fleeing. My elders think I cannot control my son. This is your last chance."

Caleb shook his head again.

"I have your surgery scheduled for tomorrow. Then you'll breed anyways. What does it matter? Don't you want to keep your powers and your mind? My people must believe that I, Adrian Madroc, am in charge and know what's best for them."

Caleb stared into his father's eyes burning with yellow fire, glad his own eyes were different. His father had abandoned his eye covers long after they settled here. They'd never had anything in common. His father had dismissed his writing. He said poetry was for sissies, but his mother had loved his poems. She'd said he had a well of beauty inside that someday a wonderful girl would fall in love with.

Well of beauty.

Well.

And the loss of his mother struck him hard again—and the thought he'd played with in his mind for years came back to him. Why *had* she fallen down the old well?

And his father had ordered him to build that new well here. A horrific idea came to him. Was his mother's death not an accident after all? *No. No!* His father couldn't have done that.

Memories flickered of the few times his father had been full of light to him, not dark. The time he'd broken his leg at seven. His father had placed his big hands on his leg and healed it. He hadn't even yelled at him for crying, then he'd picked him up and carried him home. Caleb remembered feeling safe in his father's arms.

Then when he had been nine years old he'd been sick with a raging fever. His mother was off visiting her sister and his father had stayed home from work to be with him. It was an accepted practice to let children heal in their own time from diseases they could fight off. If they didn't they contracted many more illnesses and their body's immune system became weaker and weaker, until a slight cold could kill them.

Caleb recalled from his feverish state how the light had hurt his eyes. He kept them closed while for hours his father had sat next to him pressing cold, wet cloths to his forehead and neck. Shadows of goodness in his father had been there once. Anyone with a shadow of goodness didn't kill their own wife.

"All right, Father. You're right. It's time."

His father looked at him for a moment then nodded. "I'm glad you've finally come to realize this is part of your destiny here."

"I do. I can't fight it any longer. You're right." Caleb looked at his feet, unable to bear his father's steady gaze.

"Being celibate is no fun, right Son?" His father put his hand on his shoulder. "Let someone else do the work of your hand and make our Madroc offspring from it, too." His father raised his hands to the cold sky. "For behold, I will create a new Elyon and a new Earth. The former things will not be remembered, nor will they come to mind."

But it shall not be wholly forgotten, if I can help it, Caleb thought. His father twisted the words of the human god into his own. So could he.

"And I will wipe every tear from their eyes. Death will be no more. Mourning and crying and pain will be no more." His father lowered his arms and looked at Caleb. "And you will help me show our flock they must work through this pain first in order to have their own 'heaven here on Earth', as humans say."

Caleb nodded. "I'll go now and wait for the female."

"Yes, you go."

Caleb turned away but his father called to him again. "And I'll be watching."

Caleb nodded again and made his escape.

It seemed he had no choice now but to do his father's bidding.

He was named after his murdering uncle.

Charlie didn't want to believe it. And he didn't understand how his mom could forgive her brother for killing her family and friends. He couldn't even forgive his dad just for wanting him to be normal. Charlie would never be normal—and good enough for his dad.

"But, Mom, I still don't understand why Dad tried to kill you."

His mom got up and walked to the bay window. Branches scratched at the glass pane in an eerie wail. Total blackness leeched out there, as if the world around them had disappeared.

"I thought, at first, it was because I had suppressed my powers for so long and my pregnancy brought them out, redirecting them on him. Hormones can do funny things, especially when you get older." She turned to smile at him. "Kind of like with teenagers."

"But now?"

"But now, I'm not sure." She placed her hands on the window as if looking for someone out there. "Tonight your dad said something that triggered a terrible memory."

The mystery around what he was, who is mother was, and why his dad acted so strange all swirled in his head. And then there was Adrian. Who was he, too? A guardian angel or an enemy? He wasn't sure what to think except that he needed him.

"What kind of memory?"

"I can't remember it all. I've blocked it out. I didn't want to remember. But I do know it had to do with the day my boss died at work. An employee went on a shooting spree. While the details are blurry to me now, I do know that what your dad said—'it's not me'—had something to do with that day."

"Why?"

His mother shook her head, as if shaking away the memory or trying to relive it.

"I—I don't know. I knew then but not now."

"Could your brother have said the same thing?"

"Maybe. Oh, I haven't thought of it in years. I haven't wanted to remember all the deaths. I erased details of them on purpose years ago, but I didn't want to erase the people I loved."

Charlie got up and stood by his mom. She took his hand and looked up at him. "I'm afraid someone like my brother is here from Elyon. Someone who wants to hurt us."

Charlie pulled his hand away, a crushing weight of guilt fell on him.

"Mom, I don't understand. How can someone from that planet be here now?"

"I don't know. I've tried to contact the planet for years through a belt communication device I have that was Felix's. But I feared everyone on the planet had died out. I saw the Elyons there once through the belt. I met my one uncle…and others."

"A belt to contact aliens?" Charlie laughed. It sounded crazy.

His mom nodded and went to her bedroom. When she returned she had a box. She pulled out a funny looking metal belt. It glimmered and glowed. Light moved through the burnished gray steel like flowing water. Charlie reached out to touch it. Buzzing warmth crept through his fingers. He pulled away. She put it back in the box. He wanted to try it but was afraid his secret of Adrian would be found out if he did.

The stove light glowed warm in the cozy kitchen. But Charlie felt anything but cozy. He felt cold dread inside. His mom sighed and sat down at the kitchen table. "I've had migraines and nightmares for weeks, like I had when my twin sought me out. And now your dad is acting so strange. I've been convincing myself it's my pregnancy causing all this, but I just don't know."

Charlie sat down across from his mom. He had to make it right, with his mom and dad and Adrian. Maybe he could bring them all together to talk about things. "I'm sure you're right, Mom. Let's see how tomorrow is. Call Dad then and see how he's doing."

"Tomorrow. Yes." His mom looked out the window. She was silent a long time as if thinking of another time and place. He tried to read her thoughts, like Adrian had taught him, but it didn't work. She must be skilled at blocking them, too. "And maybe by then I'll remember what those words mean. 'It's not me'."

I'm not sure if I want you to, Charlie thought, but he nodded at his mom.

Tomorrow. He would tell her everything tomorrow.

CHAPTER 20

Adrian laughed and laughed. To control the lowly human filled him with power. He hadn't wanted Ben to kill Laura, just hurt her enough so she used her powers to kill him. How tormented she would have been—and would be when she discovered he had been teaching her son his true powers.

For now he had to deal with the community elders. They filed into the meeting room and faced him around the long table. None spoke. Adrian stood up and smiled at them.

"I'm bringing the woman in. She brings my two heirs with her. They will help make this community strong again. The boy now. Her baby later. We shall groom him. You shall see."

Tollen opened his arms in mockery. "Two Madroc heirs, Brother Adrian? Really, neither child is yours."

"They are of my blood. They will be raised to take my place. Once the flock knows this, they will embrace them as their own. We will demand their love and they will freely give it. And we will provide them with some of the things they want to make them content. Things that do not break down our community."

The elders looked from one another and back to him.

"I think your naming a successor is premature," Tollen said. "And especially two. There are no rules set in place stating your family has precedence to rule after you. This isn't a kingdom but a shared community. We follow the laws our Destroyer leaders set forth for us to build a life here." A few nodded.

Adrian tried to control his voice so it didn't quiver with anger. Idiots, all of them. "We need to give the flock something to hope for. New hope in new blood. We will announce special reward offerings to the flock at the fall festival, and we will center the event around the boy's arrival. Make him the star. Have him mingle with the people. They will want to follow him, alongside me."

"What about your son Caleb?" Tollen's eyes narrowed. "You can't control him. What makes you think you can control this boy who's been raised a human?"

Adrian soothed his anger and smiled at the questioning group before him and at his nemesis, Tollen. "Because I have been grooming him since he was a young child. He is the son I should have had." *Like the one you should have had, Brother.* But he kept that thought hidden. For now.

"Our future has altered," Tollen protested. "I no longer see Elyon Destroyers in positions of power. Our fate is murky. We must reverse our fate. You have led us to this uncertainty."

Adrian had seen this also and he fought the urge to grab the fireplace poker and ram it through Tollen's heart. He took a deep breath and smiled. "We have *all* led ourselves to this. But our future will change. We will make it so."

The elders murmured amongst themselves. Tollen clapped his hands together in approval, although it seemed more mocking than submissive. "Fine. Let's see if your mission works. All who agree?"

All hands rose in the air, answering him as if he were leader. Adrian would soon find a way to make him pay. For now, he bowed to the elders and they streamed out. Adrian walked to the fire and warmed his hands over it. Everything would work out. Now he needed to check in on Caleb to ensure he carried out his duty tonight.

If not, his end came tomorrow.

He couldn't wait to see what tomorrow delivered.

Laura stretched out on her bed, so empty with Ben gone. She had dozed on and off, holding her belly. It comforted her. She was drained from telling Charlie everything tonight. He took it well. Better than she had hoped. He seemed to accept it.

And the familiar man in her dreams. *Who was he?* She needed to figure things out. She needed to remember. Why had those few words terrified her so? *It's not me.* She had suppressed her powers and memories for so long, except reading of minds. She had taught Ben how to accept her thoughts and it had brought them closer. Not now. She could use the Elyon belt to seek Ben out, but she was not ready to face him yet. And tonight she wasn't sure if she could heal again but she did. Thank God. She didn't blame Charlie for hurting Ben. He had just been protecting her.

Charlie had gone to bed but not after he had gone around the house bolting every door and window then locking himself in his room.

She closed her eyes now and forced herself to relive the deaths of all those she had lost years ago at the hands of her twin brother. There had to be a clue in their deaths. She had to remember the details.

Her parents killed when he burned their home down.

Her best friend in college savagely torn apart.

Her boss shot in the head beside her.

The night her twin killed himself.

She could remember nothing that would help her.

Twice already she got up to make sure Charlie's door remained locked. Relieved she returned to her room each time and dozed again. She closed her eyes and took herself back to the day her boss was murdered, willing herself to remember. Puzzle pieces came to her. It pained her. She watched it unfold again. Gunshots rang out in the office. She pulled her boss, Renee, under the desk. Screams pierced her ears. More shots. The screams tapered off. *It's not me. Someone is making me do it. It's not me.*

Laura opened her eyes and sat up fast, trembling. The shooter had said the same thing. Then Felix's words came back to her about her twin. *He hates the idea that you have a life of freedom and pleasure. He has sought to destroy your life. It was him who burned your house down and killed your parents.*

She got up and paced the floor. Felix had said something else. Remember, damn it!

Then it hit her like a blow to her chest.

Your brother entered the body of your co-worker to kill your colleague.

"Oh, my God."

Ben. Someone was controlling Ben.

Someone from Elyon. A Destroyer who wanted to hunt them down and kill them.

Charlie!

She ran into the hall and stumbled. *Let it still be locked.*

She fell into the door, fumbling with the handle. Still locked.

"Charlie?"

No answer. She pounded on the door. Then for the first time in years, she called upon her powers to move an object. She gripped the door handle. *Open!*

Nothing happened.

She placed her other hand on the door and gathered all her will. *Move!*

The handle jiggled.

Sweat broke out on her upper lip. She licked it off. *Come on, damnit!*

She pressed her body into the door. The handle shook harder.

Then it turned easily in her hand.

She swung the door open. Wind rushed cold across her from the open window. Her eyes adjusted in the dark.

Charlie was gone.

Ben couldn't sleep. He stood by the motel window looking at the moon, like he had years ago on a night when Laura had been lost to him. The night he had joined forces with Mr. B and Felix to kill her brother. The night those three had died in a cavern under the earth. Ben and Laura had left them there, sealed in, their story silenced forever. And then Laura disappeared.

She had left him then, afraid to commit to him. Afraid she would curse his life and he would die, as so many others she had loved. He understood how she had felt for he, too, had shut humanity out until Laura opened that door. Months went by before she came back to him, pregnant with Charlie. Now she was lost to him again.

He spent an hour driving crazy on dark side roads before heading to the only motel in town. He'd parked in front of his room trying to quell his urges. He yearned to get good and drunk, but those were the old days. He understood Charlie's rage more than his son could imagine, but he hid that side from his son. He had to. He never wanted to be a fuse to set off Charlie. He had seen what Laura's brother had done, and he believed their son could do the same.

But could someone be hunting them again? They'd had a quiet life since Charlie was born. The threat was gone. Why now, after all these years, would someone come after them?

It was crazy.

Or he was.

He looked at his hands—the hands that had nearly killed Laura. He had seen himself doing it in a fog. It had been like watching an evil character in a movie. He got up, shoved his murderous appendages in his pockets, and looked out into the dark. An owl hooted. The wind carried its mournful call to Ben. A sole creature of the forest beckoning for companionship. Ben felt the same way. He had not been this painfully alone in a long time.

Maybe there were others out there they didn't know about. Had been out there all along. Watching and waiting. Maybe that's what he had to do. Wait and see. Perhaps Laura was right. Once the baby was born all would go back to normal.

Normal.

It's the life he wanted. It's what Charlie could never be. He should accept this, for Charlie's sake. They never did get along. And what was the reason for that? He drummed his head trying to figure it out, thinking back through the years.

And then he understood.

"The reason we never got along was because I could never accept you as my own son. And you know this."

Saying it out loud drove the truth home. Could Charlie hear him?

An ache in his heart stabbed him. Did Charlie also know that Ben placed high hopes on his new son to be the kind of son he'd always wanted? He put his head in his hands.

"How can I fix this? How can I get my family back? And how can I control something I have no control over?"

Tomorrow he'd see things differently. But how could he fight something he didn't understand? It was a mystery all right. And right now he was the only threat to Laura and Charlie. No one else.

He was desperate for it to be true.

And now he stood in a dark motel, alone once again, watching the woods as if waiting for a madman to rise from the dead.

Maybe *he* was the madman.

Tomorrow. He would fix this tomorrow.

CHAPTER 21

Laura ran to the window. Cold gusts blew in like stinging daggers on her skin. She looked down at the short drop to the ground. Part of her wished Charlie had run away. Maybe he went to the forest to let loose his rage. With all her heart she wished he was in the forest finding comfort in the darkness.

Anxiety clawed up her throat.

"Charlie." She called to the wind and the dark. Nothing but the forlorn wind returned her call, taunted her. She ran through every room calling his name. Sharp pains tore at her abdomen. She doubled over and gasped. Loss welled in her from the place where her deepest love resided. She wailed with grief as she searched the house for some sort of sign of where Charlie had gone.

Or who had taken him.

She accepted the truth she had wanted to banish. They were being hunted. And her son was the first taken. The man in her dreams was real. He had controlled Ben and tried to kill her using his strength. And he had taken her son. As he had taken her baby in her dream. *Oh, my God!* Her baby. He had come back for her baby.

"Charlie," she screamed. Something caught her eye on the floor of his room. Something that didn't belong in their home. She snatched it up. A leather whip. Its handle was braided with nine leather strips tied to it. Red tinged the ends of the strips. A torture device. She held it in her shaking hands and closed her eyes, not wanting to see the images it carried. But she had to. For her son. For Ben.

Blurred scenes became sharp. Charlie as a little boy running through the meadow in the forest. A man called to him. Charlie ran to him. The man floated in the air like a vision, the pale monster in her dreams only now clothed in a gray robe.

Then Charlie was older. He stood in the meadow battling sticks and stones together with his mind power. The man watched over him, arms crossed. Then the man stood over her sleeping son in his bedroom. In their house. He was a real monster in the flesh. He pulled out a syringe and pushed it into her son's thigh. *No!* She gripped the blood stained whip unable to stop watching.

Her baby tumbled inside her, kicking hard as if he felt her torment. The man picked up Charlie and looked at her. He stared right into Laura's eyes. She gasped. He smiled, malevolent and gruesome. He pulled Charlie tighter to his chest, holding him as a father would a child. His hands looked strange. Hands with no nails. Like Charlie's.

"No, he's not yours!" Laura dropped the whip and stumbled back onto the bed.

She knew this monster now. Remembered his face. Knew his name now. It was Adrian Madroc, and he was her uncle.

She had met him using the belt to communicate with Elyon before Charlie was born. He had been so kind, so welcoming. *You are safe with us,* he had said. *Take care of your child. He is part of all of us and connects our two worlds. You may now be our only hope.*

He was not kind. He was a Destroyer. And he wanted her and her children.

In the dim moonlight words jumped up at her from the whip's handle. She picked it up and turned on the light. Burned into the handle sprawled one word.

Benevolence.

Caleb looked at the female. She had been with his father and had several children with many males, but she still looked so young.

"What's your name again?"

"Leah," she whispered. She looked at the floor, blonde hair covering half of her face.

"Leah, it's been a long while for me."

"I know." She looked up and smiled then looked back down at the floor. "Everyone knows you're saving yourself for a special female. I—I've hoped you would choose me."

Her one cheek burned red. He walked toward her and gently pushed her hair back, exposing both blushing cheeks. She stood dainty before him with full lips and large, bright green eyes. Her skin glowed luminescent in the low light of his room. Her breasts jutted out from her robe, a worthy invitation. He took her hand and rubbed the inside of her wrist. An immediate jolt shot through him. He heard her almost imperceptible groan and felt her shudder.

It had been so long since he touched a female, been deep inside their warm depths. He envisioned sliding inside Leah, warming her body with his, skin to skin. He grew hard instantly. He had hoped to not like the girl and make this a fast event, but he felt her yearning for him. He needed to make it special for her. He didn't want her to suffer because he hated his father. She was a victim in this, too.

"How old are you, Leah?"

She looked up at him. "Eighteen."

Only eighteen and already a mother many times over.

He hoped he did not make her one tonight.

"I'm ready for you, Caleb." She pulled her robe off, naked underneath, and looked at him for his blessing. He nodded and she lay back on his bed offering her body to him. He wanted her, and he would have her. He took off his robe and stood over her. She looked scared and he sensed her thoughts. She was afraid of not pleasing him, and afraid he would be like his father, cruel and rough. He saw her visions of what his father did to her and it sickened him.

Caleb would treat her like a flower instead, stroking her petals until she bloomed for him. Then he would take her. When she raged with desire and called him to her dark heat, he would possess her. This gift he could give her.

He knelt before her and spread her thighs apart, stroking her body with light feather caresses. She moaned and raised her hips to him, begging him to enter her.

"Not yet, sweet Leah. This is your night."

She moaned louder as he took her to new heights molding her skin into fiery points of pleasure. His full heart was ready to give away. It brimmed with an ache that throbbed inside him.

He couldn't give it to his sons.

He couldn't give it to Rachel.

He could open it tonight and give it to Leah.

And only when he rocked deep inside her, did he unleash his full heart on her. She took it wholly for one night. And when their bodies fit together as one he released his long pent up seed within her.

And he saw his father in his mind's eye smiling with satisfaction.

And he hated him even more.

Ben woke up. Dawn threatened. The gray sky inched lighter into his room. *Laura and Charlie.* He had to get to get to them. Work it out. Something.

He grabbed his bag and quietly headed to the motel door when a pounding rang through it. He yanked it open.

There stood Laura, her face crinkled as if in terrible pain.

"Laura, are you—"

"Charlie." She grabbed Ben. "He's been taken."

He pulled her close. Her heart beat fast against his.

He had been right all along.

Someone was stalking them again.

After fifteen years the nightmare had begun—again.

CHAPTER 22

Charlie's eyes felt so heavy as if marbles rolled around in them. His throat, dry and parched. He swallowed hard and opened his eyes. This wasn't his room. He tried to sit up, but dizziness forced him back down. A low light glowed yellow on the ceiling. The narrow room held a bed, dresser, desk, and chair. A hand stitched picture on the wall blared out its message at him in bold letters. *The wise are promoted to honor, but fools are demoted to shame.*

He stood and the room tilted. His clothes felt strange and cumbersome. He wore a gray hooded robe. Where was he? He last remembered falling asleep in his bed. *The door. Must get to the door.* He lunged toward the door handle, stumbled, and fell. His body moved in slow motion. *Mom, Dad, where are you?* He pulled himself up. Light blazed and a shadow crossed over him.

"Sweet Charlie, get back in bed. You need more time to recover."

His vision blurred. Roses wafted across him. A girl. Her soft hand led him back to the bed. He flopped down on it and his vision cleared.

"Who are you? Where am I? Where are my clothes? Where's my mom?" He tried to sit up again but she gently pushed him back and placed a cool cloth on his forehead. She had shiny, blonde hair and pretty eyes. He had never been this close to a girl. And a cute girl. She placed something on his tongue. It melted into tart liquid soothing his throat.

"Shh, now. Adrian will be in soon once you're fully awake. He will explain everything. I'm Leah. I'm here to make sure you're all right."

"Adrian. He's here? Is my mom here, too?"

She leaned down to kiss his cheek then floated away.

"Wait. Don't go. I need to get home. My mom. She needs me. My dad…"

He tried to sit up but the room raced around him.

Her shadow crossed the door again. "Dulcet dreams, Charlie." Then she was gone.

He tried to cry out but his lips stuck together. His vision blurred again.

His new world disappeared.

Charlie smelled herbs. Like his mom's kitchen when she cooked his favorite meal. Turkey with homemade stuffing. He opened his eyes. Adrian stood over him, smiling. He was real. A thrill spilled through him. Ghost Man was gone.

Charlie staggered up and Adrian placed his hands on his shoulders, looking down at him. His spicy smell covered him in home. Sweet warmth oozed through his brain like hot fudge. He felt so peaceful and a sense of belonging.

"Charlie-boy. Welcome."

Adrian's yellow eyes pierced his with intensity as if drawing something from him. His facial features became amplified in person. A mouth like a black hole, a nose like a giant pancake. His ugliness was powerful to Charlie. And his hidden power radiated from every pore, filling Charlie with awe. He had never seen anyone with yellow eyes except in the movies, or pale skin and white hair like his own.

Adrian let go of his shoulders then took Charlie's hand. Their nailless hands blended as one. They were the same. Somehow. He was like Adrian more than his own dad. What did it all mean?

"How did I get here?"

Adrian took a step back and folded his arms across his robe. His smile disappeared and his large features sank into his face. "I apologize, Charlie-boy, for having to drug you to get you here. I wanted to surprise you and your mom…and dad."

Charlie thought about what he said. Peace and belonging still surged through him, conflicting with the thought that he should be angry for being taken in the middle of the night. He didn't remember being drugged. "My mom and dad are coming. Here? But where are we?"

"Yes. They come soon. I made myself known to your mother. In a day or so they arrive. We are not far from your home, Charlie. Deep in the woods by the mountains. We're a few miles off any road."

"You showed yourself to my mom?" Charlie felt relief knowing his long held secret was now out and he didn't have to tell her. Would she be angry with him?

"Yes. She has been expecting something like this for years."

"Are you going to drug my parents to get them here, too?" It didn't sound right, but what did he know of these people and their ways? "Won't they worry about where I went? I'm supposed to be protecting my mom. My dad…well, there's something wrong with him."

"No, no. They won't be drugged. Your mom understands why you had to come here. She wants me to spend time with you. She came to understand once we spoke. She knows I am her uncle and your great uncle. We're family. We're both twins and have lost our other half. And we can help your dad. We have ways to stop his episodes. Your mom is safe, believe me."

"But why take me?"

"You belong here. You are an Elyon and of Madroc blood—my blood." Adrian's yellow eyes burned into his. *You will never want to leave, my son.* And Charlie knew it was the truth. Adrian's words and power filled him like liquid pleasure in a dream. Charlie didn't understand but accepted. That acceptance replaced any questions he had. It pulled at him and enticed him.

Adrian touched his shoulder. "You will never feel powerless again Charlie. You are meant to lead. I will show you how. But first we have preparations and work to do."

"What kind of work? You mean like cleaning?" He looked around.

Adrian burst out laughing. "No. We need to work on your powers. And the women we work on too, in a way." Adrian motioned him toward the door. "You'll soon discover it's pleasurable."

"Is this something I have to do before my parents get here?"

"We'll see. Either way your parents will be thrilled. They'll love the surprise."

Adrian hadn't steered him wrong all these years. He was family. And he understood how to make Charlie feel better, teach him new tricks, and advise him. He'd run to him in the field whenever he needed him. He'd been there for him, made him feel good. Sometimes when he'd been with him it had felt as if he were being guided to a wonderful place.

And his mom did like surprises. His dad, not so much. Charlie was relieved they would finally know about Ghost Man. Feelings for his parents were all mixed up in his brain, but he didn't want to think those thoughts. He wanted to think about the girl, Leah.

"Will I see Leah again?"

Adrian steered him into a brightly lit hallway. People bustled about with papers, laundry baskets, and food. They stopped to smile and nod to him. He found himself nodding back. Some had white hair and yellow eyes. Some had dark hair and bright green eyes. Some looked massive, their heads scraping the ceiling, and some looked short, mostly the women.

"Oh, yes, Charlie-boy. You and Leah are going to get to know each other very well."

Caleb watched as his father strode with his new prodigal son into the courtyard. The boy's eyes darted everywhere with his mouth open in wonder at the festival in full swing. He looked like his father but with smaller facial features. His face was handsome next to his father's harsh, wide lines and furrowed brow.

His father bent down to say something to the boy and their heads touched. A twinge of envy shot through him, remembering the rare times as a child his father had touched his giant head to his. A time when there'd been kindness in his heart. A time long before he had given in to his Destroyer side.

But now his father had a new son. Together they were pale twins with a bond that Caleb would never have with his father, nor did he want. Anger and sadness mixed in him. The yearning to have the same bond with his own sons burned in his gut.

His father lifted his head and laughed, flinging his arm out at his flock gathered in the courtyard as if showing the boy they were at his beckoning. The flock smiled at the boy then turned to whisper amongst themselves before returning to their rejoicing. Color and music flowed as the community reveled in their much anticipated day of celebration. Caleb did not rejoice. His mind was a tangled knot of how to use this boy to his advantage to escape the compound alive with his sons.

Dancers whirled around him, gleeful in their abandon, but he remained still. Watching and wondering. Gray robes floated and twirled about like doves in the sky, dipping away from each other and back again. Flute and mandolin players, populating a stage built for the event, swayed to their instrumental ministrations. They spilled out wandering notes, filling the air with carefree abandon. Red and gold streamers fluttered and bent in the cool breeze mixing with the final autumn leaves waving goodbye in the wind.

His father had given the flock a day to frolic in fellowship and a night to choose a partner of their own. One night of heathen love allowed. It had renewed their approval and worship of him. It would take more than a festival and free love for Caleb to follow his father with blind faith. It would take compassion and the destruction of the community's way of life. Two things his father was not capable of.

His father walked up onto the stage. The boy hesitated then followed. The musicians stopped playing and moved back. The dancers stood still. Gray robes hung lifeless. The sun covered the silent watchers in flashing light as it passed between clouds. Somber quiet hung heavy after the loud revelry of moments before. Hundreds of eyes looked at the boy wondering how he fit into their fate.

"My Elyons, officially welcome Charlie." His father's voice broke the silence. He motioned the boy closer to him, who peered at the crowd before him with wide eyes. Side by side, they looked like father and son. Caleb scanned the gatherers, who murmured approval as if they, too, knew it to be right and good.

Caleb inched along the overhang, closer to the stage. His father nodded at him. He didn't have the decency to introduce the boy to Caleb first before their world.

His father grasped Charlie's hand and raised it with his. "Charlie will help us assimilate into the human world as our churches grow. He was raised in it and now is here to be one of us. He is my great nephew. I have been teaching him in secrecy for many years and it's time for him to help lead alongside me."

The crowd's murmurings grew louder. Charlie puffed out his chest.

"Have faith." His father's voice became more commanding. The murmuring stopped. "And what is faith? It's the confident assurance that something we want is going to happen." His voice rose louder. "It is the certainty of knowing what we hope for is waiting for us, although we cannot see it far down the road. And so shall we create our new world, unseen by the human one outside of it. And we shall prosper. Won't we?"

"Yes. Yes." The cries of hundreds rang out. Their feet stomped the stone courtyard, stained by the blood of dozens. No blood filled it now, only glory.

"Come everyone, greet Charlie. Make him welcome. He is our new hope."

The flock moved toward the stage. His father put an arm around Charlie and smiled at him then steered him down the steps to meet his people. The boy's scared look became a grin as Leah came forward and kissed his cheek. His father looked over at Caleb and smiled. A knowing smile.

Caleb's stomach tightened, realizing his father's plans now. He saw Leah in his mind moving beneath him with wanton desire. Soon she would be moving beneath the boy. It sickened and angered him. He never should have given himself to her. Now the boy's innocence would be taken and with the first woman Caleb had given himself to in years.

He thrust the feelings away. They had no purpose for him. Leah whispered in Charlie's ear and his laughter rang out. Then his father moved him along through the waiting crowd. The Elyons touched the boy's shoulder and offered him their blessings, but it was Leah he kept turning back to see. She bowed to the boy and then turned and caught Caleb's eye. They stared at each other across the crowd. Then with a resigned smile, she hung her head and walked out of the courtyard.

Caleb watched the flock surge around the boy.

Change was coming.

CHAPTER 23

"We're going to Benevolence," Ben said. "We'll find their hiding place."

"The community compound is supposed to be a day's walk or more into the woods from the town, I hear. There are no roads to it," Laura said. "And no one has ever been inside. The church bought up all the land bordering the protected wilderness and they live, totally isolated, off the land."

"I remember news reports that claimed the police questioned them for suspicious behavior, but the accusations have all been unfounded, so they say. We now know why. They've most likely masterminded their success by preying on other people with mind control."

"And all these years they've been here and we never knew they were connected to me—to us. I should have known. I should have sensed it. I shouldn't have tried to forget my powers."

Ben took her hand. He had nothing to say.

"I'll work on my powers. Bring them back," Laura said. "Nothing will stop me from saving Charlie."

"We should call the police," Ben said. "Let someone know about this. What if we disappear and no one knows where we are?"

"No." Laura shook her head. "They won't believe us and they can't do anything."

Ben squinted at her. "But Laura, you're eight months pregnant going off on a trek into the woods to God knows what kind of situation. Let me go alone."

"No!" Laura gripped his arm. "I'll know what to do when I get there. He's leading me there for a reason. It's fate. And I have to help realign it."

"Who's 'he'?"

"My uncle. I know what he is now. He's waiting for me to come to him. He's been watching and waiting all these years. Now he has our son. And he wants our baby. But what he doesn't know is that he won't survive me."

Ben squeezed her hand. She was strong in mind but also hugely pregnant. He hoped she wouldn't take matters into her own hands as she had the night her brother attacked them. They had survived that night. Would they survive this? He would have died for her then—as he would now for Charlie and their unborn child.

"We can't warn them we're coming," Laura said. "And if they discover we are then what happens to Charlie?"

Again, Ben had no words of comfort. "Let's go."

They stopped at a grocery for nonperishable food items then returned home to grab backpacks and sleeping bags—and Ben's gun. Laura would only let him keep it in the garage. She didn't say a word when he tucked it in his jeans. She forced herself to go into Charlie's room and take the Swiss Army knife he kept in his drawer. She lifted it out, trembling, and sat down on his bed. The sheets were tousled as if he just woke up and was in the shower getting ready for school, ready to yell any minute for her to please get breakfast ready for him. She touched his sheets, bent down and breathed his smell. Her heart shattered into a million pieces and she ran from the room.

They left and the day hung overcast, suffocating them in its woes. They drove in silence until they reached the trail entrance and turned off the engine. Benevolence Mountain towered menacing over them.

"This is the trail leading toward their community," Ben said. "I checked the map, it ends at the protected land border and then I don't know where we go. No one does. Are you sure this is what you want to do?"

"We've got to get our son back and I'm going. I'll know how to find them," Laura said.

She pulled the flogging whip out of her pocket. They stared at it then she shoved it away and started tugging their backpacks out of the car. Ben helped her put hers on.

"Cell phone reception on the mountain is spotty," Ben said, checking his phone. "If we need to call for help I don't know if we can."

"If we need to call for help, it won't matter."

She was right. Laura headed up the trail, but Ben held her back. He placed his hands on her belly. "Promise me, no matter what happens to me, you'll take care of yourself and little Ben inside."

"We haven't given him a name yet," Laura said with a forced smile. "Not sure he's a Ben."

"I don't blame you. Who needs another Ben running around the world? Terrible hygiene, bad manners, dumb as a bag of hammers."

"Hammers aren't all bad. Builders of things. High impact. Reliable. Top performers."

He hugged her.

"My Ben is all of those," she whispered in his chest.

"I'm counting on it." He bent his head and kissed her for a long moment. A passionate kiss that spoke of another time when they had once moved into one another, lost in their own world. It was a fierce kiss. Their tongues intertwined like hands grasped together in fervent prayer.

Time to go. He took her hand. They headed up the trail to get Charlie back.

Ben didn't know if all of them would return.

Charlie was alone in his room. His robe itched and he took it off and sat on the bed in his underwear. How he wished for his jeans and T-shirt and sneakers. The shoes he'd been given were nice. Warm and lined with some sort of fur on the inside. But why the robes? Everybody looked alike. Would his parents be expected to wear them, too? But his dad was an outsider.

Adrian had said Charlie could help him lead the community. His dad could be proud of him then and see he was normal amongst these Elyons. His dad would now be the abnormal one. A delicious feeling swam through Charlie. His dad would finally feel like *he* had his whole life. A freak.

No! No! He banged his hands to his head. Guilt took over and he lay down on the bed, his head bulging with all that had happened over the day. How he wished Adrian had brought him here sooner so he didn't have to suffer all those years of not belonging.

He couldn't stop thinking about the morning and all he'd experienced. Eating the home grown food for breakfast in the dining hall. Then taking part in their fall festival and being presented to the community. Best of all he got to see Leah again. She was so pretty. When she kissed him on the cheek he felt his face burning hot. Adrian said he would be seeing a lot of her.

He'd never had a girlfriend, although many in his class did. All the other kids would be so jealous. The one time he had ever kissed a girl on the lips was at a birthday party and they played spin-the-bottle. He had to kiss Amy LeFay in front of everyone. Her lips had been wet and slobbery. He hoped Leah's lips would be different.

He liked being here. Everyone approved of him. They called him their *new hope*. He was someone. A surge of power rushed through him. Every time Adrian touched him he felt all tingly inside. Charlie rolled over on his side, trying to block out his parents. His feelings for them were so confusing now. Days ago his life had been simple but depressing. Now his life was happy but confusing and complex. He decided to go with it.

He closed his eyes but a knock jerked him awake. He stumbled to the door and opened it. A tall, dark haired man with bright green eyes stood there. He frowned at him. Charlie remembered seeing him at the fall festival.

"Your robe," the man said.

Embarrassed, Charlie reached for his robe and pulled it on. The man came into the room with a white cloth draped over one arm. Leah stood behind him. Had she seen him in his underwear? God, he hoped not. The man placed the clothes on the bed. More robes?

"I'm Caleb," the man said. His bright green eyes glowered down at Charlie. "And you know Leah already."

Charlie smiled at her with what he hoped wasn't a goofy smile. She smiled back and looked at the floor.

"Leah is here to teach you of Elyon ways."

"Like seeing into the future?"

Caleb didn't reply, just shook his head and continued to frown at him. *Who was this guy?* He had a familiar look to him. He reminded Charlie of someone. He looked at Leah, but she remained with her gaze locked on the floor.

"Does Adrian know?"

"Adrian knows everything. He is my father and his orders are always followed."

The revelation struck him. Caleb looked like his mom. Homesickness swirled inside him. "We're related."

"Yes." Caleb pursed his lips then turned and strode out the door, slamming it behind him.

Leah sighed and looked up. "Now we can have some fun." She smiled at him and took his hand. Charlie felt the homesickness fade away replaced by something else, a warm feeling that tingled with wonder and the unknown.

"Jeez, what's wrong with him?" Charlie tried to sound casual but her hand in his distracted him. His heart pumped a little faster.

"Oh, he and Adrian never got along. That's all. He's really not so bad once you get to know him."

"I don't know if I want to get to know him."

"Well, never mind him. We're going to get to know one another." She smiled.

Charlie swallowed a huge lump in his throat. "Um, okay. Do you know when my mom and dad will be here?"

Leah touched his hand. "I don't know, but we'll take care of you until they arrive. But first we have to change into our initiation robes." She picked up a robe and held it out to Charlie. He hesitated then took it.

"Why?"

Leah picked up the other robe. "So our community will know we've been bonded to one another."

"Bonded?"

"Adrian has said I am to be your first family."

"Family, like a sister?"

Leah laughed. "You're adorable, Charlie." She motioned for him to turn around. "Now we both change into our new robes back to back. It's the first step to our bonding."

"But what does that mean?"

"When each male Elyon comes of age they are bonded to another Elyon in the community before they give their seed to all. It's the one time in their lives they are bonded. Then after a period of time the bond is over and they belong to all the community."

Leah turned around away from him. Charlie stood there for a second unsure of what he was getting himself into. *Give his seed? Belong to the community?* But he wanted to please Leah. He turned around and pulled off the itchy gray robe. He threw it on the bed. He heard Leah take hers off and he forced himself to look at the wall in front of him as he put on his new robe. He hoped she didn't cheat and look at him in his underwear. Talk about mortification. The white robe hung heavy and soft and tied at the waist. A definite improvement. He ran his fingers over the yellow shooting star embroidered across the top left side.

"Charlie?"

He turned around and she stood before him. She looked even prettier in white. Her shimmery hair fell in waves on the bright robe.

"Now everyone will know we are to be bonded." She touched his star then touched the star on her chest. "Our stars have come together to reside over our heart. They have blazed in the dark to meet in light. The light we create in bonding will live on forever. Our world will be blessed with a rain of stars. A golden shower begun by you and me that will wash all darkness away."

She reached up and touched Charlie's cheek. She spoke so strange, like a poem. A poem meant only for him. He didn't know what to say. Anything he did say would come out awkward, so he remained silent.

"Today is our day of music. Tomorrow is dance."

Leah pulled Charlie toward the door.

"What's next?"

"Then it's the day our music and dance are joined. And then it's the day we're bonded. Come on!"

"Where are we going?"

"To the sanctuary. This afternoon we learn our song together. We must then sing and dance for the community before our final day."

Charlie was more and more confused but filled with longing to remain with Leah. He didn't want to break her spell which had mesmerized him. He followed her out the door. People smiled at them as they passed down the corridor and nodded as if they approved of their 'bond'. And Leah's hand felt so warm in his. He held hers tighter. They left the corridor and entered the courtyard. His breath hung frosty in the air. He shivered.

"Final day?"

"The day our family bond is complete. The day your initiation is complete." She smiled at him and kissed is hand. "No worries, Charlie. We're having fun, right?"

He looked down at her and nodded. "Right."

"Then come on. We have work to do."

Was this the women's work Adrian spoke about? He didn't know. But he didn't mind at all.

He let Leah lead him across the courtyard to the sanctuary. Her hair gleamed in the autumn sun under a cold, blue sky. Her dainty hand fit so small in his. Was this ritual some brother-sister thing? He didn't feel very brotherly toward her. And he didn't know why he was to bond with her. But he would follow her anywhere.

CHAPTER 24

Laura and Ben hiked fast up the rough trail that grew unrecognizable and disappeared altogether. The state forest markers had ended a while ago. They moved deep into the wilderness with no one around for miles. Ben stopped but Laura hiked on.

She sensed where to head, but exhaustion overcame her. She stumbled. Pain ripped through her abdomen as the weight of her child yanked down on her with each step. Ben put a hand under her elbow to steady her. His other hand held a Glock aimed and ready to fire.

She felt his fear for her, for their baby. But her fear right now was for Ben. Deep inside she knew she needed to go this alone, but Ben would never let her. She had left him and gone it alone years ago when her brother hunted them. And Ben had nearly died that fateful night. Was he meant to die then and would fate realign itself now to fulfill his destiny?

Suddenly, there in the forest floor, tracks appeared.

"Look," Laura pointed. "A vehicle's tracks." She knelt and placed her hand in the dirt and closed her eyes sensing the memories of the earth.

"What is it?"

"They have their own ATVs. It's how Adrian transported Charlie to their compound." She reached her hands out in the air. "All the way from the woods behind our house. Drugged."

"Bastard!" Ben lifted her up. "But you've got to rest."

She pulled away and took off, following the faint tracks. "No. There is no rest until we get Charlie back."

"What happens if you push yourself too hard and go into labor?"

She slowed down a bit then stopped. Ben helped her sit on a fallen log. Crows cawed overhead, stark and full of despair. Like she felt. The woods grew lighter as the sun crept overhead. A deer burst through the trees. It looked at them with panicked eyes and darted off.

Ben knelt before her and took her hands. "We'll find Charlie. We'll get him back."

"I wish I was a Seeker and could see into the future and know that for sure. I wish Felix was here to help."

"You're a Healer for a reason, Laura. And Felix would have wanted you to take care of yourself first. You carry two people I love. You need to be okay to help us find the third." He sat on the log next to her and put a hand on her belly. She covered his hand with hers. Their child pulsed inside her. A cool breeze swirled around them drying the sweat on her brow. Sunlight sparkled on Ben's face. For a moment he looked like the young man she first met, although his face was deeply etched with lines now and his hair nearly all gray.

She pulled out the flogging whip. "I wonder whose blood this is." She touched the tips. Adrian flashed before her. He had a name now. The face which haunted her dreams. There was no redemption to be found within him. There he stood naked before a mirror flinging the whip. Blood streaked across his burly chest and thighs. His tendons bulged out with each strike but he did not flinch. He smiled at himself and flung the whip harder. With each grunt he moaned and stared into her eyes from the mirror. *Laura, you are mine.* She dropped the whip, shaking.

"What is it, Laura?"

"It's his blood. Adrian's. My uncle. He flogs himself. He enjoys it."

"Sick bastard. What has he done to Charlie?" Ben got up and slammed his hand on a tree.

"Nothing. Yet. He wants him for his own."

Ben turned to her, his face tight. "What does that mean?"

"He wants him for his son. To turn him to evil."

Ben nodded. "He'll never turn him."

"Light and dark reside side by side."

"Our son is not evil." He held out his hand. "We need to go. Are you feeling well enough to go on? I can do this alone, Laura. I can save our son. *Our* son."

"No, you can't. Not from this. You don't have powers to fight with." She picked up the whip. "And he knows we're coming. He wants us to come."

"Why?"

"He's been here for years. Secretly guiding Charlie in his powers and waiting."

"Waiting for what?"

"He wants to breed his Destroyer kind and take over Earth."

"But why does he need Charlie?"

Laura looked at him. "Because Charlie has a Destroyer hidden inside him."

"A hidden element."

"Yes." It came out a whisper. She dared not tell him about the dreams. Especially the one where Adrian made love to her.

Ben stared at her. She sensed his feelings of fury and sadness.

She took his hand. "Let's go."

The air grew warmer. Fall was being forced out with the brief return of summer heat. Sweat rolled down her back. She didn't know if they would reach Adrian's world by nightfall. They still had miles to go and she was so tired.

They marched on toward a hidden enemy who watched—and waited.

CHAPTER 25

Adrian watched Leah and Charlie from the sanctuary's balcony. She led him in the initiation song. Their voices rose together in a sweet clamoring. He looked uncomfortable singing and kept glancing over his shoulder, but Leah touched his cheek and he faced her to sing louder.

Adrian was pleased. The boy would be ready for Leah's intimate instruction on the final day. He would continue to brush off Charlie's inquiries of his parents and mind bend him to think what he wanted. By the time they arrived the boy would no longer be under their influence but under Adrian's full control as his rightful son.

It pleased him that he had chosen Leah for the boy and angered Caleb in doing so. It would teach Caleb not to become attached to any one female. Their community would not grow and thrive as one body with individual families. He began to suspect his allowance of one night of free love between his people was a mistake. He had looked into the future and no longer saw himself in the White House. Laura remained a blur on the edges, as if she was being erased. *It can still be changed. I will make it so.*

He had already admonished three couples he had caught kissing and holding hands in the shadows of the compound wings. Public affection was not allowed and neither was a single partner. He had separated them, ordered them to work the latrines and garbage route for a month, and sent them to the assignment clerk to be reassigned new partners to breed with.

The one female had cried. He had fought the urge to slap the wench. Her desires did not matter. The whole of the community mattered, and he was in charge. He told the female such and she had sulked off with the others. As she did he had caught Tollen watching him from across the courtyard as if he were keeping a list of his failures to use against him.

You can't touch me, Brother.

Tollen raised one eyebrow with a half-smile. *We'll see.*

The community chooses me. Just like Manta chose me.

Only for a short while. Just like Manta did for only a time.

Adrian took a step forward, but Tollen did not retreat. *What do you mean? She left you for me.*

Tollen's half smile became a full grin. *She never left me. I was with her the day before she died. Deep within her. So, so deep inside. She couldn't stand your rough ways. I was the one who brought her to the heights of ecstasy. She had grown tired of your ways.*

You're just jealous because she chose me.

The community flowed around them, sneaking looks at their private battle. Adrian gripped his thighs and a hot pulsing in his temple pained him.

She didn't even want your child, Adrian. She was going to get rid of it.

Liar!

Confusion filled him. Tollen thought Manta carried Adrian's child, not Brahm's? Before he could spout out the true father of Manta's child, Tollen turned and strode away. Adrian's anger cooled. Another time then.

He brought himself back to the bonding business at hand and watched Leah and Charlie a little while longer before heading to his room. He knelt on the floor and let his mind soar into the woods. There he watched Ben and Laura on their trek. She was enormously pregnant and this pleased him. He waited for her child's birth with immense delight.

To have Laura and her son would be his last act of vengeance. She represented all that his brothers, Feo and Brahm, had taken from him. They had betrayed him. Both having been selected for Earth's mission decades apart. They had both lost. He had won. He took Feo's daughter, Laura, now for his mate and she would replace his true love, Brahm's wife. The taste of double revenge was sweet.

He soared in closer. She looked so lovely with her auburn curls gleaming in the sun as she moved toward him. He envisioned her naked as he had seen her so many times—and taken her, been deep inside her. Even in pregnancy, her swelling breasts and belly called to him. *Come, Laura. You are mine. We will be together. You shall be my goddess and I will be your god. And our sons shall rule our new world.*

He relished taking care of Ben. Perhaps Laura could help. When nightfall came he would have his fun with them.

Charlie and Leah walked hand in hand toward Caleb. He had been waiting for them at the combat arena. Adrian ordered him to work with Charlie on his powers as part of his Destroyer training. Jealousy streaked through Caleb as they drew closer. He had to let it go. It was not the boy's fault. Once again, his father drove his anger.

Leah saw him and looked away. She let go of Charlie's hand and walked quickly back to the compound. Charlie stood before him, massive already at fourteen. He looked like a man. He could be a formidable foe, or ally.

"Adrian said I'm to come here and work with you," Charlie said. His voice went up a notch and Caleb couldn't help but smile. The boy was not a man yet. They faced each other under the open sky in the outdoor arena. The blustery wind had died down and the September sun warmed them with its final heat.

"Yes," Caleb finally said. "I know my father has been working with you for years on how to move objects with your mind powers, but now we need to work on other powers as well."

"Like seeing into the future?"

"Not yet. But yes, Seekers can seek out people and the future. However, we can't seek out an Elyon who doesn't wish to be found."

"What about healing?"

"Yes, you'll learn that along with mind bending."

"Mind bending?"

"It's what we Destroyers do, with training."

"I want to see the future."

"Someday."

"And how can I do that?"

"You give in to hate."

Charlie nodded, accepting this premise. Caleb would not. If he gave into hate and learned how to be a Seeker he could seek out the Elyons he'd saved to ensure they were all right...and he could watch over Rachel. But he could not give in to hate just to gratify himself.

"But first," Caleb continued. "You'll learn to control the minds of others, bend them to our will. This power we wield will enable humans to help us as needed. It's how we've made it here on Earth so far. We've convinced humans to give us money, sell us land, and let us live here alone in our community, until the day we grow throughout the world. According to my father that day is coming soon."

"What happens then?"

"This world becomes a new Elyon."

"So you steal to get what you want."

Caleb smiled. "It's how we must survive. We left our dying planet for a new life. You have a saying here. What is it? Survival of the fittest."

"It's a saying meant for the wild."

Caleb threw his arms out. "Take a look around, Charlie. We're in the wild. And creating a new world is hard if we want to thrive. And we must be hard on ourselves and sacrifice. If we don't we will not succeed. We will hang our heads in shame at our failure. We are only dust between the womb and grave. But we must not blow idly in the wind. We must shape our time here to leave a legacy before we leave our bodies for total darkness." His voice grew harsher than he intended, burning with anger as he repeated his father's words.

"The wise are promoted to honor, but fools are promoted to shame," Charlie recited. "It's on the wall of my room."

"Yes. Fools here are not merely shamed."

Charlie moved closer to Caleb. "What do you mean?"

"They are punished." He stared at Charlie and let that sink in. Charlie frowned and chewed on his lip, shifting his eyes about. The boy's physical likeness to Adrian was striking. Would his mental likeness be as well? The boy seemed innocent in his youth, but he sensed deep anger in him also. Anger his own father wanted to tap into.

"Caleb, can you see into the future? Can you see my future?"

"No," Caleb said, softening his voice. "I am not a Seeker yet. My father will teach you that power."

"What about you?"

"Someday. I'm not ready yet. But we don't need to worry about that now, for today we practice healing." Caleb strode toward Charlie and pushed up the sleeve of his robe. Charlie stepped back but Caleb held his arm tight.

"What are you doing?"

"I'm going to heal you."

"But I'm not—"

In a flash Caleb withdrew a knife hidden in his hand and slashed Charlie's forearm. The boy cried out, but Caleb held him tight. Blood dripped on the arena's dirt floor. Charlie struggled against him.

"Be still."

Caleb closed his eyes and pushed his fingers into Charlie's flesh. He felt his life force pumping strong. He willed the skin to stitch together. Charlie gasped and his arm went limp. Caleb opened his eyes and wiped the blood away. The cut disappeared. The only evidence that remained was the spatter at their feet.

Charlie shoved Caleb away. "Why did you do that?"

"I needed to show you what we can do. Now it's your turn."

Charlie shook his head. "I'm not cutting you."

"This is just part of what you will learn Charlie. There is more power you will learn to use as well."

"I don't want to know."

"You must. Adrian has decreed we fulfill *all* of our powers. It's how we will survive on Earth. It's how we will stop any humans that turn against us."

Caleb felt sick inside repeating what his father had instructed and instilled in him for years. But his father was watching, listening. He would teach Charlie and appeal to him when the time came to help him. He hoped his father's new heir would also be his great downfall.

Charlie took a step back toward him, massaging his arm. He twisted his arm looking for a scar. None could be seen. "I can't believe it. I can really do this, too? I mean, I sort of did it with my mom after my dad attacked her."

"Yes. You can do this and other things." Caleb paused. "Killing."

Charlie's eyes widened. "Killing?"

"With our minds. We must be ready to destroy when necessary."

"Who?"

"People who get in our way."

"Like bullies?"

"People who could stop our cause. But while we have these powers we are not allowed to use them amongst ourselves. We cannot take matters into our own hands. If a member of the community has reasons to do so—whether it's mind bending or healing or killing—they must get permission from the elders first. We are only allowed to practice our powers here within the arena. An elder can override that law in emergency circumstances but must answer later for his actions."

"What happens if you use your powers on each other anyways?"

"You are punished."

Charlie was silent. He didn't seem eager to know what the punishment was. He took another step closer to Caleb. "I've never fit in anywhere before, you know?"

"I know. You belong here, with us, Charlie. We're cousins. We carry the Madroc blood. We're family. And everyone here is your family. And you are destined to help lead it."

"And my mom and dad?"

Caleb wasn't sure how to respond to that. He could not sense his father's plans yet for Charlie's mother, but he could guess what Charlie's father's fate would be. "I'm sure they're part of the plan."

It seemed a safe answer. For now.

He motioned Charlie closer and held out the dagger. "Show me your power."

In his mind's eye Adrian watched his sons work together. Caleb did his job well and Charlie responded with enthusiasm, after his initial shock. He healed Caleb's slashed arm then enjoyed making a young boy do his bidding with his mind bending. By the time Caleb brought out the rabbit in the cage, Charlie was ready for the killing. Power radiated from the boy.

After the rabbit stopped its struggle the boy grinned, relishing his kill. He held up the animal by the legs and waved it at Caleb who stood with arms crossed, a tight smile on his face. The death wouldn't be wasted. Rabbit stew highlighted the dinner menu tonight.

Killing was useful in so many ways.

CHAPTER 26

Night was coming. Laura moved slower and slower. She had to rest. Besides walking all day she was exhausted from practicing her powers as they moved deeper into the woods. It had been so long since she used her mind powers to battle. She moved sticks and stones together as they hiked toward their enemy. It drained her and she didn't know how she kept taking step after step, but the thought of sleeping here on the ground in the woods terrified her. She saw herself giving violent birth to her son on cold earth as Adrian watched.

They still had miles to go. They had not seen a soul since entering the woods. They trudged deep into the wild, heading toward a hidden alien enemy. The air had grown so cold. Winter blasted in driving the last warmth of late summer away. The wind stung her cheeks with icy knives.

"Laura, we have to make a shelter before it gets dark. Get a few hours of sleep."

"I know. We're still miles away."

Ben pulled logs and branches together between a thicket of trees. He checked his cell phone but they had no service. Then he made a bed with the insulated sleeping bags they had carried for hours on their backs. They were heavy duty and good for sleeping in below freezing weather. He spread one out flat and unzipped the other to cover them as a blanket.

Laura sank onto the soft flannel and shivered. The temperature was predicted to be in the thirties tonight. Her baby had not moved much all day but now, in her rest, he prodded her. Ben curled up behind her, warming her with his body.

"Once we find Charlie how will we get him out?" Ben whispered in her ear.

"We can't know until we get there."

"Will your powers be enough?"

She squeezed his hand. "We have to hope so. We'll need the element of surprise."

"These ATVs they have. Can we steal them and break out with Charlie? Can you see the layout of this compound?"

"It's fuzzy right now. I'm only getting pieces from the whip. It holds the memories of Adrian. I'll keep trying."

At least Charlie was alive. She would find him—and Adrian. Then a shocking thought swept through her mind. What if other compounds sat hidden? Like alien cells waiting to take over the world? She whisked the thought away. She had to think of Charlie now and her unborn child. And Ben. They had the promise of forever once. Did they still?

She closed her eyes.

The last thing she heard was Ben murmuring *I love you* in her ear, his breath warm and comforting on her neck. She didn't know if it could be enough to save them all.

She slept.

Leah led Charlie back to his room. His mind raced with all the events of the day. At first he felt silly singing with Leah but then he lost himself in listening to her sweet voice. After he learned the song she had urged him on. Their voices had blended as one, high and low coming together. He didn't understand the song they sang. It had to do with love and fire and seed. Something light and hopeful stirred in him being with her, a pleasant yearning of sweet anticipation that threaded through his gut.

If only the kids at school could see him now with this hot older girl. They would be so jealous. Then a different kind of yearning twisted in him. A yearning to avenge himself against them. He hoped he would get the chance.

Something dark had stirred in him when he was with Caleb. Slashing, mind bending, and killing felt good. It held power. And with power he could do anything. No one would make fun of him again. Here he was as revered as a god.

His mom and dad flashed through his head, but they seemed like two-dimensional figures now. They were part of an old life. Adrian had pulled him in to his world. In a way, Adrian had been preparing him for it for years and now had become his true father. His natural father, Ben, seemed cardboard and false, like a puppet that never knew him and only wanted to pull his own strings to be normal.

Charlie didn't want to be his father's version of normal anymore.

He looked down at Leah as they reached his door. She stood on tiptoes and kissed him full on the lips. They moved over his, so warm and soft, not slobbery like Amy LeFay's. He found himself kissing her back. He reached a hand down and stroked her hair. It fell like silk through his fingers. She pulled back and smiled at him.

"Soon, Charlie Madroc, our special time is coming."

But that's not my name! And he didn't know what she meant but he didn't care. He let his thoughts flow into hers. He felt golden just being with her. *Nothing gold can stay.* The Robert Frost poem from English class flashed through him.

"It can here, sweet Charlie."

I hope so. I don't want it to end.

She smiled at him and left him standing there watching her go.

Ben was dead.

Tall shadows dragged his body away. Her child seemed to scream inside her, but her own voice was gone, along with all hope. She fell to the ground in agony. Her child ripped his way out. A monster, as her brother had been. Like Adrian was—and like Charlie would become.

Her screams came then. Real ones. Not from within a dream. Ben hung over her, pinning her to the ground. The moon spilled across his face. He grinned at her, but it was the hideous grin of another. His hands closed around her throat, her child crushed under him. She twisted beneath him but he held her down. His ragged breaths pounded the air.

"Laura, you're mine."

She gripped Charlie's knife. It hid in her hand while she slept.

"Ben, stop!" He hesitated for a moment and she spit in his face.

His grin turned to a scowl. He removed a hand to wipe the spittle that dripped down his cheek then his hands reached up and they closed on her neck again.

He stared into her eyes with those intense gray eyes she had fallen in love with.

Now they blazed with hatred. The eyes of another. She willed this monster to be her Ben again. He would not die here in the wild by her hand. By the hand of evil.

"Kill me, Laura." Adrian's words now mocked her in Ben's voice. The same voice that had murmured desire and love to her. His hands gripped her tighter. She grew faint and let go of the knife. She would never use it on him.

"It's not me," he whispered and fell back on his side.

Her Ben!

And she heard the sobbing from her co-worker in her head from long ago. He'd crashed along cubicle walls seeking her out then, a puppet of her twin with the intent to kill. She shrunk further into the ground next to Ben, as she had then under the desk with her boss, Renee.

"It's not me!" The man had screamed over and over. "Stop it! Let me stop!"

He pulled the chair out and pointed his gun at them.

"I'm so sorry but *he* is making me do it."

"Who?"

"I don't know. But he hates you."

He shot. Once. Twice. Three times. And the back of Renee's head exploded covering her in a spray of blood.

The man lowered his gun. "Not you. He told me it's not your time yet."

The sobbing grew louder. Her own now.

"Ben, come back to me," she whispered. He lay huddled in a ball, his eyes closed. She reached for him, touched him with her healing hands. Her world grew darker. She didn't have the strength. Trees spun around her. And Ben remained so still beneath her hands.

She sent her light into his dark depths.

But her light was fading. She would not give up.

Could not give up.

The dark took her anyway.

CHAPTER 27

Adrian's flock congregated in the courtyard. The sun warmed his face with a resurgence of summer. Such an unusual late September day for a whipping. Sweat dripped down his spine. It stung his wounds from the previous night's self-flagellation. He relished the sting, the clarity the pain brought. The sun's rays grew hotter as all assembled.

The lovers were to suffer by heat today for the heat between each other. After the night of free love they did not heed warnings to stay apart. They snuck time together to wantonly mate. Adrian took great satisfaction in catching them in the act after being tipped off by one of his elders. And he was satisfied to know his elders still followed him in the laws set down, especially Tollen.

He could have no cracks in the world he'd created. He needed to ensure that Elyons would come to rule. And he, Adrian, the great leader, would be honored for creating this new world from a dying planet. He was the savior of Elyon. His chest rose with pride. People would follow him or suffer. Today's suffering came as a warning to his flock.

Charlie stood beside him silent. He wondered what went through the boy's brain but his thoughts hung now below the surface. He mustn't worry. The boy belonged with him. He had a dark heart inside, a twin to his own.

Caleb led the naked lovers in, who both cried pitifully. Caleb tied their hands over their head to the bar swinging out from the side roof. He then spread their feet and shackled them down.

Charlie looked at the ground.

"Charlie-boy, you must watch. These two shamed themselves and will be shamed here. What they have done puts our future at risk."

"Just by being together?"

"Yes, for there will be persecution such as the world has never before seen in all its history and will never see again. For as the lightning flashes across the sky from east to west, so shall my coming be, when I, the Messiah, return."

"I don't get it."

"Laws must be followed. If Elyons do as they please we will become weak and die out. We have no home to go back to."

Charlie looked at the couple waiting for their punishment then up at Adrian. "Caleb told me it's survival of the fittest."

"It's how humans survived. It's how we will survive. And you will help me lead our people toward a bountiful future. Only one with a dark heart has the power and conviction to do so. Do you want to go back to being a freak in the human world?"

Charlie shook his head.

"Can you accept your duty and the hard choices that come with leading, as I have done?"

The boy stared at him. It was like seeing a younger version of himself wrestling with his powers and desires, just as he once had. He had made hard choices and he lived with them now.

"I think I can."

A thrill surged through Adrian hearing the words he wanted to hear. The crowd stood silent waiting for him to begin. He gripped Charlie's shoulder. "Good. Now watch."

He strode toward Caleb who held the whip out to him. Caleb's narrowed eyes told him all he needed to know about his son's disapproval. The crack in his flock had to be mended. A son who did not follow the leader's law was reason for the crack to widen.

Adrian stepped back and raised the whip. That crack would be filled here.

In this courtyard. In his flock.

And through his and Laura's sons.

Charlie faced Leah at the sanctuary altar on their second day together. Their day of dance. Candles burned smoky with a thick scent of pinecones and nutmeg. Their hands pressed together as one. Her face was so close to his. They swayed to the strange music flowing around them, wild and primal.

Dark desires sprang in him. And guilt at watching the hideous whipping scene today. Guilt at not wanting to leave this place. Guilt at not wanting his parents to come. When he was with Adrian he didn't feel guilty. He felt power. But now here with soft, lovely Leah the guilt moved in.

He pulled away from her.

"What is it, Charlie?"

"Those people today. It was so awful. Why did Adrian do that?"

She took his hand, but her touch confused him and he let go.

"It's part of our world, Charlie. Adrian knows best. He has been chosen to lead us to a new world. Our planet is dead. We have nowhere to go. If we don't follow rules we'll die out here, too."

He looked at this pretty girl who spoke like a grown up. He didn't feel like a grown up.

"And you believe that?" He took a step back.

"Yes, I do. I want to thrive. I want our people to thrive on Earth. And I'm thrilled to be a part of its beginning. Adrian says soon our flock will spread. New communities are to be formed soon. We will breed with humans—and control them. Our genes are stronger and will wipe theirs out."

Leah flung her hair back. She didn't look like the sweet girl he wanted to kiss again but a warrior woman on a mission. The angles in her face sharpened. Her emotions earlier had flowed over him with sweet yearning and light. Now they drowned him in tempestuous need driven by dark desires. She crossed her arms and walked back and forth in front of him. The candle smoke wrapped around her like ribbon as if gifting her to him. The strange music throbbed on and on.

"And my parents. Where are they? Why aren't they here yet?"

She stopped pacing and her face softened a bit. "They will be here soon. Trust Adrian. Your mother and father know what you are, where you come from. They will want you to be a part of this. I'm sure your mother has been waiting for this to happen."

It rang true to him. His mother would understand. She wanted him to be himself, as long as he didn't hurt others. But he needed to hurt others sometimes in order to lead, that's what Adrian had said. Didn't all leaders have to make hard choices? Like the president who had to send people to war to kill in order to keep America free. It's what people believed in. Some had to sacrifice for the greater cause. And this was a new cause he had to believe in for his people. *His people.* Wow. He had his own people now.

"My mother, yes. My dad…well, he's another story. He wants me to be normal."

"You are normal here, Charlie. And you will be a great leader. You are a Madroc. We need you. *I* need you."

He looked at her. She looked so young, yet was so old and wise in her words. "You do?"

"I do. We all do. You are Elyon's new hope."

Doubt and fear hung inside him. It seemed like such a big responsibility. And who was he? Nobody. Nothing. But he wanted to be so much more.

"I don't know if I can do this," Charlie whispered. He let her see his thoughts. He wanted her to feel what he felt. Dark and light raged inside him. Like her. Could he follow the dark part of heart which Adrian said he had yet also embrace the good? He was just fourteen. A kid. How could he be the leader of a new world? Such a big task for anyone to take on, much less a nobody kid with zero experience.

Leah put her hands on the back of his neck and pulled him down into a deep, hard kiss. Her tongue pressed hot and soft in his mouth. He gave in and kissed her back, a kiss that unleashed the pent up longing and passion that filled his hormone-addled adolescent body. Drums beat the air in a fury infused with lust. She finally pulled her mouth away taking her heat with her. His mouth became cold and empty again.

"You can do this, Charlie. You are meant to do this. I will help you lead."

She flicked her hair with an encouraging smile. She became all girl again. His girl. He surged rich with power again. He drank from her power, Adrian's power. And his own. And he liked it. He saw how the Elyons looked at Adrian. He saw them bow their heads when he had entered the courtyard today. And it struck him now that they had been bowing to him, too. It filled him with greed for more.

Leah held up her hands again. "Come, Charlie, we must practice our dance, for tomorrow we perform before the community."

"And then what?"

She moved into him, her robe's star pressing into his like two shooting stars colliding in one fantastic explosion. "Then we are bonded the day after."

She stepped back and held up her hands again. The drums beat fire and wind around them in a swirling frenzy. He pressed his hands into hers. They swayed once more in a dream.

A dream he didn't want to end.

Laura opened her eyes. She lay on her side. Her neck burned. She put her hand to her throat and swallowed. It hurt. She sat up. Ben was flat on his back. His eyes closed. The Swiss Army knife lay next to him in the dawn light, accusing her of what she could have done. She picked it up and gripped the handle.

"Ben," she whispered. Could he still be possessed by Adrian?

He opened his eyes. She remembered the first day she had stared into them. She had never known anyone with gray eyes. They were so beautiful. A stormy sea below rolling clouds and thunder, filled with sorrow, loss, and desire. They looked at her now as they had on the first day she met him. Her Ben was back. She closed the knife and slid it into her pocket.

He sat up and held her tight. She felt his tears on her cheek. She had only seen him cry once. The night Charlie was born in pain and fear. He shook and she held him closer, murmuring in his ear that it would be all right. They embraced under the warm sun and faced a new day. The horror of the night faded.

"Laura, what have I done?"

"We're alive. He didn't win."

Ben nodded and looked at her. "It wasn't me." He touched her neck. "I'm so sorry. So sorry." He jerked away and stood up. Laura slowly stood. Her body hurt everywhere, but they had to go on.

"Time to find Charlie." She took his hand and placed it on her swollen stomach. Their child thumped inside, alive and strong. "We are stronger than Adrian. We are family. Do you remember what I told you a long time ago?"

He shook his head, unable to look at her.

"Love remembers. You didn't believe it once."

He looked at her with a pained face. "You helped me remember."

"Don't forget again. Please. For me. For Charlie." She pressed his hand into her belly. "For our unborn son."

"But what I've done…" He pressed his fingers to his brow as if to erase the deed.

"This was not your fault, and there is nothing you've done I can't accept. I told you that a long time ago. It hasn't changed. I believed in you then. And you believed in me then, too. You said I had all the human elements that matter."

"You do."

"And so does Charlie."

"I know. I need the chance to tell him."

"You'll get the chance."

Together they hastily disassembled their camp and took off through the woods again, eating as they went. Laura fought the urge to go it alone as she had long ago when Ben helped her survive against her brother. She feared Ben's death then as she feared it now. Once, everyone she loved had died. She believed then she was cursed. It's why she had left Ben. She believed then that if only one person she loved survived, she could live with herself. But what if Ben didn't survive now? And now they had a son. A son who had been taken and Ben would never back down from getting him back.

They would soon be face to face with Adrian and his people. He had betrayed her. This was her chance to end him. She would not redeem him like she had tried to redeem her brother. He was beyond redemption. She saw his plans. Saw how he kept his people in line by fear. Saw how he forced them to do horrible things to bring out their hate and evil deep inside.

She would end him. She had to—or they would die.

CHAPTER 28

Adrian stood once more before the elders. They stared at him with stones in their thoughts to cast him out. This day had to come. Too many of his flock were fleeing. The night of free love he gave them had opened a crevice that now grew wider and wider, with Tollen aiding. His people wanted the freedom to make their own choices. The freedom to become part of human society and be like them.

Stupid beings.

They were crushing the future of their new planet. Why had they come here if to fail? They only saw their own pleasure. They would be the downfall of Elyon and Destroyers. Could they not see that they needed to unite together and stand as one to rule Earth? He had looked into the future and now saw his people blended with humans as equals. Laura was still there but a mere shadow by his side. His sons were gone.

And he alone knew the reason why their females had gone missing. If they discovered the reason he would be the next stoning victim. His people accepted his brutal ways that abided by the law, but he had acted outside the law. His crimes must be kept hidden.

"Brother Adrian, the time has come to name another leader," Tollen said.

Adrian stared at him, feeling the animosity roll off his senior elder who coveted his place.

"Our flock is leaving," Tollen continued. "More have disappeared into the night. Men this time, too. You let this happen with your festival and night of free love. You gave them too much and now they want more. They won't listen and won't follow the rules of breeding. They don't respect you, Madroc."

"You mean *you* don't respect me," Adrian said between clenched teeth. Tollen stared at him. The other elders remained silent, watching him. "We hunt down the ones who have fled and lobotomize them. They will falter in cloaking their whereabouts at some point and then we break them with fear. And we implement our new community in the human world. It's time. Great success comes with great sacrifice. We must reinforce this with our people."

"It's too late. Our future is unpredictable now," Tollen said. "And we can't kill or lobotomize everyone. Soon there will be none left. Who's next? Me? Caleb?" He pointed at Caleb who stood in the corner with his arms crossed, expressionless. "Or perhaps your *new* son?"

The other elders spoke in agreement with Tollen. Their voices rose louder, in protest. Adrian thought fast. He could not lose his power. Not now when Charlie had just arrived and Laura so near.

"I name Charlie as sole leader," Adrian said.

Silence fell in the room. The fire popped and hissed as the wind raged down the chimney.

"The boy?" Tollen laughed. Anger burned inside. The fire spit sparks out on the floor as if fueled by his rage.

"Charlie is Elyon's new hope. He's my brother's grandson. My twin who was sent here to begin a new world for Elyon and—"

"And he failed."

"But he left behind his prodigy to spread his seed. And this prodigy has been raised by humans with the Destroyer in him we need to succeed. He can help us assimilate into human society and use them for our needs until they are under our power. They will then have no choice but be dominated by us. I have seen him perform with the promise of this, right, Caleb?"

Caleb stepped forward. "Yes. I'm training him."

Another elder spoke up. "And he has proven himself?"

"Yes," Caleb said. "He is a willing Destroyer. And eager to learn."

"Even killing?"

Caleb nodded. "Yes."

"A small animal he killed, I hear," Tollen said, waving his hand as if he were already in charge. "What about humans? Can he mind bend and kill humans if ordered?"

"He will soon enough, Adrian replied." Caleb glanced at him, a puzzled look on his face.

"When?" Tollen questioned in a mocking tone.

"Within the day. Trust me. I have planned it. He is my blood. And his mother is on her way. She will help Charlie lead."

"And what if this female doesn't want to be part of our community?"

"Then she will die."

The wind rattled the windows. Cold had blown in, chasing the warmth away that teased them for a day. Snow threatened now.

"And he is to be bonded with the female, Leah, tomorrow?" an elder finally said.

"Yes," Adrian said. "Today they perform for the community. Tomorrow they will be one and Charlie will be one of us. Let him show his true colors. If he does what I think he can do—let him rule. The people are drawn to him."

Adrian let the elders talk amongst themselves.

"Name Charlie as leader," Caleb appealed to the elders. "Do it at the bonding ceremony. It will be a double message to the community. And my father will guide the boy. Elyons are eager for change. And Charlie is their new hope."

"It's true," spoke up another elder. "They flock to him. Haven't you seen? They touch him as if they believe he is their new savior come to lead them into our promised land."

"Even if that land is a desert with no water?" Tollen frowned at the elder.

Caleb held up his hands. "They would drink the sand then. They don't know the difference. They are blind. They need us to lead them." The elders turned to him. "I say, let Charlie be named the new leader of our community."

"He *is* the rightful heir to the mission that came before us," another elder said. "It's a sign. We can look into the future once he's ruler and see how he'll change our fate for the better."

The others joined in. "Fate." "Destiny." "Meant to be."

"My father began our great community," Caleb said. "You would all be in hiding back on our dying planet if it weren't for him. Now Charlie is the one to help us move into our next phase. The people will listen to him and, with us shaping him, it's a win-win situation."

Adrian nodded at his son. But could he trust him? He had lain with the female. Something he hadn't done in years, and he was training Charlie properly. But Caleb had no desire to lead himself. He was too weak in mind and heart. Perhaps he wanted the boy to lead to move the responsibility of leadership away from himself. Charlie's heart was full of dark. And dark was what they needed to steward them into a new world.

"Aye," one elder said. More echoed the same. Tollen had not won this time. He nodded and gave his blessing. For how long, Adrian couldn't know.

Tollen would only win over his dead body.

And that would never happen.

Caleb knocked on Charlie's door. Time to take him to the sanctuary ceremony with Leah. The boy answered with a hopeful face, but his smile fell when he saw who it was. Jealousy reared its head again as Caleb thought of Charlie bedding Leah. He had to remind himself that his anger was for Adrian and not for this innocent boy taken from his home and molded in his father's likeness.

"It's time. You and Leah are to perform."

Charlie nodded and stepped out into the corridor. They walked slowly to the sanctuary through deserted halls. Caleb had precious little time to speak with Charlie alone. The entire community waited for them.

"Charlie, you're meant to be here. You know this, right?"

Charlie looked at his feet as they walked. "I belong here."

"My father wants you to lead."

"I know."

"Do you know what this means?"

Charlie looked at him. "Adrian said that being a leader comes with hard choices to make."

They stepped out into the courtyard to cross to the sanctuary, but Caleb put a hand on him to hold him back. "And sometimes those hard choices can change if you choose." A chill had settled in the air. It snaked its way into his robe, filling his insides with dread.

Charlie stared at him. "What do you mean?"

Caleb looked around to make sure they were still alone. "You don't have to give in to your dark side to rule. There are many who believe otherwise. Many who want to live a human life. A life of love and free will. A life where they can blend in peacefully."

"But the kids back home call me a freak. I *am* a freak." He thrust his hands out. "No one there looks like this. No one there has the power to do what I can do except my mom and she hides it. And no one there likes me like Leah does. No girl ever will."

Caleb thought of Leah instructing Charlie in the ways of breeding and bile rose in his throat. The boy didn't know what he must do with her when their bond was complete. He would then become a man. Ceremony music drifted across the courtyard.

"You can be powerful without giving into hate and evil. And just because you have power doesn't mean you should use it."

"Why not?" Charlie's voice rose. "I like it. I'm good at it. Others like me for it. I belong. Maybe it's you who doesn't belong. I mean, why doesn't your father choose you to lead with him? Huh? Maybe you're not so powerful. Maybe you're really not a Madroc."

Caleb grabbed his arm. "True power is giving yours up to help the greater good. True power is in helping others. My father doesn't understand this but I do."

Charlie jerked away from him. "Yeah, well no one has helped me until now. Not my mom or my dad. Adrian and Leah helped me. I thought you wanted to help me, too. You showed me how to use my real powers. Why show me if I'm not to use it?"

"Adrian's way is not the only way. We can change things. You and I. Some doubt my father's leadership. Now is the time to make a change."

"I don't want things to change. My whole life I didn't fit in. I like fitting in."

The music grew louder. "We must go. They are expecting us. Don't say a word of this conversation to anyone."

Charlie frowned as if debating the wisdom of all that Caleb had revealed.

"Promise me, Charlie."

"Why should I?"

"I can show you more powers."

Charlie was silent. The music grew faster in its tempo calling to them. "Leah's waiting for me. *She* wants me to be what I am."

"I do, too, in a different way. I can show you."

Charlie shook his head. "I want to be what Adrian wants me to be. He doesn't think I'm a freak. He's the dad I should have had."

He strode away from Caleb and stood at the sanctuary door. He hesitated then pulled the door open. Music and light blared. Leah waited for Charlie at the altar. His father stood at the podium above her and the community waited for their new leader.

In Charlie's final words hope dimmed in Caleb that together they could change their world. Hope for the boy. For his sons. For his very life.

CHAPTER 29

Another day in the woods got them closer to Charlie. They had to be close now. They spent another night in the cold, this time Laura had the knife in her hand and the gun by her side. She kept jerking herself awake, afraid of waking to Ben pinning her down with a monster in his eyes. She shook with exhaustion as they trudged along, her energy almost depleted. The baby took any reserves she had left. She swayed on her feet and Ben grabbed her arm then took in a sharp breath.

A shot of adrenalin rushed through her as a building thrust itself before them, forbidding in its immense octagonal shape. They stopped and huddled behind a massive oak tree. Music floated to them. It moved slow in tempo then rose in a frenzied pounding. Chanting voices clamored with it. Laura gripped her knife in one hand and Adrian's whip in the other and closed her eyes.

What she saw sickened her. Images of Charlie mind bending, slashing and healing, then killing a poor rabbit. Worse was that her son enjoyed it. Then a crowd flowed around him. Touching him. Wanting him. Her heart ached. A pretty girl kissed Charlie, and a great stone plunged deep into Laura's heart. This was the girl Adrian had chosen for him. *No. Not my son.*

But these weren't the memories of this whip. These were images Adrian showed her now. He knew they were here. She closed off her mind with the desperate regret she had ever let it open.

"Sounds like a church ceremony," Ben whispered.

"It is. The whole community is in there but a few guards around the perimeter." She opened her eyes. "Adrian has chosen a girl for Charlie."

"A girl?"

"To bond with. To breed with."

"Oh my God. He's only fourteen." He pulled out his cell phone. Still no signal. "Damn."

"There's no one to call, and they know we're coming."

"Our one chance is to shoot our way in. We use your powers to fight them off, steal one of their vehicles, grab Charlie, and get away before they catch us."

Bolts of pain smashed through her head. Laura dropped the whip and knife and clutched her head. Adrian was inside her, tormenting her. She tried to fight it off, but the pain grew too great.

Ben shook her shoulders. "Laura, what is it?"

"They're here."

She opened her eyes and cried out. The dull gray light pierced her with blinding torment. She fell to her knees and looked up.

Ben leaned over her. "Laura!"

Shadows crossed over them. They grabbed Ben. Ben yelled and fought them off as he held on to her. Then his hands disappeared. In her darkness she saw him struggle, but she couldn't move. Adrian had paralyzed her. She felt herself being lifted up. Many hands carried her. They gripped her flesh tight. Her baby quaked inside her. The pain wracked her head like a tight fist slamming into her.

They took her to her new master. *Yes, take me instead.*

I intend to, Laura.

Please, let my son go. Let Ben go.

Your son is mine. As you are. Together we will rule. And Ben's time on Earth is done.

No!

She tried to fight him off but the darkness took her again.

Music beat in Ben's head, thumping painfully alongside the throbbing in his body. His eyelids were weighed down. He couldn't make the connection on how to open them. Or how to move his arms and legs. *Laura. Charlie.* Where were they?

He pushed the boulders up from his eyes. Excruciating light poured into his brain. Gray forms swayed around him. He tried to focus. They came into view. Hundreds of people filled an enormous room that arched up in a round ceiling. Candles lined the walls with flickering flames straining to be free from the cold wax imprisoning them. Like him. He wasn't tied down then remembered the needle being jammed into his leg. Drugged.

Charlie stood at a wooden altar covered in red cloth. A woman stood before him. They pressed their palms together. The music yielded to a murmuring ballad. Their voices pierced the church with words of obedience and duty. They moved in a sensual dance. And behind them stood a monstrous man with raised arms. Pale, like Charlie, but fierce looking. Adrian. The people around him floated like lifeless specters in submission to their earthly master.

The music stopped. The woman and Charlie kissed. They turned to face their audience, holding hands. Damn it. He was powerless to rescue his family. This had all gone wrong so fast. It was a blur. The woods. Attacking Laura. Being taken.

He slowly moved his head to the left. Laura sat a few feet away from him. Her head lolled to the left. Her enormous belly rose, a tender protrusion vulnerable to their captors. Had they drugged her, too? And their child. He screamed inside, thrashing his body about in his mind but it would not bend to his will. He looked at Laura sending his thoughts to her. *Wake up, Laura. I can't do this without you. Help me save our son.*

Laura lifted her head. Her eyes caught his. Together they turned to watch their son who stared at them without recognition.

Had Charlie become what he was meant to be? A Destroyer?

Charlie looked out at the Elyons who witnessed the ceremony.

His heartbeat quickened as their intense acceptance of him enveloped him, as did his yearning for Leah. It grew into a great ball of want that rolled through him, filling him up. And now Adrian had announced his leadership of the community as his rightful heir. Power swept inside him like a river of lust. Lust to be loved by the community—and by Leah.

Across from the sanctuary his mom and dad watched. They had come to witness his transformation. Pride surged alongside power. His mother accepted him, like she had her own brother. And his dad would now see how powerful he had become and see he wasn't a freak here.

Adrian touched his shoulder from behind. A thrill crashed through him like thunder in his veins. His true father. *Time now, Charlie, for your human dad to pay for all those years he didn't accept you.*

Yes, Adrian was right.

"You must prove yourself to our people, Charlie." Adrian's hand pressed heavy into his shoulder, transmitting his omnipotence to him. "We have an outsider here. One who does not belong. One who must die today."

Hundreds of heads turned toward his dad. Revenge and love twisted inside him. *Can you accept your duty and the hard choices that come with today?* Adrian's words came back to him.

Once they called him a freak. Pod man. Not anymore. Not here. His eyes swept past Caleb who frowned at him, his jaw jerking back and forth.

"You've been trained to kill," Adrian said. "Here in this place, before all, can you do what you were born to do, Charlie Madroc?"

Charlie looked at his mom and dad. They sat there staring at him. They didn't protest. Conflict hung on the edges of his mind. But he was born to do this. His dad has just been a weak human necessary for his creation. The hard choice now faced him.

Leah gripped his hand tighter and nodded her approval.

The crowd pulsed before him, urging him on.

Adrian smiled at him. *I am your father now, Charlie.*

And in his dark hidden heart a righteous power raged.

He knew what he must do.

Fury and loss raged in Laura. She could not move or speak. The drugs they'd given her rendered her powers near useless, but she did sense the thoughts of those around her—and of Charlie. His feelings burst inside like a disease shifting in feverish waves from revenge to love to godly self-empowerment. *Do the right thing, Charlie. Help us turn the people against Adrian.*

She had to save her first born. He had been turned against her and Ben and was now announced as leader of this Elyon flock with the devil as his mentor. Her uncle.

The one she saw so long ago on a faraway dying planet. The one who pleaded for her, with kindness in his eyes, to help them assimilate into human society once they reached Earth in their final mission. The one whose true mission lay in being a Destroyer to wipe out humanity.

Ben sat near her, paralyzed as well. His presence provided her with small comfort in their desperate situation. And Charlie just stared at her as if he had forgotten her. *What had they done to him?* Her child. Her sweet boy who had given his whole heart to her when young. He had shared his hurts with her as a teenager. Tears of despair fell from her. She could not wipe them away as she had once wiped her son's tears away when he hurt. Had he truly become like her brother had been? Remorseless and full of hate? It was a stake that pierced her heart and severed her son grievously from her.

Charlie placed his hands on his head and closed his eyes.

No, Charlie!

The crowd stopped swaying. Silence hung in the church like a gun aimed, ready to shoot.

Ben shuddered in his chair. His head flopped down. His body convulsed. She felt pain radiate around him like blazing fire. Like when her twin had tried to mind-kill him long ago. Ben didn't die then. He couldn't die now. Laura refused to believe this could be his destiny. Fate would not be realigned. She closed her eyes and sent her life force and healing into him. She willed him to live. But she was so weak. The drugs had dulled her powers.

She battled with her son who was killing the one man she had ever loved.

His dad.

CHAPTER 30

Ben was dead.

She last remembered being dragged away by men in gray robes. Then she passed out. She awoke now after they shoved her into a narrow room and slammed the door. She stumbled and fell on her stomach on a lumpy mattress strewn on the floor. Pain shot through her and she hugged herself, rooted in deep loss. She cried for Ben. Her first love. And for Charlie and her unborn child. She had to be strong for them now. Adrian had one son. He would not get the other. *Please dear God, don't let my child be born in this place. Help us get home.*

She pulled herself up by a chair, the only other thing in the room besides a dangling light bulb and window too narrow to squeeze through. A slit in the wall to tease her with. Like the bolt on the outside of the door. There was no escape from this room. She tottered to the window where sunlight flickered. It called to her with its gentle glow, painting her prison with warmth. The woods crept vast and deep before her. Woods like where she had met Ben the day he caught her singing in a tree.

She had to find a way to get Charlie and escape.

But he had killed his father.

She cried harder.

And with this chilling realization came the knowledge that there was nothing Charlie could do that she could not forgive, just as she had accepted Ben's failings before she met him. She accepted Charlie's now. It was not his fault. Her heart broke for her son.

The door opened.

Adrian loomed over her. Vile hate sprung inside her. She lunged for him but fell. He caught her. She twisted away. Agony seared her with his touch. His dream image flashed before her where he had been deep inside her, pleasuring her. She wanted to throw up. She backed up to the wall and leaned into it.

He smiled at her. His large features stretched wider across his monstrous face. His yellow eyes coveted her.

"Laura Fieldstone. I've waited so long for this. Your unborn child is mine. And Charlie is mine. He is on my side and will make a great Destroyer. I have been grooming him for years for this moment. You are all Madrocs now."

She shook her head. Hate froze her words. He moved closer to her and put his hands on her stomach. She closed her eyes. Sick images coiled in her brain of things he had done, enjoyed doing. And things he planned to do to her. Finally, she opened her eyes.

"Thank you for bringing my whip back." He pulled it from his robe's pocket and caressed her cheek with its straps. Its cool leather sent chills through her. She cringed, her muscles tightening as if they, too, wanted to shrink and disappear.

"We are both twins, Laura. We are each the more powerful half of a duo. We survived. Our twins did not. We are the strong ones. Together our power can rule."

His face was so close to hers. His breath pulsed hot on her cheek. She turned her face away looking for something to fight back with. The chair! She reached her mind out to fling it at him but all it did was wobble back and forth from her weak state. In a flash, he reached one hand out and grasped it. He steadied the chair and smiled at her.

"My dear Laura. You can't win against me. Your fate is here. I've seen into the future. You will breed with me. And soon we will go out into the human world and launch our communities there. The humans stand no chance against our powers. We will use them as needed and our genes will wipe out all humans on Earth and a new Elyon shall shine in its place."

"Never," Laura whispered.

"We are creating a new world here and you *will* be part of this."

"No."

"Then you will die."

She stared into his jaundiced eyes burning with a crazed passion. There had to be an escape from this monster. She had survived too much to not survive this. She would discover his weakness and kill him with no regrets.

This fact shocked her. She had been a forgiving person, one to find the redeeming qualities in all. Even her brother, who killed so many people she loved, had a tiny place in his heart where love could grow. Only that place was kept empty and starved for love his whole life by those who imprisoned him. Her acceptance and love of him in the end was not enough. He believed he was beyond redemption.

"You lied to me when we spoke from Elyon," she whispered. "I thought you were good. You said I was Elyon's only hope."

"And you are, my Laura. You will help me rule a new Elyon. Let me bring out your Destroyer gene. We'll be united and you will come to love who you truly are—a Destroyer."

He gripped her arms. His pod-like fingers pushed into her flesh, a precursor to what awaited her. He would soon be filling her with his hateful sex. She felt faint and moaned. He let go.

"You kill me and you kill my unborn child. If you want to make him yours then why kill him?"

He crossed his arms and laughed. Blue veins pulsed through his neck. "I wouldn't kill our child, Laura."

Her legs shook. She slid down the wall to the floor. Were all her dreams to become realized? If she did not accept his offer she would die, leaving her child here to be raised by a mad man. She closed her eyes to get away from his hideous face and plan, but he pulled her up and pressed her to the wall.

"Open your eyes, my Laura."

She did as he said and stared into her destiny. Why had she come here if not to save Charlie? Ben was dead. Loss overwhelmed her, but Adrian gave her no reprieve. His hardness pressed into her stomach. Nausea overcame her and she shrank into the wall. Her child let loose a fierce kick inside as if he knew that this was not the man who had fathered him.

Adrian laughed and felt her child. He pushed deep into her abdomen and she bit her lip. "He's feisty. My new son. A Madroc. Like Charlie. A Destroyer, too. I know it."

Laura looked up at him, helpless as he pinned her to the wall. "He's not your son." Her voice broke. "He's Ben's."

Adrian let her go and stepped back. His smile became a sneer. "Ben? You think Ben conceived this child? A useless human who had a vasectomy? I think not, Laura."

Goosebumps ran up Laura's arm. "What do you mean?"

"I'm your baby's father, Laura. I have been all along."

"Only in my dreams, you bastard."

"It wasn't a dream, Laura. I was there in the flesh. Many nights for months I came to you when your Ben was away on assignment or at a convention. I was there the night he slept in the guest bedroom. I mind bended you, made you think you lay in a dream state. But they weren't dreams. I plunged so deep inside you. Deeper than Ben ever was. You thought so yourself. I filled you up with my seed. It's our child."

She shook her head. Horror filled her at what might be true. "No." It came out not like a sound, but like a prayer.

"You moved beneath me with such wild abandon. You offered yourself to me fully. Such lust. I can't wait for us to be together again. In the flesh."

"No."

"Yes."

She looked out the window. This child was hers and Ben's. A child conceived in love, not hate.

"No. I would rather die," she said quietly. "I would rather my baby die."

"Your death can be arranged. Is this what you want?"

Hope fled fast inside her. She made sure to keep her mind closed to Adrian's probing powers. Her only hope was to go along with his plan. She needed to buy time. She needed an ally. She needed Ben.

"What do you want from me?" She turned back to the monster.

"I want you to breed with me, Laura. We're destined to do so. I'm carrying on my twin's legacy, as you can fulfill your twin's legacy. We survivors will live out their destinies. You're meant to be with me and lead our people into a new world. But humans cannot know of our presence or plan. If they do we'll be locked away, experimented on. Like your brother. Like your son will be. Do you want that for him?"

She shook her head.

"So, it's a simple answer." His muscles bulged and flexed in his neck, dominating and powerful as her brother had been. He, too, had once stood before her like this with her life on the line.

"You are a Destroyer inside, Laura. Give in to the hate." He held up his hands. "If you want to live, be what you are."

Long ago Felix had said those same words to her. *Find your powers again because the evil is coming. And he is coming for you next time. If you want to live, be what you are.*

He had been right and now the same evil threatened her life and all she loved once again. She stared into Adrian's vengeful yellow eyes, but no words came to her.

"I'll ask you one more time. Will you offer yourself to me?"

She had no choice. For now. And the words came to her. "Yes, I will."

He loosed a deep, guttural laugh. "And since you accept my invitation, I'll let you have one last special night as a reward. Lucky for you that you thwarted your son's own power. For now."

He banged on the door. It opened and a man was flung on the floor before her.

Ben.

And he was alive.

Laura clung to Ben. They held each other on the dank mattress after Adrian left. The light began to fade from the narrow window, but a tiny bit of hope still sparked inside Laura. Faith renewed itself inside her that they would find a way out of here. And then horror replaced it. She would have to tell Ben that Adrian's child grew inside her. *No, no.* She couldn't tell him now.

But she hadn't known Adrian had been inside her. It had been a dream. And she had kept her eyes shut each time thinking it was Ben, except once when she opened them—and saw the monster pleasuring her. He *had* been deep inside her. She *had* enjoyed it. How many times had she been with him? She wanted to be sick.

"Laura, did he hurt you? Did he…?"

"No," she whispered. He held her tighter and she felt him draw a deep breath. "I thought you were dead."

"Never. The bastard can't kill me."

"I tried to stop Charlie—"

"It was Adrian who brainwashed him. He made him do this. Our son is somewhere inside waiting to be found again."

"We have to find a way to get him back. If we can turn him away from Adrian he can help us bring Adrian down. I know it. I feel it. Adrian has placed all his hope on Charlie for his new world. He announced it to his people in their church."

Ben stretched out beside her on the sagging mattress and groaned. Bruises darkened on his face. Dried blood ran across his cheek. They had beaten him badly. Laura placed her hands on him and willed healing into his body. He stroked her hair as she practiced her power, but she was still impotent from the drugs.

"The drugs affected my abilities, Ben. I—I don't know if I can heal you all the way right now."

"Laura, my Laura. It's okay."

"How do you feel?" The bruises had faded somewhat on his face.

"Better."

The sun sank. The woods grew gray in the window above them. The lonely light bulb spilled garish light across them.

Ben put his hand on her face. "Tell me how we can save our family in this godforsaken place. This is what hell is. I know it. Those robed men took me to a room and beat me. They followed Adrian's orders like robots. The worst part was they did it all in silence. Like crazy cult members. But they didn't kill me. Why?"

She put her hand over is. "I don't know. Adrian might have plans for you." She had to buy them time. And she couldn't let Ben know all that had transpired between her and Adrian.

"He spoke to you. What did he say his plans for you are?"

"He wants me to help him lead his people to a new world. I let him think I'll be part of his community. Charlie is his new hope. Tomorrow I'll ask him to let me see Charlie, as a gesture of goodwill. I'll see if I can get inside our son's mind, turn him back to our side."

Ben looked at her. "Why did he put us together tonight?"

Laura moved into him and closed her eyes. "I don't know."

"He has another son. Did you see him in the church?"

He has another son coming soon too, Ben. But she kept those thoughts hidden. "Yes, he called him Caleb. He said Caleb was training Charlie in Elyon ways. I saw him in my vision, too."

"Maybe this Caleb can be turned against Adrian. He didn't look too pleased Charlie was named leader."

"Tomorrow. We'll find a way to fix this tomorrow."

"Promise me, Laura, you won't let him touch you." He pulled her deeper into him. She felt his heart throbbing against her chest. "I'll kill him if he does."

"Never, Ben. Only you can touch me. You made this." She moved his hand across their child who waited to show himself.

But what if Ben learned Adrian had impregnated her? She had to keep a spark of hope that Ben's seed had found its way into her womb. But could she love her baby no matter whose son it was?

She placed Ben's hand on her breast. "Love me."

He looked at her, shocked. "Here? In this place?"

"Yes. I need you to make everything all right for one night."

He buried his face in her breasts, loving them with his lips. "One night."

Yes, just let me have one more night.

"Tomorrow we'll get Charlie back. We'll find a way to get out of here. We'll survive."

She held his hand, flashing back to the first time she had intertwined her fingers with his and the day they shared secrets buried inside them that forever linked them. Her parents killed by a house fire, his crushed by the spaceship that landed one night and changed their lives.

And she gave herself to her first and only love, one last time.

Ben moved into her as he took her on the worn mattress. He gently stroked her, kissing her belly that rose toward him over and over. She wanted him to pour into her. She imagined his seed spiraling up into her uterus, connecting with their child, making him their own.

As if she called to him, Adrian appeared before her. She closed her eyes as Ben moved across her body. She didn't want to see Adrian while her husband made love to her in their cell. But he remained in her mind, watching, smiling as Ben ebbed and flowed into her. It might be the last time to be with her husband. The next time she offered her body it may be to a monster. He would plunder her. And she would let him.

She would do anything to save her family.

CHAPTER 31

Charlie stood at the altar. The Elyons had gone and Adrian and Caleb remained with him. Leah had kissed him with the promise of more and left. For now she didn't fill his mind. His mind hurt with all that had transpired today.

Had he really killed his dad?

He had wanted to. His dad had been weak, like Adrian had said. His killing him proved Charlie was more powerful than him. Hate flowed through Charlie like a golden honey, soothing and sweet. It filled him with power and lust and want. It had felt good to send his hate into his dad. He watched him twist and writhe in pain, and when they dragged his dad away relief surged through him. His mom had cried out in his mind to stop, but he couldn't stop.

What had he done? Grief welled in him alongside revenge. The two mixed like oil and water in his heart. His dark heart. He *was* like his mom's twin who had killed so many she loved, like he killed who she loved today. Was it meant to be? Adrian had said so.

He stared at his hands which looked like Adrian's. Like Caleb's. Like so many others here. He had power in this place. And he had used his power to kill his dad. He had hurt someone weaker than him. It's what bullies did. And in that thought, sweet power filled him. He'd never be bullied again.

No going back now. He was a Destroyer. Today he'd proved it.

"You fulfilled your destiny today, Charlie-boy," Adrian said, echoing Charlie's thoughts. "Your human father's purpose in this world was to provide passage for your life. His purpose is done now. Your mother understands. Her place is here with us now. Like yours is. All you've been through has been leading up to this day."

Charlie looked at Caleb seeking his thoughts, but he revealed nothing.

"I killed my dad."

Adrian moved in front of him and pressed his hands on his shoulders. "Look at me, Charlie." Charlie forced himself to look into Adrian's flattened face and yellow eyes, and it filled him with a sense of righteousness. What he had done today was his passage to a new world. If he didn't accept this role and his duties then his people may die out.

One human's death is so small compared to preventing an entire species' extinction.

Adrian's thoughts curled inside his head. Yes. He was right.

Smoke drifted down from candles that burned low, sending long shadows across the sanctuary. "I am your father now," Adrian said. "It's meant to be. And Caleb is your brother. He will continue to train you and help you realize your full potential. And your mother will be here with us, guiding you as well. We are all Madrocs."

Charlie looked at Caleb, who nodded. "Why me?"

Adrian flung his arms outward as if claiming the world to be his. A haze of smoke from sputtering candles encircled him like a halo. "You were conceived from despair, Charlie. Your mother was conceived in desperation before my brother died in his ship's crash. You are half human, half Elyon, and my blood. You have a true Destroyer heart, not like some." He frowned at Caleb. "Some of us are weak and incapable of carrying out our destiny, no matter the hard choices. Remember what I said about hard choices, Charlie?"

"It comes with power."

"Yes. And today you made a hard choice. You have the power. You were created in darkness and shall lead us out of darkness. Are you ready?"

Fear and exhilaration exploded inside him. "I'm not sure."

Adrian frowned. "You need to be sure, Charlie-boy."

Caleb stepped forward. "Let me take him to the arena. We can work on more skills. That may help. Right, Charlie?"

Silence stood between them. Finally Adrian nodded and smiled at Charlie. "Good idea. I know you've had a difficult day and this is all new to you."

"Yeah, new," Charlie mumbled.

"You need time to adjust and accept. It will come. But don't take too long. Our time here grows short. We need to move out into the human world undercover and begin our mass generation."

"Charlie understands, don't you?" Caleb stared at him.

"I do."

Adrian nodded, apparently satisfied.

"Come on, Charlie," Caleb said.

"Yes, go with Caleb. Work on mind bending today. It's what you'll need most in the human world to get what you want."

Charlie nodded and slipped behind Caleb who strode fast as if he wanted to get far away from the sanctuary and what happened in it today. He turned back once to see Adrian facing the altar, his arms raised. His immense outline glowed celestial in the candlelight, a godly figure to be worshipped and feared.

And Charlie did both.

Charlie stood on one side of the arena with Caleb. On the far side a man and woman stood like figures on a stage waiting for their cue.

"Will I learn to see into to the future today, Caleb?"

"No, that is the final power to learn when you fully commit to being a Destroyer."

"Can you do it?"

Caleb hesitated, as if not sure what to tell him. "No, not yet. Right now Adrian says it's time for you to learn how to get others to do what you command."

"What does that mean?"

"Hard choices, Charlie. These two volunteers are here to do anything you mind bend them to do. No matter the consequence. You may meet humans out in the world you need to control to carry out a mission."

The man and woman nodded at Charlie. Both were dressed in jeans and tops, like humans. Like Charlie had dressed days ago. They looked strange to him now. He had gotten used to a path of gray robes wherever he went. It had become comforting.

The couple smiled at him, waiting.

"Once you send your thoughts to them then you can control them with speech. It's no different than mind bending to kill. Send your thoughts to the husband first. He is angry with his wife. She has left him and stolen all his money."

Charlie pierced the man's mind and his smile turned to a frown. He twisted around to the woman.

"And let the wife know she is angry at him for being a drunk and beating her." Caleb urged him on. "She wants a divorce."

The wife turned to her husband and shouted at him. "You drunk bastard. I hate you."

"Now tell him to smack her and yell at her to shut up."

Charlie commanded and watched in awe at the couple playing out his orders.

"Go on Charlie, make it up from here."

A thrill spurred Charlie on. *Hit her again, husband.* He goaded the man on. *She needs to be punished.*

The man did as Charlie said. The woman shrieked.

Wife, smack him back.

She did, leaving a red mark across her husband's face.

Run, wife. Husband go after her. Pull her down. Kick her. Yeah!

His playthings acted out their parts, grabbing and hitting one another. Blood flew from the woman's nose. The couple scrambled over each other in the dirt. This was like creating his own action movie.

"Now it's time for the husband to take her down, Charlie," Caleb said quietly.

Charlie had forgotten Caleb stood there. He was so entranced on the scene he had created before him.

"You mean…?"

"Yes. He has a knife. Make him use it."

Charlie watched the couple smack each other around some more.

Husband take the knife and plunge it into your wife's chest.

The man pulled the knife from his back pocket. He popped open the blade. The woman screamed. And screamed again when her husband plunged it into her chest. Blood seeped down her shirt.

Again, husband. Get her good.

Adrenalin rushed through Charlie like a racing train. Power filled him like never before. His head pounded with the intensity of it all. His fists clenched, squeezing the rush deeper into him.

The man stabbed the woman over and over as she clung to his legs. She sank to the ground, covered in blood.

"Stop," Caleb ordered. The man stepped back and looked down at his kill. Caleb strode to the woman and placed his hands on her. The rush flew out of Charlie as fast as it had come. *What had he done?*

He ran over to the woman. "Is she okay?"

Blood spattered the dirt floor. The husband smiled at him, wiped his bloody knife on his pants, popped it shut, and slid it back into his pocket. Caleb moved his hands across the woman's chest, his hands stained with her blood. Only it was Charlie whose hands should have been stained. He had forced this man to murder his wife.

"She'll be fine," the man said, rubbing his hands together. "Not the first time she's almost died for the sake of our community." He laughed and put his hands on his hips. Charlie felt sick. At this man's words. At his own actions. He *was* a Destroyer. Like his mother's twin. Caleb continued to work on the woman. She opened her eyes and smiled. Caleb helped her up. She looked down at her shirt.

"Another one ruined. Good thing we've stolen plenty of human clothes." She laughed and the man joined in.

Caleb walked them to the arena gate. "Good work. You can clean up now."

They left, leaving Charlie to stand in a ring of blood.

Mom, where are you?

"Charlie?"

He looked at his hands. Clean. But he felt dirty. He had made a person stab another in a murderous rage.

Caleb rinsed his hands under a spigot in the wall. "Are you okay?" He looked at him.

Charlie nodded, not feeling okay at all. "It seemed like a game. But it was real."

Caleb dried his hands and walked over to him. "Yes. It's a very real and dangerous game. Our people have done these things many times in the human world to get what we need to survive here." He put his hand on Charlie's shoulder.

"Kill for real?"

"Yes, and other things. Mind bend to get money for supplies, to get humans to do what we want, to erase their memories. Once we make our mass exodus and settle into new communities out there we can mind bend humans to be part of our community and breed with us on a planned scale. Our genes will overpower human genes and Earth will be a new Elyon. If we want to survive we must consider our situation one of life or death...as my father says."

Charlie shook Caleb's hand off and walked away. He looked into the woods that surrounded them for miles and miles in their own world. "And it's what Adrian wants."

"Not just Adrian. But the leader of the Underground Destroyers who directed his group before we came here. Adrian was chosen to lead our mission here by their laws and grow our people into a new world of our own design to ensure the strongest gene pool."

"And slowly wipe out all humans?"

"Yes."

"What if we go out in the world in peace and let whatever happens...happen?"

"Then our genes will become diluted over time without a controlled plan. We might not know who has Elyon powers and who doesn't. Some may turn against us. Some may or may not have powers, or know they have powers. And they wouldn't know why they had them unless we showed our true selves. And eventually they might accept these new talents if it happens over many decades, or centuries."

"Like America's melting pot."

Caleb looked puzzled. "Melting pot?"

"It's what we call America. People came from different countries all over the world to find a new life. And we all blended together."

"And did it have a good outcome?"

Charlie wasn't sure how to answer. He bumbled around in his head for memories of social studies class. "Well, yes, I guess. People loved America so much they wanted to come here for a new life."

"So then…this melting pot might work here."

Charlie thought about it. "But people won't know who Elyons are. If they find out they'll think we're freaks."

"I watched one of your movies, *To Kill a Mockingbird*. A man with dark skin. A man who once might have been a slave of humans here in America, right? And now others like him hold down jobs and have homes like anyone else here, isn't that true?"

Charlie's head hurt from trying to make sense of all this, of what Caleb said, and most of all of how he felt about it all—and himself. "Yeah."

"And so if people here can go from thinking of this different looking man as a slave, a criminal, and eventually as an upstanding citizen, could they think the same about us?"

"I don't know. It's not making sense to me. Let me think about it."

Caleb moved toward him and put his hand on his shoulder again. "Think about it. But keep your thoughts to yourself."

"I know. Adrian taught me how. And my…dad…he taught me stuff, too." He looked at his feet. "I killed my dad, didn't I?"

Adrian squeezed his shoulder. "No, Charlie. He's not dead. He's alive."

A web of light pierced Charlie's dark heart. "But Adrian said he was dead."

"Yes, well, he was mistaken."

"Can I see my dad?"

"No, Charlie. Now is not the best time." Charlie didn't know what that meant but left it alone. He wasn't sure if he wanted to see his dad after what he had done to him, but his dad was alive. That's all that mattered.

"Come now." Caleb clapped his back. "Let's get some food."

Charlie sighed and followed Caleb out of the arena. Exhaustion wrung his energy out of him. Using his powers for the dark side tired him out. He looked back once at the accusing blood dark on the dirt.

He wondered how much blood someone could lose and not survive. The idea sent a delightful shiver through him.

And that scared him more than anything.

CHAPTER 32

The door banged open. Laura's eyes snapped open as consciousness slammed into her abruptly. She was sucked back into their nightmare. Three robed men pulled Ben off the mattress. One of them was Adrian's son, Caleb.

"What are you doing?" Laura struggled to her feet. Sleep still carried her in its thick blanket. Dizziness engulfed her and she fell back on the mattress. The men held Ben firm but he shoved them away and lunged for the door. "Ben!"

One man pulled him back. Ben punched him in the face. Blood sprayed down the man's gray robe. Laura pushed herself up and beat at the man with her fists. "Leave him alone!" He shoved her down on the mattress. Their attackers remained silent in their mission.

"Don't hurt her, you bastard!" Ben got another punch in before the second man overpowered him and held his hands behind his back. Ben grimaced, trying to twist away but couldn't break free.

Caleb moved toward Laura. "Are you okay?" He reached out his hand to her then pulled it away.

She shook her head. "Let him stay with me, please."

"I can't." His face looked pained as if he wanted to. "Adrian has ordered him to be eliminated."

"Bastards." Ben kicked his captor in the shins and the man groaned. In a flash the other man swung a knife out from under his robe.

"No!" Laura stumbled up. The knife gleamed in the sickly light then plunged into Ben's chest.

Again. And again.

Ben sagged in the man's arms. His knees fell to the floor. And Laura fell with him. She cradled his head. "No!"

But his head did not move.

He was gone now. For real.

Caleb pried her away. "It wasn't supposed to be like this."

His companions dragged Ben away. A bloody trail followed him out of the room. The last thing she saw was his face, peaceful in death. He left her here in this foul place. This time he would not be coming back.

Caleb set her down on the mattress. The last place she had loved her husband. Her Ben. Her savior from long ago. He'd said she saved him, but he had saved her, too. She couldn't save him now when he needed it most. She put her face in her hands and cried and cried. She only had her baby now, still safe inside her.

She felt a hand, soft on her hair. When she looked up Caleb closed the door behind him. She heard it lock in place.

And then pain drove a spike through her abdomen. Water gushed.

Her baby was coming. A month early.

God, please no. Not in this place. It was her dream all over again, but now she was here in this prison where her family had been cleft apart. She had to keep her child inside her, but he was forcing his way out.

She smashed her fists on the door. "Help me, please." She screamed for help over and over. "I need help. My baby is coming. Please."

But no one came.

She dragged the mattress to the wall, panting in pain, and eased her swollen body down onto it. Heat hit her in waves. She unbuttoned her shirt and pulled it off. Then she unstrapped her bra freeing heavy breasts that waited to be suckled by her child. Coolness washed across them. She fought back a sob. Ben had washed them gently last night with his tongue and lips.

She pulled off the rest of her clothes preparing for her child. The chilled air hit her nakedness like a stranger violating her every crevice. Charlie had come fast. This child wanted to as well. She leaned up against the wall and pulled her legs up. Another contraction hit her.

Breathe. Breathe. She heard Ben's voice as he had whispered to her weeks ago in Lamaze class. A day when all was right with the world. She had her Ben. She had Charlie. They were a family.

She prayed now no one came to help. She wanted to see her baby. Hold him. Keep him to her breast. *Let it be Ben's.* She'd love him no matter who his father was. He would have a chance like Charlie had. But did Charlie have a chance now?

More pain sliced through her. She screamed and rocked on the dirty mattress she and Ben had christened with love. Their love came now, hard and fast. She pulled her legs up with her hands underneath and willed the pain away, but all her energy went to her child's fierce need to exit her body. She embraced the pain.

Her baby ripped her as he hung inside her small canal, pushing his way out. She felt the top of his head, warm and wet and pulsing in her hand. He throbbed between her legs, enormous. The pain grew so intense she had to fight to keep from fainting. Deep pressure racked her body.

Push. Push.

Oh, God, if you're in this place come to me now. Don't let me die like my mother. Don't let my son die!

And Ben came to her then, squeezing her hand as she screamed, *don't let him be a freak!* Only it was Charlie's birth. She prayed with Ben—but then he was gone.

"No. Don't leave me here alone."

The pain became a great flame that scorched her flesh as the musky scent of her sweat and blood infused her. The room grew hotter. Blood gushed between her legs. It flowed into the dingy mattress.

Adrian appeared before her as a ghost. He shimmered in the gloomy light. She cursed his image.

He smiled at her as she suffered. "You can do this, Laura. If you're strong enough. Feel the pain. It's yours to be enjoyed. I need you to be strong."

"You'll never get him," she whispered.

"Your son is mine. As Charlie is now. As you are. And soon you will bear more sons for me."

She closed her eyes to him, focusing on the workings of her body. When she opened them he was gone. A great wave of pressure rose through her abdomen. Her son stretched her flesh beyond her widest point, tearing her with his feral need to be cast from her body.

"Push, Laura," Ben whispered to her. "It'll be fine. I promise. Push!"

The baby blasted out of her in an explosion of blood and mucus and came to rest between her legs. She shuddered with the release of this wondrous being from her deepest core and picked him up with shaking fingers.

He cried out and so did she.

He had the face of Adrian.

White hair sprung thick on his tiny head, and his nose was wide and flat. She held him to her breast christening him now with her tears. She had given birth to a monster, but he was still her son. She wiped his face clean with her shirt. Yellow gleamed from the slits of his eyes and her heart seemed to skip a beat. His lips rooted about and she gave him her nipple. At first she had to show him how then he took to it, drinking of her life. Her aching groin throbbed with the fierce connection of her child latched to her breast.

But could she love this child? Revulsion at bringing him to life spilled through her, to know this evil had grown inside her for months. To know Adrian had really been deep inside her, pleasuring her, filling her with his seed. Her body had betrayed her.

She had wanted to believe it was Ben's child. It had been so in her dream. She put his small head in her hands. It would be so easy to bash it against the floor and kill the son of Adrian.

She squeezed her baby's head, pulled him away from her breast.

She had given him life. She could take his life.

Harder she squeezed. She held him away from her, trembling inside.

The floor was cold concrete. A few seconds is all she needed to do it.

Bash. Bash.

She could see his blood run, could end him before he became like his father.

Her son wriggled beneath her hands, mewling for food and warmth.

She lifted him high above her, readying for the force to smash him down.

Horror twisted up from her gut as madness threatened to take over. *Oh my God, what am I doing?*

Was she a Destroyer inside, too?

She pulled her son back to her breast, shaking over what she had almost done.

She touched each toe, each finger, blessing each one. "Benny, my little Benny."

Love filled her heart in naming her son, replacing the hate. Her finger traced a faint heart-shaped birthmark on his thigh. "You weren't created in hate. You were created in love and born in love, my sweet child."

Sorrow cut through her. Ben would never hold their child. Never know him. But then he had been saved from knowing the ugly truth— this child was not his but an alien devil's. She rocked with her baby. Cramps hit her as the afterbirth slid out of her. She lay in blood and filth, but she was alive. Her child was alive. And she was the one who could save him from his destiny here.

Then the door opened.

Adrian stood there, smiling down at her with his hideous face.

"You are strong, my Laura."

"No." Laura held Benny tighter. She had to protect him from her captor, his true father. She tried to get up, but her body failed her and her child was still attached to her.

Adrian moved toward her. "He's mine. Can't you tell? I told you I was deep inside you, Laura."

He knelt before her, his monstrous presence threatening the one thing she had left to live for. She had lain with a monster and bore his son, but she would not give up her child.

"Let him live. Please, let him live," she whispered, shrinking back.

His yellow eyes burned into hers, windows to hell. He pulled her son from her. Steel glinted in his hand.

He swung up and Laura screamed.

Then he swung down and severed the umbilical cord, as he had in her dream. He *was* a monster.

"No!" Laura struggled to stand but fell back. Her bloody and wailing baby branded Adrian's robe with bright red streaks. His hands were now painted with her blood, her son's blood.

He looked at her child. "Like father, like son. You've done your work well. He is my bloodline and soon we will work on creating a new child."

"No. Benny!"

Adrian swung around and with her wailing child, slammed the door behind him. The lock slid into place. She crawled after him and banged weakly on the door but finally collapsed on the floor praying this monster let her baby live. And for the first time she prayed for her own death so she wouldn't know the fate of her children.

She welcomed death. But he did not come for her.

CHAPTER 33

Laura opened her eyes. A woman stood over her with a sheet.

"We need to clean you up."

Laura let herself be pulled up. Her naked body was sore, her flabby stomach still swollen.

Benny was gone. Her Ben was gone. Charlie was lost to her. Nothing mattered.

The woman wrapped the sheet around her, led her to another room with a stand up shower, and instructed Laura to wash herself. Blood still trickled from her. But Laura just stood under the steady stream of water that washed away her husband's touch and her child's existence. The woman sighed and washed her as a mother would a child. The water stung where she had been ripped open by her child. She didn't want to heal herself. She needed the pain. No one could take that away.

She cried as the woman's hands moved over her. And then her tears dried up. No use in crying. Deep resolve settled tight within her. And hate.

"You need stitches," the woman said after washing between her legs. "I am not allowed to heal you. Nor must you heal yourself. It's forbidden." Laura didn't want to heal herself, even if she could. She wanted to suffer. As Ben had. The woman dried Laura off, gave her underwear with a heavy pad to soak up her blood, and dressed her in a robe then told her to wait on the bed. A man came in with a bag. He looked at her with cold eyes.

"I am the doctor here. You need stitches. I am told you are to heal like any human would. There is to be no special preferential treatment for you." He moved forward and placed his bag at the foot of the bed. "Open your robe, remove your undergarments, and open your legs."

Laura did as she was told. He handled her expertly but with no kindness. She bit her lip to keep from crying out from the pain. He had no anesthesia and she felt each stitch sliding in and out of her tender skin. He injected her with a drug, to keep her powers dulled he said. Then he packed up his bag and left without looking at her. The lock clicked once more. She had no power to undo it.

She curled up on the bed. Her heavy breasts dripped with milk for her son. She crushed them to her chest fighting the urge to cry. Her breasts would soon dry up leaving no evidence she ever had a child. But there was no room for sorrow here. She must fill herself with hate, but her body and mind were so tired. She dozed.

The door opened. A short, plump woman came in carrying a baby. Laura jumped up from the bed. The woman reached out the baby to her.

Laura shook her head. "Where's my son? This baby isn't mine."

"No child is yours here. You will nurse all the babies who need it. Now sit in the rocker and take this child. When he is done I will bring you another."

Laura stared at the woman and the child. "No. I—I can't."

The woman frowned and tapped her foot. The baby cried. "If you do not take this child I will bring enforcers in here to tie you to the rocker and force this child to your breast. We all have our duties here." She pointed to the rocker in the corner, homey looking and covered in quilt patches, like something Laura had at home to nurse her little Benny. They had picked out a gliding rocker for the nursery. Blue and green. Laura sat down in it and the woman placed the baby in her arms. Laura stared at the little one. A boy with blond hair. He gurgled and her heart tugged. The woman impatiently opened Laura's robe and took her breast.

"I will do it," Laura said. She pushed her nipple into the baby's mouth. He blindly moved around it then hung on tight, sucking greedily. A deep heat tugged inside her. Whose child was this? And what woman was feeding her Benny?

The woman left. She came back with food and water, looked at Laura, and left again. Each time the door locked in place with heavy bolts.

Laura watched the little face that drank life from her, and she prayed that her own son was getting love and life from someone, too.

She had lost her husband, but she would get her sons back.

Adrian stood outside Laura's door and watched her in his mind's eye before he went in. He enjoyed watching her nurse. She waited for him, so lovely in her robe. Her long hair hung in soft waves and curved around her bare breast. She smiled at the baby who tugged on her nipple and she kissed his tiny fingers. She then moved the child to her other breast, placing it in the newborn's mouth who took her life with force.

Adrian grew hard watching her. He would have her soon. He hoped the night he had given her with her husband fueled her hatred of him. He needed her hate. Somewhere inside her lay a hidden element. A Destroyer element. And he would bring it out.

He had just come from watching another woman nurse his and Laura's baby. His people burst forth with life. His Elyon flock would continue to breed and build a strong community in numbers and power. And Laura would provide him with more sons soon enough but first someone else would prepare her for his special time with her. She was sorrowful from losing that human husband. Adrian had no patience for sorrow. He needed her submissive and strong in body and mind when he took her.

She was the powerful mate he had dreamed of for so long—his twin Feo's offspring. Feo had been dead forty years now, since he was eighteen. It had been Feo's fate to crash, punishment for not taking Adrian with him—as it had been Adrian's fate to destroy Brahm's chance of going to Earth. In ending Brahm's dream, he now fulfilled his own.

Then the memories of two dead women who took his children to the grave would finally fade away. For now, Laura's two sons comforted him and eased the pain. This pain he did not want to feel. The pain of having lost something. But in Laura he could accept this loss. *A table is being prepared before me in the presence of mine enemies. My cup runneth over. Laura will make it so.*

He opened the door. She looked stricken to see him. Her vulnerability washed over him like an enticing lover. She quickly covered her breasts while the baby suckled.

"Hello, my lovely Laura."

Her rage at him burned bright. And hate. She had so much hate. It served her well here.

"Murderer. Where is my baby?"

The child in her arms began to cry at her shouting and she stroked his head soothing him.

"He is being fed by another. As it should be. We do not connect to our children here as you humans do. Such a waste of energy and power. Giving in to these sentimental emotions. Treating your children as pets. Disgusting. We only work with them when they mature, to train them in our ways."

"Your evil ways." She bent her head to the baby. "You're a monster." A single, solitary tear fell on the swell of her breast. He grew hard again thinking of her moving beneath him.

"I am what I need to be and so shall you be."

"And what is that?" She looked up. Her eyes shone with loss and loathing.

"You will be a breeder like all females here."

She closed her eyes as if to shut out his presence. He caressed her with his eyes, drinking in her loveliness. Even so recently after birth she cast a glow. It made him want to devour her body and mind. He took a step forward and her eyes jerked open. "I—I need some time."

"Tomorrow you begin."

"Tomorrow? I've just given birth. My body is torn and sore. I can't." Her voice fell away. She pleaded with her eyes. "Please don't make me do this. I've lost my husband, my sons. Please."

He pointed a smooth finger at her. A slow green pulse throbbed from the end of it. It grew brighter. "I don't need to be inside you to pass my seed on to you, Laura. I can create our child within you like you were created, with the power of transference." The green tip beat faster in rhythm, seeking out her womb to fill.

Laura's insides quivered thinking of him impregnating her. He was all powerful, whether he used his finger or his sex. Bitter saliva filled her mouth.

He lowered his finger and laughed. "But I'd rather feel myself inside you—again." He moved beside her and touched the long curl that curved around her breast. He ran his fingers along the tender, rounded slope. She flinched, a prisoner, bound by duty to some other woman's child and his power. He smiled at her. She looked away.

"If you accept your duty with honor I will heal your body and discontinue the drugs the doctor has been giving you. You will have your powers back, but you must be careful, Laura. One misstep and your baby suffers. Charlie suffers. And you, most of all."

Laura caressed the baby's head and rocked slowly, her choices racing through her brain. She looked at him. "And if I don't agree?"

"Then you will be torn apart by a lust filled male with no care for your birth ravaged body. I have the perfect male in mind. He has been withheld from breeding in punishment and is eager to take a female. And he hates humans. He will enjoy taking you, Laura. He will make you suffer and bleed worse than you did last night pushing out your baby. You may not survive." He shrugged.

She held the baby tighter to her, rocking faster now. "And if I do my duty, will I breed with you tomorrow?" She spat out the words.

He laughed. "No, I'm saving you for later. The man you'll first mate with will be gentle with you. He won't ravage you like I will, my Laura. I will consume you. We are meant to be. It's fate. Can't you see? We are two twins coming together as one, with Destroyer strength enough to rule the world."

She closed her eyes again and nodded. She began to hum.

"How do you choose, Laura? Gentle or hard?" He waited as she rocked and hummed.

"Gentle," she whispered and continued her humming.

Her eyes remained closed and he left her then, in full submission to him. He had waited seven long years for this moment. She would replace all he had lost—and more.

That day two more children were brought to Laura to nurse. She fed them her milk and as much love as she could. She rocked the babies to her breast all afternoon, comforting herself as much as them. It was all she had in her stark room of imprisonment, along with the plans that began to form in her mind. Adrian's son, Caleb, had a seed of good in him. In her brief moments with him she'd sensed his conflict. It lay murky beneath his surface, his thoughts clouded.

And Adrian. She had to let him think she would submit to him. Although the thought of it filled her with terror. He had said he had another male in mind for her before he took her. She felt sick thinking about giving her body to another man as she grieved for the one man she had ever loved.

Her Ben. Her soul mate. Grief overcame her again, but she had to live now for Benny and Charlie. She cried until she had no more tears.

The woman who had washed her appeared again and took the baby away. Then she returned. "I'm here to heal your body. Adrian has ordered it. No more drugs will be administered to you. Within the day your powers will return, but I must warn you there will be immediate consequences if you use them against anyone here or to escape. It is futile. Tomorrow you will begin breeding again."

The woman frowned at her as if Laura was certain to cause trouble. Laura nodded.

"Good. Now remove your clothes and lie down on the bed."

Laura obeyed. A chill passed over her naked skin. She closed her eyes. The woman's hands moved on her, kneading her swollen and traumatized flesh. Laura flinched. At first it hurt then the pain flowed away. Energy restored her. The woman pushed her legs open and massaged her most private places. Laura took herself to another place far away to escape this violation of her body.

She remembered Ben the first day she met him, as she sang in a tree at the lake near her childhood home. He had scared her with his intensity then. He had caught her as she fell from the tree with his arms, and his eyes. She had fallen in a spiral into those gray marble eyes. They had held her in a rolling storm of wild-hearted passion. He had swept her away then as Charlie had the day he was born and looked into her eyes with his brilliant, blue ones—and as Benny did today with his yellow ones. They all owned her fiercest love. She had belonged. She once had a family.

She dozed. A click woke her up. She opened her eyes. The woman was gone. She stood and looked down at her body and passed her hands over herself. Her stomach was flat again. Her stitches gone. Her breasts small and compact. She squeezed them as if to bring milk forth again. None came out. They had dried her up and erased Benny from ever being.

But he did exist.

She drew on her robe and looked out the tiny window. A fierce wind whipped the trees. Gray sky hung heavy like a blanket waiting to smother her. The promise of Indian summer had been snatched fast by winter calling. The weather was tormented here as well, conflicted over who it obeyed—and unable to escape its master's bonds.

Hate seethed inside Laura as her energy grew stronger within her healed body. She watched the woods as the angry wind punished it. Laura would find a way to do the same to Adrian.

She had made a promise to Ben she had to keep—that Adrian would not survive her.

CHAPTER 34

Adrian stared at the mirror. He raised the whip higher. Each lash drove pain deep into him. He moaned with his need for it. His muscles flexed. His blue veins pulsed fast, raised on his pale skin. He painted himself with blood as his father had done many times.

Harder. Harder.

He had to make himself stronger than his father. Only then could he be the master of the man who'd terrified him—and the master of his own weakness.

He tried to imagine Laura's face beneath him as he covered her body, but his father's face drove hers away. It hovered over him as he had clawed long ago at the walls of the dank well, shivering in its sludge. He recalled every word.

"Please, Father, don't leave me here again tonight."

"You will suffer for your weakness. It must be driven out of you. No son of mine shall be weak."

"There're things down here, Father. Slimy creatures swimming about. And it's s-s-so cold. Please."

His father had smiled at him then. A terrifying smile holding the promise of pain. The moonlight slashed his face in two. Dark and light. His enormous nostrils flared.

"They are hungry, Son. Your flesh is tasty to them. Embrace the pain they bring. You must endure pain to inflict pain. This is what we Destroyers do. Your brother, Brahm, is too weak. A useless thing. He'll never make a Destroyer but you, Son, have power in you. You are a true Madroc. And you and Feo are my legacy."

"I don't know if I can be a Destroyer, Father. P-p-please." Something brushed his leg and he screamed. Panic raced through him. He grabbed at the slimy rock but kept sliding down. He had tried many times to break down the rock walls with his powers and climb out, but it was too fortified. His father knew this for he had built the well.

"Weakling." His father's robe swirled and disappeared. Only the moon watched him now, silent and accusing.

"Father!" Teeth bit into his legs and buttocks. He thrashed about in the water, screaming. The teeth moved away. His screams became sobs. He stared at the moon. The one light in his prison. He watched it as it watched him.

"I will survive," he yelled to the moon. "I will survive."

The teeth returned. He bit his lip. *Don't cry!* He kept his eyes on the luminescent orb above him. The bites increased. He remained still and let the creatures eat on him. And his hate grew. Hate for his brother, Brahm, who never had to suffer for being weak. Hate for his twin, Feo, who was rarely punished for being weak. If he could have shared the well in punishment with Feo he might have been able to stand it.

They had been best of friends until Feo went to Earth without him. His own twin had betrayed him as so many others.

And in that well Adrian had sworn that he would never again be punished for being weak.

He would come to rule with hate.

As his father did.

As he did when his wife refused to become a Destroyer. She was weak and there was no mercy for being weak and bearing a weakling like Caleb. If Manta had gotten pregnant with his son instead of Tollen's, what would he have been like? *Oh, my love, how could you have betrayed me so?*

Manta wasn't supposed to be at the laboratory that night. She was supposed to secretly be with him. But they had fought that day, like too many other days. She refused to leave his brother, Brahm, and resign her post on the mission to Earth. She was part of a select group to start a new life there and message back for the others to come. She was leaving Adrian to go on the mission of his dreams and worst of all going with his brother. How he hated him. Brahm had everything he desired, the chance to lead a mission to Earth—and Manta.

He grasped her arm, but she jerked away. They were alone in her house while his brother worked at the laboratory on the day shift readying the ship for Earth.

"Stay here with me," Adrian pleaded.

She looked at him with a sad smile. "Your wife may be dead now, but I am already married to another Madroc. Why should I stay? To remain your secret lover and give up my dream of going to Earth?"

"We can leave this place. Start over in another town."

"There is nowhere else. Elyon is dying with no sun. An ice age is coming. We have no future here."

He pulled her to his chest. She didn't resist this time. "I have no future without you," he whispered.

"Brahm is a good man to follow. We can find a new place for our people to start over."

"You don't love the good. You are dark inside, like me. Give in to what you are destined to be. You know you want to."

Her tears wet his shirt. She didn't disagree. He moved his hands across her face. He bent down and parted her lips with his tongue as he stroked her breasts, tantalizing her nipples into hard points.

She winced.

"Manta, what's wrong?"

He stopped stroking her breasts but still held them as they swelled larger in his hands—and then he understood. "You're pregnant aren't you?'

She pushed him away and looked at him with sad longing. "It doesn't matter."

"Doesn't matter!" Adrian's rage boiled over. "You must stay here now. You can't risk our child's life. I know it's mine. You haven't slept with my brother in months." He gripped her arms. "I won't have Brahm raise my child."

She struggled then went limp, defeated. "Adrian, don't you think I've been living in torment over this? But I'm going on this mission. Brahm will be the father. You will stay here and raise Caleb. He needs you. Someday we'll be together again. I know it." Tears spilled from her lovely green eyes and dripped onto breasts soon to nurse their son—his son.

"It's a boy isn't it?" Adrian raged. He shook her and she cried harder. "You're mine. Mine!"

"It's not meant to be, Adrian."

"If we're both free we can be together. There's only Brahm in the way now. I can take care of him, too."

Manta's face cracked with shocked realization, and she pushed at him wildly. "You killed your wife?"

"For you. For us."

"No, no." She slapped his face over and over. "I never wanted this!"

He grabbed her hands and she hunched over crying. "Let me go."

"Never."

Then her whispered words cut him deep. "It's not yours."

He sensed the truth. "Tollen!"

He shook her and she cried harder, nodding. "Before you."

"Lying wench!"

She didn't deny it. Her final betrayal.

And then a haze fell over him. Her sobs faded. He drew his sword of power. She was his. No one else's. And he would make this child his. He stabbed her over and over. It felt so good and he wielded his weapon, aiming for her core. Her skin was so soft between his teeth. Blood flowed and it fed his thirst. Her scent filled up his every crevice. Deeper he devoured her, claiming his son, and a burning wave of lust and envy and hate crashed through him.

Faint screams floated on the air. They grew louder and louder, igniting him with terror. It drowned out the pleasure that pumped from him with fury.

Her screams shattered his ears. She lay beneath him, bloodied and shaking.

"What have I done?" Adrian withdrew his drained power and stood over her. She curled up on her side, gasping. Blood trickled from his bite marks livid on her skin.

"Get out. Get out!" she screamed between sobs.

He had gone too far. He grabbed his clothes and ran for the woods. It was the first time he ever tried to drive the weakness away himself. He slid down the rungs into the well. The very well he had pushed his wife down into. He left her there to die weeks earlier, lying broken and crooked on cold stone begging him for mercy. He had none to give. He knelt now on the stain of her blood and lashed his back and sides with a sapling branch, striking himself as he had struck the one person he had ever loved.

And when he had punished himself enough he sought her out.

She had to forgive him. She had to stay.

But she was dead—killed in an accidental explosion that afternoon in the laboratory. His brother, Brahm, had just been injured. She must have gone there to lose herself in her work and forget what he had done to her. If they hadn't fought, Manta wouldn't have gone to the lab, she would have been safe in bed with him. Instead he had violated her and drove her to her death.

Harder. Harder.

He flung down his whip and shouted in anger. He didn't want to remember those times.

His wife was dead. His mistress was dead. His unborn child was dead.

And his father was dead.

He had died of old age, a peaceful death for such a tyrant. He had ruled as region leader with ruthlessness and torment, his Destroyer genes and swelling underground uprising hidden from society. His father had been crafty in deflecting his true mission. And innocents suffered unknowingly because of him. It was the law of Destroyers.

They had been crushed once and nearly killed off in a civil war. They retreated in secret, planning to come back and rule all of Elyon someday. They had given in to their Destroyer genes that all Elyon's possessed deep down inside. Most turned away from their true destiny. They did not allow hate to trigger their true fate. But hate consumed Adrian and he faced it full on. He became what he was meant to be, and he was now meant to rule Earth.

But his plan was crumbling. His flock diminished and not all by his hand but by their own will. The humans in the outside world would become suspicious and harder to mind control as their numbers grew. The community elders held an emergency meeting. They planned to send their trusted people out into the human world to gauge human suspicion of the Elyon community.

It was time to have Charlie lead with an edict. He needed the flock to believe in the boy because he would change their future. They accepted him, and he would let the flock choose their mates as a new law. Charlie would announce the edict. He would be their savior and they would stay.

He stepped into his shower and washed the blood away. He did not flinch from the wounds.

It was time to call Caleb in. He had a new duty to perform.

CHAPTER 35

Caleb stood before his father in his room. A lonely candle burned. Shadows of gray flame flickered across the walls seeking escape. He eyed his father's whip hanging next to the candle. The idea of whipping himself made him sick. It was enough that his father whipped him.

His father saw him look at the whip and smiled. "You have one, too, Son. It's a shame it's never been used."

Caleb looked him in the eye and muddled his thoughts. "I don't need to whip myself to be strong, father."

"You never will be strong unless you follow my path. You will never rule. You must endure your own pain before you can inflict pain on others."

"Like Charlie will? Your replacement prodigy?"

His father frowned. "Yes, he is a true Destroyer. You, sadly, are like my brother."

"I'm glad. I loved Uncle Brahm. I was sad for him when Aunt Manta died. *Your* lover."

His father smiled again. He stood taller and Caleb felt his powerful wrath radiate from him. "He was an idiot."

"And don't forget, Ben and Laura." Caleb smiled even as fear clung to him.

"Ben is dead." His father moved closer to him and placed his hands on his shoulders, glaring down at him. Passion and fury rolled off his father straight into Caleb's heart. He willed himself to remain still and return his father's stare.

"Yes, I know. I buried him."

"Good."

Adrian moved away and Caleb's heart slowed. How he wished for one moment he was a little boy again being carried home in his father's arms. No fear. No hate. Just love. Those days were long gone. His father had given in to his Destroyer gene and killed the man inside he'd once cared for—the father who'd once cared for his firstborn son.

His father now sat in the chair by the window. It was of wide planks from the largest oak in the woods with arms that gnarled up into giant fists. A chair for a king, a punishing potentate with a thirst to kill.

"And what of Laura?"

"This is why I've brought you here, Son." Adrian gripped the arm's fists. His own fists engulfed them. "She is to be yours…for a night."

Laura appeared to him in his mind, begging him to let her husband stay. He remembered the softness of her hair as he touched her before he left her in grief. He'd raced off to his room then to secretly use her confiscated Elyon communication belt before handing it over to his father. He had to know Rachel was all right. He had found her asleep on a cot in the basement of a church's homeless shelter. She looked so peaceful asleep, and so free. His heart was full in knowing this, and he hid all this from his father who stared at him now waiting for his response.

"Why, Father?"

"She is filled with grief over the death of her stupid human. I need you to soften her grief and prepare her for me. She will be mine and I need her strong again. You have a soft way about you. The women seek you out so why deny them?" He grinned. "Leah certainly enjoyed you."

"And you enjoyed watching didn't you?"

"I did, yes. And I will enjoy watching you with Laura. If she submits with passion and ease you can reward her with seeing her baby. Do your job and I may reward you with what you've been seeking."

Hope and fear swam together inside Caleb. "What do you know about what I seek?"

"Your sons, of course. I will allow them to spend time with you and get to know you."

"You would do this?"

"Yes."

Caleb couldn't trust his father, but the thought of hugging his sons and talking with them filled him with joy. "When do I go to Laura?"

"Tonight. After your training with Charlie."

"But she's just given birth."

"I have healed her body. It's new again for you. It's her mind that needs renewing now. She must be turned to the Destroyer side. She has it in her to become a powerful Destroyer. Her brother had it. Charlie has it. And I do." He smashed his fist down. "As you do but deny it."

"I will go to her tonight."

"Don't forget, I will be watching."

Caleb nodded and left his father on his throne. He saw it on fire and his father in it, strapped down as he had been strapped down and brought here against his will.

The vision gave him deep pleasure.

Charlie stood in the arena and inhaled Leah's scent. Roses floated fragrant about her. They kissed again. Cool air rushed over them. He awkwardly put his arms around her. She moved into him. He felt her curves soft against him and a jolt rushed through him. Was this love?

He had seen other kids at school making out in the halls and groping each other at dances. He'd wondered what it was like. And this pretty girl wanted him. He wanted to show her off to the jerks at school. But he'd never go back there again.

A leaf spiraled down into her hair. He tugged it out. She pulled away and smiled at him, her hair gracing her face like a framed painting.

"Tomorrow is our day, Charlie." He reached out and took her hand, fumbling. His cheeks felt hot. She laughed. "You're so sweet. Tomorrow will be special with you. More special than any others I've been with."

"What do you mean?" Jealousy filled Charlie. She had other boyfriends? He didn't want to think about it. It hurt too much.

"You'll see. It's all good." She kissed his cheek. "Caleb is coming."

She looked past him. Her smile faded.

"Why don't you like Caleb?"

"I never said that." She let go of his hand and hid her hands in her robe, staring at Caleb. "I'll wait for you over here." She moved toward the end of the arena. A cold gust blew after her. He shivered, cold now with her warmth gone.

Caleb strode toward him, glancing at Leah with a frown. "We have work to do. Adrian has ordered it."

Charlie stepped back. Caleb's anger hit him like a punch to his chest. "What's wrong with you?"

Caleb smoothed his robe down and looked up at the gray sky. "I'm sorry. I'm on edge."

"Is it Leah?" He looked over at Leah who seemed far enough away to not hear them.

"What do you mean?"

"You guys don't like each other."

"That's not true." Caleb looked away. "I like her very much."

Jealousy rose in Charlie again. "I get it. You *like her*, like her."

"I did once. But it wasn't meant to be."

"Yeah, because she's mine now."

Caleb nodded. "And now we must work."

Charlie's anger fled as fast as it arrived. He sighed. "Fine."

"Today you learn a new power."

"What?" He tapped his foot, eager to get on with it and find a hot meal. Using his powers drained his energy. He needed to eat all the time. But he also wanted to prove himself in front of Leah. She smiled at him, waiting.

"How to bring the mortally wounded back to life."

Charlie stopped tapping his foot. That was worth working for. "Can you bring back the dead, too?"

"No," Caleb said, after a pause.

"Well, it's cool anyways. So what are we going to do?"

"We attempt to kill someone first."

Charlie looked at Leah and back at Caleb. "Who?"

Caleb waved Leah to come over.

"No," Charlie whispered.

"Yes," Caleb said quietly.

So that's why she had waited.

Leah touched his shoulder. "Caleb has done this many times before. It will be all right. A person can be brought back before their life drains completely. I trust you won't let me die, will you?"

Charlie shook his head. He couldn't speak. She unzipped her robe. Beneath it she wore a plain white dress. She turned away and hung her robe on the fence. Then she brushed her hand through her hair and stood before them. Her hand trembled. Caleb looked at her. She nodded. Charlie looked back and forth between the two of them.

"Charlie, when I am done you will follow my instructions explicitly. Do you understand?"

Charlie stared at Leah.

"Charlie?"

He nodded. Caleb pulled a leather holder from under his robe. He drew a long blade from it.

Charlie's breath came in quick gasps. "Why like this?"

"I need to show you how to save someone before they die, Charlie."

But he couldn't watch. He turned away. He was afraid of being sick, right there in front of Leah.

Caleb pulled him back. "You must watch. This is the hard that comes with our good."

Charlie felt faint. Leah took his fingers in hers and smiled. "I'm ready, Caleb."

Caleb swung the knife.

Again and again.

Charlie cried out. Leah gazed at him, a soft smile on her face as if it were all okay. He gripped her hand until she closed her eyes and let go. She had never made a sound. She lay crumpled at his feet. Blood seeped scarlet through her dress, branding her in near death. He fell to her, crying.

Caleb stood over him. "Now I show you how we save her before she dies."

CHAPTER 36

Ben opened his eyes. Again.

He was on his back. He licked his lips and tasted dirt. How long had he been here, under the ground? He twisted his body on the cold, mud floor. His chest throbbed and he couldn't move his legs. He pushed himself up on his elbows. Light slanted down from above him somewhere.

He remembered where he was. Underneath the whipping shack. It's what Caleb has called it. The screams that came later pierced his head. He covered his ears to shut it out, but they went on and on. He watched the shadows of a poor victim through the cracks in the floor and could do nothing. Not if he wanted to live.

He remembered the pain—and seeing Laura's face for the last time. Then being pulled from the earth and Caleb bending over him as he coughed dirt out from his burning lungs. He had flashed in and out of consciousness as moonlight danced overhead and Caleb carried him through the woods. Then he was placed in this dark hole. He thought he had arrived in hell, only to find he was alive but still in hell.

He felt around for the water Caleb had left and drank greedily. He touched his hair caked with dirt. Adrian's son had pulled him from his grave and brought him back to life. Why? Ben tried to pull himself up on the few rungs on the side of the earth cellar leading up to the ground. He managed to raise himself up and push up on his wooden ceiling, but it wouldn't budge. Too weak. He had to get to Laura. And Charlie. He fell back and slammed his fist in the dirt. If he couldn't move his legs, how could he to save his family? And where was Caleb?

Then Laura's words came back to him.

Love remembers, Ben. Hold on to that.

And he did. He warmed himself with her vision of their first night together when she had told him that. She had given herself to him then, moving beneath him like unspoken poetry. He had never been so inside someone. They had moved into one another, creating something good from so much bad.

After their heartbeats slowed, he withdrew from her and fell back into bed.

"Laura, my Laura," Ben whispered into her hair, holding onto her warmth. He didn't want to ever be cold again. "I've never made love before."

"What do you mean?"

"I never made love, only hate. Hate for myself."

She placed a hand on his chest. "Why do you think that?"

"No one ever showed me love before. I haven't known love since my parents died. I guess I forgot what it was."

"Love remembers."

"Does it?" He shook his head. "I don't know if I believe it."

"You have to believe it."

"Nothing is certain in life," he said. "And you can't count on people or love. You can only count on yourself."

"I don't believe that. I can help you remember how to love. I want to try."

He closed his eyes. He had no answers, but he wanted to try again.

"Love does remember," he whispered now, but she didn't reply.

Cold swept across him stealing her warmth.

"Laura?"

She was gone.

The door to the shack creaked open. Ben lay still. His heart thumped unevenly. Light poured down on him. Caleb appeared. He climbed down the rungs and knelt next to Ben.

A cool, wet cloth moved across his face.

"You are safe here. For now. I created this cellar when I was ordered to build this shack. No one else knows it exists."

"Laura. Charlie. Are they okay?"

"Yes."

Ben closed his eyes. He had never been a praying man, but he prayed now. *God, take care of my family. Let me see them again. Let me see my new son. Let me find my son who's lost to evil and bring him back.*

"Can you move your legs?"

"No. What's wrong with me?"

"You were dead. For quite some time. I couldn't heal you fully. I don't know how long it will take for your body to recover."

"How did you find me?"

"I buried you with the help of the men who killed you. I went back for you later. Alone."

"You buried me…" The awfulness of being pressed deep in the earth sickened him. "Why save me?"

"I'm not my father."

"My cell phone," Ben said.

"My father smashed it to pieces."

Ben's hopes sunk.

"But I used something Laura had before I had to hand it over to my father."

"The belt."

"Yes."

"Laura said they were coming," Ben said.

"I snuck in my father's room a few times over the years to use his belt. I wanted to communicate with Elyon and see if our people still survived there. I saw them once, through the mist, but never again. My father never used his belt to contact Elyon. He did not want them tracking him. But he did use it to contact your son here on Earth, for years."

"To turn him away from me—and into the likeness of himself," Ben said as devastating awareness sunk in. His son had already been lost to him long ago because of this monster. Was it too late to get him back?

"Yes."

"Could there be more of your people on the way? Good people who can stop your father's madness?"

Caleb shook his head. "I used Laura's belt to seek them out. I saw no one."

Ben clutched Caleb's robe. "Please. You've got to save my family."

"I'll do what I can. I wanted to move you tonight. Release you into the woods, but you can't even walk."

Caleb pulled out some food from a bag and placed it on the floor. "Here. Eat. It may help you regain your strength."

Caleb got up to go but Ben pulled him back down. "Does Laura think I'm dead?"

"Yes."

"What about the baby?"

Caleb paused for a moment, his green eyes shone in the light that filtered down from above. "The baby is a healthy boy."

Ben grabbed his arm. "He was born? In this place?"

"Yes."

Grief tore through Ben and then sweet hope. "But he's alive. Laura's alive."

"Yes. Now rest. And be quiet. I'll be back later when I can to check on you. Things are not safe for me now either."

"Why?"

"My father hates me. I am not the Destroyer he wanted for a son."

"But Charlie is."

"Yes. He's been preparing him for years for his role."

Ben let go of Caleb's arms and sank back into the cold mud. It permeated deep into his soul.

"Let Laura know I'm alive. Please. She needs hope."

"How do I tell her? My father's eyes and mind are on her now."

"Just tell her…tell her that I'm her match. She'll know."

Caleb nodded then climbed the rungs and closed the wooden door over his world.

Ben needed hope, too, but he had no idea how to find it.

Leah walked Charlie back to his room after she had changed out of her bloody clothes. She held his hand tight knowing he had been disturbed by what he had seen. More so than the stoning. No one could know which stone killed those people. They all did but none did. And those traitors deserved it, right? Adrian said traitors couldn't be tolerated. As leader, Charlie needed to make the hard choices. But could he order someone to be stoned to death?

And Leah. He had held her hand as Caleb stabbed her. And yet here she was next to him. Pretty, smiling, and so alive.

They went down a hallway, passing a room with a woman crying in it.

"No, no," the woman yelled. "I don't want more babies!"

Charlie peeked in. A man bent over her, his finger tip glowed green. A woman held her arms down on the bed while another held her legs. She thrashed her head about. The man touched his finger to hers. She screamed once and then sobbing took over. Leah pulled him away and led him toward his room.

"What was that?" Charlie looked at Leah, but she would not turn to him she just walked faster.

"Transference." She said no more and he didn't ask, but she gripped his hand and slowed down. A pretty girl, his age, passed by and gave him a flirty smile. It didn't make him feel good as it once would have. He only felt dread.

They stopped at his door and Leah reached up, her soft lips grazed his.

"Come in?" He looked down into her green eyes. He had never seen eyes so bright, like an emerald sea. She nodded and stepped inside, sitting down on his bed. But he stood over her. He wanted answers.

"You nearly died today. I let it happen."

"It happens a lot, Charlie. Don't let it bother you. It's what we do. It's power."

"I'm not like that."

"You are. You know it."

He shook his head at her.

Leah's eyes narrowed and she pursed her lips. "Don't you want to lead? Rule our people on our new planet?"

"I—I don't know. It's all happening so fast. I don't think I can do this."

She stood up and grabbed his arms. "You can do this, Charlie. I'm taking a chance on you. I offered myself up for you."

He stepped back. "What do you mean?"

Her face softened and she took his hand. "Caleb had the possibility once to lead. And Adrian's leadership is in jeopardy. But you, Charlie, are meant to be a great leader. You are the one. And with me, together we can rule a new world. Don't you want to?"

He pulled his hand from hers. "You did what you did today just to prove to me how powerful you are?"

"It's what we do," she repeated. "If you can't do it, you're targeted as weak. I know you're not weak."

He looked at the floor. "What happens to the weak ones?"

"They're lobotomized."

He sucked his stomach in so tight it hurt. "They cut out part of their brain?"

"Yes. But they're still bred."

"What do you mean?"

She laughed and moved into him. He didn't move away this time. She was so warm and soft. He felt the special feelings stir inside him for her. He wanted this feeling, not the feelings of chaos and helplessness and doubt.

"They make babies together, Charlie."

He froze. "Because they want to?"

"Everyone here breeds to grow our numbers. The weak ones do, too. Some by physical contact. Some by transference of their spirit, like you just saw."

A memory flickered in him. *Just like how his mom's mother got pregnant. She claimed to be a virgin. No one believed her.*

"Is this what we're supposed to do on our final day?"

She stroked his hand and nodded.

"By transference or—"

"No."

His brain couldn't wrap around what that meant for him. He was just fourteen. Make a baby? On purpose? A girl in his school had gotten pregnant. She had been fourteen, too. He had seen a porn movie once at a friend's house. The people in it had been moaning and doing it in weird positions. The men's penises were huge. His wasn't that big. Would Leah expect it to be?

He had jacked off enough but to think about being with a girl made him feel powerful and terrified at the same time. To see Leah naked. To be inside her. He had no idea how to do it right. His anxiety deepened.

"Do we have to do…that?"

"Don't you like me?"

Sweat broke out on his upper lip. God, did he like her. But fear mixed with the sweet feelings of desire. He couldn't answer so he nodded. *Mom, Dad, what should I do?* Inadequacy rushed through him.

"Where are my parents?"

"Why?" She frowned and stepped back.

"I need to know."

"They await our final ritual tomorrow in the sanctuary where we are to be bonded."

"I want to see them now."

"You can't. Adrian forbids it."

"Tell me where I can find them."

"It's not my place to tell you." She reached for him again but he moved away.

"You say 'they' so that means my dad is okay, right?"

She didn't answer but moved toward the door. "I'll see you in the morning. All will be answered then. You'll see. Things will be fine. You'll be our leader. And I'll be your girl, Charlie Madroc."

"My name is Charlie Fieldstone." And saying it out loud drove his confusion over where he truly belonged.

She just smiled at him, but it didn't warm his heart.

It froze it. As if the old Charlie had already died.

CHAPTER 37

Laura waited in the rocking chair for her lover.

She ate little of the dinner left for her. Her stomach hurt from clenching it over and over. Bits of her old life swirled through her head. Her powers still had not fully returned. She kept trying the lock on the door without success. Would the government know what this place was and come for them before it was too late? But they hadn't known about this hidden society for years. Why would they come now? But she had to hope. There had been government agents watching for these Elyon beings before. Someone had to be watching now. Waiting for them to return. Waiting for a sign.

She pulled her white robe closer wanting to keep her nakedness contained beneath it which would soon to be offered to a stranger. Her one hope was to appeal to someone for help. If she could find Benny she might have a chance at escaping this place with him and coming back for Charlie. Her heart hurt to think it, but Charlie had tried to murder his father. He was her son, but she couldn't trust him. And that hurt worst of all.

She closed her eyes and rocked. The door creaked and then shut. A click sounded on the other side. Someone outside had locked them in. She opened her eyes.

It was Caleb.

She stood and faced him. He stared at her, a pensive look on his face as if he too had been ordered to do this. She forced herself to put her life in a box and lock it in her heart. Her body was a mere vessel to be used to save her family. She was just a woman here with a man. Nothing more.

"You," she said.

He nodded. "My father has ordered it."

"And his orders are always followed," she said sarcastically.

He nodded. "Or we die."

"You, too?" Her heart felt for him even being the enemy. She couldn't read his mind but she could read his heart. His heart hurt too.

"Yes. I follow orders, too. If I don't I will be punished. My father is a master mind prober. Keep your thoughts to yourself. More importantly, my father follows the Destroyer law to control breeding to build up our numbers before we enter the human world."

"And this makes it right?"

He stared at her. "It's what my father has been chosen to do. Lead us. And now he has chosen Charlie as leader."

Laura's legs shook. She sat back in the chair. Charlie was lost to her then. Caleb knelt at her feet. She leaned back in the chair and stared at him. His rugged face was appealing, his soul naked on it. He looked nothing like his father. He reminded her of Felix who had been a good man forced to commit awful acts for the government, but he had kindness in his heart. Just like Caleb. Felix was long gone but Caleb was here now. His bright green eyes bore into hers like lost jewels floating at sea, adrift here in this place. She sensed he had other plans. She wanted to know them.

She forced her tears away and smiled at him. "I will do what you want. I only ask one thing."

He pulled her up and stared down at her. His hands covered hers. They were larger than Ben's. She bit her lip. Her thumb grazed the inside of his wrist. His pulse was quick. He was nervous, too.

"What is it?"

"I want to see Charlie and my baby."

He looked at her as if weighing his decision. "If you submit tonight I will take you to see your baby but not Charlie."

Laura swallowed a sob and pressed Caleb's hands to her face.

"It's time, Laura. I will be gentle," he said softly.

"What if I get pregnant?"

"That is the intention here. However, Adrian plans to impregnate you. He senses your fertile time of month in a few days. Then it will be his turn. He likes to share and he wants me to prepare you for him so you are a willing partner.

A fist closed around her heart. *Not if I have something to do with it.* Hate drove away the heartache.

"And what of Charlie. Is he to breed as well?" She closed her eyes at that ugly word. Breed.

Caleb hesitated then nodded. "Tomorrow he will be initiated."

I won't let that happen.

Neither will I.

Her eyes flew open. His words punctured her brain like a searing bright ray of sunshine. Her powers were returning.

"Did you hear me, Laura?"

She nodded.

"Are you ready now to do your duty?"

"I'm ready."

He held her, infusing her with his smell of burnt pine and hay. Musky and male. She closed her eyes and wished it was Ben. She would make his every touch Ben's. Caleb untied her belt and pushed aside her robe's collar. The cool air tickled her breasts, but she kept her eyes closed. Her robe slid off. She shivered and heard his robe fall. Then his hard body was pressed into hers.

"Adrian is watching," he whispered in her ear. She stiffened and opened her eyes. She didn't know where to look. His muscles bulged everywhere. So she looked into his kind eyes. He stroked her back and his thick staff rose up against her stomach. Her nipples hardened despite herself. She tensed and moved away, but there was nowhere to go.

"What do I have to do?"

"Offer yourself to me."

He led her to the bed. She lay down on it. He stood over her, a mammoth young man of strength and power. "I don't think I can do this." She closed her eyes and squeezed her legs together.

"Laura, look at me."

She opened her eyes. He eased his bulk down next to her on his side and took her hand. His fingers were smooth and nail-less like Charlie's. Like Adrian's. Caleb's pale skin glowed in the dim light of her room. His muscles flexed as his body pressed into the length of her. She had never felt so vulnerable in her life. She thought of the first time giving herself to Ben as a shy young girl and tears rose up again. This time she let them go. She turned into Caleb's chest and cried. He held her in silence until her tears stopped. He wiped them from her cheeks like a gentle giant. She was painfully aware of their nakedness crushed together.

He moved closer to her. *Laura, we'll pretend.* His words came to her like a whisper in her mind. *Can you pretend?*

She nodded, relief flooding through her. "How can you be so good in this place?"

Then he whispered in her ear so she barely heard him. "I could choose to give in to my Destroyer genes, but it doesn't mean I desire it. It's why my father hates me. And Charlie can choose, too. His destiny is not set in stone." His words touched her. Maybe Charlie had a chance.

"How can you do these things your father orders?"

"I have my reasons. Two of them," he said cryptically.

And she knew he understood her heart.

He raised himself up and knelt over her. "It's time," he said in a loud voice. She hesitated then parted her legs. He smiled. She forced her fear and sorrow away and clung to the new hope inside her. She smiled back. He lay on top of her but kept his weight off, except for the male part of him that pulsed on her thigh straining for release. He stroked her neck and hair and gazed in her eyes. "Beautiful Laura."

She hesitated then wrapped her arms around him and felt ridges. "What's this?"

"From whippings. It's nothing."

She traced the raised skin, as she had traced Ben's scars. Caleb winced. "Some are fresh."

"Yes."

Hatred flowed through her with vengeance. Adrian whipped his own son. What would he do to Charlie?

She raised herself up on her elbows. "Let me see."

He twisted to the side. *Dear God.* So much pain he had suffered. Like Ben. Both of these men tortured and scarred. She sensed Caleb's deep empathy for the weak and innocent. This is why he suffered in this place.

I prayed to God, Laura. For years.

Our god?

Yes. He's supposed to be a loving god. He gave up his only son to be sacrificed for the greater good.

You sacrifice, too.

Not enough…never enough.

She reached up and for the first time since meeting Ben, she kissed another man. Her lips moved over his marked flesh tenderly, wanting to erase his scars. He turned back to her and covered her soft body again with his hard one. His lips moved down her neck. He hesitated when he reached her breasts.

Close your eyes and pretend I'm Ben. His words flowed across her brain. She did as he said. His warm breath caressed her breasts but he did not touch them, as Ben once had and never would again. Adrian appeared before her. Watching. Smiling. Waiting for his turn. He left but watched from afar.

Caleb's scent enveloped her. "Let me be your Ben."

She sighed and Ben came to her. Loved her. Encouraged her. Wanted her. He was with her now in her private world. A world with no sorrow or pain or loss—only love.

Caleb pushed open her legs and raised her hips with his hands. And he was Ben taking her for the first time long ago. She had moved with him then in the firelight. Caleb blended with Ben and he bent toward her, his hair fell soft on her cheek. *I'm going to pretend to penetrate you, Laura. I need to make it look real. I'm sorry.*

She nodded quickly and kept her eyes closed, praying he would honor his word. She couldn't suffer being violated. One night ago her husband had taken her in love and her child had burst from it in love.

Caleb's body moved over her, pulsing so close to her heat. He wrapped his arms under her back and pulled her closer, kissing her trembling stomach. He slid then—not into her but falsely over her skin, between her buttocks. His groin pushed into hers slowly then rocked with hers, pounding her soft mound and stroking her bottom. Thrust, after rhythmic thrust they were connected by pliant skin. She moved into him as he rode her, his hard body everywhere. He was inside her—but he wasn't—stroking her longer and deeper.

Like Ben had their first night together at the cabin. The wind had rattled the windows over and over with a screeching wail, rising with intensity as her heart beat did. She flowed beneath him now once again, meeting him half way in the firelight as its shadows leapt and bounded over them. The fire roared up hissing flames. Laura cried out with each fervid thrust that filled her body—and her heart.

His warm lips pulsed on her neck between ragged breaths as her breath matched his, linked by a fiery need to lose themselves in the sliding of skin. He rose and fell over her as their heat fanned their desire. He pressed her to him, his chest flattening her breasts as he strained against her. His hardness rubbed faster and faster beneath her. The bed shook. "Laura." He held her tighter. Wet warmth covered her bottom as he shuddered against her.

Ben was gone.

Caleb fell on her chest. *I'm sorry. I couldn't contain myself. You're so lovely.*

She put her arms around him. *It's okay, Caleb.*

His heart raced against hers and his sweat covered her chest. Adrian's face appeared once more. One eyebrow raised, mocking her. Then he disappeared.

Caleb pressed his head to hers. *Ben is your match.*

Laura's heart skipped. *He told you that.*

"Yes," he said aloud.

"You said *is*." She clung tight to him, wanting to believe.

"Yes."

He raised his head and looked at her with tenderness. "Time to go see your son."

Laura stood in the nursery next to Caleb. Two women rocked in corners nursing other women's babies. They glanced at her then dismissed her. They had their own jobs to do, and their own worries. She scanned dozens of tiny heads. There he was. Sleeping, content in his crib. She had memorized the path from her room to this place, as she memorized the details of this room.

"Hold him, Laura," Caleb said. "He is yours, no matter who fathered him."

So he had seen the likeness, too. She went to her child and stood over him, afraid to touch him, afraid to love him. Hate shot through her as she saw his name plate. *Madroc*. No first name. Just the last name of the devil.

Ben, will you accept him?

Benny murmured in his sleep. He was just a baby, not a monster. And then love washed over her with a mighty maternal force. She picked him up and his sweet, baby smell poured into her. Her breasts ached but she had no milk to give her son. He snuggled into her neck and she smiled at Caleb.

"Thank you." It seemed surreal she had been so intimate with Caleb and now she was here with her child.

"It's the least I could do."

"Can I see him again?"

"No. Bonds are not allowed between mothers and fathers and their children. A baby is taken away at birth and placed in the nursery. Most do not even know who their children are."

"But you do."

"They are my likeness. It wasn't hard."

Hatred flashed through her for Adrian, for these Elyons—her people. What kind of world did she come from where such evil reigned? And yet, they had good, too. Good and bad, like on Earth. And good in Caleb. In Charlie. In her. And even in her dead twin, X-10. He never had a chance to be good. His goodness was crushed—hidden—as these Destroyers hid their evil from the world. X-10 was like Adrian but not. He'd never wanted power like Adrian, he'd just wanted to live free and in peace. Perhaps Charlie would choose the same.

"How do you stand it?"

"That pain is fleeting. It does not fester and live on like other kinds of pain."

And then it was clear. Caleb had children.

"Your children?"

He nodded. "Twin sons."

His two reasons. Twins. Like she had once been. "Where are they?"

"Being raised by a community of women in another part of the compound."

"Do you ever see them?"

"Just in passing in the courtyard and at meals. When they become older I may be allowed to train them. Someday I imagine being with them, in another place but…"

She couldn't fathom his pain. She kissed Benny's head, not bearing to say goodbye. She would come back for him.

Help me, Caleb. Help me, escape. Get me to Ben.

He didn't answer, just looked at the women nursing. They stared at her.

"It's time to return to your room, Laura."

She placed Benny back in his crib, so small and helpless. It took every effort to turn and leave him behind.

She followed Caleb back to her room. His wide frame covered the hallway. Charlie would grow as big as him soon.

Caleb opened her door and stood in the doorway. She reached up to hug him. *Help us escape.* She squeezed him harder. *I know you're good inside. Help me get Benny and Charlie and Ben.*

I used your belt, Laura.

She drew in a sharp breath. *Did you travel to Elyon?*

Yes.

What did you see?

Nothing and no one.

No building? No ship maybe? I saw…something.

Only an empty land.

She let out a defeated breath. *Perhaps they really are all dead.*

Or perhaps they're on their way here—now.

Her heart jumped with the thought.

Caleb took her hands then, so big and warm. He slipped a square folded piece of paper into her palm. He squeezed his hand over hers. "I must lock you in now."

I'll set you free tonight, Laura. Work on your powers. Be ready.

His words filled her mind.

Then screams shattered the quiet.

Caleb took a step back and slammed her door. The lock clicked in place.

She pounded on it. "Caleb!"

But all she heard was his footsteps running away and the wrenching screams of someone being tortured.

CHAPTER 38

Adrian was in a foul mood.

He knelt and looked at the perfect bottom that faced him waiting for his mount. He still couldn't make himself rise to the occasion. This was the third attempt at relieving himself. His frustration boiled inside. He needed release and the female was prime for fertilization. He moved into her. She pushed back into him eagerly. He squeezed her hips, she moaned, and he grew to full length. He pushed between her thighs. Her entrance waited, glistening like a pearl to be treasured. He pushed in and instantly shrunk. He yelled and pushed her away.

Her head twisted around, eyes wide with fear.

"You can't arouse me, wench. What good are you for breeding?"

She put her head down. "I'm sorry. This can happen with the elder males. I've birthed many children. I'll do better."

Adrian straddled her. "You think *I* am a weak, old male?"

"No—no. I didn't mean that. Let me help you."

A dark film descended over his vision. "Help *me*?"

The body beneath him swam in a blur of water. He was in the well again of his father's making and this female made him weak with her lush body taunting him—as the moon above had once taunted him, as Manta had taunted him with her leaving and infidelity.

There was no escape then for his being weak, and there was no escape now from his body's failings. The female had to suffer, as he had suffered, to become strong.

"Your body disobeys me, female," he whispered in her ear. "I pour out my vengeance upon those who refuse to obey me. Now it is yours."

His hands closed around her throat. A wild need for release overtook him.

"Writhe and groan in your terrible pain! You are exiled from my land."

The female bucked beneath him, her screams garbled. He plummeted into pure bliss and ravished the dark depths he coveted. He bit with primeval hunger as he had been bitten long ago in that cold well. The water flowed around him as it once had, and he tore into what was his to now devour. Howling in ecstasy, he slid in glory amongst the crimson waves.

Panting, he pulled his head up. The water he held the female under cleared. He stared in horror at what he had done. She sprawled unmoving before him. Her skin shredded from his raging feast. He fell back, his chest slick with blood. He licked his lips, tasted her, then leaned over and threw up. He had killed them in a rage before but never this. His crime would be found out. How could he cover this up?

Manta's trembling bloody body flashed before his eyes.

Thunder crashed at his door. "Father, let me in. I heard screams. Who's in there?"

"Go away," Adrian mumbled, weak from his outburst. He looked away from the female, sure he would be sick again.

The door burst open. He squinted in the harsh hallway light. Caleb's face appeared. "Father, what have you done?" He knelt to the female, felt her body, and listened to her chest. He pulled away, his robe smeared with red. "You killed her."

"She challenged me!"

"Killed her," Caleb repeated. "Like a wild animal."

"You would have done the same. We are the same. Admit it."

Caleb shook his head. "Never." He closed his eyes and placed his hands on her.

Feet slammed along the hallway. Shocked faces stood in the doorway.

"We heard screams. Brother Adrian, are you all right?"

Tollen and the brothers stood over him, realization dawning on their shocked faces. They dragged him and Caleb up and held them, staring at the murder scene.

"No, let me help her!" Caleb tried to twist away from his captors.

"It's too late to save her," Tollen said coldly. "You and your father killed her."

Adrian wiped his mouth and his legs shook. His rage had depleted his energy. "She made me do this."

One of the elders bent down to the female. "Yes, she's dead."

Tollen crossed his arms and smirked at Adrian. "Even you cannot escape such a crime, Brother Adrian. You are a savage beast and must pay. And Caleb. I didn't expect this from you."

"I just got here. I found this," Caleb said. "Let me heal her!"

"Her blood soaking you speaks otherwise. You can't save the dead." Tollen tipped his head to the others. "Take both Madrocs here to a cell."

Caleb struggled against the elders as they held him back. "No. It wasn't me. I can save her!"

"Traitor," Adrian screamed. "You'll be the downfall of us all." He lunged at Caleb, but his son jerked away and the elders' grip tightened. "The well awaits, Son. It will serve you well—as it served me, as it served your mother."

"No one serves you," Tollen said and shoved him back.

"Put my son in the well, Brothers. Kill his weakness. His mother was weak, like him. I made sure death came for her. Let it come for him."

Caleb grabbed his arm. "You murdered my mother."

"She deserved it. A traitor, like you."

"You led the search party. You let me find her." Caleb's voice rose.

"Not pretty in death was she?"

Caleb's fingers pressed hard into his arm. The elders pried them apart.

"And your death won't be pretty either, Son."

"You can't kill me, Father."

"Enough of this family spat," Tollen said. "You'll both be silenced soon."

"Brother Tollen, ask him about the bodies in the bog," Caleb said in a deep shaken voice.

"The females taunted me," his father screamed. "Don't you see? They needed to be punished. They are weak. All of them. I am not. I am the strong one. You'll see."

"No, *you'll see*, Adrian. You took matters into your own hands, *Brother*," Tollen said. "What you've done was not a sanctioned punishment. Nor other crimes you may have committed."

"Like killing Manta—and your unborn son?" It felt so good to say it out loud. Vengeance flowed through him like wine to a drunkard.

Tollen took a step back, steadied himself with one hand on the corridor wall. "My son?"

"She told me. It was yours."

"No."

Adrian laughed. "Yes. She wasn't supposed to be at the lab when it exploded. We were together. But when she told me she was pregnant with your child, I punished her. Plundered her body of betrayal. Tore into her like a feast!" He laughed and laughed as Tollen's face became cracked armor. "I left and so did she, to go to work and erase her punishment. But her punishment wasn't over. Death came for her that day. I made it so!"

Tollen's fist came fast and hard. No mind probe for him, only a rock to his face with the full force of hate behind it. Pain flashed and blood flew from his nose as he fell on the concrete floor. Again and again his enemy's fist battered him, until the others pulled him away.

"Take him to a cell and guard him," Tollen said, his usual calm voice quaking with rage. "Tomorrow he will answer to the flock. Caleb, we'll deal with you now."

Adrian swayed as his people yanked him up. "I'll bend down the heavens and rescue you all! I'll deliver you from the power of our enemies."

"There are no enemies, Father, but yourself," Caleb said. "And we will rescue ourselves from you."

No! His son was wrong. "The mountains will smoke beneath my touch. I shall let loose my lightning bolts like arrows and scatter humans to the ends of the Earth." He raged against the arms that held him, but the elders held him tight.

"Deliver me from evil men," Caleb shouted at him as they led him away. "Preserve me from the violent, which plot and stir up trouble. Their words and actions sting like poisonous snakes. Keep me out of their power. Throw them into deep pits from which they cannot escape!" Caleb's words followed him as they dragged him away like a dog to be punished. "And then you will be destroyed, Father, by the very evil you planned for me!"

He could not be destroyed. Yet Adrian looked into the future now and saw himself as a mere ghost and the shadows of his people behind him. He had used hate to squelch his weakness, but had he doomed himself to lose Laura? She and her sons were his destiny. They would take his pain away. But he still had to face his people. Would they turn against him or stand with him?

If he were to be with Laura he had to win them over.

The screams stopped.

Laura unfolded the note Caleb gave her. It was a hand drawn map of the compound laid out in detail. There was her room, Charlie's room, Adrian's room, and the nursery. Caleb had put a key with the number of steps between the major gathering places. There were several sleeping quarters with hundreds of barrack-style beds as well as single rooms, three eating areas, a kitchen, a storage area, a courtyard, a garage, a training arena, and the sanctuary.

Caleb's sorrow struck her then as she gripped the map. His memories were etched into the paper he had passed on to her. His pain and emptiness. And love. He had so much love inside him to give away. His heart overflowed with it. He saved it for his sons. His face appeared before her. He grimaced in pain with each strike of a whip. His torso jerked with the fiery lashes.

She flinched trying to shut out the vision. The whip disappeared and his naked body bent in beauty. His back rippled with the grace of a swimmer pushing toward a distant shore. He moved between the legs of a woman who moaned with desire. He loved her like the gentle giant Laura had witnessed. Then his pleasure melted away and he knelt by his bed sending a prayer up to be with his sons.

She shook away the visions to study the map again. There at the bottom of it, marked in red near the kitchen, was a tunnel. Adrian's secret underground tunnel. Caleb wrote that he had found it years ago. Adrian must have planned for an escape at some point if he needed it. According to the map, it traveled under the compound to a place called the whipping shack and then far out into the woods. The key estimated it to end a half a mile away from the compound. It must have taken a lot of time and effort for Adrian to create such a long escape route with his powers, unseen and unheard from the community. And now, with a sense of justice, it would be her family's road to survival.

Shouts and yells distracted her from the map and she shoved it in her robe pocket, waiting for her door to burst open. It never did and the sounds faded away. She wondered where Caleb had run off to and what horrible things had been done to that person to cause them to scream in such pain.

She pulled out the note again and flipped it over. In neat, block handwriting Caleb's note read:

Lovely Laura, I will persuade Charlie to leave with us tonight. I'll unlock your door with my powers, lead you to the escape tunnel, and show you where to get Ben. At the end of the tunnel Adrian has a vehicle in hiding you can escape with. Keep hope alive. You'll see Ben soon. If anything happens and I do not appear, do whatever you can to escape. Yours in service, Caleb.

His words *Lovely Laura* and *Yours in service* resonated in her mind. He was a kind soul who did not belong in this place.

Her pulse raced thinking about what lay ahead. Silence hung over the compound. She breathed deep. She needed to practice her powers.

New energy pulsed through her. And joy over Ben being alive and being with him soon.

She stood tall and ran her hands over her body, trim and strong again. She held her hands out and moved her mind to the few objects in her spartan room—a chair, a jug of water, and a glass. At first they quivered and then hovered in the air. She closed her eyes, confidence growing. Sweat gathered in the arch of her back.

She worked into the night. She needed to undo the lock herself.

She set herself a goal to do it before the bell tolled two.

Ben woke up again. The dark encased him like a safe refuge. If he wanted to live he had to leave. Caleb wasn't coming back. Something was wrong. He shivered. It had grown colder. He had no idea how long he had been dozing. His legs throbbed. He bent his knees and flexed his feet. He had to find help. Save his family. Urgency screamed inside him.

Laura, speak to me. But none of her words came to him.

He would die for her now as he had sworn long ago. She had all the human elements that mattered.

I was lost before you, Laura. You and Charlie keep me found. I don't want to be lost again.

He saw her clear in his mind stretched out by the firelight as he had their first night together. He watched her then as shadows leapt over her curves in a wild dance, her chestnut hair flowing like burnished gold before him. They connected in pain and need, and he didn't want to leave her that night—or ever. But she had set him free with one word. *Stay.* And he had.

He knelt now and reached his hand out to steady himself. Wet earth crumbled in his fingers. He pulled himself up on the rungs. His head hit the wooden door above. In disorientation, his legs trembled and he fell. He pulled himself up again and braced his hands on the wood. He waited, listening for movement. No light shone down. Wind howled above him.

He shoved hard. The door lifted up. He collapsed on the floor of the shack. Dizziness engulfed him and icy wind cut into him. It raged around the poorly insulated building. White blew across the one window. Whips hung on the wall and hooks dangled from the ceiling. Ben's stomach turned, visualizing the torment doled out in this shack.

He stood. His legs stayed, but his chest threatened to crack open with each breath from where he had been stabbed. Death hadn't taken away his pain. It now exploded inside him. He opened the door. Steel knives of frigid air sliced into him. He staggered back and gripped the door's edge. Snow swirled, beating at him.

A face appeared through the snow. A gray robed man lunged at him. "What are you doing here?"

Ben lurched as the man shoved him back into the shack, and alongside his weakness, fury blasted through him. He punched the man in the face. In the seconds the man staggered back, Ben grabbed a hook off a ceiling chain. They circled the shack, eyeing one another.

"Human, you can't take me down." The man lumbered around him, a hulking figure.

A piercing pain lit across Ben's head as the man probed his brain. The pain intensified. The man came at him. Ben dodged right like a drunkard and swung hard. The hook sunk into the man's back. He screamed and fell to the floor. Ben stumbled back and fell to his knees. The room spun. The pain dissipated. The man flopped down and was still. Blood spread in an incriminating stain across the light gray wool of his robe.

Ben crawled to him, shaking from adrenalin and the cold. He searched for the hidden door. Finally, his fingers felt a notch in the wood. He lifted the latch to the cellar and with all his remaining strength, rolled the massive man into it. He crashed with a thud. Ben stared down at his victim, the man's hands crossed his chest as if posed in death. *God, forgive me.* Then he slammed the door down to hide his crime and stood up.

Laura, help me now.

But she remained lost to him. Thinking more clearly, he took another hook and pulled down a whip from the wall. They may come in handy.

Then he stepped out into the gale.

Dizziness grabbed him again. He staggered out into the winter abyss. Step by step he headed away from the Elyon world and toward his own. The trees held him up when his legs could not. The cold snarled inside him, claiming him, but he would not give into it.

It could not have him. Not yet.

Caleb waited in his cell for the elders to make a decision on his punishment.

He was exhausted and powerless. They had drugged him to dull his powers. He didn't care. He could think of just one thing over and over.

My father murdered my mother.

The deep loss he'd felt hit him afresh after all these years. His beautiful, loving mother. She had been the softness that protected him from his father's hardness. Tears welled in his eyes. It had been so long since he cried. He cried now and wiped the tears away angrily. His loss as a young boy drained away, replaced by anger.

What would happen now? The elders had questioned him for what seemed hours. He had detailed every step he had taken in the last day. They had prodded deep into his strained relationship with Adrian, thinking he had partnered with his father to torture, rape, and kill females.

"Our people may be assigned partners to breed with, but you know rape and murder is a line not to be crossed," Tollen had said, frowning down at him. "We do not take matters into our own hands. We do not become like the human beasts that perform such atrocities. Ours is a shared community. And those who violate our rules are punished by law, not by vigilantes."

"You mean murdered by law," Caleb had said, staring at the blood stains on his robe.

"Punished for justice. And you shall await yours."

They had left him them. He heard the bell toll one a.m. now. He had to get out of here and help Laura. Ben counted on him, too. He smashed his fists on his thighs. His plans were unraveling.

His door opened. The elders filed in.

Tollen threw a robe at him. "Change out of those bloody clothes. We have decided you are innocent of this crime. We believe you came across your father's act by chance. You are exonerated. As you know, your powers will return in time."

Caleb changed his robe and stood. "Thank you. What of my father?"

"Tomorrow he will be punished in the courtyard."

"Stoned," Caleb said. A numb feeling mixed with a deep seated relief washed over him. His father had murdered his mother and built the well here to do the same to him.

"To death."

"Will Charlie still be leader?"

Tollen smiled at him. "No. I am."

The elder had wanted his father out for a long while. "My father had promised me I could spend time with my two sons."

"It's not allowed at their age."

"I prepared the female, Laura, for him. My sons were to be my reward."

"Your time on her won't be wasted. She will be mine now. And if she doesn't comply she will be eliminated."

"Let me be with my sons."

"We'll see."

Caleb looked at the grim faces of the elders. He had no choice but to wait. For now he had to help Laura and her family. It's what he did. Set the oppressed free. Except himself. He was imprisoned in a world of hope to be with his sons. He had planned many times to escape with them but the logistics had too much risk. His sons didn't even know he was their father, and if they were caught escaping they could all die.

"Let me go back to my room and rest."

"Not yet. You will come with us. I have ordered Charlie to the sanctuary. He will be informed of his place here now. And since you have worked with him, he will be your responsibility now."

Caleb nodded and followed the elders out of the room. Laura would have to wait.

CHAPTER 39

Charlie stood at the altar in the sanctuary. The brawny Elyon who woke him up to bring him here stood silent, flexing his giant muscles.

Candles burned low on the walls. Black smoke drifted from them in a murky haze. Stars flickered above in the glass dome skylight. A dead Elyon world hung in the universe up there watching over this new one being created. The courtyard bell rang slow and steady.

Clang. Clang.

Two a.m.

Footsteps echoed in the corridor outside. The giant door swung open. Caleb entered. Behind him stood the community elders.

"Charlie-boy." The tall elder smiled at him. The way he used Adrian's nickname for him sent a shiver across his stomach. "Remember me? I'm the head elder, Brother Tollen."

He nodded. "Why am I here?"

"I have an announcement. Adrian has committed a heinous, unsanctioned crime. And with the preparation of his disposal—"

"What does that mean?

"—you are no longer in charge of our Elyon community."

Charlie stepped away from the altar. "Where's Adrian?"

Caleb shook his head slightly at him as if to silence him. Suddenly, everything felt so wrong.

"And your place is one of a menial worker now." The elder continued on, ignoring him. "You will be assigned to Caleb and do whatever he assigns you. You will no longer have your own room but sleep in the quarters with the other males. All who second this say, 'Make it so'."

The elders responded in unison, nodding. "Make it so."

"But Adrian—"

"Adrian is not here to protect you anymore." Tollen paused. "He will be stoned to death at sunrise."

Charlie shook his head and stepped back. His new father was to die? Caleb's father. Why did Caleb just stand there?

"No. No."

"Yes. And you will help us do it."

"I can't," he whispered.

"You will. Or you mother will suffer. Your baby brother will suffer."

Charlie took another step back and stumbled as he hit the altar steps. "Where's my mom? Is she okay?" The words *baby brother* hung in his head.

"She's fine. For now. And so is her new son. Elyon's new son. Soon she will produce more new sons. With me."

Charlie's world tilted. He strode to Tollen, fists ready to smash the man's face in.

"You can't do this. My father won't let you. You're not in charge. You're nothing!"

The elders took a step back, but Caleb stepped forward and grabbed Charlie's arm.

Tollen smiled at him. "And which father is that, Charlie-boy? Your pretend father, Adrian? Or your dead human father, Ben?"

Charlie pushed against Caleb, but he held him tight. His eyes burned into his begging him to stop. *Charlie, calm down. Trust in me. I will help you.* But his rage burned too bright. He struggled against Caleb. The Elyon guard held his other arm.

"My dad isn't dead. I didn't kill him in the sanctuary."

Tollen twitched his lips. "He's dead now. Adrian ordered it."

"Liar!"

"And Caleb killed and buried him."

Caleb's hold loosened on him. Charlie turned to face him. Hate filled him as never before. Caleb's face revealed the truth. Nothing was as he thought. And everything was his fault.

"Charlie?" Leah's soft voice broke through Charlie's despair.

She stood like a golden dream in the doorway. Light radiated around her. She walked into the sanctuary and her light faded.

"Ahh, Leah," Tollen said. "Thank you for coming. Charlie and you are no longer bonded. You see, Adrian has committed a terrible crime and must pay for his sins. I am now leader. Charlie will be assigned elsewhere. Your services with him are over."

Charlie swallowed hard. Leah couldn't be lost to him, too. "Tell them, Leah. We're supposed to be…shooting stars, right?"

She shook her head at him and moved closer to Tollen. "Poor Charlie. Sorry." Tollen stroked her hand. She smiled up at the old man. A smile she had given Charlie many times. She gave it away now. "I go where the power is. You no longer matter."

"Caleb, take Charlie to his new quarters," Tollen said. "The bell will ring in a few hours for Adrian's stoning." Caleb nodded and tightened his grip on Charlie's arm. "Leah, I'll expect you in my room within the hour."

She nodded and Tollen and his group left.

But Leah lagged behind. "Too bad about you and me, Charlie. You're adorable. We'd make handsome sons, to add to the ones I've had already."

Charlie looked at her, hating her and loving her. She had babies? She was a mother? How could he have ever thought she was an angel? She had used him. She wasn't any different than the girls back home. He never had a girlfriend before. He had never been used before. But now he felt that pain. He bit his lip. It stung like the thought of her kisses now did. He shoved his hands in his robe pockets and forced them down, stretching the material tight. It didn't matter that he looked like the Elyons here. He would trade all of it to be home in his house with his Mom and Dad. Right now even the bullies seemed more appealing.

"I hate you," he mumbled.

"Good. Hate is stronger than love. Hate will serve you well here."

"Forget her, Charlie." Caleb pulled on his sleeve. "We have to go."

Charlie yanked away. "And *you*. Killer! You killed my dad."

"No, I didn't," Caleb said and let him go. "I buried him after. And then…"

"And then, what?"

"I didn't kill him."

"I don't believe you."

Leah flounced her robe and twirled to leave. "You and Caleb can fight out your own battles. I'm done here."

"Why are you so mean? I thought you liked me?"

She turned back. "I did, Charlie. But now you're useless to me. Like Adrian." She shot a smile to Caleb. "And Caleb. All you Madrocs loved me but now you're not worthy of me."

"Don't listen to her, Charlie." Caleb pulled at him again. "She can't love anyone. She's a Destroyer to the core. She has no emotion except to care for herself. She only wants power."

"Caleb's right. I follow the leader. And neither of you are it anymore. Goodbye Charlie." She laughed then moved toward him and pressed her warm lips to him. He hated himself for letting her kiss him but he did.

He stood frozen but Caleb didn't. He shoved her away from Charlie. "Wench. Leave us alone. Go be a whore somewhere else."

She stepped back, her eyebrows in a line of lightning. "At least I'll be at the top. I won't be trash at the bottom like you two freaks."

That last word slapped Charlie like a whip. Her hair spun in the candlelight like a golden web as she turned toward the door. Her slender figure moved away with grace. But his hate grabbed her back. He sunk his mind into hers. She grabbed her head and cried out.

"Don't ever call me a freak. You *bitch*."

She let go of her head and turned to face him. "I am stronger than you, Human."

Pain splintered through Charlie's brain. His neck snapped back like a baseball bat had hit him. He grabbed his head and sank to his knees, pleading with her in his mind to stop.

"No." Caleb ran to her.

Candle sticks flew from the walls and bludgeoned Charlie, adding to his pain.

Leah smiled at him as she killed him. "You can't hurt me, Charlie."

"But I can," Caleb grabbed her arms.

The bell tolled the half hour. Two thirty. Where was Caleb? Something had gone wrong.

Laura sat down, frustrated and out of breath. She had been moving objects in her room but couldn't get the door lock to budge. It had a long, heavy handle on the outside that slid into place. She wiped the sweat from her neck and brow.

She stood again and pulled her robe tighter around her thin waist. It felt strange to not have Benny inside her. Soon she would have him in her arms. Her breasts ached thinking about his needs. She squeezed them to shut out her sorrow then flung her arms in the air. She strained her muscles as energy flowed through them. *Let my powers return!*

The bell tolled three a.m. *Where was he?*

She reached for the lock in her mind. She envisioned it easing across, slow and steady. Inch by inch. Smooth steel sliding against wood.

Move, damn it.

Minutes passed. Sweat trickled down her spine.

Click.

She rushed to the door and placed her ear to it. Silence. She turned the handle. The door popped open. She grabbed it so it didn't creak and let out a huge breath. She peered through the widening crack. Shadows filled the corridor from dim lights that lined the ceiling.

She unfolded Caleb's map. She traced the way to the nursery. Left, left, and a right. Three halls away. Fortitude filled her—and fear. She pushed it deep down inside her. She would hide it until she needed it to fuel her ability to face whatever she might be tested with.

She stepped out into the corridor feeling more naked and vulnerable than she had with Caleb. She tiptoed along the wall, praying she didn't encounter any Elyons. The dark stretched forever. She passed door after door. She slunk on, feeling braver. The community was tucked away for the night.

After another minute she faced the nursery. The lights glowed softly. It looked like any nursery in a hospital ward. Like the one Charlie had been in. Peaceful and full of new life. One woman nursed a baby in a rocking chair in the corner.

Laura took a deep breath and strode through the door toward Benny. Her heart raced. She almost had him. She reached in the crib and pulled him to her chest. She peeled back his bunting and checked. His heart birthmark branded him with her love. He was *her* Benny, *not* Adrian's. She smelled his sweet hair. He opened his sleepy yellow eyes and gazed into hers. She lost herself in her son.

"What are you doing?" The nursing woman stopped rocking and stood up, the baby latched to her breast.

Laura held Benny tight. "My breasts are full. I need to release my milk."

The woman moved closer. "You're that human, aren't you?" She put her baby in its crib.

Laura shook her head. "Of course not. I'm nursing this one in my room. Goodnight." She turned away, but the woman ran up behind her and grabbed her arm.

"Stop! You are that human." She touched Benny's head. "And this is your baby."

Laura pulled away. Her heart wouldn't stop pounding in her chest. Benny began to cry.

The woman glowered at her, tightening her hold on her arm. "You can't take him. He belongs to the community. I'm calling the head nurse."

Laura smiled at her. "All right." The woman looked surprised and her grip eased.

"Come with me." The woman turned away, heading toward the door.

Laura followed. She held Benny with one arm and swiped a glass bottle from under an empty crib. The woman saw her movement and jerked around. Laura smashed the bottle on the edge of the crib, shattering it. Benny cried from the noise.

"What are you—"

Laura shoved the jagged glass into the woman's neck.

She pushed it in deep. Anger fueled her force. Exultant fury exploded in her and her heart raced, not from horror at what she did—but triumph.

The woman staggered back, tried to scream, but blood spurted from her sliced artery instead of a sound. It splattered across Laura.

Benny's cries grew louder. Another baby cried out.

The woman fell to the floor, twitched, and was still.

Laura struggled to drag her off to the corner with one arm and dropped her next to the fridge. Heaving for breath, she wrenched it open and grabbed four bottles of breast milk from the shelves. All she could fit in her pockets. She hoped it was enough.

Benny's cries softened. "Shh, my sweet boy." She buried her face in his neck. Her pulse slowed. She had never thought herself capable of hurting someone. She had never murdered someone before. But her child's life depended on it.

She turned away from the bloody woman and pulled out the map with one hand. It was damp from the cold bottle and ripped as she shook it open. She quickly assessed where Charlie's room was and fled from the slaughter with her son.

One more son to rescue.

She was running out of time.

Pain stabbed Charlie's head.

Leah's figure struggled with Caleb's. They hovered over him in a blur.

He hugged his knees to his chest, wanting to die. The world became black. He drifted away. Through the darkness a high-pitched scream cut through his brain. Leah's. And then silence. Was he dead? Smoke drifted across him. Did they have candles in heaven? Was his real dad there, too? His eyelids felt so heavy, like blankets protecting him.

He slowly opened his eyes. The pain receded. White swirled in the sky light above. He struggled to get up.

Caleb lay on his side, moaning. Candlesticks were strewn about. And Leah. She lay sprawled by the altar. So still and quiet. He stumbled to her and knelt down. She had no breath, no life. He touched her fair hair, her face. He wanted to see her eyes one more time. Sobs filled his chest, trapped. He refused to release them.

"Caleb, help me."

Caleb moaned, stretched out his arm. "I—I can't. She drained my powers. Too weak."

"You killed her," Charlie whispered.

"She was killing you." A coughing spasm racked his wounded body.

"How can I save her?"

"Maybe she still lives. Do what I taught you."

Charlie moved his hands across Leah's still body. He had hated what she did, but he couldn't let her die. "It's not working for me. You've got to help me!"

Caleb pushed himself along the floor to Leah's body. A gash oozed blood down his face. He placed a hand on her leg and closed his eyes. His hand shook then he sank his head on the floor.

"Caleb!" Charlie shook him.

"Sorry…"

"I'll heal you. Bring back your powers."

"You can't bring back powers from a mind killing attack. My energy must restore them on its own. It's fate."

"Fate?"

"For her to die. She would live to wreak more pain on others for power."

"What are you talking about?"

"There will always be someone like her. Like my father. Like Tollen. I must stay and make sure it doesn't happen. For my sons."

But Charlie didn't listen. He kept working on Leah. He caressed her face with shaky hands, kissed her cheek. He willed life back into her body like Caleb had taught him. He used his mind to heal her, as he had healed his dad with his mom a thousand years ago at home.

Home.

He let the sobs go then. He was only fourteen. Just a kid who needed his mom and dad. But his dad was dead. And soon Adrian would be dead, his mentor who looked like his true father—had become his true father. And now both fathers were gone. If he saved Leah it would be something good out of all this bad.

"Leah, come back to me. Don't go. I don't hate you." He forced his powers into her, willing her broken body to mend, but she remained still.

Caleb raised his head and struggled to sit up. "I thought I might have loved her like Rachel. She fooled us both. She had the true Destroyer seed of hate festering in her. She grew strong on it. Like my father. She would never stop spreading her evil."

"She can change. If we save her. I don't know who Rachel is, but I need to save Leah!" He put his ear to her chest. Nothing. He rested his head on her, trying not to cry.

"I used to pray to your god. He has abandoned us in this place," Caleb said. "There is only suffering here and death."

"I don't want this anymore," Charlie cried upward to the stars in the skylight. "I can't be a Destroyer." Saying it out loud made his old life and all he had lost well inside him. "It's too late. I don't even know where my mom is and my dad died because of me. Now Leah." He looked down at her as if she might respond.

"I know where your mom is."

"I don't believe you." Charlie wiped his cheeks. Heavy despair weighed him down, suffocating him in grief. All he had was gone. His family. His home. This girl he cared for. He stood and picked up Leah in his arms. Her hair fell like a silky sheet. He placed her on the altar and smoothed down her robe then folded her hands over each other, as he had seen done in the movies when a loved one dies.

Caleb stood. "We've got to go. The community will awaken soon. And I made a promise to your mother."

"There is no promise."

"Yes, there is. I promised her to bring you with me. To help you all escape. Including your father, Ben."

Charlie stepped toward him. "Stop it!"

Caleb placed his hand on his shoulder. "It's true. I dug him up. I gave him life again."

Charlie shoved him back. "You're lying! You and Leah told me it's not possible to bring the dead back. Maybe it's *you* who wants to be in charge, isn't it? I thought you were my friend, my family."

"I am, Charlie. Let me help you. We are family."

"No. I have no family. I have nothing." Charlie punched him in the face.

As the adrenalin urged him on he realized he liked hitting far more than mind killing. The feeling of fists slamming into flesh felt good. Caleb stumbled back but kept his hands at his side. Charlie jabbed his fist into Caleb's stomach. He bent over in pain but still did nothing.

"Come on, hit me," Charlie yelled.

"No, Charlie," Caleb said, gasping. "We're all we have. We need to get your mom and Benny now. And Ben."

"Lies. I have no one." Charlie crumpled to the floor. "I *am* no one."

He remembered his mom hugging him. He remembered his dad carrying him to bed as a kid, when he'd pretend to be asleep just to be in his dad's arms.

The years flashed through him of time spent with Adrian. Of meeting him in the field where he had guided him, been there for him when he had no one—and all this time he had been leading him here to the dark side.

Then the truth hit Charlie like a thunder bolt—why he and his dad had never gotten along. He thought it was because they were so different, but it was because Adrian had been turning him against his dad for years.

And in that truth he understood he had never truly known his dad.

His dad—who had come to rescue him and died doing it.

His dad—who had faced Adrian's power and didn't back down.

His dad—who was more a hero than he had ever imagined.

His dad—the sort of father he had always wanted. He'd had him all along.

How could he have followed Adrian? Been so brainwashed to want to kill and like it? He couldn't go home and he couldn't stay here. His rage fled and self-loathing replaced it. He swallowed hard, tasting his own bitter self-hatred. He had no good in him anymore. And there was only one thing left to do.

He drove a dagger into his mind. Fire blasted hot.

Stab. Stab.

Let there be pain then let there be nothing.

He closed his eyes and fell to the floor.

"Charlie, no." Caleb grabbed him. Shook him. "Stop!"

But he didn't want to stop. The nothing took him.

CHAPTER 40

Adrian awoke and stared at himself in the small, cracked mirror in his cell. Dried blood painted his face in ceremonial marks. The taste of the female still covered his tongue. She had paid for his rage. Now he would pay for what he did, according to Elyon law. Tollen had proclaimed it. He would die by stoning after sunrise. Clarity of thought came with the release of his crazed anger over the female. He had to escape this place, but he had no powers. Tollen had taken them away by drugging him. He remained naked and his chest itched with caked blood as he stretched.

The cracked mirror directed him what to do. He pulled it from the wall and placed it on the floor. One smash of his fist cracked it into dozens of pieces. He took the largest piece.

A guard's voice called out. "What's all the noise in there?"

Adrian banged on the door. "I'm sick. Help me." He coughed and gagged, pretending to throw up.

Silence then a snort followed. "You can stay sick until your death."

"If I die before then you'll pay the consequences."

More silence. Then a click. Adrian held his stomach. The door opened.

The guard held a knife out. "You don't look sick."

Adrian moaned, doubled over, and fell on his side. He rolled his eyes up in his head. A robe rustled. Breath blew across his face. He focused his eyes on the guard and grinned. The guard's eyes widened. He scrambled for his knife and opened his mouth to call out but not before

Adrian reached up and sliced his throat. Blood spurted in a jet. It sprayed across his face and chest, adding to his crimes.

The male grabbed at his throat and fell back on his haunches. He bled out in seconds. His legs and arms writhed then were still. Adrian removed the man's robe and put it on. He dragged the guard under the cot and peered out the door. The hallway was empty. All remained asleep.

His chest swelled. Even without powers he was a powerhouse. He had killed with just his wits. Energy flowed through his veins. He could survive and start over. He had lost Laura and her sons...for now. He would find them. They would still be his redemption. His powers would return and he would start a new community. Be almighty again.

Heaven is my throne and Earth is my footstool. My hand has made both the Earth and the skies, and they are mine. And all shall tremble at my word.

If only his father could see him now. There would be no well of punishment, no whippings from the heavy hand of his paternal oppressor. He would show him that he was the strong one. Not his brother. Or Caleb. They were weak. They needed love, like these despicable humans. Love didn't bring power, it brought pain.

He glided down the dimly lit hall, an obscure ghost quiet but deadly. He headed to his tunnel to escape and seek sanctuary amongst the humans.

Then Manta blasted into his mind from the grave, alive in spirit now.

There can be love without pain. Her lovely face hovered. Her hand grazed his cheek.

He shook it off and stumbled. *Leave me be. You made me hurt you. You were leaving me for my brother and bearing Tollen's child. You betrayed me. And you died for it. And I made Brahm pay by stealing the ship and claiming his mission as my own, with my own people.*

You only hurt yourself, Adrian, she whispered. *You're still hurting yourself.*

I hurt you worst of all, Manta. He punched himself in the gut, forcing a new pain to replace the emotional one that drove spikes into his heart.

I forgive you.

Those words stung hard.

Why? I killed my wife for you so we could be together. I attacked you, the one woman I loved. I led you to your death, your unborn child's death. I've tried to redeem myself with Laura and her sons, but I can't make her love me. But I will not give up.

He heard footsteps and stopped. They moved away and he continued on. Not so far now. Soft lips moved on his. *You were cruel, Adrian. Hate filled you. It still does. It destroyed your ability to love. You can end the cycle of your father. Don't give in to your genes. It's not too late.*

He closed his eyes and put his hand on the wall. *Stop it.*

But she continued to appeal to him from the darkness she hovered in. Her energy haunted him. Her hand held his. So much wretched love. It burned in him anew. He had forgotten the glorious feeling of it—and the agonizing suffering from it.

Adrian, you can start a new world here with love. Elyons will follow. Don't let your hidden Destroyer element dictate who you are. There is also love hidden inside. Let that dictate what you are. Let it lead your people. You deceived Caleb to bring him here. Let it be for something good. There is more power in sacrifice than ruthlessness. The true strong ones are those who are vulnerable by choice.

He shoved her hand away and strode faster down the corridor. One more turn and he would be at the storage room. The secret door there led to his safe passage to the woods. It had taken him months to complete. Night after night of working when the newly formed community slept. Pounding through rock and earth with his mind. Inch by inch and foot by foot he had carved his crossing to another life. The day for that was here.

He slipped into the storage room and pushed aside the shelves of supplies, pulled up loose wooden planks from the floor, and lifted the latch to his freedom. Cool air blew up from his sanctuary. *See, Manta, you are wrong. Being weak does not pay.* He climbed down into darkness and sent her away.

But she would not leave. *There is no one here with you. No one follows you. Your so-called strength has left you alone. And this will be your downfall. You loved me once. You were kind once. Find that loving part of you and embrace it.*

Anguish struck him. He didn't recognize the feeling at first. It rose inside him like an angry animal. He fell to his knees on cold dirt. He was alone. So alone. As he had been in that cold well. *Let these feelings go. Release me from this pain.*

Something wet touched his cheeks. He reached his hands up. What was this? Tears. Horror filled him at the evidence of his weakness. He rubbed his sleeve across his cheeks.

Manta's fingers traced his back. Her touch burned into him, not like the whip's agonizing pain but with agonizing healing. *Why do you suffer so at your own hand? You have punished yourself enough. Go forward with love and make all the wrongs you have done right.*

Her face appeared again and soft hair moved across his cheek. He put his hand there, wanting to feel her on him one more time. He smelled her skin, tasted it, and held it close to him.

Only you can release you, Adrian. I love you.

And she was gone.

He cried out for her. *I love you, too. Don't leave me again.*

He reclaimed the pain he thought he had long ago discarded. He stood. Blackness filled his every crevice in this pit of his creation. He slid his hands along the tunnel wall and forced himself to run on again, toward freedom.

Then a voice called to him from far away. Manta? No, Laura. She came to him. Had Manta sent her to him as his second chance? He didn't know. But he knew what he had to do now.

Snow swirled thick around Ben. It piled up to his calves and grew higher. He reached the fence that surrounded the compound and pulled himself up and over it, ripping his side on barbed wire. He gasped in pain and fell hard on the other side. Dizziness slammed into his head but he fought it off and stumbled on through the wilderness, shivering. He held Laura's love warm inside. It kept him going. And then, he heard her calling to him. *We need you, Ben.*

And he held Laura in his arms once again. The ground quaked beneath them. He wasn't in the woods anymore. Another time and place came to him. She smelled of sunflowers. Running, running. Up he carried her through a tunnel of dark earth. Ben tripped. Snow blew white across his filthy hands. Why was snow in this tunnel of long ago? Throbbing pain burned his torso. The ground shifted beneath his feet. He tripped and crashed down, slamming Laura into the mud. So cold and wet.

She moaned, unconscious.

Up. Up. He went again.

Pine struck his nose and he breathed deep to will his dizziness away. He slammed into trees. Their spindly arms pushed him around in circles. Playing with him. Why didn't they show him the way? Icy snow beat his face and hands.

Up. Up. He went again.

Dead. They were all dead down there under the earth.

He had to leave them behind. But not Laura. Never Laura. He held her tighter. Anger and fear fueled him. The wild woods grabbed him. Tore at him until he bled. Like Laura's twin had bled him. He shoved the taunting arms away, angry to be held back.

He bounced off earth walls and cradled Laura's head to his own. Then light spilled ahead. A great rumbling bellowed below him. The ground shook and he stumbled on heading for the light.

Laura. Charlie. They were being held by a maniac.

Confusion flooded through him. How could Charlie be here? He wasn't born yet.

Laura's moans grew. He ran on, lurching sideways and, with a gasping leap, flung himself on the ground. The shaking took over. He crawled. Each movement forward shot pain in his head. The earth fell behind them, crushing all below. And Laura's screams matched the cry of earth falling. Final darkness came for him, strong and permanent in its grasp. He fought it away—again.

Ben, we need you. Charlie needs you. Come back to us. Ben looked down at Laura. Snowflakes painted her cheeks and glistened in her chestnut hair. Her eyes were closed, her lips did not move.

Charlie's dying. Help me.

He had to get to them. Had to turn back. "I'm coming, Laura."

He blinked and she was gone. His arms hung empty. Cold pushed its icy fingers into him. The snow stung his eyes, penetrated every crevice. He was alone in the blizzard. Laura had never been in his arms. They weren't in the tunnel. Could he save her now like he had once in that tunnel long ago? The night the earth fell and crushed their friends— and Laura's brother—with it. This time he could fail. If he did his family would be lost and he would be alone again. Like the little nine year old boy he had once been whose parents were crushed under a spaceship.

He couldn't lose his family again.

He wouldn't live through it this time. He wouldn't want to.

Charlie's room had been empty. Laura used the map to navigate down darkened hallways to reach the sanctuary. She heard voices and shrunk against the wall, gripping Benny. He cried out and she gave him a bottle to suck. How she wished she could feed him. *Oh, Ben, we're coming. I'm bringing our sons to you.*

And a blast of arctic ice chilled her.

I'm coming for you, too.

Ben's words came to her but swirled away with snow. He was somewhere so cold and white. Wasn't he hidden away as Caleb said? She had to get out of here and get to him. She shook the vision away and eased to the edge of the sanctuary door. A body sprawled on the altar and two figures, outlined by candlelight, tangled together.

Charlie! And Caleb was shaking him.

"No!" She ran toward them. "Let him go."

Caleb turned to her. "He's killing himself."

Caleb placed Charlie on the floor. She knelt at his side. Benny's sobs were muffled against her skin. "Charlie, please, don't do this." He was killing himself, like her twin had—only he had succeeded. She couldn't save her brother from himself that night long ago, but she had to save her son.

She placed her hand on his head. He was still there, inside somewhere. She stroked his face. Her beautiful boy's face. Her son who had been through so much. She should never have turned her back on her powers. It blinded her to their enemy who was here all along.

"He couldn't save Leah," Caleb said. "He said he had no one."

But you do, Charlie. You have me.

She willed life into him. Love coursed through her with a hand on each son, one who just had his first breath and one who was drawing his last.

Caleb knelt beside her and placed his hands on Charlie's body, too. "Leah took my powers but they're coming back. Come back to us, Charlie." She stared into Caleb's eyes as he willed life into her son with her. Such kind eyes. He was the sort of man Charlie could grow to be.

"Yes, Charlie. Don't leave me. Not now. I need you. Your dad needs you."

She kissed his face, his fingers. Beautiful strong fingers.

We'll get you the surgery. We'll make you look like you want. I promise you.

He looked like a man, but he was still her child. She felt his pain inside. It was so hard to be a teenager who didn't fit in. She wanted to look into his eyes and tell him he did belong. He belonged with her and Ben and Benny.

She felt a spark inside him. Benny gurgled against her. His tiny life force surged in her and she passed it from one son to another.

"You have so much life left to live."

No life. A whisper in her head.

"You couldn't save Leah but you saved me," she pleaded with him. "If it weren't for you I'd be a lost soul, too. I wouldn't belong. But because of you I have your dad and you and now Benny."

I killed my dad.

No. Your dad's alive. Waiting for us.

Not true.

Yes.

Caleb placed a hand on her shoulder. "We need to go. Others could find us here. I'll carry him."

"No, he's coming back to us. I hear him." Then she whispered. "Be brave, Charlie."

Being big doesn't mean you're brave, Mom.
Being big of heart does.
I have no heart.
You do. The biggest of all.
I'm a freak.
No. I thought I was, too, once. But your father showed me I have all the good from both worlds. To him I was the most human person he knew.

No good. I'm evil, Mom. Like Adrian. Like your brother.

Lots of good, Charlie. There is nothing you've done I can't forgive. My brother chose dark. You are stronger than him.

"Choose life, Charlie. Open your eyes and meet your brother."

And he did.

His eyes moved to Benny. He reached up a hand and touched his brother's fingers. "He's so tiny. He's so…Adrian." He looked in shock at Laura.

"He's your brother."

"Big Brave Blue," Charlie whispered.

"Like you." Laura squeezed his hand.

Caleb helped Charlie stand. He swayed and looked away. "I'm a Destroyer."

"We all can be. Human or Elyon," Caleb said. "But it's not who we have to be."

A door slammed somewhere. Voices carried to them. "Let's go," Caleb said.

Charlie grabbed Caleb's arm. "Leah, you've got to save her."

Caleb picked Leah up and placed her gently under the altar's curtains, hiding her. "I'll come back for her. I promise."

"You can bring the dead back to life?" Laura stared at him, not believing.

"Yes. It's how I saved Ben."

"Promise?" Charlie looked back at Leah.

"Promise."

"If we let her die we are no different than Destroyers."

Caleb nodded and pulled Charlie away. They left the sanctuary and darted down dark hallways through the giant maze. The community was coming to life in the early dawn hours. Her murder would be discovered soon. Twice they stopped and hid in shadows as people went about their daily business.

Laura gripped Charlie's hand as they ran. And he let her. She didn't want to ever let go.

CHAPTER 41

They came to the end of a corridor.

Caleb looked behind them then slipped into a door that seemed invisible in the dim light.

"It's an old storage room not used anymore. They shelve things here we've outgrown but we may have future use for."

Charlie and Laura moved into the room. Light from a small window bathed them in gray. Daylight grew. Snow blew hard at the glass, scratching to get in. Caleb pulled a door up from a hidden latch on the floor.

"Someone's been here," Caleb said. "The shelves have been moved."

"Adrian," Laura said.

"The Elders locked him up. Maybe he was here earlier…" But it bothered him anyway.

"Let's hope."

Caleb nodded. "The tunnel is down here. And this is where I leave you."

"No, Caleb, come with us," Laura said.

"I can't. I have to save Leah. And I need to be with my sons."

"But you aren't with them now," Charlie said.

"I have faith I will be soon. Someday we will be together."

He put his hand on Laura's. Her tiny hand held such strength. The vision of them pressed naked together again flashed before him. He bent and kissed Benny's cheek, his breath warm on Laura's breast, as it had been once. She shivered and he knew she felt their time together, too.

"He will grow into a fine man, like Charlie." Then he straightened up. "Give me the map."

A door shut somewhere. They all tensed. Listening. Silence held them captive, and the snow that blew against the pane with little ticking sounds was the only thing they could hear. Laura unfolded the map. They spoke in softer whispers.

"Follow the tunnel until here. See the whipping shack? There's a door in the tunnel wall. It leads to a cellar under the shack." He looked at Laura and then Charlie. "This is where Ben is."

"For real?" Charlie grabbed the map scanning it.

"Yes. Adrian had him killed and buried. I went back and dug him up and brought him there to heal him. He suffered greatly, though and is not all well yet. It will take time."

Laura placed a hand on Caleb's arm. "That was difficult for you."

"Yes," was all he said. "Then continue on through the tunnel. It will end more than a quarter mile past the whipping shack. Beyond the fence perimeter. There is a vehicle there, fully fueled. It's not hard to figure out how to use. Adrian hid it for his escape. It's now yours."

"Then where do we go?" Charlie looked out the window. "It's a blizzard out there."

"Head east. It's six miles to the road that leads into Benevolence."

"Six miles?" Laura said louder, then whispered, "We'll die in the storm."

Caleb pulled out a bin. He handed them two thick hooded robes lined with fur. "I hid these here long ago in case I needed them to escape in the winter."

"There's an extra one there," Charlie said.

"For my other son. I planned to leave with them."

Laura took the robe, clasped Caleb's fingers for the two brief seconds they touched. "Thank you."

He nodded and she looked into his eyes for the longest of moments. Then he pulled out a glow stick and snapped it. It lit up green, much brighter than a Halloween one.

Charlie grabbed it. "Thanks."

"You'll need it down there."

Charlie put his robe on over his old one, but Caleb motioned to Laura to wait. He pulled down a cloth bag hanging on a peg, ripped a large piece off. Laura understood. A sling for Benny. Caleb wrapped it around her and crisscrossed her chest. She folded the sleeping baby into his new cocoon. Then she put her new robe on. It was bulky but warm. Benny fit snug inside.

"Hurry now," Caleb said.

Charlie hesitated then hugged him. "Thanks...for...not being like Adrian."

Laura touched Caleb's face. *You will get the chance to be a father to Jeremiah and Josiah.*

He smiled down at her. *I hope.*

The snow beat at the window urging them on. *And someone will love you back deeply someday, Caleb.*

He wanted to believe it. *Someday.*

"Come on, Mom," Charlie eased his tall frame down the trap door. Laura followed him, nimbly stepping down with Benny strapped to her.

She looked up at Caleb before she disappeared into the earth. "I won't forget you."

"Good luck. I'll pray for you." He wondered if he'd ever see her again.

"I'll pray for you, too."

Then she dropped into the darkness.

They were on their own.

Ben tried to move his feet. They were down there somewhere but he couldn't feel them. The snow packed tight in every opening. He tried to move his stiff fingers then shoved them back under his armpits. He thought he was heading back to the compound but he was disoriented.

He would die if he didn't get shelter soon. But he could die at the hands of the Elyons, too. Laura had called to him. He had no choice.

Laura, where are you? Talk to me. I'm here. I'm coming back for you.

Trees caught him as he stumbled. A raging world of white tore at him. Another time appeared before him. He, Charlie, and Laura had been housebound in a blizzard. They had no power and no heat. Darkness descended as the storm beat at their door. The snow piled up four feet high. The storm of a century. Charlie had been ten.

They wrapped themselves in blankets and played board games by the fire, roasting hot dogs and marshmallows. He recalled his son's laughter. It burst out all night and he felt comforted knowing his son thought he was funny. Laura lit candles and they winked in the windows as snowflakes flew at them trying to get in.

When it came time for bed Charlie hugged him and told him it was the best night ever and could they do it again? But they never did. That world of white had been warm and content. A world he hadn't wanted to end. Or his time with his son. In the morning their disconnect had returned, cold as the bright winter sky that hung over the blowing sea of snow drifts.

Ben blinked. Charlie and Laura were gone. He fell to his knees and struggled to get up. Each breath like a fist slamming into his chest. Tears streamed down his face from the frozen wind.

"Laura," he yelled into the storm. A yellow haze grew overhead, blurred by the artic onslaught. The wind slammed into him and he grabbed onto a tree. A rescue helicopter? Could they fly in this weather?

He peered up as the yellow grew larger. The wind knocked him to the ground

It was no helicopter.

Adrian moved stealthily in the dark. And Laura's voice carried to him. Charlie was with her. Then he heard a cry. She had her baby as well. How could they have known about the tunnel and escaped? And if they knew, who else did? It had to be Caleb. It did not matter. She was here and coming to him with her sons. Manta had sent them to him.

He flexed his hands willing power back into his drugged body but it was useless. He had never been drugged before, never been at the mercy of others. Tollen would pay for this like his brothers, Brahm and Feo, had paid for their betrayals. Perhaps not now but someday. After he had taken Laura and their family and built a new life, she would see she belonged with him, not a weak human.

Charlie would help him. Adrian had been there for him all these years from afar and now with him in the flesh. He had turned the boy on to his true nature. He could not turn back now that his wings had unfolded. Charlie wanted to fly with him.

Laura's voice floated toward him like ghostly echoes, haunting and fleeting. He stopped and waited for her. And as she came to him Adrian saw her naked before him in his mind, chestnut hair gleaming in candlelight. Her nipples rose pink and luscious and he nipped and sucked them, rolling them on his tongue. She quivered beneath him and he delighted in her trembling limbs seeking release. Her smooth skin moved into his and he licked the sheen glistening on her from their tangled meshing. She opened her deep, brown eyes then and gasped as pleasure spiraled through her, and he pushed deeper into her.

He grew hard thinking of her moaning with lust and longing beneath him. And when he had shot his Destroyer seed into her womb a new child would grow. They were a powerful pair, each a twin who had survived. Together, they doubled their strength. Those in their way would die.

She must accept the Destroyer side of herself. It hibernated in their genes since the beginning of time. And as humans were once primitive cave people, so were Elyon Destroyers. They had once ruled their planet with fire and fist. Survival of the fittest reigned for them, too, long ago when their civilization began. And it would be so again.

Laura's voice grew closer, wafting over him. He waited for her to come to him.

He had waited seven years for this. He could wait a little longer.

Charlie led the way through the dank tunnel. Sickly verdant shadows rose and fell on the packed mud walls as the glow stick lit the way to freedom. The stagnant air smelled old and unused. Charlie's head brushed the ceiling and dirt fell. Bits caught in Laura's mouth and musty grit rolled around her tongue. She spit it out, leaving a metallic tang behind, and adjusted Benny who slept soundly.

Her eldest son charged through this black hole seeking out what he sought to save. She sensed his guilt and sorrow and his need to right his wrongs. She struggled to keep up with him as Benny weighed heavier across her chest with each step. She held out her hand to steady herself, running her fingers along the knobby edges of their safe passage. In some spots her hands came away wet from slimy water that ran down.

Memories took her to another tunnel where she and Ben had run for their lives years ago. The men she loved, and her tormented twin she wanted to love, were crushed to death that night. She left them behind then. She would not leave behind her men today.

"Charlie, slow down," she whispered. His shoulders jerked as if she had startled him. His steps slowed and he fell in beside her. The tunnel was barely wide enough for both of them.

"Got to get to Dad…if what Caleb said is true."

"I believe him." Laura put a hand on his arm. He squeezed her fingers for a brief moment as if making a pact for it to be true.

"It's all my fault he's here underground. All alone and hurt, if he's not dead. Like Leah."

"He's not dead. I feel his spirit."

Charlie stopped and turned to her. "Do you?"

She nodded.

"Why don't I?"

"I don't know. Perhaps you aren't as in tune to him as I am." She smiled at him to quell his worry. "You shut him out quite a bit after all. When we get out of here—and we will get out of here—you can make it up to him."

"I want to." And he took off walking fast again.

They half jogged in silence for a bit. She had no idea how far down they were but they would be found missing soon.

"Charlie, maybe Leah isn't dead. Caleb said he could revive her."

"But how will I ever know?"

"She meant something to you."

"I never had a girl like me. Crazy in this place, right?" He slowed and looked at her, biting his bottom lip.

"Did you…do anything with her?"

"Mom."

"Please."

He looked away and shook his head. "We kissed. We were supposed to be…like shooting stars. Dumb."

She took his hand. "Not dumb. Special."

"Yeah." She stopped pressing him.

They jogged in silence then Charlie spoke again. "I wanted to be a Seeker, like Adrian."

"To see into the future?"

"Yeah, but now I'm not so sure I want to know the future—the world's or mine. I think it may be better to just to let the future happen, you know?"

Laura's heart swelled with love. "I do know."

She was going to say more, when a dark haze filled the tunnel before her, darker than the earth clutches that held them. Shadows and light blended in a twisting kaleidoscope. She pulled Charlie back. Evil hung in the damp air like a poisonous spider waiting to ensnare them with its vile venom.

"What is it?" Charlie bent down to her.

"How much further?" she whispered back, dread filling her throat like water rushing in a drowning boat.

"It doesn't look far on the map."

She took the glow stick from Charlie and inched forward, motioning him to be quiet and still. The dim light lit the few feet in front of them then faded to the black beyond. Water dripped from the ceiling. It fell on her forehead, cold and lifeless. The kaleidoscope cleared. A draft blew across her as if someone had moved. Someone waiting in stillness. A predator poised to catch its prey.

A rusty smell snaked up her nose.

Blood. Death waited for them ahead. She fought the urge to turn back and flee.

Scrape. Scrape.

It was so faint yet struck her ears like a cannon shooting off. Charlie flinched. He'd heard it, too.

She stepped back as Charlie lunged forward.

"No!" She reached out for him but he was gone.

He sprinted away into the darkness. A thwack echoed through the tunnel. Then a thud. The ground shook. She screamed and ran into a darker hell.

CHAPTER 42

Caleb walked fast through the halls. He wanted to run but didn't want to cause suspicion. Elyons flowed around him heading to their day jobs. Many called out to him in greeting. They chatted around him about the blizzard. The lights flickered. They buzzed again about the generator, but Caleb just nodded and hurried on his way.

His mind jumped with all that had transpired and what was yet to come. Irrational thoughts clouded his reasoning. Of Leah rising from the dead on her own. Of Adrian going on a rampage and killing Elyons randomly. And of Adrian stalking Laura right now, but it was impossible. His father had been drugged and locked in a cell. *Stop it.*

He stretched and cracked his knuckles. He felt like his body was split in two, needing to be in many places at once. He wanted to save everyone but how could he? With Tollen in charge things would be different. Could he get his sons back? Could Laura and her family escape, and if they did, what did that mean for their community? Would the world discover them? Could he start life anew with his sons in the human world? All the possibilities rushed through him, fueling his adrenalin spike. *One thing at a time now.*

He stopped by the infirmary and while the dispenser was distracted, stole a drug syringe. Just in case. He reached the door to the courtyard. The quickest way to the sanctuary. White blew across the once bare stones. The cleaners had been hard at work clearing the snow, but a fresh inch covered it already and more blew down. He peered through the frozen frenzy. Laura and her family were in it now trudging through this madness back to their life.

He flung open the door and shoved it behind him as the storm grabbed him. He ran to the sanctuary door, head down, and nearly fell through the door as a gust shoved him in. The sanctuary remained empty. Candles flickered lower. Only the scratching of the snow on the skylight broke through the quiet. He pulled aside the curtains under the altar.

There she lay in death. He pushed the strewn candlesticks aside and pulled Leah out onto the floor. Her hair flowed around her peaceful face, pale in the candlelight. The snow on his robe melted and fell on her cheek, like tears she would never cry again unless he revived her.

He wiped the snow away, pushed up her robe sleeves, and massaged her arms. They were cold and stiff, but she was still beautiful. And evil. He breathed life into her. Willed energy to once again flow into her limbs, for blood to pump through her veins. He felt his energy draining as he passed her his life force. He had to for Charlie and for himself. This is what he did. He saved lost souls.

Pink infused her skin. Her neck pulsed once again with life. She arched her back and gasped, taking in a deep breath. She opened her eyes, shocked to see Caleb. She reached up a trembling hand and placed her fingers on his face. He peeled them away.

"You're alive, Leah. It's what Charlie wanted."

"You too."

He looked down at her with disgust. "No."

She lifted her face to his. Her soft lips, warmed by blood, moved across his lips. "You saved me even though…"

He pulled away. "Even though you tried to kill Charlie and me. You're a murderer. And you'll have to answer to Brother Tollen now."

She smiled. "I can answer to you right now."

She unzipped her robe and slipped out of it. The sight of her breasts and dark mound seized him and filled him with need. Lust raged in him like a dam let loose. *Why?* Murderous female! And then she knelt on the floor, her bottom presented to him. And between those luscious legs her dewy slit beckoned and beguiled him. He wanted to plunge into her. He gathered his robe up and mounted her. *What was he doing?* Wild urges overcame him. He bent over her, grabbed her swaying breasts and squeezed them until he thought he would explode.

No! This is wrong. And a big mistake to open his mind to her.

You want me, C-a-l-e-b. She sang in his head.

Bad. But he couldn't stop. Didn't want to stop.

He gripped her hips, poised to ravage her. His engorged tip throbbed to enter her.

Then pain crashed in his head. *Now you'll die.*

He moaned and fell on his side. She stood up, pulled on her robe, and smiled.

"I'm too strong for you. Weak is what you are, like Adrian said. And now he's weak, too. Like father like son."

He pushed through the pain. She bent down and stroked his hair.

"Sweet Caleb. Too sweet for your own good." Her lips brushed his cheek.

And he jammed the syringe into her neck, pushing down on its plunger. She shrieked and fell back clawing at it. Pain still raged in his head but lessened as she huddled on the floor. He grabbed her leg and shook her with all the strength he had.

"Bitch," he said. "That's what humans call a malicious, promiscuous female."

"You're so dead," she whispered.

"Or a female dog," Caleb continued. The pain disappeared as her hold left him. He got to his knees. The room tilted. "You're both I think. Willing to get on all fours and do your seduction act to get what you want no matter the cost to others."

He stared down at her as she moaned. The drug would knock her out soon for a few hours, rendering her powers useless. He did what Charlie wanted, what he had to do. He didn't take life. He saved life.

She was a strong Destroyer. She had come back from the dead with frightening strength and determination. He thought of what she could and would do by Tollen's side and it terrified him. Together they could lead a new Destroyer Uprising on Earth.

Then he thought of her being lobotomized and it brought him even greater pleasure than the night they had together. She had used him. He could have loved her as he had once loved Rachel. He had let his cautious guard down and let his emotions take him to another place. If he ever found Rachel again he would find that place again.

"Seductive witch," he said to her. "Now you'll be powerless."

He tried to stand, but his legs buckled and he fell on top of her.

"And you'll be dead." Her face skewed in hatred as she struggled to push him off.

He braced himself on her to get up and out of the corner of his eye the blur of her arm swung down.

Something hard crashed down on his skull. Fire cut a searing path through his head.

The alarm bell gonged. Over and over. It's metal peal clanged an urgent cry.

The last words he heard whispered were, "Forever dead."

CHAPTER 43

A truck seemed to pin Charlie to the floor. Fire burned his lungs. Air. He had to get air, but a knee on his chest held him down. A bug skirted across his hand. He yanked it away and struggled against the massive body covering his own. The smell of sweat and copper swept over him, alongside a cruel laugh. Adrian. Light grew in the dark. Green pulsed on the walls. His mom's screams echoed around him. Adrian pulled him up and clamped his arm across him, trapping him to his chest.

"Get off me!" Charlie yanked his arm off and stumbled back. *Too easy.* His mom grabbed him. Benny screamed. Adrian's face loomed in the dim light like a hollowed out skull. His mom slid along the tunnel's walls tugging at Charlie to follow. Adrian moved with them in a circle, side stepping in the battle arena.

"We're getting my dad—*my real dad*—and getting out of here. You can't stop us," Charlie said. The jagged tunnel walls cut into his back as he slid along it. His mom held his fingers tight, pulling him.

"Is that what Caleb told you? He lies. The human lowlife, Ben, is dead and buried. Rotting in a grave. Crawling with worms."

Charlie punched him in the stomach. Adrian staggered back, bent over. Charlie smashed a fist to his head and Adrian fell on his knees. "And that's for making me like Leah."

He kicked Adrian in the chest. The bastard fell on his side. "You were never like my dad. Maybe he's only human, but he never taught me to hurt and kill people. Even if he could, he wouldn't."

"You're my son…Charlie…Madroc."

"Fieldstone! It's Charlie Fieldstone, you bastard!"

His mom tried to drag him back, but rage fueled his powers.

Laura dug a hand into Charlie's arm as he continued to beat Adrian. Benny's wails urged her on to flee. Adrian grabbed Charlie's leg. They tumbled on the floor, a mass of muscle and fury. Their shadows flew on the walls like demons trying to escape hell.

And hate exploded inside her. She shot a spiral of fire into Adrian's brain. *Die, you monster!* Adrian's screams echoed through the tunnel. She blasted him over and over with her rage. *You can't have my sons.*

Mine. You're mine.

Never.

You're a true Destroyer. Hidden inside.

No.

Hate is life, my Laura.

Love is life. Not your Laura. Ben's Laura.

He's dead.

No. You are.

Her hatred grew. Adrian was right. She had the Destroyer gene in her. She wanted to tear him apart, limb from limb. Make him suffer. It had felt good when she killed the woman in the nursery. She wanted to feel the same way again with Adrian. It exhilarated and terrified her at the same time. She stood now on a high wire looking down. And she would be doomed if she jumped off and gave into her murderous rage. She had to inch her way back to the safe harbor of her heart where love resided.

Love would save her. Hate would kill her.

Adrian's sick thoughts snaked inside her head. They filled her with defeat and aching misery and swelled through her like a black wave of refuse. She didn't want to feel that way. She released her hate, along with his wretchedness. It exploded out of her like black poison. She heaved for breath, clasping Benny to her. Adrian's darkness spewed in her.

She grew faint. Her hold on Adrian was sucking the power from her.

"I told my brother a long time ago that I know about hate," she whispered. "And it's short lived—like you. Love lives forever."

"Useless now, aren't you?" Charlie smashed his fists into Adrian over and over.

Adrian's massive body twisted on the earth floor. "Charlie-boy."

"Stop. Calling. Me. That!" Charlie kicked him with each word. Laura collapsed on her knees, clutching Benny as she drowned in Adrian's black soul. Her attack on him was sucking her away to his dark side.

"Mom! What's he doing to you?"

The stale air burned her lungs as she tried to breathe.

"It's me," she whispered. "I can't keep him down."

Charlie hauled Adrian up. "Stop hurting my mom." He shoved him against the tunnel wall.

Adrian opened his eyes. "She's mine."

Charlie pummeled him with his fists. Laura watched but couldn't move. She could barely hold Adrian hostage with her mind powers as his yellow eyes gazed at hers in the sallow light.

Like Benny's eyes.

Like her twin's eyes. His had held torment and self-loathing and desperation.

Adrian's eyes held only hate. He stared at her in contorted agony and desire as her son smashed into him.

Laura felt herself spinning into black nothing. She had to let go. And she did.

Charlie, we need to trap him in the tunnel. Bring the ceiling down. Your dad needs us.

Let me kill him first.

No. You're not a killer. Not a Destroyer.

Charlie turned to look at her. His face was a mask of hate and revenge.

He nodded and flung Adrian down then dragged her away. Benny wailed louder. They backed up into the tunnel. Something flitted past her. She stumbled. A whirring filled her ears. A mass of winged black rushed past her. Wind blew across her.

Adrian stood. His trembling finger reached for her, seeking to fill her womb again. It shook with his need but didn't turn green this time. Somehow, his powers had left him.

No! I won't accept another child from you!

Then the bat frenzy roared around him, beating at him as if angry he filled their space. He became a blur of muscle and wings.

"Now, Charlie," Laura yelled.

Packed mud blasted down. The ground quaked beneath her feet.

Goodbye, Adrian Madroc.

No!

He lunged for her.

Dirt slammed into Adrian's body. Bats exploded around him. Laura and Charlie's face faded. Their light moved away with them. Blackness engulfed him.

"No, Laura!"

But she disappeared, headed toward freedom. He was barricaded in. And he couldn't break through it. He ran forward and smashed into a wall of wet rock and earth. He slid his hands along it. Bashed into it again and again. Shrieked with madness.

He slid down and leaned on the crashed down wall. Stone fists poked into his back. The bats left him. A rotten smell filled his nose. Something had crawled down here and died. Death accompanied him. Perhaps his own soon. Silence enveloped his every crevice, sucking the air out of him. The crushing weight of no escape struck him with terror and his body ached from Charlie's blows. A reminder that his prodigal son had left him. As Laura had. As Manta had.

Manta, come back to me. Help me. Save me.

He banged his hands on his prison wall of mud and rock. Sharp points pierced his flesh. He banged harder, forcing the pain to fuel his energy. Gasping, he leaned on his cell and wiped his face.

No! Tears are for the weak.

Like the tears he had cried as a child chained in a well under a night sky with only the moon for a friend. No moon befriended him here. The dark was so solid he floated in its giant space.

Manta, show me the way to Laura.

Light flickered. A flame in the sable silence. Calling to him. He heard her voice.

Adrian, you must accept your fate. Love was once yours. Not now. You've killed it inside you by tormenting others.

I was to be our people's prophet and offer them new life here on Earth. Like the Jesus these humans worship. He gave them new life, new hope. I can be Elyon's god.

Jesus led his people in love, not hate.

Love destroyed Jesus. I will not be destroyed.

Hate has already destroyed you.

Manta's light moved closer to him, but other voices crowded her out. "He can't be far."

The light grew larger, brighter. It bounced off the walls rushing toward him. Feet thundered toward him.

Manta.

Goodbye, my love. It floated like a wisp of hope in his heart. Then she was gone.

The cold sunk into his feet on the tunnel floor, as it had in the well his father left him in long ago. He was powerless and alone now as he was then. He wept openly. It felt good. He smeared his tears, tasted their salt mixed with blood. Its tangy bitterness fed him.

"There he is. Grab him!"

The sun filled his eyes. A halo surrounded it. Figures shimmered around it. Hands yanked him up. Fingers bit into his flesh.

Tollen's face appeared, grim. "Your end has come, Adrian."

He stared at him and continued to weep.

He couldn't stop.

CHAPTER 44

Sleet pelted Ben's cheeks. Snow numbed his body, creeping over him with its death chill. He lay on his back, paralyzed with exhaustion and cold. His dry, aching throat burned from thirst. The yellow light became a blinding white above him, piercing his eyes.

He had failed his family. Death could take him now.

Was this the good light that took you to the other side?

Unlike the dark that threatened to take him to the other side long ago. A night on Oahu when Samoan brutes had tied him to a rock and whipped him again and again, intending to rape him and throw him off a cliff.

The howling storm tore at him with icy fingers. They wanted him. Like the Samoans had wanted him that night.

S-n-a-p.

The crack whipped across his back. Streaks of fire cut into him like snow burning him with its frozen bite.

S-n-a-p.

"Motherfuckers!" He cursed them, twisting away from his tormentors. How did they find him again here in this godforsaken place?

No one will hear you scream, brah. This is a haunted place. Your screams carry away on the wind.

The wild mountain wind raged around him and shrieked in his ears.

Ben screamed but it carried away in the storm. He flung himself on the snow, pulling at the ropes that held him. He was so tired. Death called. Like it had that night when Felix saved him from those monsters torturing him on a Hawaiian mountain. Felix had physically set him free only to wander lost inside himself, until Laura came into his life and set him free in his heart.

"Laura. Charlie." He had to live for them. Cold grit crusted his eyes as he strained to see through the white everywhere. Light blinked from above. Was that the bustle of Honolulu in the distance? Drifts moved around him, changing shape with the wind. Snow piled on him, pressing on him. His raspy breath spewed out clouds that were whisked away. He couldn't stop shivering.

And then the cold slipped away. The frigid soldiers attacking him put down their arctic weapons. Warm flowed into him. The light beckoned him. It grew until it filled the sky above him.

A lightning flash zapped the air. Dark shapes moved through the swirling madness.

A hand caressed his face. A gray blur hovered over him.

And then he hung in the wind, lighter than air.

Another flash. And he was gone.

Laura and Charlie ran on. Toward Ben. Toward home. Adrian's howls faded. Her heart thudded inside like a hand mixer on a metal bowl, beating fast against Benny who had quieted down.

Charlie's anguish pumped into her. "Charlie, you're not like Adrian."

Silence.

"Or my twin brother."

More silence. "You named me after him."

"Yes." She tugged at his shirt. "I wanted something good to come out of all the bad."

He slowed his pace and looked at her, his face a disturbing green from the dim light of the glow stick. "Like canceling out the evil things he did?"

"Yes."

"But I *am* like Adrian, like your twin. I tried to kill Dad. I did other bad things—and I liked it."

Laura put her hand on his arm to stop him. They stood facing one another, but he wouldn't meet her eyes. "My twin never had love. He didn't know what to do with it when I offered it to him. And Adrian was surely raised by hate. You've had too much love in your life to give in to the darkness. Genes do not make who you are—environment does. You can overcome your genes."

Charlie looked at her. "I want to, but can I?"

"You will."

"Maybe it's what Caleb's been trying to do all along."

"Yes."

"I've been wrong about a lot of stuff." Charlie sighed.

"You're just fourteen. You're supposed to be wrong about stuff. It's how you grow up. I *want* you around to grow up. We all do wrong. It's how we embrace the right afterwards that matters."

"I got sucked in by evil."

"You were taken advantage of by Adrian. He swayed a young boy to his evil force. He's responsible, not you."

"And he made me like Leah. I thought I loved her."

"Someday someone will love you so deeply and you'll belong to each other and in that you'll discover all the good hidden inside you. Love brings out our good. Hate only destroys it. You can choose love, Charlie. It's what makes us strong. Hate only makes us weak."

"But Adrian isn't weak. He's the most powerful person I know."

"No, he is the weakest because he used his powers to cause pain. Those who use their powers for good, even at their own expense, are the strong ones."

"Like Caleb."

"Yes." Laura squeezed his arm. "Caleb has true power in healing not in destroying—as Adrian does. Caleb has a brave heart. To do what's right. And so do you. Now, let's go get Dad."

"Will he still want me? I mean, I tried to—" His voice broke.

"Of course. There's nothing you could do that would stop us from loving you."

He nodded and they ran on. Not far.

"It must be here." Charlie stopped and held out the glow stick. At first glance it appeared to be the same wall of earth that encased them. Charlie frantically scraped the dirt away. "A handle."

He tugged. Laura pulled with him.

The door creaked. Charlie wrenched it open.

An underground hole. Light slanted down from above. They were under a building. Cold gusts blew down through the cracks.

"Ben?"

A body lay there. A breath caught in Laura's chest.

Please don't be Ben.

Caleb opened his eyes. The alarm bell gonged from the courtyard. Then it stopped. He pulled himself up on shaky legs. The back of his head throbbed. He stretched his neck. Pain ripped through him. He put his hand up and pulled away sticky blood. Near him sprawled Leah, one hand outstretched toward a candlestick. She didn't get far before the drugs knocked her out. Evil harlot. The fact he nearly plundered her again made him sick even though she had manipulated him to do so. He placed his hands on his head and willed the pain and wound away.

His thoughts ran dizzy through him. Had Laura and her family's absence been discovered? He didn't know, but he did know someone would come into the sanctuary soon and discover him and Leah. He dragged Leah back under the altar and hid her under the curtain.

"Stay there forever, wicked wench, and when you awake you'll be as weak as any human for a while."

He looked up. Blue sky gleamed cold through the skylight, as clouds raced frantic across it. The storm had passed. *Safe passage to you, Laura.* He ran to the altar door but as he turned the knob it swung open. Tollen and the elders stood before him. The cobblestone courtyard had been shoveled clean. It gleamed in the new sun as workers wheeled in the stoning gates.

"We've been looking for you, Caleb. Why are you in here?"

Caleb looked at the curious faces before him. He closed his mind off to them.

"I was restless," he lied. "This place is peaceful."

Tollen looked behind him. "It doesn't look peaceful."

The candlestick.

"They fell. Sorry I didn't put them back on the altar."

Tollen pushed Caleb aside and strode in, his flock flowing behind him. He leaned over and picked up the candlesticks and set them on the altar. Sweat sprung on Caleb's upper lip. *Stay still and silent under there, you devil's trollop.*

"We have more important things to discuss. Your father has killed a guard and escaped. We raided his room and found cryptic drawings. We believe them to be a secret tunnel he created long ago and we found him there."

Tollen bent his head and squinted at him. The elders stood behind him, united.

"This is terrible news." Caleb chose his words carefully, praying Laura and her family made it out. His leg muscles tightened as if answering his own urge to flee.

"Yes, indeed. Terrible for him, too. On top of that, the humans are missing. And a slaughtered female has been found in the nursery."

Sweat now trickled down Caleb's back. He folded his hands across his stomach, as the elders did, straining to look calm. "And you believe my father killed this female and hid the humans away?"

Tollen smiled at him. A knowing smile, as if he knew Caleb played games with him.

"We believe the human, Laura, killed the female in the nursery to take her baby. When we caught your father he was ranting that the humans had escaped through his tunnel. We sent a search party out just now to find them. But I have a question for you."

"Yes?"

"How did the humans know about the tunnel? Did you know about it and escort them there?"

A dozen pairs of eyes stared at him, wanting to accuse him. "I did not," he said sharply, trusting he sounded indignant. "I know my place here."

"As you should. For your sons."

The hairs on Caleb's necked prickled, his fear mixing with his sweat now.

"We scanned the storage room where the tunnel leads from. Memory traces of you are there."

Caleb thought fast. "Well of course I've been in there. Part of my job is to review our inventory and store things in there not in use anymore."

"I see." Tollen moved away from the altar and paced across the sanctuary floor. His minions waited as cones of silence. Caleb took the opportunity to sidle closer to the altar and stand in front of it.

Leah sighed. A soft breath that floated out. Caleb sucked in his stomach.

Tollen stopped pacing and looked up with a frown.

Caleb sighed and the elder's frown disappeared. "And what will you do when you find the humans, Brother Tollen?" His heart thudded hard inside as he forced a concerned, dispassionate look on his face.

"Charlie will be lobotomized and work as a cleaner. Laura will die. She has taken the life of an Elyon."

"No." It came out a tortured plea.

"No?" Tollen raised his eyebrows.

The elders shook their heads, pursing their lips, a conglomerate of one mind subservience.

"I mean, they could be our ticket to the human world as Adrian planned. They would be useful in assimilating our community in human towns."

"Perhaps."

The sweat now rolled down Caleb's neck. "And I could oversee this. They respond well to me."

"Are you sure you don't want the human female for yourself?"

Caleb shook his head. "I like blondes."

Tollen nodded. "Like Leah. She defied me. She never came to me last night. Have you seen her?"

Caleb shook his head. His palms were now sweating. He wanted to wipe them on his robe but didn't dare. "Sorry, I have not."

Tollen stretched out his arms. "Come now, Caleb, your help is needed." He took him by the arm and led him toward the door. The elders murmured behind him, falling in step.

"Where are we going?"

"It's time to present Adrian to our community for punishment."

"Stoning."

"Yes, and you will throw the first stone."

Caleb stopped. "I cannot."

Tollen turned to him. "Even with all he's done to you, Caleb?"

Caleb shook his head, stepped back and tripped on an elder who pushed him away.

"No. He's my father."

"He killed your mother."

"Yes." It came out a whisper. He looked at the floor. "But he spared my sons."

"I see. Then you will not cooperate and do what is asked of you?"

"No." He looked up at Tollen who watched him.

"So be it. Then you will be drugged and locked in your room until the execution is over. And then you will be brought out to dispose of your father."

"No!" Caleb shoved Tollen into the door. It banged open, slamming onto the outside wall. Cold rushed in from the courtyard. The elders pulled him back but he punched Tollen in the face. The elder teetered back but didn't make a sound. Caleb tried to punch him again but guards rushed in. They held him back.

Tollen wiped his mouth where a spot of blood oozed. "I knew you wouldn't do your duty." He jerked his head to the guards. "Drug him, take him to his room, and lock him in. Perhaps later he will change his mind."

Caleb struggled against the arms that held him as he shot pain into Tollen's brain. From his peripheral vision a hand drew back. Too late. A syringe plunged into his neck. He stumbled, tried to yank it out but dizziness overcame him.

"Jeremiah and Josiah!" He shouted their names out loud for the first time as a prayer to a human god.

The last thing he remembered was being dragged across cold stone, the wintry air on his face.

CHAPTER 45

Laura's sighed with relief looking at the body of man that lay on his side before them.

"It's not Dad," Charlie cried.

Laura held him back and knelt in the mud floor next to the large man. A hook protruded from his back. Had Ben killed him and fled? She traced the earth, trying to feel Ben. He had lain here, hurt and so alone.

Ben, we're coming to you. We're free.

Laura. The light is taking me. I'm sorry...I failed you.

What light? No, stay with me, Ben.

Love you. Tell Charlie-boy I will always be with him.

Hang on, Ben.

Goodbye, my Laura.

"No!" And he was gone.

Charlie stepped over the man and climbed up rungs on the walls. He banged on the ceiling and pushed a door up. Cold light blinded her and snow drifted down with a frigid wind. He looked down at her. "Come on, Mom. Maybe Dad escaped. Let's follow him."

"Get back down here, Charlie! Caleb said there was a vehicle at the end of the tunnel beyond the perimeter."

"But Dad might be out there, hurt!"

"We go through the tunnel. I have to save all of us."

"But what about Dad?" She looked up into Charlie's eyes, so full of eagerness to save his father and prove himself worthy.

"We need to survive first to save him. Hurry back down here, before someone comes along."

Charlie looked around. "There's no one here. This looks like a torture chamber."

A bell rang out. It blared through the silence. Over and over it gonged.

"Charlie, get down here now."

He nodded and quickly backed down the rungs.

They returned to the tunnel and jogged on through its dark depths.

"Mom, why'd you yell 'no' back there?"

"I put all my hopes on the fact your dad would be here."

"Me too."

She was glad he believed her. Because she believed Ben was truly dead this time.

And he wasn't coming back.

Adrian hobbled in chains as they led him to the stoning gates. The cold buffeted against his naked flesh. He couldn't stop shivering. The snow blew in drifts around the compound as the sun adorned him on his way to death. The cobblestones blurred beneath his feet. Each step full of icy pain.

The pain seemed far away though, locked in another part of himself, along with his powers. His time was done. Time held no chance of reinventing himself in the human world to create a new community to rule.

They locked him in the gates. His legs and arms were stretched taut, wide open for all to target. The shackles bit into his skin. His once loyal followers stared at him. They held no grief in their faces. Tollen stood by, alongside the other elders. He had wanted to take his place and now he had. Adrian hoped for Tollen to find himself in the stoning gates soon, his flaccid manhood torn to pieces. Adrian grinned at his successor.

Tollen did not grin back. He turned and faced the hundreds gathered to do their duty.

"Fellow Elyons, we are called here today to punish one of our own who has strayed. He has savagely murdered members of our flock."

The crowd swayed and murmured their anger.

"Justice is here though. The elders have agreed. And I will lead you into our new world. A world where all will be accepted and listened to. And we will go out into the human community and make it our own. Earth shall be Elyon someday and we are the founders."

The flock nodded in unison.

"Now come, my people, and pick your stones."

Where was Caleb? His son, who so hated him, would miss out on his end.

His people surged forward and stepped to the stone pit. Adrian watched as they chose their rocks to smash at him. At first they would fling softly then their rage would sink in and they would pummel him with power. His fingers broken. His nose cracked. His eyes, blinded and torn, stabbed with sharp edges. His testicles mashed to pulp. His kidneys and liver ruptured. He would bleed to death internally, unless his skull was crushed first.

He looked to the blue above. A glorious day to die. The clouds sailed over him. The sun embraced him although the wind battered him with steel knives. He closed his eyes to pull the sun's warmth to him when the first blow struck like a bullet to his chest. He stiffened and looked toward the sky. It was so wide open, so beckoning. So free.

Pain attacked him. He grunted and jerked. He would not cry out. Sharp stone bit into him. Over and over. Like the invisible creatures in that well.

Make the pain yours, Son. Accept it. Don't be weak.

He tried to drive the voice away, but his father's angry face reared. It rose over the well. The dark encroached upon him. The world of white faded away. Stars appeared above.

Don't leave me here to die, Father. Please.

You must suffer for being weak.

Teach Brahm or Feo, Father, please. I'm not weak. They are.

You are my true heir. You are the strongest one of all.

But he was here now. His people had turned on him, yet they adored Caleb. Why? Because he helped the weak? Didn't that make him weak? And Laura. How he had wanted her. They had created life between them. Like he and Manta had done. He and Laura could create more sons. Why couldn't she love him? Why couldn't she give in to her Destroyer side? Strong Laura. She had survived him.

The creatures nipped at his legs with fire from their carnivorous mouths. They bit into his most vulnerable places. He twitched to make them stop.

"Father, please. Don't leave me here!"

Embrace the pain they bring. It's the only way you can be a Destroyer and rule.

They're hurting me, Father. And it's s-s-so cold. Please. I don't know if I can be a Destroyer.

Weakling!

His father's face swirled away. The stars receded and the sun blinded him once again.

"Father!"

Teeth chomped away at his legs and privates. Tore chunks from him. His blood ran. He thrashed about, screaming. He stared unblinking at the light above. It burned into his bleeding eyes. He watched it as it watched him. He kept his eyes on the golden orb above. The bites increased. He remained still and let the creatures eat on him as he once had.

And his hate grew. For himself.

And he would die from hate.

As his wife had.

How fitting.

The cold had melted away. Warmth radiated through Ben. His pain was almost gone. It throbbed far away, barely touching him. Silence filled his head with blessed peace. There was no wind, no blowing snow to sting his frozen face. No soaked jeans plastered to him with a chilling grip. He half slumbered, connected to life again. Soft light gleamed through his sleepy eyes.

Laura! Charlie!

He jolted awake and sat up. A gray robe had replaced his clothes. He lay on a padded table in a round room. Sloped walls shimmered midnight blue. He was thrown back to the night Charlie had been born. The maternity rooms had been so tranquil and softly lit to soothe women in labor.

Except the night Charlie was born, Laura's serenity had turned to fear. He recalled staring at his son's head pushing his way into the world between her quivering legs and Laura screaming in agony—and mad horror. *I don't want to see it! He changed inside me. I know it.* She had gripped his arm as he wept alongside her. *Don't let it be a freak.*

Ben loved Charlie no matter what he was, and he needed the chance to tell him. He jumped off the table and swayed. Must get to Charlie and Laura…and their baby. Were they okay? Fear spurred up his throat. Had to get out of here. Where *was* here? Part of the Elyon compound? Something told him it wasn't.

Food and drink waited for him on a table. A cheeseburger and pickles. A human offering. He hesitated. They had saved him. They wouldn't kill him now. He gulped the food down as he ran his hands along the wall, looking for a door.

"Let me out. I have to save my family." He pounded on the wall. Its light kept a steady pulse. Stars flickered in and out. "Help me!"

The light became still. Ben stepped back. A picture formed on the wall. A face appeared before him. An Elyon face. White hair flowed into his pearly skin. Yellow eyes watched him. Sympathetic eyes.

"Why am I here?"

The face spoke to him yet its lips did not move. *You would have died out there, Ben Fieldstone.*

Tiredness swept over him.

"Thank you for saving me but I need to get to my family."

Soon. They come.

"No, now!"

His fell on one knee. His side ached. Dizziness flooded through him.

Your body is not fully recovered from your death experience.

"I don't care. Let me out. They will die."

Not if we can help it. We have traveled a long distance to reclaim our people from the evil Destroyer Uprising. Laura and Charlie are part of our new world here. And your new son.

"Our baby! He's okay? How can you know?" Ben struggled to get up, but he found himself floating, being carried on nothing. They placed him back on the table.

He is fine. We see many things. We see the present. We see the future.

"My sons…" He now had two chances to make it right. He hadn't been there for Laura in her darkest time of need. He needed a lifetime to make it up to her. *Let us have a lifetime.* But for now he was so tired. The light was fading.

Your people are near. We hope they will accept us in our final hour. If not, we accept our end.

I accept you.

So tired.

Rest now, Ben Fieldstone.

And he did.

Light appeared in the dark. A tiny dot. It grew and grew. The floor of the tunnel angled up. They neared the surface. They ran faster. Benny gurgled from being jostled. They had reached the end of the tunnel. White blinded them. The storm had passed. A crystalline landscape spread before them. Heavy blankets of snow glittered untouched. Birds' feet marked it with their scattered pictures. A cold gust blew soft flakes past them. They swirled and played as if glad the blizzard had left them behind. It presented a surreal scene from the dark and danger they left behind.

Laura pulled Charlie back. Their captors could be waiting above to snatch them.

"Got to find the vehicle Caleb told us about, Mom."

She put her fingers to her lips. He nodded. Together they searched the walls of the tunnel.

"Here," Charlie whispered. She squinted in the dark, her eyes trying hard to adjust from the blinding light of the snow back to the inky black of the tunnel.

Deep in the recesses of the wall he had found a hole. Inside it sat a bulky form. Charlie pulled its cover off to reveal an all-terrain vehicle of some kind. It had a long wide seat that two people could easily sit on and three wheels.

Thank you, Caleb. And Adrian.

They wheeled the vehicle out to the end of the tunnel. Its key hung from the ignition. Laura looked up at Charlie. He got on the front. She settled in behind him. Benny protested at being squished. She soothed him.

"Get us out of here, Charlie," she whispered in his ear. She sensed his same trepidation at heading out. Underground they felt safe. Now they were exposed.

"There's a compass on the dash," Charlie said.

"Caleb said to head east."

"How do we find Dad?"

"First, we need to get safe. Your dad would want it."

Charlie nodded then turned the key. The vehicle started up with a hacking rumble then smoothed out to a dull roar. He pressed his foot on the gas. They blasted forward into the bright world before them. He gunned it. They launched out of the dark and into the glaring sun, slamming down onto a drift. Wheels spun then they sped forward over the snow. It blew around them angry to be parted. No one attacked them. No shouts of alarm called out.

Laura hugged Charlie tight. Benny's cries punched the air, but she had no choice but to hang on. Her eyes teared up from the freezing wind. Fall had been taken out by winter. A strange, early snow for here. Trees flashed by. Charlie deftly wound between them. Pride welled inside for her son. He had been through so much and now guided them to safety like a man.

She dared to peer behind her. A world of white enveloped them. Nothing more. Her heart began to slow. They were going to make it. She breathed in deep. The air had a crisp, ozone snap to it making everything pure and clean. She needed to feel clean again and not think of Ben being dead. He was alive until she saw his lifeless body before her. She would not let him go until she touched his cold, dead face.

The woods opened up and Charlie stayed a straight course. They were alone in a lifeless landscape. Snow shot down from trees as branches split and fell, not ready for the heavy burden placed upon them.

Wooden screams wrenched the air. Blowing snow scratched her face. Her knuckles were raw from the cold. The frozen landscape held them captive in its terrible beauty.

She peered behind her again. Their tracks were visible for anyone to see but only stark trees contrasted the draped world behind them. They roared toward civilization. She turned her head back when movement caught her eye.

Two shapes behind them. They grew closer. Gray figures on all-terrain vehicles.

"Charlie, faster! They're after us."

He bent his head down and increased his speed. The vehicle tipped dangerously.

"Hang on, Mom."

She looked again. They were gaining.

Hatred surged through her. They had come this far. Nothing would stop them now.

Charlie slammed on the brakes and turned hard left. Laura slid. Her foot slashed through the snow. She screamed, trying to hang on. The cold air burned her throat. Charlie grabbed her from behind with one hand. When she looked past him she understood why he turned.

A wall stood before them. A great hull rose above them arching toward the sky.

And it was not of this Earth.

CHAPTER 46

The ceiling moved in and out above Caleb. He focused on its blurry tiles in the dim light that stretched in from his tiny window. One square. Two square. By the time he counted twenty tiles the ceiling had cleared. He staggered out of his bed. So many faces reared themselves. Laura. Charlie. Ben. And his father. He was dead by now and Caleb couldn't stop it.

The door opened. He squinted at the bright hallway glare. Tollen and the elders.

"Time to put your father to rest, Caleb. Are you ready now to do your duty?"

Caleb's tongue stuck to the roof of his mouth. "Yes," he finally said.

Tollen moved in to the room. "Then I'll return your powers to you. The people respond to you and you are a hard worker. You normally do your duty without being asked. Will you answer to me now?"

"Yes."

"Give me your arm." Tollen yanked up Caleb's sleeve and pushed a syringe into him to counteract the first drug. A humming swelled inside Caleb. It rose and quaked then moved away. Strength filled his limbs and mind.

"Come." Tollen led the way.

"What about Laur—the humans?"

The elder turned back to him with a smile. "They have been spotted outside of the perimeter. They will be back in our custody soon."

Caleb followed his new leader, his thoughts jumping about in his head.

He wanted to help Laura and her family.

He wanted to earn Tollen's trust to be with his sons.

He wanted to breathe life into his father. He had hated him, yes, but deep down he had loved him, too.

He could not do all these things.

Perhaps it was time to choose.

He was tired of saving everyone and not himself.

Laura hung onto her son. He raced between the trees alongside the giant thing looming over them. It appeared two stories high casting a shadow of gray light. Charlie bent lower over the handlebars urging their ride on. The Elyons had turned with them. They were so close she saw their faces. They kept glancing at the building that hung over them.

The engine sputtered and the vehicle jerked. Violent snow sprayed up.

"Mom, something's wrong!"

The vehicle slowed and then sped up. It bucked and lunged forward then slid on its side, one wheel in the air. She gripped Charlie harder. They skidded across crusty caps. Their enemy headed straight toward them now and would reach them in seconds. Mad men who wanted to imprison them again. Or end them.

She hung on to Charlie as they crashed along, banging into trees.

The Elyons were closing in.

Two hundred feet.

One hundred feet.

Their vehicle spit out black smoke and died, slamming into a snow bank. She jumped up, swung a leg over the seat to get off, and fell deep in the snow. Charlie dragged her up. Benny's screams tore into her. Charlie grabbed her hand. They plunged through the merciless snow. It pressed heavy against her legs with its glacier grip. They headed to the wall that trapped them. The Elyons stopped their vehicles, were dismounting. They would reach them in less than a minute. The snow was so deep and there was nowhere to hide.

"There's no escape," she said to Charlie.

"Wait! There's a door here. It's some kind of ship. Come on."

He pulled her along, but she sank to her knees. She clutched Benny who whimpered. She faced their captors. They slowed their pace through the snow.

Charlie was yelling at her to get up. *No.* She had to end this now. She stretched out her hands. Sent her mind out. A killing machine.

And then a great blaze of lightning flashed.

His father hung in the stoning gates.

Bruises painted his body in gruesome strokes. Blood streaked his pale torn skin. A violent death. More so than Rachel's. She had been bruised but not gashed and gouged with rock. His father had been battered to death with hate and revenge. His big head hung down, defeated. His massive muscles flexed no more. He could never hurt anyone again. His father's flock had once worshipped him and accepted the rules he enforced. They had followed him here for a new life as Destroyers where they believed they would not be persecuted. But they had been, by one of their own.

Caleb hadn't wanted to come to Earth under these circumstances. He'd wanted to come here and be equal partners with humans. But he'd also wanted a life back home, even if he was ostracized by the other kids for not using his healing powers. They didn't understand he wanted to feel pain as humans did. He wanted to suffer as the humans did, to understand them. And now here on Earth he was forced to live a life as a Destroyer.

He had to believe that a Destroyer could reverse his own fate.

Could defy genetics. Could be good. Could heal. Could love.

He had one day hoped his father could. Now that would never happen.

"Go on now, Caleb," Tollen said. "Remove the executed."

"Where will I bury him in this snow?"

"You won't. You will carry him to the tree line and leave him there."

"The animals will ravage him."

"Yes. They will tear him apart and pick his bones clean. An appropriate end for a wild animal such as himself."

Nausea swirled in the pit of Caleb's stomach thinking about his father's flesh being torn asunder and chewed on by snarling wolves. He moved forward and unshackled his father. Blood spattered the cobblestones beneath him. His father's stiff body fell into his arms and he staggered back and summoned his strength to pick him up. He used his sleeve to wipe the blood from his father's face, so at peace in its stillness. Had he ever known peace? He had never seen his father with his eyes closed. He didn't look monstrous, just sad.

Hurry. Choose, Caleb.

Snow began to fall, soft this time. It floated down and dressed his father's cold body. The flakes did not melt. He had been left out here dead for some time. Guilt spawned a seed of love inside Caleb. He had been drugged and slept while his father was battered to death. He looked at Tollen and the elders. Other Elyons had stopped to watch as they went about their business again. Back to baking and child care and laundry—

after killing. They watched him now, wondering if he would have the same end as his father.

Choose.

"Why are you hesitating, Caleb?" Tollen demanded. "Follow orders or there will be consequences." He crossed his arms. The elders murmured.

More of the community came out to see what was going on. And still he stood before them with Adrian's body in his arms. He looked down at his father.

There was only one choice to make.

If he let his father die then he could never be the father he had hoped to be for his sons. He would be giving into his Destroyer gene— and that would destroy him.

He carefully placed his father on the cold stone and closed his eyes.

"What are you doing?" Tollen's voice rose loud and angry. A hate-filled murmuring swelled around him but he focused on his task. Laughter echoed in his ears. "You can't bring back the dead, Caleb."

The laughter grew as others joined in. Caleb ignored them. He looked up once. His sons watched him. They did not laugh.

He molded his father's body in his hands, cleansing it of pain and suffering. He willed life into him, inch by inch. Imagined his blood pumping through his limbs.

Please, Father, come back to me a renewed being of light not dark.

He felt movement under his fingers and opened his eyes. Color rushed back into his father's cheeks and chest. Veins pulsed like rivers of blue once more against white skin.

The crowd gasped.

"Look."

"It's an Elyon miracle."

"He brought him back."

"He's our true Elyon leader!"

"Yes. Yes! Caleb Madroc!"

Tollen shook his head, as if not believing. "You're wasting your time, Son."

Caleb looked up. "I am not your son."

"No, you're mine." Adrian clutched Caleb's arm, his eyes wide with something Caleb had never seen before in them. Fear.

Caleb helped him stand up. The crowd before him became silent. Then their voices rose up in outrage. "Kill him again!"

Adrian hung his head.

"No," Caleb yelled over them. They were silent once more and stared at him. Waiting. "Let him go. He is nothing now. His reign of pain is over. Let him be in misery. Let him flee as so many others did. Alone."

He let go of Adrian. His father tottered, his naked body weak and pathetic. The snow fell again. Mad flakes bashed at them. Tollen stood there, clearly unsure of how to react.

One elder stepped forward. "You're our true leader, Caleb. You brought him back to life. You've evolved to the higher form our scientists predicted we'd become someday. You can lead us into our new world where we will belong. It's destiny."

Tollen shook his head and held his hand up. "No need for haste! We don't know what just occurred. The elders must meet in chambers to investigate before a new leader is decided upon."

But the Elyons swarmed to Caleb, pushing Tollen aside.

"No meeting. We know what's true and right!" "Yes, true." "Brother Caleb is meant to lead!" "New world." "Our new hope."

The Elyons surrounded Caleb. They squeezed his arms, kissed his hands, and pushed at him from all sides. Then Leah stepped out from the sanctuary. She stumbled toward the courtyard, dazed and weak. She joined the surge, not knowing what was going on.

The crowd lifted Caleb up. All the elders nodded, except Tollen. Caleb watched him standing off to the side, a deep frown of anger splitting his face. The snow embraced Caleb in a frenzied celebration along with his people as they held him on their shoulders. He was stunned. This was not what he envisioned. Then a feeling burst inside him. He almost didn't recognize it.

It was hope.

He could be with his sons.

He could be a father.

He could lead his people into a world where they could live in harmony with humans, sharing the Earth as one gift.

His sons came into view. The crowd swelled toward them with him over their heads. Jeremiah and Josiah looked up as he passed by, eyes as green as his, and they smiled at him. He reached out his trembling hands and touched their soft black hair—the first touch of his children he loved and had never known—and then he was swept away from them with the crowd.

He calmed his emotions and spoke to them as they paraded him in the snow. "Elyons, we can change our destiny. We can live in peace, not pain and fear. We can overcome our Destroyer ways and not hide what's inside us anymore. If I can bring back the dead, think of all the other things we can do someday—you can do. Good things."

Their agreement flowed around him. They had been ready for a change.

"Our hidden element can be the light we never knew we had. Charlie had it. I have it. My Uncle Brahm had it. It will be hard but we can reach out to the human world and embrace them— and hope they'll embrace us back."

Tollen stood still, watching. "Elyons, don't be so quick to judge or to believe these new ideas."

"Caleb is the true leader and his words are truth," another elder shouted back over the crowd. "He will bring us into the light and out of the dark. He can bring the dead back to life. He can bring us into a new life."

Caleb's people cheered and carried him from the cold into the warmth of the compound.

Then it struck him. In the chaos he had lost his father.

He was gone.

Adrian's limbs spasmed from the cold.

His people had shoved him aside like garbage to get closer to Caleb, their true leader marked by destiny. His own son who he had marked as weak. He had stumbled off then in shock and wandered into the woods. He reached the community fence and struggled to pull himself up and over it. His flesh ripped on barbed wire. The pain no longer felt good. It no longer made him strong. Weaker he grew.

Twice he fell and began again. Finally, he dropped down on the other side and lay there heaving great breaths as his body grew numb. Could he make his way to Benevolence and convince a human to take a naked stranger in? He stood and staggered forward.

He tried to see into his future but it was now a blank space.

His people were gone. Laura and his sons were gone. And so was he.

He wept from the loss, his tears like fire on his frozen cheeks.

The snow surrounded him like a false welcome blanket, cruel in its glittering luster. It stung his feet and calves. At first it burned and he clung to the pain. Then cold spread throughout him and he felt nothing. He had died today and yet now lived.

The pine trees shook the unwanted snow from their branches. It covered him and soon melted to a chilled glaze covering his body. So tired. Needed to stop for a rest. He didn't know where he headed but something pulled him along.

Manta. Laura. Where are you?

But neither answered.

He trudged on when a voice inside his head smote him down.

Weakling!

He dropped to his knees in terror, haunted by his father's voice. *Yes, father.*

Go to the well. Now.

This was where his subconscious had been leading him. He staggered up, numb. His feet were cut from scraping on shards of snowy ice. He left bloody footprints with each step.

Trees held him up as he lurched along. Not far. He had built it to punish Caleb, the weak one, but now Caleb was strong—and *he* was weak. His father had said so. It had to be true. His entire life had been a lie. Wretched self-loathing devoured him.

The cover to the well waited for him. He wrapped his hands around the handle, his fingers blue. *Help me, father.* He strained. His fingers jerked and he slid the cover off.

Get down in there, Son. Face your fears. You will never be anything if you're weak.

Yes, Father.

Adrian slowly backed down into the well. His feet slipped on the rungs and he fell, crashing down into the icy realm with a splash. Caleb's words crashed into him with truth, 'Deliver me from evil men. Throw them into deep pits from which they cannot escape.'

The cold blasted him in his pit of suffering. He screamed in agony. He shook and tried to hold still. He would not thrash. He would be strong. He could suffer like Caleb and be strong.

Do not fight the pain. It will give you great power, in life and death. Let hate rise you up.

Yes, Father.

He embraced his suffering this time. He would not beg for release. He looked up at the wintry sky. The sun hung over him gracing him with its rays.

Manta, come to me.

They had created warmth in their love. He had known love once.

But she did not come to him now.

Snow kissed his face. As Manta once had.

So much softness.

He drifted away in it.

CHAPTER 47

The fire-bolt streaked across them. It struck their two pursuers and they were sucked from the air into a portal on the side of the wall. Their screams severed the silence. A blinding flash burst and they were gone. A scarf swirled and glided down. It landed and then the wind took it and flung it away again. It skipped across the drifts and disappeared.

Charlie dragged Laura up, but she floundered in the snow.

"Run, Mom! To their ATVs."

She stumbled after him. Exhaustion gripped her as she struggled to move through the deep snow. Benny protested against her with each step.

"Charlie, there's nowhere to go."

"They're gonna kill us now." He yanked her arm heading toward the dead Elyons' vehicles.

"No," she said and pulled away from him. "They would have killed us by now. They saved us."

Panting, he jerked around. "Who?"

"The ones in the ship. They've come again."

The gray mass shone under the sun. At first it looked like one solid construction but looking closer there were seams in it. They ran in uniform shapes. Like entryways.

And then one of the seams glowed. Its square outline radiated light.

"Mom, look."

They clung to each other. Awe flooded through Laura at the possibilities of what this ship meant. She gripped her eldest son's hand while pressing her youngest to her chest. The seams glowed brighter, radiating out.

"Mom, let's go!"

Charlie's fear swept over her as he pulled on her. But she was not afraid.

"No. It's our destiny."

He stood still, accepting her words. "It's opening."

They stood in the snow amongst trees that had grown on their world for millions of years. Wood giants that had died and replanted themselves with seeds in the wind, as humans evolved and civilization grew around them. They stood and watched as this thing, surely from another place across the universe, opened itself up before them like the massive unveiling of a new world. It was real, not just in her dreams. She was a bridge to it.

The seams broke away. Light poured out. The massive door opened before them like on a giant hinge.

"Oh, my God," Charlie whispered.

"They must have a god, too," she said. Charlie nodded, not taking his eyes off the ship. Snow pillows floated down from the trees. The scent of pine wafted across. The placement of this foreign thing hung surreal in the serene wintry wilderness. It wouldn't be hidden for long.

The door unfolded. Yellow light spilled from it. Figures grew before them.

Laura stood with her sons and waited for their destiny, helpless and amazed.

The community had gone back to work after celebrating the coming of Caleb. He now gathered with the elders in the sanctuary.

Tollen was silent and resigned it seemed to his reduced stature. He now spoke. "When did you know of your special powers to bring the dead back?"

"I've been aware of them since I was a child."

"Why wait until now to show our community this?"

The elders looked at him, waiting. "My father was the leader. I did not want that role. I did not want to give in to my Destroyer gene. I wanted to help those less fortunate."

"What of those who died naturally?"

"I figured it was their time to pass peacefully. Their fate."

The elders nodded except Tollen.

"And all of our executed people buried up on the hill—"

"Most of them I dug up, revived, and set free."

"They are out there amongst the humans?"

"Yes." Rachel appeared in his mind and his heart ached.

"And Adrian?"

"I no longer sense his presence in this world. He is out there in the woods."

"Dead."

Caleb nodded and stood taller. He could rule. He never wanted to before but now his father had met his end. Destiny. And after this meeting the first thing he would do was begin his own destiny—visit his sons.

"It's time for a new era for Elyons," he said louder. Hope filled him with strength. "It's time the humans knew us. We must co-exist in harmony. We must trust they won't turn their backs on a civilization in need, even one that came under malevolent forces. Those forces are gone now. It's time to take a risk. Stop hiding. Start being part of this Earth, not hidden but in full view. Stop giving into our Destroyer genes. It does not make life, it destroys it."

"We risk much," one elder said.

"Yes. They'll discover what we're capable of," said another. "Use us as experiments."

"Maybe not," Caleb said. "There are too many of us for them to hide. Perhaps they'll come to understand there is much we can learn from each other. And there is Laura and her family. Have you informed her pursuers to retain her?"

"Yes."

A male burst into the sanctuary, out of breath.

"You found the human, Ben? Is he all right?" Caleb had seen him in his mind out in the snow and sent another party to bring him in to safety. Laura and her family would be reunited. Like he hoped soon for himself. First he had to take care of business.

The male shook his head. "No, but a ship has landed."

They all stared at him, as if not believing. Caleb's heart pumped loud in his ears. "An Elyon ship?"

"Yes. A mile past the perimeter. Our people messaged back and then communication was cut."

"Do they have Laura and her sons?"

"I don't know."

Caleb looked at the elders. This changed everything.

"I'm going." He strode to the door. "Alone."

He spoke to the wide-eyed messenger on the way out. "Put the community on lockdown. Everyone return to their rooms."

The messenger nodded and rushed out.

Tollen grabbed him as he passed by. "Careful, Caleb. Our people would hate to see their new leader struck down because of a miscommunication. Do you understand?"

Caleb felt the animosity roll off the elder who gripped him. He stared into Tollen's angry eyes and shook away the hand that held him. A force filled him like he'd never felt before. Strength resonated through him. He could truly make a difference now and relieve his people of the dark that had imprisoned them for so long.

"There will be no miscommunication," Caleb said in a low, steady voice. "We will meet our people with truth in our words. There will be no more lies and deception—and death. Do *you* understand, Brother?"

Tollen held his stare then stepped back and folded his hands. "Yes, Brother Caleb."

Satisfied with the elder's submission, Caleb nodded and ran out the door.

He would have to wait to be with his sons.

They came to Ben in his dreams.

An Elyon looked down at him with kind eyes. He had dark hair like Caleb but eyes like Laura. He spoke with his voice this time.

"Adrian hijacked our ship readied and bound for Earth years ago. We had peaceful intentions. We did not know he was an Underground Destroyer. He came here with his own evil purpose."

"He wants my family."

"No longer. His time is done. We've been working for years to create another ship with our limited resources so that we could come here. This is where you must help us, Ben Fieldstone. You and Laura and Charlie. This is our last chance to survive. Elyon is a ticking time bomb, as you say. Few survivors remain. The last few years have plunged us into an ice age."

"I will help you. My wife is part of your world. And my sons. If I ever see them again." His voice cracked. The Elyon placed his hand on his arm. A strange hand. Like Charlie's. Pale, smooth, and without nails. Warmth melted into him. And love. It overwhelmed him.

"You will, Ben."

He woke up. *Laura.*

Energy poured into his body.

"I have to rescue my family." He jumped up. They had to hear him with their omniscient presence.

And they did.

Your family comes to us. As do your people.

A door slid open. Yellow light flooded in. He had not seen a door there before. He wiped his mouth and ran out. A figure stood there. The one from his dream. The being held out his hand and smiled.

Come, Ben Fieldstone.

And he did.

Laura looked up at the open door to another world. She stared at the shadows that watched them from above. The government would find them. They had to be watching and waiting, as they always had. Adrian had come undercover. These Elyons did not. What would that mean for her and her family? Would her own government imprison them, experiment on them, as they did her twin?

Her pulse ping-ponged inside as if trying to find release. Charlie's rushed fast too from his wrist as his hand wound tight around hers. Benny's tiny heart beat fast and steady into her breast. All her hearts were here. But Ben's. His wild and loyal heart had been silenced forever somewhere behind her.

Engines rumbled far in the distance. They looked behind them.

"Mom, more of them."

Then a great light flashed.

The last thing she saw were Charlie's eyes wide open. *I want to live.*

And they were sucked away like the others.

Caleb pushed the throttle on the vehicle faster, pushing it beyond the limit across the snow dunes. The vehicle rocked. He leaned into a turn, avoiding a tree. He sent his mind out seeking these humans he had come to care for, but he found no human life in the vast white wilderness. Charlie and Laura could be blocking themselves from being sought out. The baby was too small to be sought. He had no will yet. But where was Ben? Dead?

And then his past and future rose before him. He slammed on his brakes then sped up. His people were here.

He raced toward the ship then skidded to a stop. He jumped off his vehicle and waded through the snow toward it.

Laura. Charlie.

He looked up at the open door that welcomed him.

CHAPTER 48

Charlie still gripped her hand. They were in a long tunnel. Yellow light glowed all around them. They were in the ship. They weren't dead. Cold blew behind them and then faded as the door they came through sealed shut.

Charlie bent to look at Benny. "He's okay. We're okay."

"It was a transport system."

They walked down the tunnel. It felt supple and soft, molding itself to their feet as they walked.

"Where are we going?" Charlie tugged on her sleeve. Silence hung all around them like they were in their own peaceful bubble floating away.

A gray figure appeared far away. It took shape.

A familiar figure that held her world.

Ben. Wonderful, alive Ben.

She ran.

Yellow shimmered around him.

He took her in her arms. She breathed in, drawing his smell deep in to her memory, tucking it away forever.

"They saved me," he whispered in her hair. "Like you did long ago, Laura. I got another second chance." They embraced until Benny's cries of protest pried them apart. Ben reached his hand down to touch him but Laura stepped back and held her crying son to her chest.

"We all need second chances."

He looked at her puzzled. She stared at him, holding this moment close before he saw what she had born into this world.

She offered him their son. "Benny."

Ben looked at him then back at her. He touched her son's fingers to his own. Benny's cries slowed. *That monster…did this. He was with you…inside you…in our home. In our home! They weren't dreams.* He snatched his fingers away and stared at her, a frown cutting his forehead in two.

No, they weren't. She couldn't bear it if he couldn't accept this. She reached an arm out, desperate for his love and acceptance, but he stepped back.

"That monster tore our family apart." Ben closed his eyes as if the sight of Benny sickened him.

"No. Never. It's over. He couldn't stop us from being family." She dared to believe he could believe it, too. Benny was the only good thing to come from this place.

"Come on, Dad," Charlie pleaded.

"Hope needs a second chance, too," Laura whispered.

"It must be the desired outcome," Ben finally said and opened his eyes to stare at her.

"Destiny." She smiled at him.

"Fate."

"Forever." Laura handed the baby to him.

Ben hesitated then took their son, and she thanked God for bringing them all together.

"Your son," he said and smoothed down Benny's hair. A curl popped up. Benny cooed and twitched his pink fingers.

"*Our* son. He grew with us as our son."

"I wanted to be with you, Laura. I—I wasn't there for you when you needed me most." His voice broke and he quickly handed Benny back to her, as if he couldn't stand to touch this baby that was made inside her by a monster.

"We can accept this child and break the chain of evil. Love overcomes all, doesn't it?" *Please tell me it does.*

"Like love remembers?" he said sadly, but it whispered into her open heart.

She nodded and the great pain that threatened to split her apart melted away. "Love remembers."

Ben looked over to Charlie, who stood on the side shuffling his feet.

"Dad, I'm, I'm—"

Ben grabbed him and hugged him.

They stood there for a long time and while Charlie stood taller than his dad, he still cried in arms like a little kid. Charlie had finally let his armor go.

"Charlie-boy, you're all I want you to be," Ben said, his voice cracking.

"Normal?"

"There's no such thing as being normal. Not on any world."

"Like being big doesn't mean you're brave—only big of heart does?"

Ben laughed. "That's right, Charlie-boy."

"I'm sorry I've been so hard to…love."

"Love is hard, but you don't ever give up." Ben shared a look with Laura over Charlie's shoulder.

"I wanted to give up."

"I know. I'm sorry if I made you feel this way."

"Not you, Dad. All these years, Adrian had turned me against you. I'm so sorry."

"I'm sorry, too, but now we have a new chance to begin again."

"New beginnings," Laura said and moved into her men. Hearts connected. All different but sustained by love.

She had said she would survive the evil that preyed on them and she did. They all did.

Their hearts were as one again.

"What now?" Ben turned to her. They stood in the tunnel, unsure what to do. "I don't know. But you can't hide a ship like this in the wilderness forever."

"Who'll find us?" Charlie looked at them both.

"Military Special Forces," Ben said. "First responders. I'm sure the government's been watching for them to come again."

"How will they be to us?" Charlie looked at Laura, his voice rising and panic in his eyes. "They'll find out about the Destroyers and what they've done…can do. What *we* can do."

Laura put her hand on Charlie's. "Human or Elyon. Good can win out. It's never too late. And we can hope. It's all we've got. And each other." She had to trust it would be enough.

Cold covered them.

"Look," Charlie pointed. "The door is opening again." He ran toward it.

"Wait, Charlie!" Ben ran after him. She followed.

Ben yanked Charlie back from the door but Laura peered down.

Caleb stood below.

He looked up at her. His bright green eyes bore into hers even across the distance. She opened her mind to him, but he spoke first.

Adrian is dead.

Three little words. They emboldened her with faith for a future.

"Caleb?" Ben moved forward. Charlie waved down at him. He waved back.

"He saved us," Laura whispered.

"All of us," Ben said.

You can be with your sons now, Caleb.

Yes, we're free now.

All of us.

We need not be weary of living anymore.

A humming grew beneath their feet. A ledge pushed out from the door entrance. It grew into an arched metal path beneath their feet with guardrails to hold on to. It extended to the ground and the humming stopped.

Elyons filled the space behind them. They were ready. They had traveled across the universe for this. A final chance to live.

The three of them held hands. Laura headed down the path first. They walked toward a new future for people everywhere and the Elyons followed. She connected them to Earth. Caleb watched her descend. She neared the ground and she stared into his eyes as he grew close. She would keep their intimate moments hidden in her heart forever. He had been kind to her in a place that had held no kindness.

Then a great bashing noise cut through the wintry air. The cracking of trees thundered in a deafening split as if ripped apart. A battalion of tanks smashed through the woods. Men in full-body white suits and helmets moved stealthily between the trees, blending in to the arctic landscape, guns poised. They were surrounded on all sides now, with the ship behind them.

Ben wound his fingers tight through hers. She clung back. They all froze on the path.

Tell your people to stay still, Caleb.

He nodded.

"Mom, will they shoot us? Shoot the Elyons?"

"No." But her heart pounded when she said it.

The tanks rolled to a stop, guns aimed at them. Watching and waiting. As they had been for years.

Human facing alien. Would this be a new beginning or an end?

Their breaths hung in the air in terrified anticipation.

Caleb flicked his eyes back and forth from Laura to the army that stood positioned to kill them.

Then a figure stepped out from behind Laura and her family on the path.

Uncle Brahm.

I'm here for you, Son.

With his presence and words the seed of hope planted inside Caleb swelled and grew. He had never truly belonged on Elyon or here, but he had belonged with Brahm. And for the first time in a long, long time—even with guns locked and loaded to kill him—he felt like he was home.

"Stop!" a loud voice boomed over a tank speaker.

Soldiers moved between the trees, guns ready to fire.

Laura held up her hands. "We're here peacefully. We've been taken against our will but not by these people here."

An armed man stepped out of the tank and raised his gun. He trudged through the snow, his gun steady on them, and stopped a few feet away. Caleb couldn't see his face behind his shield, a faceless human holding his fate in his hands. The snow whipped up in frenzied waves battling with the sun that pushed the clouds away and held the promise of warmth on Caleb's shoulders.

Brahm's voice rose loud over the sudden thundering silence. "Our planet is dying. We are a peaceful people but for a few dissenters."

"Stand down," the man yelled, swinging his gun at Brahm. His comrades followed his line of sight. The wind scattered the snow in violent bursts.

"Please, help us," Brahm said in a deeper voice. He bowed then looked at Caleb. *Our moment is now. Starting a new path for our world to follow.*

If this world accepts us.

Have hope.

You bring it with you.

The soldier shifted his feet and moved closer. "I'm in charge of this operation. We're here to secure and quarantine this area." His tinny voice cut through his helmet, adding to their divide.

"We need shelter," Laura said. Her baby cried out at her breast. All eyes and guns twitched toward her.

The man spoke into a device. Immediately the remaining soldiers rushed in. More humans in white suits and helmets, carrying equipment. Tents were set up. Hoses connected. Lights installed. And a small group descended upon them. Laura held her baby closer. Ben wrapped his arms around the little family.

"Don't hurt them," Caleb yelled.

Then an engine rumbled on the wind. Louder it raced. A vehicle rocketed through the air from around a tree. It headed straight for Caleb.

Tollen. And two small, dark heads.

Jeremiah and Josiah! My sons! No!

Caleb saw the hate on Tollen's face. Faster he sped toward him, with his sons.

In slow motion Caleb saw Ben push his family down.

He heard high-pitched screams carried on the wind.

He saw Brahm dragging their people back up the ramp.

He saw the human soldiers take cover and raise their guns.

The ATV launched off a crusted drift of snow and hung in the air. Two pairs of frightened eyes stared into his.

"You'll never get your sons," Tollen screamed. "They'll die as mine did!"

Guns blazed.

Caleb threw himself left, avoiding death by milliseconds, and smashed hard into packed snow. Smoke exploded across the woods. Tollen catapulted off his ATV, dragging the boys with him. They struggled against their kidnapper. More shots rang out. Tollen jerked back. The ATV sputtered and was still.

So was Tollen. His blood seeped around him in a red wave.

And then he stood.

Caleb pushed himself up and ran to Jeremiah and Josiah, struggling against the deep snow. They huddled together, heads down.

A soldier yelled. "Stop!"

Tollen lunged for Caleb's sons, grabbed them by their hoods, and dragged them back.

"No!" Caleb tripped on a chunk of snow and fell to his knees. He staggered up.

"Stop or I'll shoot again."

But Caleb couldn't. Just a few more steps.

Rat-tat-tat.

Tollen twisted in the air and flew back and Caleb stumbled. His sons looked up. He reached out for them but couldn't move.

Laura was yelling, but he couldn't hear her words. Pain radiated into his legs and one arm. He fell on his side. The cold sliced into him like a razor. His own blood spilled outward. Flakes floated around his head. The world blurred.

Laura's sobs punched the air's painful silence after the deafening gunfire.

He lifted his head to look at the soldier in charge. "Please. They're my sons."

The man shook his head. "Be still!"

"No. I need to save the one you shot."

The soldier jerked his gun at Tollen. "He's dead."

"I can bring him back to life."

He took a chance and started crawling toward Tollen.

"Don't make me shoot you again."

Out of the corner of his eye the soldiers took a collective step closer, their guns poised in a succinct line. He sensed their anxiety of this unknown. One shot from them all and he'd be gone in a second. There'd be no one to bring Tollen back.

Rachel, come, unwrap my heart and set me free in you.

But she remained lost to him. The trees rocked and the white turned black. He couldn't stay awake. He placed his face on the snow. So cool and welcoming.

Laura's words floated to him through blessed darkness. "It can't end this way."

"Don't screw this up," Ben yelled. "You'll be damning yourselves with these people from another world."

"I'm part of their world, too," Laura pleaded. "I can heal this man. His name is Caleb Madroc and he has the power to bring the dead back to life. His people came here for a new life. Don't end it before it's begun!"

Silence covered Caleb like the numbness that crept across his limbs.

And then soft hands moved across his legs and arms. They touched him with tenderness, filling him with a life force. It grew like a light inside, warming his soul.

"This is the only thing I can give you," Laura whispered. Her breath pulsed across his cheek. Snow crunched. More hands moved across him. He opened his eyes. Charlie worked his body.

And his sons.

They knelt before him in the snow and placed their small hands on his face. Such warmth in such cold.

"Father," they said in unison and his heart cracked wide open.

His skin stitched up. His wounds stopped bleeding. His life force grew strong. "Must. Get. To. Tollen," he rasped out. "Before it's too late."

Laura and Charlie helped him up. He lumbered to Tollen and bent down to him.

He willed life back into the one person who wanted him dead.

Tollen opened his eyes, focused on him then pursed his lips. "Dead! You should be dead. Your sons dead!"

"So should you," Caleb said. A piercing pain stabbed his head. A black haze covered his sight. He punched Tollen in the face with all his might before the pain took over. His former leader crashed down, unconscious.

He jerked Tollen up, holding his arms back, and yelled to the soldiers, "Take this one and drug him, otherwise he'll kill you with his mind powers." The guns were lowered. He sensed the fear and wonder in the soldiers. Their helmets gleamed in the wintry sun, revealing nothing behind their shields. Some shuffled about, fear and unease in their hearts. Caleb shoved Tollen toward the leader who grabbed him and dragged him away.

The men in white moved forward again to quarantine them. Whatever that meant, they were in it together. It had to be a better life than what his father had given them, an honest life.

Laura locked eyes with Caleb then took a step toward the army. Holding her family's hands she walked with them toward their new world. A world of good. He had loved her in the brief moments they had. She had unraveled his heart to be filled again. And he could now give his full heart away—to his sons.

He looked down at them. *I'll find your mother.* They nodded and each took one of his hands, fitting perfectly in his.

There was nothing to hide now. The world would know what he was.

Laura turned back to smile at him, and he stepped toward his future.

~ * ~

Message from the Author

Dear Reader,

Is there a writer gene and is storytelling genetic? I like to think that we either are storytellers or we aren't.

When I read pieces of my work in public, I often forget how dark my writing can be. One event coordinator noted the comedy in my reading about heads popping in vices and whatnot as I peered up with innocent eyes.

This led me to wonder if there are sub categories of the writer gene just like there are sub genres in writing. If there is a "dark" writer gene, well, that fits me perfectly. I like writing from the dark places. To spiral my characters into tragedy—with a dash of hope. On the page I can act out horrific events by evil people and never get arrested. My blood pumps a bit quicker. My fingers fly faster over the keyboard. My husband wants to know how I can write this stuff.

Ancient history was full of folks inducing pain in real people, not just characters on the page. Back then people acted out their aggressions upon the unfortunate ones, who were ripped to shreds by lions, skewered gladiator style, and tortured by medieval stretch rack.

We're so much safer today reading and writing about tormented characters. If more people would lose themselves in dark writing instead of dark action, we'd all be better off. Plus, there is just wicked fun to be had in writing the evil and tormented characters.

This brings me back around to the question, if the writer gene does exist then are writers predisposed to write what they do? Dark fiction, young adult, fantasy, science fiction, romance, memoir. What in our writer gene predisposes us for that? If my son writes some day from the dark places I will know why and probably enjoy it immensely. My husband? Eh, not so much.

~ Donna

About the Author

Donna Galanti writes murder and mystery with a dash of steam as well as middle grade adventure fiction. She is the author of the bestselling paranormal suspense *Element Trilogy*. She also writes for children and is the author of two fantasy adventures series with *Joshua and The Lightning Road* and *Unicorn Island*. She regularly presents as a guest author at schools and teaches writers through her online Udemy courses. Donna has lived in fun locations including England, her family-owned campground in New Hampshire, and in Hawaii where she served as a U.S. Navy photographer for Fleet Intelligence Pacific. She now lives with her family and two crazy cats in an old farmhouse that sadly, has no ghosts. Visit her at elementtrilogy.com and donnagalanti.com.

~ * ~

If you enjoyed this book, please consider writing a short review and posting it on your favorite review site. Reviews are very helpful to other readers and are greatly appreciated by authors, especially me. When you post a review, drop me an email and let me know and I may feature part of it on my blog/site. Thank you.

donna@donnagalanti.com